WHO SOWS THE

REAPS THE WHIRLWIND

HENRY S HOLLOWAY

J H GROUP

British Library cataloguing in Publication Data

A catalogue record for this book is available from the British Library.

ISBN 978-0-9562323-0-4

Front cover by David Abraham

This is my first published novel
and it is dedicated to my wife Doris.

With thanks to 'Ginge' Mather
late of the RGBW,
who introduced me to the story
of Blair 'Paddy' Mayne.

'They sow the wind

And reap the whirlwind'

Hosea Chap 8: 7

Lt Colonel Blair 'Paddy' Mayne was the most decorated soldier in the British army in World War 11.

Churchill did have a network of spies known only to him and the Major.
It was known as 'The Secret Circle'.
Josephine Butler was the only woman member of The Secret Circle.

The Right Reverend Fraser McLuskey was Paddy Mayne's Padre in 1 SAS Regiment when he fought in France.

The incidents described in this novel are entirely fictitious.

SOW THE WIND, REAP THE WHIRLWIND

Chapter one

The funeral cortege took over an hour to pass. It was one of the largest funerals the province had seen. The procession of mourners made its way slowly down the road towards the churchyard, passing onlookers who were sometimes four deep. Houses and shops along the way had drawn their blinds.

Representatives from the Army, including the SAS, the Legal Profession and the World of Rugby were present. At the end of the procession three people walked with their heads bowed, as though they were trying to hide their faces. One was a beautiful, elegant woman in her early fifties. Her name was Marie Aveline and she linked the arm of her daughter Andrea.

Andrea bore an uncanny resemblance to her mother, and if anything she was even more beautiful. She held the hand of a tall, handsome boy.

Lt-Col Blair 'Paddy' Mayne DSO (3 Bars), Croix de Guerre, Legion d'Honneur was laid to rest on the 15th December 1955. He was the most highly decorated British soldier in World War 11. His final resting-place was Movilla Churchyard in Newtownards, County Down, and the town where he was born on the 11th January 1915.

It was a sombre occasion, and after the committal, mourners drifted away. Finally, in the early afternoon, Marie, Andrea, and her son were standing alone. They looked around them, taking in the unfamiliar scene. Then hesitating slightly, they walked slowly and reverently to the graveside, which was covered with a board festooned with wreaths. They stood silently for a moment, the cold December air bringing a flush to their cheeks. Andrea looked at her mother and saw the tears trickle slowly down her cheeks. The boy looked at the wreaths and then quizzically to his mother.

"I think it's time now mother," Andrea said.

Then she looked down at her son. "Come Patrick, we'll soon have to go."

Andrea removed a glove, and putting her hand in her pocket, she pulled out a silk handkerchief. She looked at her mother, who nodded, as she wiped the tears from her eyes.

Andrea took the handkerchief and knelt down, and raised the board with the wreaths, and held her hand over the open grave. She opened her hand and dropped the handkerchief. As it drifted down, a torn French Franc note fell away beneath it, to rest on top of the coffin. It was immediately covered by the handkerchief. Then Patrick picked up some soil, and threw it over the coffin as Andrea lowered the board again.

Andrea looked again at her mother. "Mother we'd better go. The taxi's due anytime." She said.

As they turned to leave, a man came towards them. The Right Reverend Fraser McLuskey, Paddy Mayne's Padre from the SAS, had said the prayers at the funeral service. After the committal, he had gone back inside the church for a moment of quiet reflection. As he made his way slowly past the gravestones, he fixed his eyes firmly on the two women and the boy.

He was a tall man, handsome and well built, with an open and friendly expression on his face. But there was deep sadness in his eyes.

He smiled as he held out his hand to Marie. There was warmth in his voice, compassion in his eyes as well as the sadness. "Marie," he said gently. "I'm so glad to see you, and you too Andrea. So very glad you came. I was looking out for you, but you know, with the crowd."

Turning, he smiled at Patrick and Andrea, who smiled back. "It's been a long time Fraser," Andrea said.

"You never met Patrick," Marie said as she looked at her grandson. "But we've told him so much about you. He wants to be a Padre, just like you."

Fraser laughed and ruffled the boy's hair. "Paddy would be glad you came," he said.

Marie smiled warmly. "We had to come. It's been so long since that awful War when Anton died." She paused, and almost whispered, "And then of course my son Jacque."

She hesitated, realising that Fraser didn't quite know what to say. "It's all right," she went on. "We have Patrick now."

Patrick looked up and smiled.

Fraser looked at Marie, hesitating in case he said the wrong thing. But he had to say it. "Patrick has his father's looks," he said looking at the boy.

"More than that," Marie said. "His father's temper as well."

"And he's as strong as an ox," Andrea said, punching Patrick on the shoulder. "He can almost beat me at arm wrestling already."

"Can he now?" Fraser said. "Then he's certainly Paddy's son."

Fraser put his arm around Marie. "Are you stopping over until tomorrow?"

"I'm afraid not," she said. "We've to catch a flight to London now, and then on to Paris in the morning."

"That's too bad," Fraser said. "There's so much to talk about."

"Why don't *you* come and see *us*? There's plenty of room in the Château," Marie suggested. "You know I've asked Paddy and you before."

"It's always a tempting thought," Fraser agreed.

"A lot of the old gang are still around," Andrea added.

Fraser hesitated, thinking.

"Well that's it then mother," Andrea said with enthusiasm. "We'll have a reunion! What do you say Fraser?"

"That *is* tempting Andrea, and we can have an arm wrestling competition," Fraser said nudging Patrick in the ribs.

"I'm serious Fraser," Andrea said.

She turned to her mother. "What do you say mother. It's ten years since the war. Wouldn't it be great to get everybody together again and talk about old times?"

Marie shook her head. "I don't know Andrea. Not everybody wants to talk about the old times. It will rake up forgotten memories and not always good ones."

"We could lay some old ghosts to rest," Andrea said faintly.

Marie turned to Fraser. "What do you really think Fraser? Is it wise to go back over it again?"

3

"Some of the lads talk about it, others don't," Fraser said. "For me it seems like another world all together. But I don't want to forget what it was like. War's a terrible thing, there's no mistake. But if we can learn from it, then that's all to the good and we can only learn from it if we talk about it. It's not good to forget. I've found that it's the people who bottle it up and don't talk, who can't cope."

"You mean like Paddy?" Marie insinuated.

"Paddy was different from anybody I've ever known, especially in the war. You know that," Fraser countered.

"So you're saying yes Fraser?" Andrea said eagerly.

Marie raised her eyebrows, a faint smile on her lips.

"I'm in favour Andrea," Fraser said. He looked at Marie. "But only if you agree."

"Yes do," Patrick interjected. "Say yes. I want to."

Fraser gave Marie a squeeze. "This has been sprung on you. Paddy's funeral will have affected us all in different ways, and it wouldn't be the same without him." He took his arm from around her. "Today's not the time to decide, but for what it's worth I'd say yes. I've put it off for too long. It was Paddy really that held it back. So think about it and let me know. You have my address and if you do decide to go ahead, I'll arrange things at this end. I know I can speak for a lot of the lads and many of them would love to go back."

"I'd like to meet them again," Andrea said. "For old times sake if nothing else, and I'm sure I saw one or two faces here today that I recognised."

"Maybe," Marie said. "But we'd better go Fraser," Marie said. "I can see the taxi is waiting to bring us to the airport. We'll think about a reunion and let you know, I promise."

Fraser kissed Marie on the cheek. "Don't leave it too long now, will you?" he said.

He embraced Andrea and held out his hand to Patrick and frowned when he felt the strength in the boy's hand. It reminded him instantly of the first time he shook Paddy Mayne's hand. "Until we meet again - in France," he said

Fraser stood and watched as they got into the taxi. It was quickly out of sight and Fraser's last view was of the young Patrick looking back through the rear window. He wondered if he *would* ever see them again.

Paddy Mayne's death came as a great shock to his many friends, especially to those who had served with him in the SAS during the War years.

His untimely death came in the early hours one morning when he crashed into the back of a parked lorry. He came out of the War virtually unscathed but he found it almost impossible to cope again with civilian life. It was Fraser McLuskey who sent word of his death to Marie and Andrea Aveline. Fraser was the only person who was aware of the special relationship between Marie and Andrea and the big fighting Irishman. With his commanding officer Lt Colonel David Stirling he stood head and shoulders over friend and foe alike.

That night, Fraser McLuskey was tossing and turning in bed. The War he had come through and in which he nearly died, was never far from his mind. But that night memories came flooding back. Some were memories he had never shared with anyone, not even his nearest and dearest. They were memories of a doctor and her husband, seriously wounded during the British retreat to Dunkirk and her daughter and son, and many others, including Paddy Mayne.

Marie was the daughter of a French doctor and an Upper Class English woman. Her parents had met at a garden party when Marie's father had been studying medicine in London. They fell madly in love. In the 1920's Marie studied Medicine at the Sorbonne and there she met a French count who was also studying Medicine. They married and had two children who grew up to be bilingual.

Marie made many friends at University and one of them was to have a major impact upon her life in later years. Josephine Butler had a brilliant mind and a superb physique and she was also English.

Josephine's father sent her to France when she was a child of eight, partly to curb her exuberance. She was the only 'Protestant' in a Catholic Convent but her schooling was exemplary and she excelled at everything. To all intents and purposes she became a French woman.

When her schooling ended she decided to read Medicine and Sociology at the Sorbonne. For Marie and Josephine it was a fateful decision.

At the Sorbonne Josephine and Marie became close friends, sharing each other's enthusiasms and dreams for the future. When University days were over and their training completed they went their separate ways. Josephine became involved in a Cancer Research Unit situated in the Rue des Invalides in Paris. She worked there with a leading surgeon called Thierry de Martel.

During the Munich crisis in 1938 Josephine decided to return to her native Britain where she joined First Aid Nursing Yeomanry (F.A.N.Y) a voluntary organisation. With the prospect of War looming F.A.N.Y was disbanded as a voluntary force and became a paid occupation for the volunteers. In F.A.N.Y Josephine became a driver for V.I.P's. After the air raids in London she was drawn back to medicine again but couldn't settle and felt she could be of more service in F.A.N.Y.

She was later drafted into the Ministry of Economic Warfare (M.E.W) in Berkley Square where she became involved in dealing with maps of Europe. She was not aware of it at the time, but the work she did was invaluable to the Special Operations Executive (S.O.E).

Josephine's particular gifts were noticed, and her credentials were brought to the attention of one man in particular. At the end of February 1942 she found a letter in her in-tray. It was marked 'Top Secret'. The letter instructed her to go to a place called Storey's Gate. She had never heard of the place, but she discovered that it was a secret place forty feet under ground in Whitehall where among other things the War Cabinet met.

There, to her absolute amazement, she was introduced to the Prime Minister, Winston Churchill. Josephine, the English doctor, educated and trained in France before the War became one of Winston Churchill's, elite 'Secret Circle'. She was the only woman in the organisation of twelve members; none of whom knew each other.

So secret was the 'Secret Circle', that neither the War Office nor MI5 was aware of its existence. It was Churchill's closest ring of intelligence agents.

Following her meeting with Churchill, Josephine underwent intensive training, including learning to drop out of an aircraft as it flew four feet above the ground.

In the latter months of 1942 Josephine Butler – code name Jay Bee – flew on the first of over fifty assignments into occupied territory. Her first assignment was on the express instructions of Churchill to find out what the attitude of the French to the Germans was. The Parisians had by then been under military occupation for over two years.

The reports sent back from France, and Paris in particular, often presented two different views. It was difficult for Churchill to know exactly what the true situation was and he needed a first hand report from someone whose views he could trust.

Jay Bee's first flight into France was in a black painted Westland Lysander. The Lysander was nicknamed 'the Flying Carrot' because of its shape. There was no reception committee because nobody knew she was coming, so nobody could betray her to the Germans. The Lysander touched down briefly and before she knew it she was alone.

She had already decided who her contacts in Paris would be and they had priority. One week was not long for all that Jay Bee wanted to achieve but she did it, apart from one visit. She was desperate to visit her old friend from University, Marie Aveline. She knew that Marie's husband Anton had joined the French Army as a doctor at the beginning of hostilities and she wanted to know how they were *all* bearing up under the occupation.

Marie lived in her husband's family home – the Château Aveline – just outside the village of Chantilly. Jay Bee took a train from Paris and after an uneventful journey in a train filled with a mixture of French civilians and German soldiers she arrived at Chantilly.

The Château was three miles outside the village. This was nothing to Jay Bee for whom a twenty-mile hike was child's play. In well under an hour she came to the Château. It was as if she was in another world. Everything was quiet and peaceful. The road up to the Château from the main road was a narrow, single line cart track. It was lined on either side by tall trees. Jay Bee walked slowly but purposefully and for the first time on her journey to France she had a lump in her throat!

She had taught herself to keep her emotions under tight control and never to reveal, by her facial expression, what she was feeling or thinking. When the door opened and she saw her friend Marie for the first time in years she knew immediately she had given herself away. But in that split second she consoled herself with the knowledge that her life wasn't hanging in the balance just then.

Together they burst into tears of laughter as the joy of seeing each other so unexpectedly overcame them both.

The mood changed quickly as Marie's eyes darted about her and she tugged Jay Bee's sleeve, pulling her into the hallway.

"Josephine I don't believe it," Marie cried. "How did *you* get here? What about the Germans? Weren't you stopped and questioned? What on earth did you say?"

Josephine laughed delightedly. "The same old Marie, you're still asking questions and never waiting for an answer. My but you haven't changed a bit."

"Of course I have Josephine," Marie laughed. "Look at the lines and wrinkles. Two children and an invalid husband take their toll. But come into the lounge and have a drink and tell me what this is all about."

Marie led the way and as she entered the lounge she turned to Josephine. "There's a War on or didn't you know?" And she laughed. "The Germans have been everywhere. The Resistance blew up a railway line near Chantilly."

"That wouldn't please the Germans, Marie."

"No, but it's happened before. The trouble is that every time it happens they round up suspects in the locality and bring them in for interrogation. It's not much fun for those they take in. That's why I might have appeared a bit anxious when you came to the door."

"I thought you seemed a bit apprehensive," Josephine said with concern.

They sat down in front of a blazing fire after Marie had rung a bell. In a few moments a young woman entered. "Two glasses of Cognac please, Nina," Marie said to her.

The girl left and there was silence for a moment. They both stared at the fire.

"What has happened to Anton?" Josephine asked suddenly. "You said he was an invalid."

"The War Josephine," Marie said. "He was with the British as they retreated to Dunkirk. There were so many wounded on both sides. He became separated when he refused to leave a badly injured British soldier. The others had to go because the Germans were closing in. Anton was taken prisoner and he was being marched back from the fighting when a shell exploded nearby. German soldiers were injured, but none of the British. Anton went to the aid of the Germans and he saved the life of an Oberstgruppenführer (General)."

"Wow," Josephine said genuine awe in her voice.

"Well he would have done the same for anybody. But then a few days later Spitfires strafed the camp." Marie paused, a slight tremble in her voice. "They weren't to know French and British prisoners were there. Anton was helping a French soldier when he was hit in the back by a bullet."

Josephine reached across and held Marie's hand. "I'm so sorry Marie. "What an awful thing to happen. Where's Anton now?"

"Well it's good fortune really. The General whose life Anton saved gave instructions for Anton to get the best treatment. When the time was right Anton was moved here, and I'm looking after him. With a little help of course," she added.

"Well that's a blessing," Josephine said.

"More than you think," Marie agreed. "It also means that the local Nazis have instructions to leave us alone."

"And what about the children; they must be very grown up by now."

Marie smiled. There was sadness in her eyes. "Yes," she agreed. "They've certainly grown up. Andrea's a nurse in the Hospital."

"And Jacque?"

Marie couldn't hold back the tears that welled up in her eyes.

"He's not ….?

"No, no," Marie said quickly. "You're thinking he's dead." She hesitated. "Sometimes I wish he were."

"No Marie, you mustn't think that."

"You don't understand. He's young and impressionable. He's in Germany because he believes in the German philosophy. He's become a Nazi, Josephine, a collaborator. I just don't know my son any more."

"Oh that's awful," Josephine said with remorse. "That's terrible."

"What makes it worse is that the locals have begun to ostracise us and they know what Anton did for the General. It doesn't matter that he treated French and British as well. He made no distinction. And they know I get special privileges from the Nazis. They even hurl insults at Nina, she's my housekeeper, I couldn't do without her, bless her."

Just then Nina brought the drinks and excused herself again.

"I hate this War, Josephine, and I hate the Nazis and all they stand for. No, that's not strong enough I loathe them. I loathe them for what they're doing to ordinary people. Even French people are turning against each other. Sometimes they're like rats in a cage. Nobody knows who to trust. They're tearing families apart."

"And what about Andrea; how is she?"

"She's a survivor Josephine. She works long hours and I think people see her as a compassionate nurse and that saves her, and maybe that just about tips the balance in our favour, as far as the locals are concerned. Maybe I over reacted a bit. They're not really that bad, and it's hard to blame them."

Then Marie looked straight at Josephine. "You must tell me why you're here Josephine and how you managed it. It's incredible."

Josephine looked seriously at Marie and then at her watch. She shook her head. "Please don't ask Marie, maybe another time. But I

10

must ask you one thing. Don't tell anybody I was here, not even Anton, and I'd love to see him, and I really would, especially in the circumstances."

"But Josephine," Marie protested, when suddenly the door opened and a beautiful young woman came into the room. Immediately Josephine saw the striking resemblance. Andrea was so like her mother. She was five foot eight, slim with shoulder length auburn hair and deep brown eyes and incredibly beautiful. She smiled instantly and warmly.

"Aunty Josephine, I don't believe it's possible," Andrea laughed delightedly. "Don't you know there's a War on?"

Josephine stood up. "You were just a child when I last saw you," she said. "So you remember me?"

"Of course I do," Andrea said. "Auntie Josephine. What are you *doing* here?"

Josephine laughed. "Here we go again."

Andrea frowned and Marie said. "It's better not to ask, Andrea!"

"I'm sorry," Josephine said. "It's just a question of the less said the better and as I asked your mother could I ask you not to tell anybody you saw me?"

Andrea smiled and there was something in her smile that gave Josephine confidence. "Are you getting back all right?"

Josephine nodded and looked at her watch again. "I really must go. I have to walk back to the Station to catch the train."

"Can't you stay for something to eat?" Marie hoped.

"Another time Marie, another time," Josephine said as she finished her drink.

They walked to the front door in silence and just as they were about to part Andrea stepped between them out onto the driveway. "I'll come with you to the Station," she said to Josephine.

Josephine was going to protest but saw the determined look in Andrea's eyes and she acquiesced. Marie and Josephine embraced for a brief moment and then Josephine and Andrea walked away. "I'll see you again Marie," Josephine said. "I promise."

They walked down the single-track driveway in silence.

11

"It should be all right Josephine, can I call you Josephine?" Andrea said as they came to the road. "We won't see any Germans here and anyway they wouldn't bother me. Most of them know me." She hesitated. "I presume you have papers?"

Josephine nodded and smiled. "So if I was a German and asked you what you did, what would you say?" Andrea prompted.

"Well I'd tell them I was a doctor of course, what else?"

"Of course," Andrea agreed. "What else?"

Andrea persisted. "But that's not why you're here, is it?"

Josephine ignored the question. "What do *you* do at the Hospital Andrea?"

"I look after the war-wounded."

"And in your spare time?"

Andrea pursed her lips. "What makes you think I have any?"

Josephine shrugged her shoulders. "Don't you?"

"Not much," Andrea confessed. "I help with father, when I can."

They walked quickly for a few minutes. Then Josephine said quietly. "I'd love to know what you're thinking Andrea."

"And I you Josephine," she retorted.

"All right," Josephine said. "We hear a lot about the French Résistance in England. Is there much evidence of it here? Your mother said they blew up a railway line."

Josephine could almost hear Andrea's heart beat faster. Andrea stopped. "Is that why you're here?"

Again Josephine ignored the question and instead asked Andrea another one. "Your mother seems concerned about Jacque. Do you share Jacque's views? About the Germans I mean."

Andrea walked on. "Jacque blamed the British for my father being paralysed. I blamed the Germans. I still do, every time I see father I blame the Germans."

Josephine took a deep breath and then very precisely asked. "Are you involved with the Résistance Andrea?"

It was Andrea's turn to evade the question. "My mother needs me," she said. "She'll be sad that you couldn't stay longer."

"Yes I realise that," Josephine said. "I'd do anything I could for your mother, but right now I've to return to England."

Andrea stopped suddenly and grasped Josephine's arm and pulled her around to face her. "All right," she said firmly. "I've been in the Résistance from the very beginning. When Jacque turned on his own family, I joined them."

Josephine let out a sigh of relief. "At least we've got that out of the way. Now tell me, how deeply involved are you?"

Andrea raised her hand up to her chin. "I'm in it right up to here," she said.

They walked on. "So *is* that why *you* are here?" Andrea asked.

Josephine found herself thinking very fast. None of this had been planned, but she was thinking of the future and her role within Churchill's Secret Circle. The War was young and Josephine had a gut feeling it would go on for a long time.

"I want you to do something Andrea," she said finally. "Forget this conversation ever took place. This *is* very important. You never saw me. I want you to go straight to the Hospital and you mustn't come to the Station with me and don't tell your mother *anything* of this conversation."

"But my mother is our leader, Josephine."

"Oh no," Josephine said. "She mustn't. It's far too dangerous. If anything happened what would become of your father?"

"They know what they're doing," Andrea said with a note of rebuke in her voice.

"We should have had this conversation back at the house," Josephine said.

Then she continued. "All right, I'm going to have to get in touch with your mother, but I must get back to England first. There's a pre-arranged pickup for me and I can't miss it. Now I want you to trust me, I know your mother would. How many are in your Circuit? And how safe is it?"

"There are twelve of us and as far as one can tell it's very secure. I'd trust every one of them with my life."

"What do you have in the way of arms and explosives?

13

"Not much, just a few hand guns and a couple of sub-machine guns and very little explosive."

"And ammunition?"

"We have very little."

"So I take it you've not done a lot."

Andrea shrugged. "We're willing, but yes, we haven't done much. Generally we work on our own and we're not involved with any other Circuit, though mother has had contact with one."

"That's great," Josephine said. "I want your Circuit to desist from *all* Résistance activity. Don't do anything. Make whatever excuses you have to, to the others, but stop everything. This is very important. Now will you do that for me?"

Andrea hesitated. "I don't know. Why should we? We didn't know you were coming so this could be a trick!" She laughed nervously. You could be working for the Germans. I mean, what authority have *you* got? And anyway, we are nothing, so small. Why would you want to bother with us?"

Josephine looked intently at her. There was a mixture of admiration and concern in Josephine's eyes. She smiled. "Andrea, except a corn of wheat!"

Andrea drew a deep breath. "Falls to the ground and dies it remains only a single seed. But if it dies it produces many seeds."

She stopped. "Yes," she continued. "I remember my Bible. It's in the Gospels I think."

Josephine smiled. "Let's find a gateway," she said.

Safely out of sight, Josephine lifted her skirt and turned over the waistband of her panties. There was a small slit in the inside of the waistband. She extracted a piece of neatly folded paper and unfolded it and handed it to Andrea.

The note read:

To whom it may concern.

The bearer of this note is engaged in vital War business. Please afford her ever possible assistance. Your help will not go unrewarded.

14

Signed

Winston S Churchill

Andrea stared at it for a minute. "Churchill?" she whispered.

"Yes," Josephine said. "I have to confess that I'm thinking on my feet right now. But I have a feeling I'm going to need you and your Circuit. It's better for now, if as a Circuit, you 'die', but only for now. When I get back to England I'll arrange for a drop of arms, ammunition and plastic explosive for your Circuit. You'll need a secure place to store it and you must keep its location secret for the time being, from all but those who absolutely must know. I'll also arrange for training for you and the members of your Circuit. And you'll need a radio and someone trained to operate it."

"Why are you doing this Josephine?" Andrea asked.

"It's all for the War Effort, believe me," Josephine said. "And it may help me enormously. Now will you please agree?"

"All right, I agree," Andrea said. "But there is one proviso; there is one bit of unfinished business I alone must take care of."

"So long as that's all, and you are especially careful. I'll return shortly with a radio and some initial supplies," Josephine said. "And you and your Circuit will get your chance. It may be weeks or months but it won't be until you're ready and the time is right."

"If you're sure," Andrea said.

"I'm sure," Josephine replied. "Now if I am sending someone to meet you, I want you to have something that will allow you to know that they're genuine."

Josephine opened her purse and took out a French Franc note and tore it in half and gave one half to Andrea. "Keep that safe," she said. "If I send someone in my place they will carry the other half of the note. Don't trust anybody without it."

Josephine and Andrea parted company. Andrea went straight to the Hospital and Josephine to the Train Station. From there she had an uneventful journey to within five miles of her pickup point. She walked the rest of the way.

15

During her training the RAF insisted that when returning home, agents should set up a series of flares so that the pilot would know the direction of the wind. Josephine had argued that that was impossible and dangerous when you were operating alone, and she always operated alone. Instead she had practised signalling with a torch and she used a different sequence of flashes each time she was picked up. The system worked well for her and after her first assignment into France it wasn't long before she was reporting personally to Churchill.

Chapter two

Jacque Aveline, Marie and Anton's son was an intelligent but highly impressionable young man of twenty. He was tall, well built and very strong, with dark wavy hair. He was also, like his father, very handsome. When the War started he was studying Engineering at University. At first he was highly indignant and swore to take up arms and oppose the invaders. His mother persuaded him to wait, and he did.

He was, however, influenced by a group of Fascist students who had been planted in the University the previous year. When his father was taken prisoner, and then paralysed when a Spitfire strafed the camp, he was easy prey. The Germans soon convinced him that they had been protecting his father and that it was the British who were guilty of leaving him paralysed. Marie was distraught when he announced that he was accepting an offer to continue his studies in Berlin. His sister Andrea pleaded with him not to go, but it was all to no avail, and in the heat of the moment she swore she would never speak to him again.

His studies in Berlin amounted to indoctrination and he soon became a Nazi. He had been singled out right at the beginning of his University career. He already spoke a smattering of German and his quick mind enabled him to become reasonably fluent in a short time.

Jacque was recruited into the Abwehr. The title meant 'Foreign Information and Counterintelligence Department'. It was the German military intelligence organisation. The head of the Adwehr was Navy Captain Wilhelm Canaris, later Admiral Canaris. He was a shrewd and brilliant Spymaster but he was to be executed by the Nazis near the end of the War for treachery. His second in command was General Hans Oster, who suffered a similar fate, and it was Oster who took Jacque under his wing.

Jacque's training by the Abwehr was much more thorough than that given to many of their spies. The vast majority of German spies who were sent to Britain were quickly detained. Many of them were executed, imprisoned or turned against the Germans. Some of them became double agents. The fault lay with the Abwehr itself, in that their spies were not properly prepared or trained. They made simple mistakes like carrying a packet of German cigarettes!

How much of this was due to ineptitude and how much to Canaris's disillusionment with the Nazi leadership has always been open to question. There's no doubt that Canaris and others in the Abwehr were involved in, or supported the Black Orchestra, the underground movement in Germany opposed to the Nazis.

Jacque Aveline was certainly treated differently from others, and some supposed it had something to do with his father saving the life of the General. Neither the General, or Canaris, was in the Nazi party, and that fact alone was significant. Jacque appeared to have an aptitude for undercover work and he soon became an efficient radio operator and expert in the handling of arms and explosives. He was also trained to search out and trap enemy spies, in the process learning many of the guises they used to try and avoid detection.

The final period of Jacque's training was devoted to the art of silent killing. In that he also became proficient.

During his period of training there were occasional visits home. On his first visit he called to see Andrea at the Cottage Hospital. She refused to see him and would not go home until he left for Germany again. His mother Marie barely spoke to him, but reminded him that because of the incident with his father and the General, the community already gave the family a wide birth. She reminded him also of the fact that his having turned over to the Germans exacerbated the situation. Jacque had little sympathy and went back to Germany, determined to show his family who was on the right side!

Whilst Marie was deeply saddened at her son's attitude and the reaction of the immediate community to their situation, she recognised the positive side and was determined to do all *she* could to get back at the Germans through the Résistance Movement. She knew the Germans would never suspect *them* of collusion with the enemy forces inside or outside France. With the help of Andrea, Marie began to build a totally trustworthy Circuit.

It was with misgivings that she listened to what Andrea told her of her talk with her old friend Josephine. How she longed to talk to her herself, to explain that she was absolutely certain their Circuit was beyond the reach of the Germans. However she agreed with Andrea to put a hold on their activities and to ask all the members of the Circuit to do likewise. She had agreed to give Josephine no more than three months to get back. After that she was determined that it would be business as usual!

When Josephine returned to England she reported to Churchill, and she then found herself alternating between M.E.W and Storey's Gate. Churchill was already planning her next mission into France and the man Churchill and Josephine referred to as the Major was co-ordinating the lose ends. It was the Major who had introduced Josephine to Churchill at the beginning.

At the same time Josephine was working out how she was going to give support to Marie and her Circuit. She had told Churchill of her meeting with Marie, but not of her intended plan to personally supply and supervise their contribution to the War Effort. She confided all of that to the Major a week after her return.

A car picked Josephine up from her flat in Sloane Street where she had moved after joining the Secret Circle. She sat in the back beside the Major. It was 06:30.

"Bright and breezy as usual," the Major said.

Josephine smiled and laid her head against the soft leather of the back seat. She had slept badly the previous night. She turned her head and looked at the Major. He was of average height but with a striking military bearing, almost as if he had been born a soldier. His handsome features would have appealed to many women and his quick friendly smile drew them to him. He was however strictly a one woman's man. His wife was in the Women's Royal Air Force (WRAF). Josephine liked men with a quick mind and the Major was one of the brightest she had ever known. She admired him greatly and looked up to him.

"I've been thinking," she said above the drone of the engine. "I've a name for Marie's Circuit."

The Major raised his eyebrows.

"The Doctors!" she said.

The Major smiled. "I'm sure it's original," he agreed.

"I need your help with this sir," Josephine said.

"Go on," he encouraged.

"I want to supply them with a radio and arms and explosives, and to train them in their use. And I want to bring what I can the next time I'm over.

"And you've someone in mind for this training?" And he smiled again.

"There's our man with De Gaulle's Free French Army, in Scotland."

"And you think we could spare him? Even risk losing him?" the Major asked.

"If *you* say so sir," Josephine was quick to add.

"Hm," the Major said. "I'm not sure Winston's going to like this."

"But do we have to tell him?" Josephine asked.

"Oh yes, quite definitely," the Major said emphatically. He thought for a moment. "Just exactly why are you interested in this particular Circuit?"

Josephine thought for a minute. "We need Circuits like them all over the Continent. We especially need Circuits we can trust, that haven't been tainted, where there's minimum risk of infiltration by double agents or traitors. If I'm honest I also want somewhere where I can be safe in an emergency."

"That all sounds reasonable," the Major agreed.

Josephine smiled. "Well I'm led to believe that I'll be back in France frequently, and every time any agent or I return, the risk of being detected goes up. And I also have a special concern just for old time's sake. I wouldn't want to see anything happen to Marie or her family."

"Well in that case Jay Bee, we'd better do something about it," the Major said.

Josephine soon found herself travelling back to the Scottish Highlands where she had done most of her training. Because of the nature of the task ahead of her it was agreed that she should make all the arrangements herself. She was apprehensive, as Churchill had insisted that Lieutenant Pier Gaston of the Free French Army should not be *ordered* to go. He insisted that such a task could not be placed in the hands of anyone other than a volunteer, in the same way that Josephine was a volunteer.

She checked into a Guesthouse near Arisaig on the West coast of Inverness-shire. It was late evening when she arrived. The proprietor was a friendly woman in her forties. Her husband was in the Merchant Navy. Josephine took to her immediately because she didn't ask any questions about what she was doing in Arisaig.

The morning after her arrival she ate a hearty Scottish breakfast. She packed her rucksack and left the house at 07:30. The Major had given her a pass and a letter of introduction. She walked the seven miles to the group of large houses, which had been taken over by the S.O.E. The road was quiet and the air crisp and cool. It suited her to walk because it helped her to stay fit. She wore stout walking shoes, a tweed skirt and a heavy woollen sweater and carried a pack on her back.

Security at SOE Headquarters was tight but her pass and the letter of introduction allowed her through. She was introduced to Captain William Taylor who had been seconded from 11th Scottish Commando.

He stood politely when she entered his office and shook hands with her, checked her pass, and read her letter of introduction and returned them to her.

"You come with impeccable credentials Miss Turner," he said in a friendly manner. "But your letter tells me nothing of what brought you to the Scottish Highlands and Arisaig in particular. It seems most unusual."

Josephine's real name had been changed in the letter.

"Yes I'm sorry Captain," she said. "It must seem that way. However I'm afraid that as my letter states, I'm not at liberty to discuss my mission with anyone other than with Lieutenant Pierre Gaston."

"I understand," the Captain said. "We're used to all manner of secrets up here."

The Captain stood up and went to the door. "Corporal Williams," he roared. "In here please."

Almost immediately there was a knock on the door and the Corporal came in. "Corporal," he said. "Bring this lady to the Compound and find Lieutenant Gaston for her."

Josephine stood up and followed the Corporal out of the room where they got into a jeep and drove off at speed. The journey was about five miles over narrow winding lanes. They came eventually to a barbed wire enclosure. Armed soldiers guarded the entrance. Inside there were a number of wooden huts and groups of soldiers in training. The Corporal was waved through and he drove straight to one of the wooden huts. Josephine hopped out of the jeep as the Corporal went into the hut to be followed out immediately by the Lieutenant.

The Lieutenant was tall and well built. He had a moustache and gleaming white teeth, which shone when he smiled. Josephine felt right about him straight away. She took to his handsome rugged features. "Lieutenant," she said. "I'm very happy to meet you at last. I've heard a lot about you."

"Thank you?" he asked in impeccable English.

"You may be thanking me too soon," Josephine said. "Is there somewhere we could talk?"

"I'll take you to my own room," Gaston said.

Josephine followed him, while the Corporal remained in the jeep. There was a puzzled look in his eye. Gaston walked quickly away from the hut in the direction of a group of soldiers doing physical exercises whilst in full marching kit.

"I can see you keep them fit," Josephine said. "Are they Commandos?"

"Yes they are," Gaston said. "We're putting them through their paces for a special operation."

As they neared the group Josephine unmistakably heard one of the soldiers call out. "What's the bleeding army coming to, women recruits next. I ask you."

Gaston smiled and looked at Josephine. "Hope that doesn't annoy you?" he asked. "We see very few women up here."

22

Josephine stopped. "Well yes, as a matter of fact it does," she said. "Don't they realise what women are doing in this war?"

Gaston called out to the men. "Get that man over here," he shouted.

There was a grumble of discontent from the soldiers who were all carrying rucksacks and one reluctantly broke ranks and came towards them. Gaston looked at Josephine who smiled slightly and winked. "Will you allow me to handle this?" she asked.

Gaston nodded as the soldier came towards them. "How good *are* they?" Josephine asked, as the man approached.

"Pretty good," Gaston said. "Even though I say so myself."

Josephine put her backpack on the ground as the soldier stopped a few feet away, wondering what the fuss was all about.

She looked at the soldier. "Please remove your rucksack," she said.

The soldier looked at Gaston. "Do as the lady says," he told him.

"Now we're about equal," Josephine said looking at the puzzled soldier. "You've a knife and I'm a German sentry who's about to reach for a gun and shoot you. What will you do?

Again he looked with puzzlement in his eyes at Gaston. "Take your bloody knife out and kill the sentry," Gaston growled.

Josephine could see the look in the soldiers eyes change. Then he smiled. "OK, is that it?" he said.

"Do what the Lieutenant says," Josephine said. "Take your knife; I'm assuming you have one! Take it and kill me if you can."

The smile left his face and he reached for his knife. "I'd take this seriously if I were you," Josephine said.

The soldier lunged at her with the knife, much faster than she expected, but it was still not fast enough. In a flash she had him in an arm lock and swiftly knocked his feet from under him. He fell to the ground and Josephine pretended to remove a knife from her belt and strike him through the heart.

Gaston laughed out loud. "That'll teach you McKerr. Now get up and rejoin the men."

There was a roar of laughter from the soldiers as McKerr marched sheepishly back. "Very impressive," Gaston said. "That was very impressive indeed." The Corporal in his jeep simply shook his head.

In the Lieutenant's room Gaston poured coffee from a percolator and motioned to Josephine to sit down. "So why all the mystery?" he asked.

"I'm sorry Lieutenant, it's just that one can't be too careful," she said. She handed him her letter of introduction.

Gaston read it quickly and handed it back. "So what do you want with me?"

Josephine smiled. "You're French."

Gaston nodded.

"But you also have a reputation, Lieutenant."

Gaston held up his hand. "If we're going to get to know one another you'd better call me Pierre."

Josephine nodded. "And please call me Josephine." She hesitated for a moment.

"There's no secret about the fact that the Allies will one day invade Europe. Until they do we need to harass the Germans at every opportunity. Already in France there are Résistance Circuits. Some are well organised. Some have had training and others are relying on their wits. Security's a major concern because there's so much infighting and resentment between the different factions. There are those who would think nothing of betraying their friends, if it suited their own ends. It's the war. It does terrible things to people."

"You don't need to tell me Josephine," Gaston said. "I've seen it all."

"Yes," Josephine continued. "I know you have; I have obviously read your file. There's a Circuit outside Paris, Pierre. I know its Leader and her daughter, but that's all. I can't tell you why, but they're to be trained to make them as effective as it's possible to be. We want them to be the best. You'll probably find they're just ordinary French men and women, nothing special, but they'll be committed."

"You said, '*you* will probably find.' Are they coming over here?"

"No," Josephine said. "*You* are going over there."

"Is that an order?"

24

"No," Josephine said with a faint smile. "You can get up and walk away now. Nobody will know anything of your decision. Nobody will try to coerce you."

"So what does it entail?"

"First of all I need to know if you'll go. It will most likely be for three months. There'll be absolutely NO visits home to family or friends whilst you're there. When the job's over you'll return to your unit and carry on as before. You'll not be able to return to France, at least not until it's been liberated. You'll be expected to carry a suicide pill. If the circumstances demand it you'll be expected to take it rather than put lives at risk. Nobody can *make* you do that of course."

"I think I'd prefer to stay here," Gaston said gravely.

Josephine looked disappointed. "But I'll go nonetheless," he added.

"I thought you would," Josephine said. "Arrangements will be made for your transfer to London. You'll be given lodgings there while you're being briefed and while preparations are made for you to go to France. In all probability I'll go with you just to make introductions. The rest will be up to you."

Josephine returned to Storey's gate and busied herself getting ready for her next flight to France. Gaston came down two days later and Josephine met him at the Train Station. She brought him to a temporary flat in Sloane Street, close to her own.

The next day the Major came round and met Gaston. With the introductions over they got down to details. It was the Major who took charge.

"I've arranged for the radio you asked for Josephine," he began. "I think that rather than involve too many people it would be best if *you* instruct them in its use."

Josephine nodded her agreement.

"From what you tell me, this Circuit has limited access to arms and explosives so we need to rectify that immediately. They can't be trained with wooden guns. The Sten is the best we have for the type of fighting the Résistance will be involved in. They're cheap and only cost the Government thirty shillings each. The problem is smaller

25

manufacturers are not always as careful as they should be and some fall below standard. As a result when they're fired they can burst the barrel and kill or maim whoever fired it. Anyway I've arranged for you to bring a small shipment with you. It will include handguns, Sten Guns, plastic explosive and detonators. Your Sten Guns will be the best and if there's anything else within reason you think you may need Pierre, let me know."

"How do we get the arms to our destination?" he asked straight away.

"The drop zone's fairly safe because we never used it before," the Major said. "You'll fly over in a Lysander and the pilot will land and taxi. He won't stop. So you'll have less than a minute to offload the shipment of arms and get yourselves out, because inside a minute he'll take off again whether you have offloaded or not."

Josephine looked at a slightly worried Gaston. "It's OK," she said. "I've flown with him before and trained with him. There'll not be any trouble."

"Will there be a Reception Committee?" Gaston asked.

"None is planned," the Major said. "It's our policy. Nobody in France will know you are coming. So if there is one there, you can take it that it won't be friendly, but we've arranged for one of our agents to hide two bicycles for you. The agent has NO idea what they are for or when they will be used. It's the safest we can provide."

"And if that agent is arrested in the meantime? Is there not a danger he might talk?" Gaston suggested.

"I'm glad you're taking security so seriously," the Major said. "And you are correct of course, but the bicycles will only be left hours before you arrive, and five miles from were you land. The agent also has very clear instructions to remain in hiding for forty eight hours, immediately he leaves the area."

"And getting everything to our destination?" Gaston asked again.

"That will be down to both of you when you get there," the Major said. "But I believe you'd be better to hide most of the shipment and return for it at a later date. Obviously you can't bring it on the bicycles. And you'll need to establish a safe place for it nearer Chantilly, and that could take time."

Josephine was ready to break off the meeting and she stood up and Gaston followed her. "Just a moment," the Major said. "There's something else."

Gaston shrugged his shoulders and sat down. Josephine remained standing.

"It's like this," the Major said, looking at Josephine. "When I brought this idea of yours to the PM it was entirely your own idea – your baby if you like. Of course at the time he didn't appear impressed one way or the other. But in actual fact he was *most* impressed. Not so much at your initiative but at the possibilities. The Circuit you've identified has taken on a new and vital significance. The PM has instructed me to inform you that he wants this Circuit to be given *every* possible support. Nothing will be too much trouble. He believes that the time will come when it will play one of the *most* important tasks in the whole War against Nazism. It goes without saying of course that this is of the utmost secrecy but neither of you can know at this stage what role this Circuit may play."

The rest of the morning was spent working out the finer details of Gaston's trip and then the Major left them. Josephine and Gaston spent the afternoon in London and managed a picture in the evening. Their trip to France was planned for the following week. Flights were only undertaken one week on either side of a full moon to give as much visibility as possible.

In the days that lay ahead Josephine was kept busy at M.E.W. and in further consultations with the Major. She had one brief meeting with Churchill to update him on their progress and also to prepare her for her next trip to France. He made one comment about the Circuit that she had adopted as her own.

"Jay Bee," he said. "The future of the Free World could rest on the preparations you make." And he drew long and hard on his cigar and blew the smoke towards the ceiling. He appeared deep in thought for a moment. "I have a mammoth decision to make," he said. "And I can tell nobody!"

In the meanwhile Gaston enjoyed the sights of London, such as they were. He also worked on a training regime for the Doctor's Circuit in France.

Chapter three

They took off in the Lysander on a moonlit night, one-week later. The flight was surprisingly uneventful, as was the drop off for both Josephine and Gaston and the supply of arms and explosives and the radio.

As the Lysander cleared the drop zone, Gaston and Josephine manhandled the container of arms to the edge of the field. Gaston was armed with a Sten Gun and Josephine with a pistol. They crouched close to the hedge and waited for an hour before moving again. When they were satisfied that the noise of the aircraft had not drawn any attention they hid most of the arms in a ditch covering them with branches and dead grass. They examined their handiwork briefly with a torch and then they checked their map to find the location of the bicycles.

They found the bicycles almost five miles away, hidden in a deserted barn a hundred yards up a narrow cart track. They only carried the radio and personal weapons because they had a four-hour cycle ahead of them. The night was cool and dry and the moon allowed enough light to ride safely. For security they cycled about two hundred yards apart.

They had been cycling for almost two hours. The night remained bright but some times the moon was obscured by cloud for minutes at a time. As a consequence Josephine, who was in front, was then hidden from Gaston's view. On those occasions Gaston cycled faster to catch up with her.

Suddenly Gaston found himself in darkness again and he increased his speed but as he drew closer to Josephine he caught his breath. There was the unmistakable sound of voices ahead of him. He cycled very slowly until he could just make out the shadowy outline of people on the road. One of them shone light.

He left his bicycle on the grass verge and walked slowly up the road. Suddenly the darkness was lifted again, as the clouds passed and Gaston just had time to climb a gate into the adjoining field before he was seen. He walked quietly along the roadside hedge and then over a barbed wire fence running at right angles to it. He was soon within fifty yards of where Josephine had been stopped on the road.

Josephine had been pleased with their progress and after two hours cycling was beginning to imagine that they were going to get to the Château without any incident. It was as she rounded a slight bend in the road that she saw the German army car stopped with its engine running. She drew her breath as she braked suddenly, but it was too late. The cloud was just passing over the moon and there was still enough light for her to be seen.

The soldier, who was the driver, had been standing at the side of the road relieving himself. He turned just as he buttoned his fly and saw Josephine about to get off the bicycle. He quickly opened the back door of the car and pulled out an MP38 sub-machine gun.

He pointed the gun menacingly at Josephine and shouted. "Come here, we want to talk to you."

Josephine hesitated and then getting off the bicycle she pushed it towards the car. Her heart was pounding. This was her first real test because her radio was in a suitcase strapped to the back of the bicycle, as was her pistol. The soldier walked slowly to meet her.

"Why are you out so late?" he demanded. "Show me your papers."

Josephine knew it was strange for anyone, especially a lone woman to be out at five o'clock in the morning. I'm a doctor," she said. "I ran out of petrol so I borrowed my patient's bicycle."

"Where are your papers?" he demanded again, shining a torch in Josephine's face.

Josephine's mind raced. She didn't know whether to try and bluff her way out of the situation or attempt to get her pistol from the case when she was looking for her papers. If she *did* manage to shoot the soldier she knew there could be more in the car than she could handle. It was a split second decision.

"They're in my case," she said. "Please hold by bicycle."

Before he knew it the soldier was resting his gun on the handlebars of the bicycle while Josephine rummaged around in her suitcase. She took out her papers and handed them to the soldier. He pushed the bicycle back against Josephine as he took the papers and shone his torch on them.

Gaston was watching the goings on through the hedge, Sten Gun at the ready. Suddenly the passenger door of the car opened and another man got out. He was in his late fifties with an obvious military bearing.

"What's the matter Karl?" he said gruffly.

"It's a woman Herr General," he said. "She claims she's a doctor." He hesitated. "Her papers appear to be in order."

"Then let's be on our way," the General said. "We're late enough as it is."

The General turned back towards the car, then as an afterthought he turned and said to Josephine. "Where are you going?"

Josephine thought it was better to tell the truth. "I'm going to Chantilly," she said. "I am staying with Doctor Marie Aveline and her husband Anton."

Josephine caught the glimpse of a faint smile on the General's face. "I know Doctor Aveline," he said. "And her husband Anton. We shall give you a lift."

"No, there's absolutely no need," Josephine protested.

"Nonsense," the General said. "Any friend of Marie's and Anton's, is a friend of mine."

He turned to Karl. "Put her bicycle in the boot."

Josephine's protestations fell on deaf ears. She removed her suitcase and then to her surprise the driver held the front passenger door open for her. She got it and as she did so she looked behind her at the General to thank him. He was not alone because there was a young and beautiful woman beside him. She smiled at the General and said thanks and nodded at the young woman. Then with the bicycle in the boot and the suitcase on her knee they drove away.

Gaston smiled to himself as he felt the tension easing and he went back to his bicycle to continue his journey alone.

The rest of the journey to Chantilly was quiet and uneventful for Gaston. It was even hard to imagine there was a War on. He made his way cautiously up the driveway to the Château in case the German staff car was there. All was clear and at 07:00 he rang the doorbell. Andrea, who was already dressed in her nurse's uniform and ready to go to work, opened the door. He could see the look of relief in her eyes and immediately knew that Josephine had arrived safely.

Two hours previously, Andrea had nervously answered the doorbell in her dressing gown. There had been so many stories of early morning calls that were the prelude to disaster, torture and death. Sometimes people just disappeared.

"I don't believe it," she had cried with joy as she saw Josephine standing before her and the German staff car driving away with the General waving. She beckoned her into the hallway and closed the door. "We didn't believe you would come back, at least not so soon," she said. "But how on earth did you meet up with *him*?"

"I said I would come back," Josephine scolded her. "As for the General, that's another story. But who was the gorgeous young woman with him? Not his daughter surely?"

Andrea smiled. "Let's just say, that's his little bit on the side. She is beautiful, and her name's Madeleine Boussine. Her husband was in the French army, and we think he was killed. Nobody seems to know for certain."

Just then Marie ran down the stairs, pulling her dressing gown around her. "I thought I heard a commotion," she said. "What a joy Josephine, to see you again so soon."

Marie brought her into the lounge where Josephine had sat the previous time. She rang the bell and Nina came, dressed already and breakfast was ordered.

Josephine looked in the direction Nina had gone. "She *is* all right Marie?" Josephine asked.

"I'd trust her with my life," Marie assured her. "Anton was very good to her mother when she was dying of cancer two years ago. If for no other reason, she would never do anything to compromise us. But why are you back so soon? What's happening?"

Josephine laughed. "Will she never stop asking questions? I'll tell you all in due course. But my first concern is for my colleague Gaston. He was just behind me when I was stopped. He knows where to come to, but one can't be too careful." She shook her head. "I do hope he's all right. He came with me from England and he's French and he's going to stay for a while."

Gaston was relieved to arrive safely and more so when Andrea opened the door to him and he realised that Josephine was safe as well.

When Gaston was seated, Josephine became serious. "There's something I must tell you Marie," she said. "It's very important and it does require your agreement."

"Go on," Marie said smiling. "I'm listening."

The Prime Minister has asked me to personally take charge of your Circuit."

Marie immediately protested. "But Josephine."

"Wait a minute Marie. I know this seems like a liberty, even a cheek, but please hear me out. This came as much of a surprise to me as it does to you, but there are reasons and I can only share them with you. Nobody else I'm afraid, not even Anton must know that I'm in charge, nor the reason. To all intents and purposes you'll continue to be in control, but I'm asking you only to act on my specific instructions and the reason is this. The Prime Minister has plans for this Circuit, so that it may play a vital role in the war. And he's asked me to tell you personally that it's his specific wish that you agree to this. He's also given me a hand-written note, which you must burn as soon as you've read it."

She handed the puzzled Marie the brief note which she explained was written in Churchill's own hand.

It read.

To M

Your friend Josephine Butler is acting wholly at my request. I would consider it a great act of faith and courage if you would kindly agree to follow my instructions through her.

Should you agree to do so, you have my word that everything possible will be done to enable you to carry out the duties, which may be required of you and your brave comrades. I will never forget, whatever price you pay, whatever sacrifices you may be called upon to make.

I will always be in your debt.

Winston S Churchill

Marie read the note through again and again. "He decided your code name should be M," Josephine said.

"How can I refuse?" Marie said, as she crumpled the note up in her hand and threw it into the fire.

Chapter four

General Hans Oster was pleased with the progress Jacque Aveline
had made within the Abwehr. He had become one of their most
reliable agents, was intelligent and willing to learn and above all, he
was always seeking to ingratiate himself to Oster. Throughout his
time with the Abwehr he had made more arrests than almost anyone
else. He enjoyed his growing reputation and he tended to operate best
when he was alone. However General Oster was aware of two
blemishes to his character. He was too fond of violence, and he had
developed a reputation for drink *and* women.

Hans Oster had risen quickly within the ranks in the army, due
mostly to his administrative ability. However when Adolph Hitler
came to power in Germany in 1933, Oster immediately aligned
himself with high-ranking Officers of the Wehrmacht, who secretly
opposed the dictator. When Oster became deputy director of the
Abwehr, under Admiral Wilhelm Franz Canaris, he continued this
secret resistance. Not only was he plotting against Hitler but also
against the heads of the secret Police, Heinrich Himmler of the
Gestapo and Reinhard Heydrich of the *SS* and *SD*.

It was not long before Oster encouraged Canaris, his chief, and
another Abwehr spymaster, Erwin von Lahousen to join him in his
conspiracies.

Admiral Canaris had little to do with Jacque, partly to maintain an
air of mystique, and he was happy to leave his protégé in the hands of
his deputy. The time came when Oster informed his chief that Jacque
was ready for a special mission known only to them.

Early one morning Jacque was wakened from his sleep by an urgent
knock on the door of his flat. The young woman, lying naked and
asleep beside him, did not waken from her drunken stupor. Jacque
threw the bedclothes aside and stumbled to the door, drawing a towel
across his middle with one hand and grabbing his Luger pistol in the
other as he did so. Two men in plain clothes greeted him. One of
them looked at his watch and shook his head.

"Put that thing away and get dressed Jacque," he said. "We'll wait for you in the car and the General says don't bother to shave."

The other man went into the flat and looked at the naked woman on the bed and the empty drink bottles on the bedside table and swore. "You'd better get her out of there," he said."

Jacque was startled at the sudden intrusion into his privacy, and he'd been involved in enough early morning raids to feel a twinge of apprehension. He knew both of the men and realised he had no option but to comply with their request. He dressed quickly, shaking the woman on the bed several times in an attempt to waken her. When he had dressed and she still lay asleep, he pulled her roughly off the bed and across the floor, to the outside of the flat. By this time she was groaning in protest. Jacque ignored her protests and simply went back and gathered her clothes, and threw them in a pile on top of her and closed the door behind him.

The men were waiting in their car as Jacque came out. The rear door of the car was open and Jacque climbed in. Nobody spoke as the car drove off. Jacque realised quickly that they were heading for Abwehr Headquarters and the sense of panic he felt began to ease. He was brought to the office of Admiral Canaris. Canaris was sitting behind his desk and he looked up as Jacque stood before him and saluted, "Heil Hitler." The Admiral returned the salute and gestured with his hand and Jacque took the seat that was offered.

"You've been wakened earlier than usual?" Canaris said.

Jacque mumbled. "I was just about to rise," he lied.

"All this money we give you," Canaris said. "I'm afraid it's going to your head."

Jacque knew that the state of his room with the stale smell of smoke and drink and the whore he'd spent the night with had already been reported to Canaris. Not only was there no honour among thieves, there was little honour among agents of the Abwehr. Jealousy was rampant in the Department. Jacque knew there was no point in trying to cover up. "Perhaps I have over indulged on occasions," he agreed.

"Hm," Canaris said. "We've lavished a lot of time and money on you Aveline. I hope it's not going to be wasted."

"Not at all sir," Jacque said. "You must know I'm ready to serve my Führer in any way I can, and after all I was led to believe that General Oster was more than pleased with my progress."

"Up to now perhaps," Canaris said. "But are you ready for something much bigger, something much more important? Something Aveline, that's vital to the War Effort, to the Abwehr and especially the Führer?"

"I'm sure I'm ready for whatever tasks you or the Führer set before me," Jacque said with confidence. "I wish only for an honourable end to this War for my beloved France, and of course victory for Germany."

"And are you ready to give up your drinking and your whoring for the love of France?" Canaris asked dryly.

"Admiral," Jacque said quietly. "Those things were simply a mere distraction; something to fill in time." He hesitated. "One can't afford to have many friends when one is working for the Abwehr. But I can assure you, that such behaviour's already a thing of the past." He moved uncomfortably in the chair. "I'm ready Herr Admiral, to do your bidding and to serve my country and my Führer."

"Very well Aveline." The Admiral looked around him for a moment, and then he called out. "Hans!"

General Oster came in immediately, as if he had been waiting at the door ready for the call. "Take a seat Hans," the Admiral said.

The General nodded and sat down in the corner of the room, his eyes on Jacque. "Are we alone Hans?" the Admiral asked.

"Our section's clear Sir," Oster assured him.

Canaris pale and tired looking turned to Jacque. "What I'm about to tell you Aveline is top secret and the success of this 'operation' depends on that. You must not under any circumstances discuss it with anyone."

He opened a drawer and removed a red folder and then looked Jacque straight in the eye. Jacque held his gaze for a moment and then let his eyes fall to the desk and the red folder that now lay open before them. Oster pulled out a packet of cigarettes and slowly and thoughtfully lit one, drawing the smoke deep into his lungs before blowing it towards the ceiling.

Canaris folded his hands in front of him as they rested on top of the folder, and he lay back in the black leather chair, relaxed.

"Twenty-two years old. You were born on the 15th August 1919, the year after the Great War, the son and first child of Doctor Anton and Doctor Marie Aveline. You've a sister Andrea, two years younger. Your mother was English and your father French so you've always been bilingual?" Canaris looked up briefly and Jacque nodded.

"With English and French connections isn't it strange you should side with Germany?"

Jacque shook his head. "France has always been my country," he said. "That's why I've sided with Germany because Germany holds France's future in her hands and I want to be part of that future."

"But your family doesn't share your views," Oster butted in.

Jacque swung round in the chair. "They shall come to see I'm right. One day they'll thank me. And they'll thank the Führer."

"You've not been home recently though, so are you comfortable going home as things are?" Canaris asked.

"We're barely on speaking terms," Jacque said. "And that's because of my views of course. We were close once, before the war, and even at the start when I went to University. My sister is *very* anti-German, but my mother and father are less so."

"Your father was a surgeon in the French army, but I know he saved the life of one of our Generals," Canaris said. "Now your father's paralysed after the British strafed a column of soldiers where he was a prisoner. It must be difficult for your mother, even though she's a doctor."

"Yes," Jacque agreed. "My father depends on her, but the German army have been good to them. That's what really frustrates me, people only want to look for the bad in Germany, and they forget how much good there is."

"There's good in everyone," Canaris said. "But there's also bad. We look at the French people, and I'm not forgetting you're French. We look at you French and we see a people divided. Some welcome

38

us, others tolerate us and of course some hate the sight of us. Of those who welcome us there are those who actively help us, like you for instance. Then there are others who are happy to see us where we are, but they don't show it. They are, as it were, sitting on the fence, afraid to commit themselves to the War Effort, just in case things go wrong and they find themselves on the losing side."

Canaris looked sternly at Jacque. "I'm glad to see that you've chosen not to sit on the fence. Your records show that you've eagerly participated in seeking to round up those French people who are against us. You've not shied away from your responsibilities, even though it has meant you're ostracised from your family and your community. Your conduct has been admirable, and you've been an exemplary agent of the Abwehr."

Jacque felt smug as he smiled his gratitude, but it was to be short lived.

Canaris leafed through the red folder on his desk. Then he looked at Jacque and pointed with his finger at the top of a page. "That is except perhaps for one incident. You remember the village of Verberie?"

Jacque looked up startled. He felt the blood draining from his face. He was conscious of Canaris and Oster watching his reaction. The whole bloody episode flashed before his eyes in an instant, as a drowning man is supposed to see his life flash before him as he loses consciousness. He was horrified when he realised the incident had come to the attention of his superiors, but how?

British airmen were sometimes seen parachuting on to French soil from their stricken aircraft. The Germans knew from the wreckage of the planes and the remains of the aircrew in them that a number of them survived. Those who landed safely were, if they were fortunate, picked up by the French Résistance and spirited away along various escape routes. Hardly any Allied aircrew were thought to make it without assistance.

Jacque was drafted in by his superiors to investigate one suspected escape route. It was a routine operation and was ordered by a sub-section of Abwehr. Neither Canaris nor Oster were aware of it, nor indeed was it even considered worthy of their attention. They had much bigger fish to fry!

Along with two colleagues, Jacque began his investigations, but after three weeks they were no further on. They had their suspicions but despite numerous arrests and interrogations they had discovered nothing, except that circumstantial evidence and a sixth sense pointed to one family in particular, the Desjardines. They were farmers, living in an isolated farmhouse. There was a husband and wife and three sons. Because of the size of the farm the two older sons had avoided military service for France and later, deportation to Germany. Then one night a Halifax bomber crashed on farmland near to the farm on the outskirts of Verberie.

When the Germans arrived they found the pilot dead in the cockpit, but there was no sign of the rest of the crew. The surrounding area was searched that night and in the morning, but the crew had vanished. Jacque's greatest fear was that the Gestapo would be called in and that they would succeed where he had failed. So, desperate not to lose face, Jacque visited the farm again.

A detachment of *SS* Soldiers was with him. He ordered the two older sons to be brought to the barn whilst he interrogated the father and mother. He hadn't been told about the younger son. The parents were beaten almost senseless but they said nothing. Now in a heightened state of anxiety Jacque and his two colleagues went to the barn where they used the same treatment on the sons.

Aware that he was getting nowhere and conscious that the *SS* was observing him, Jacque finally ordered the two brothers to be strung up by the ankles to a rafter in the barn determined that they should talk. Despite the horrendous torture they revealed nothing and eventually they choked to death on their vomit. Disgusted with the outcome and fearful the parents would talk Jacque ordered that they should be shot as an example to the rest of the community of what would happen to anybody who collaborated with the enemy.

Jacque was not to know that the younger son, François, witnessed the whole episode whilst hidden in the hayloft. He had lain silent and frozen with fear. It was two hours before he dared to move. When he did, his first thought was of his parents. He raced to the house and found them on the kitchen floor shot through the back of the head and his mother had been raped.

In a panic he ran back to the barn and looked up at the ashen faces of his brothers. He smelt the vomit around their faces and he knew they had soiled themselves. The smells were never to leave him. He turned to walk away as fear began to grip him, but he wanted desperately to cut his brothers free. He was terrified the Germans would come back and didn't dare to do it.

Then as he turned he noticed a white handkerchief on the ground. He bent and picked it up and wiped the faces of his two brothers with it. Absentmindedly he put it in his pocket as a kind of memento to the brothers he worshiped and a reminder of how they died.

Then he ran for his life across the fields, afraid to be seen by anyone. He was confused and angry, blaming himself for not having the courage to intervene and try and save his family. He was afraid to tell anyone what had happened in case word reached the Germans that he had witnessed the whole affair.

If he had not run for his life when he did, he might have died in the fire that followed. When Jacque had left the scene of torture, rape and murder, he began to have doubts about what he'd done. He returned later and set the farmhouse and outbuildings ablaze to destroy the evidence.

Attempts were made to name the culprits but it was all to no avail. Captain Jacque Aveline and his accomplices in the *SS* managed to keep their identity a secret. However, as a consequence of his actions, Jacque got himself a notorious nickname.

In the days that followed his family's brutal murder, no matter how hard he tried, François couldn't erase the memory of what he's witnessed in the barn. A deep-rooted hatred of the Germans and all they stood for began to consume his whole being. Nobody in the locality believed the fire was accidental, but there was nothing to suggest it wasn't. All anyone knew was that the family *had* been under suspicion by the Germans. Everyone assumed that François had also died in the blaze, but rumours soon began to circulate and German *SS* troops were blamed, and one man in particular whom they couldn't put a name to.

In the weeks that followed François Desjardine decided to change his name to François Debré. He became adept at living of the land, remaining hidden by day and furtive by night. He watched and observed from his hiding places during the day and listened when he could. Whenever the need arose he raided farmhouse kitchens, hen coops and byres and gradually his anger and hatred gave way to a desire for revenge. The time was soon to come when he knew he had to be armed. Having lived on the farm he had a certain familiarity with guns but he had not acquired the art of relieving the enemy of theirs. Neither was he skilled in the art of unarmed combat but farm labouring had left him as strong as an ox. It was well known that his older brothers would not have willingly picked a fight with him.

Unknown to Jacque an *SS* Corporal had photographed the beatings and torture of the two brothers and their subsequent death as they hung upside down from the rafter. Later, one of the *SS* soldiers, perhaps because of a sense of remorse, but more likely because of a desire to ingratiate himself to his masters, or even because of the fear of reprisals, obtained copies of the photographs and handed them over to General Oster.

Nothing was said to Jacque about the incident or the photographs but they were filed away in his personal records.

Now he was forced to admit to the atrocity. He tried desperately to bring facts to bear to justify what happened. "It was an unfortunate happening," he said rather lamely. "But ... but there have been no further reports of an escape route in that area. The action may have been brutal but it does appear to have had the desired effect. Surely that proves it *was* the Desjardines who organised the escape route and now they're gone they can't talk. And I did cover my tracks. I mean the fire saw to that. Nobody could ever prove it was German soldiers."

"That may be so," Canaris said. "But people put two and two together and they blamed the occupying forces anyway. Make no mistake about it. And it may also have served to further alienate the community. You do know they call you the Butcher of Verberie!"

Jacque was conscious now of his heart beating in his chest. He tried to remain calm and started to take deep breaths. Canaris and Oster noticed but carried on regardless.

"And," Oster interrupted, "it may have simply driven the escape route further underground. Counter productive wouldn't you say?"

Jacque was unsure as to where the conversation was leading. "I acted in the way I thought fit at the time," he said.

"Next time give it more thought," Canaris said dryly. "Incidents like that do not serve the cause. Among other things they leave the perpetrators open to blackmail."

"Too blackmail?" Jacque repeated.

"What do you think would happen if these photographs got into the hands of the Résistance? Hm?" Canaris asked.

"Photographs?" Jacque whispered.

Canaris handed Jacque a photograph of himself leering into the faces of the brothers as they hung by the ankles. It was obvious they were dead. Jacque felt himself shiver. "But how would the Résistance get a photograph like this?" he asked. "I don't understand. Where *did* this photograph come from?"

"The *SS* photographed the incident, just for their records as they often do," Oster told him. "Sometimes it's just to gloat about it afterwards and sometimes they use it as evidence that they actually carried out the atrocity. Some of them like to be certain that *they* get the credit you understand. How we came by the photographs doesn't concern you.

"But you asked me how would the Résistance get this photograph," Canaris said. "Well, I don't think the *SS* would give it to them because it would serve them no purpose. But they might be tempted to do with them what *we* might do. They might use them to blackmail you into doing something you would otherwise refuse to do! And likewise, if you were to act, shall we say in a way inappropriate as far as the *Abwehr* was concerned, then *we* might find it convenient to let the Résistance around Verberie have a copy."

43

Jacque looked from one to the other. "But I would never," he said with conviction.

"I know," Canaris said. Then he smiled benevolently. "Because if you did, the Résistance would find you and my guess is that they would have something very special lined up for you, when they caught up with you."

Canaris folded his arms and look keenly at Jacque. "Now Aveline," he said quietly. "We've two very special missions for you."

He held out his hand to Jacque for the photograph and as Jacque reached it to him Canaris said. "In the meantime we shall look after that, and the others."

"What exactly are the missions," Jacque asked, relieved that they appeared to be getting off the subject of Verberie.

Canaris looked across to Oster who lit another cigarette and then he drew his chair closer to Jacque. "They are two separate missions but they could be interconnected. The French are divided in their attitude to us, so too are some Germans who don't support the War Effort, and some are even plotting to overthrow the Führer!"

Jacque looked askance. "Yes, truly," Canaris said.

"It's important that we know who these people are," Oster continued. "And it's important that we have evidence against them so that they can be brought to trial and punished. Public trials are important because they serve to deter others."

"And you want me to help you find these traitors?"

"Just one," Oster said. "General Scholtz."

"But .... my father saved General Scholtz's life. He was critically wounded after my father had been taken prisoner. There must be some mistake because I've met him and he's not a traitor."

"We hope there's been a mistake," Oster said. "We're not sure, but we want you to find out for definite. Except, and let me remind you, you mustn't tell *anybody*, and I mean *anybody* what your mission is."

"Otherwise," Canaris said. And he held up the photographs. "This one's rather good don't you think?" And Jacque could feel the blood draining from his face again.

44

"You've been chosen because you've met the General, and because your family's close to him. It shouldn't be too difficult for you to find out what the General *really* thinks and believes."

"I don't know," Jacque said hesitatingly. "I told you that as far as my family's concerned I'm 'persona non grata'. They wouldn't trust *me*."

Canaris smiled. "I'm sure you'll find a way. After all you can be whoever and whatever you like. As far as we're concerned you can change sides, as many times as you like."

"Just so long as you never forget where your *real* loyalties lie," Oster added.

"You mean a double-agent? But if I do that and the Gestapo were to take me in for questioning?" Jacque asked quietly.

"They'd only do that if they didn't accept your papers as genuine," Oster said calmly. But we've thought of that eventuality also. Your best option of course is to make sure they don't! I'm sure you don't need us to tell you what the Gestapo can be like."

"Even we're afraid of them," Canaris said with a slight smile, and Jacque didn't know whether to believe him or not. "So just to cover ourselves, as well as having the photographs, we'll have a warrant out for your arrest."

Jacque sat bolt upright. "These are dangerous times Aveline, but I'm sure there's no need to worry. The warrant won't be issued unless it's *really* necessary. That is, unless the Gestapo take you in for questioning. You see we have no doubt that you would talk."

"Never," Jacque said desperately.

"Nearly everybody talks," Canaris said. "It's nothing to be ashamed of. The human body can only take so much. It's a very special person who resists the worst the Gestapo can do."

Canaries hesitated. "But then I'm forgetting am I not. You've seen first hand what the human body can take, and still stay silent. But then you were not as subtle as the Gestapo, nor as persuasive, I hesitate to suggest."

Canaris closed the red folder. "And now we must address this other rather distasteful business. Within a radius of about sixty kilometres of Chantilly a lone assassin has been killing German Officers. There's a similar pattern to these killings. The Officers are usually high ranking, not just your ordinary Captain, so you shouldn't be in danger from him! They're singled out when they're either alone or with just one or two people. Not a single clue has ever been left behind. Sometimes the shooting has taken place in a hotel, sometimes in a main street, sometimes an ambush in the country in broad daylight. The assassin *has* been seen on more than one occasion, but his face is always covered and he's always made a clean getaway. It's almost as if the assassin knows where his next victim is going to be, so that he must have inside information."

Jacque pursed his lips and frowned. "And has nobody the slightest idea who this assassin is?"

"A lot of people have been interrogated for various crimes in that region, especially for being in the Résistance. Anybody who has broken under interrogation either by the Gestapo or by us has also been questioned about this assassin. Nobody has volunteered *any* credible evidence."

"What about a reward?" Jacque said. "The French are the same as everybody else when it comes down to money, if there's enough of it!"

"We've offered 100,000 francs," Oster said. "But there's been no response."

Oster leaned forward in his chair and looked intently at Jacque. "It's very important that this assassin is caught. Please understand that. General Scholtz is well known as a high ranking Officer and a very valuable one to Germany. We can't afford to lose him to an assassin's bullet before we know for certain whose side he's on."

"Enough of this," he said turning to Oster. "Hans, we'll give Aveline the rest of the day off. I've no doubt in my mind that he'll not let us down."

He turned again to Jacque who seemed a trifle relieved. "Don't be alarmed by anything I've said," he told him. "We'll give you more details of the task ahead tomorrow."

Oster rose from his chair and opened the door. "Call for a staff car Aveline, they'll be expecting you, and they'll call for you again in the morning. And bring everything with you that you'll need because you'll not be back in the flat for a while."

Jacque stood to attention with a clear "Heil Hitler" and left the room in a cold sweat and with his mind in a whirl. He was beginning to regret he had ever set foot in Germany.

When the door closed behind him Oster sat down again and pulled out another cigarette and lit it.

Canaris look his friend straight in the eye. "What's your honest opinion Hans? Will our plan work?"

Oster sighed. "It's our best option Admiral and I believe Aveline still loves life enough to do everything he can to succeed."

"Well I'm convinced Scholtz is a good man," Canaris said. "He's one of the best and certainly not a Nazi, and we need him on the right side. When the time comes we will need him to work with us to oust Hitler and his nest of vipers. But we've got to keep our backs covered. I just wonder if Aveline learns the truth will he back us. Or will we have to eliminate him?"

"Aveline will stick with those he thinks will win," Oster said. "That's why he's sided with Germany in this wretched war, and I believe he still wants to impress us, so he'll try hard to get the evidence because he's got the impression Scholtz may be guilty."

"Which means he'll be kept involved long enough for us to get Scholtz committed," Canaris said. Then he looked at his watch. "London's most insistent that we've things in place very soon. Hess has done his bit, and Heaven help us for having to rely upon him, but his flight to England was enough to convince Churchill we were deadly serious. We mustn't let the grass grow under our feet though, so the sooner Aveline gets moving the better for us all. Now I must leave you Hans. I've a meeting with Goering and Himmler, God help me.

Chapter five

Standartenfuhrer Otto Kramer had a penchant for young boys. As a Colonel in the *SS* it was not too difficult for him to satisfy his urges. He usually played on the fear the French people had for the *SS* and the Gestapo. His favourite ploy was to seek out a young boy whom he took a liking to. It was usually, but not always, from a home where the father of the boy had died or else had been sent for forced labour in Germany. He preferred the boy's father not to be around.

Once he had identified a boy he would bring his mother in for questioning on some trumped up charge or other. All kinds of threats were then brought to bear on the poor mother until she was at her wit's end. At that stage Kramer would then offer her a way out. It was a stark choice, which was, 'Either you bring the boy to me when I want him, or these charges will stick and you'll end up in a Concentration Camp and I'll have your son anyway!"

Invariably the boy's mother choose the lesser of two evils. Then when a particular boy ceased to amuse Kramer he simply didn't call for him any more. Both were left in no doubt what would happen if they ever mentioned to anyone what had taken place.

To most of his colleagues Kramer was simply a pervert, but such was their own fear of reprisals that none of them dared to speak up. Then Kramer made a mistake. He had just abandoned one boy when he took a fancy to another. Unknown to him the next boy was actually a cousin of the last one. They lived in adjoining villages. The father of the second boy was believed by the Germans to have died in the fighting in the early stages of the war. In actual fact he was with the Maquis.

The Maquis was made up of Maquisards, men who had burned their bridges behind them. When the Germans imposed compulsory labour service in the western European occupied countries in 1942, they fled their homes. They lived like outlaws in makeshift camps in forests. They would have been shot had they shown their face to the enemy. They camped out in wild and mountainous districts, hence the name

Maquis from the Corsican term for bush or shrub. When Kramer took a liking to Andrée Cohen's son his mother couldn't cope. She confessed to her sister what had happened. After they'd compared notes with one another they decided to send word to Andrée.

Andrée was determined to set out straight away to seek revenge for what had been done to his son, but his fellow Maquisards put pressure on him to desist. Instead they put the word around in a fairly tight select circle that a certain *SS* Colonel was on their hit list.

Word reached the ears of one man who had already assassinated a number of high-ranking Officers in the region around Chantilly.

On the evening of the day that Canaris set out to meet Goering and Himmler, *SS* Standartenfuhrer Otto Kramer set out for a meeting with Standartenfuher Klaus Richter. The meeting had been convened by Himmler who was becoming increasing alarmed at rumblings within the ranks of the Wehrmacht.

Meetings like that were held in secret but one man came to know about it. He chose his spot carefully because he expected a substantial bodyguard with the Colonel. The spot he chose overlooked the route the Colonel would have to take. He had made his preparations the night before and because he always worked alone he had to be very sure that he could make a clean getaway.

He lodged a sub-machine gun securely; about twenty yards from the road at a sharp right-hand bend, where the convoy would have to slow down. The gun pointed in the general direction of the road, but it was not critical. Then he covered it with bracken and grass. He attached a thin wire to the trigger and ran the wire across a field that sloped sharply upwards for about a hundred yards.

The ground dropped off then and just behind the rise the assassin left the end of the wire, attached to a log.

The next evening he returned to the same spot and lay down on the ground overlooking the sharp bend. He checked that the wire was still in place. He laid out his sniper rifle, resting it on a tripod and waited. The Germans were known for their punctuality and he knew exactly when the convoy would arrive. Right on time two motorcycle outriders drove up the road to the corner. A black Citroen car followed two hundred yards behind and two more motorcycle outriders followed another hundred yards behind the car.

The leading motorcycles slowed and rounded the sharp bend and as the car approached, the sniper lined up his rifle. Then just as the car was nearing the bend, he pulled the log gently and the sub-machine gun blazed into life. The bullets fired harmlessly into the ground, but that did not matter. As it was still firing the sniper fired a single shot, hitting the Colonel in the chest and he died instantly.

The driver accelerated fast, fearful of more shooting and the motorcycle outriders, unaware the Colonel was dead, raced ahead also, followed by the other two. It was only after they had driven for half a mile that the driver slowed down. The motorcyclists pulled in beside the car, horrified to see their Colonel dead.

They looked at each other and without saying a word raced down the road again to the site of the ambush. They had heard the sub-machine gun but not the rifle shot. Whilst one remained on the road searching the countryside the other three and the driver of the car forced their way through the hedge. They had not gone far when they noticed the wire.

They traced the wire and found the sub-machine gun and then looked up the field on the other side from where the sniper had fired. They knew they faced a hopeless task, that the sniper would have vanished.

The following morning Jacque was picked up by an Abwehr staff car and driven to Abwehr Headquarters. Neither the driver nor his companion spoke throughout the half-hour journey. Immediately he arrived Jacque went straight to his office where Oster was waiting for him.

"I took the liberty of letting myself in," Oster said, looking around the sparse office. "I trust you slept well?"

"Yes Herr General, thank you," Jacque said, not wishing to confess that he had tossed and turned all night. He set his suitcase with all his worldly belongings on the floor.

The office was sparse. A drab grey metal filing cabinet stood in one corner. A simple desk with a typewriter and a wooden chair behind it was at the end of the small room, against the painted brick wall. A large clock hung on the wall, keeping perfect time. There was a photograph of Jacque's father in army uniform on the windowsill but none of his mother or sister. A picture of Hitler took pride of place on another wall.

"You'd better sit down," Oster said.

Jacque took the only seat behind the desk and looked up at Oster who stood over him, waiting.

"You've been back to France since joining Abwehr," Oster said. "And there was no problem with that, except from your people. You had our backing and support then if anything went wrong. This time will be different. What you must understand is that what you're doing; you are doing for the Führer. There's no glory in it, at least until this War's over. Nobody can know what your mission is, you understand that?"

"Yes, I do," Jacque said, desperate to convince Oster.

"The situation's this," Oster said to reinforce his argument. "If it's known that we suspect General Scholtz then other 'organisations' may deem it their duty to eliminate him, before we know the truth for certain. Others may not search as diligently for the truth as we would. Then a good General would be lost for nothing, and make no mistake about it, whatever his political affiliations turn out to be, he's a good General. Now if it turns out that you find evidence that Scholtz *is* a traitor, then it's equally essential that *nobody* is aware of your findings apart from Admiral Canaris and me."

Jacque was getting the drift of the argument, but at that early stage of the War, when as far as he was concerned there wasn't a German alive who didn't idolise Hitler, he was finding it hard to come to terms with it. "You're arguing that if the General's a traitor, he won't be alone in his treachery!"

"Exactly," Oster said with a smile. "And that kind of treachery needs to be rooted out. If the General's a traitor we'll use him to catch the others."

"Others," Jacque gasped.

51

"Of course," Oster said. "The Führer's convinced there's a conspiracy and it's our duty to find the culprits. I repeat one last time, absolutely nobody must know of your mission, either before or after its completion. If you're ever in any doubt as to whether or not you should tell someone just remember Verberie!"

Jacque drew a deep breath. He'd hoped he'd heard the last of Verberie but it seemed that it was going to haunt him for ever.

"Now," Oster continued. "I said a moment ago, when you returned to France, you only had the French to worry about. They were not going to stop and ask why you were not in the French Army or working for the Germans, a fine healthy young man like you. And if the Gestapo stopped you, you were working for us. But now if the Gestapo stop you, you need to be well prepared. They may very well ask you why you're not in Germany. So your story has to convince the Gestapo if they stop you."

"And do you have a cover for me?" Jacque asked.

"Just as you were acting on behalf of the Abwehr during the Verberie incident, you'll be acting on behalf of the Abwehr on this mission. Except of course, as far as the Gestapo or indeed the French Police are concerned, you're engaged in something else, quite legitimate! We mentioned the sniper to you. He's a real threat to us and you must also address that issue. It also so happens that we've information about the whereabouts of another Allied escape route, so as far as anyone else is concerned you're involved in both those problems. You're not investigating General Scholtz."

"And can I know where this supposed escape route is Herr General?" Jacque asked.

"Of course," Oster said without hesitation. "And there's nothing supposed about it. We know it operates in the region of Chantilly!"

"Chantilly," Jacque gasped. "But that's my home town."

"Oh so it is," Oster agreed. "Is that a problem for you?"

"I … I suppose not," Jacque agreed.

"Good," Oster said. "Because that's where General Scholtz is based at the minute, so it should simplify things for you, especially as the General's a friend of the family."

"But what do I tell my family?" Jacque asked.

"As far as your family's concerned you can be working for the German Ministry of Information. You may of course also tell General Scholtz about the escape route, and indeed enlist his help, and he will be all too aware of the sniper."

Oster raised his eyebrows as he spoke. "Has ... has there been a development?" Jacque asked, hesitating as he spoke.

"An *SS* Colonel was ambushed and shot last night by our lone sniper. Himmler is not amused," Oster said.

That afternoon Jacque set out by train to Paris and from there back to his home at the Château Aveline at Chantilly.

His journey was interrupted several times by air-raid warnings and on one occasion by a derailed train - the result of sabotage. There was no transport at the Station so it was late the following evening when he arrived at the Château, apprehensive about the welcome he would receive.

He set his suitcase on the ground, and not having a key he rang the bell and waited anxiously. Nina the trusted maidservant opened the door. "Master Jacque," she cried, with pleasure she didn't try to hide. "You didn't tell us you were coming."

Jacque picked up his suitcase. "I thought I'd surprise my parents," he said. And then as an after thought he added. "And you also of course."

As Nina stood back Jacque stepped inside and looked around the hall. Then he turned and looked at Nina. It was almost two years since he had seen her and she was just seventeen then. Now at almost nineteen she had changed. He noticed her hair was different and she had filled out a bit. She was no longer the skinny teenager he'd remembered but a remarkably beautiful woman with a striking figure and a lovely smile. At five foot ten she was almost as tall as he was.

"You've changed," he said.

Nina blushed and turned her head. "I'll tell your mother you're here," she said.

"For the better," he called after her and she waved her hand in the air as if to dismiss his remark, but she smiled secretly to herself

He went into the lounge and waited. A few moments later his mother entered the room. She hesitated at the door; frowning and Jacque walked over to her. He reached out his hands and held his mother's and kissed her on the cheek and smiled. "Not a very warm welcome," he said quietly.

Nina was behind her. Marie turned and said to her. "Take Jacque's case to his old room Nina, will you please?"

"No," Jacque said. "It's heavy, let me." Then he looked at his mother. "I'll be down shortly mother and explain."

Jacque lifted the suitcase and walked to the door. He stopped and looked at Nina. "Well," he said. "Aren't you going to show me to my room?"

Nina smiled and Marie noticed how they looked at one another. As they left Marie was sure she heard an unmistakable squeal from Nina. Marie shook her head in disapproval.

She was looking out of the window when Jacque returned alone. She turned as Jacque entered. "It's been a long time Jacque," she said with a hint of bitterness in her voice. "Why now?"

Jacque ignored the question. "How's father?" he asked instead.

"You know he's not been well," Marie said. "And your being away hasn't helped him. If it hadn't been for Andrea I'm not sure I could have coped."

"But mother," Jacque said. "You know if I hadn't chosen to go, the Germans would have taken me into forced labour anyway. I'd have been working all this time in a munitions factory or something. And I wouldn't be home now either."

"What *have* you been doing Jacque, and *why* choose this time to come home?" Marie asked.

"I've been working in the Ministry of Information," Jacque lied. "I've managed to keep out of the military side of things. You and father shouldn't have been so upset. The Germans aren't as bad as people make out."

Marie sighed. "So are you home for good? Or do you plan to go away again?"

54

"My superior was in touch with General Scholtz," Jacque said. "It was over some internal matter to do with billeting German Officers and my name came up in the conversation. The General made some comment that father's health had deteriorated and General Oster my superior, suggested I should go home for a while to see him. You see they still think a lot of father considering what he did for the General."

"Yes I know," Marie said. "The General *has* been good to us, and we've been generally left alone."

"Well as to how long I stay depends on how father is, but there's also the possibility that my work could be carried on from home. If you don't mind, that is!"

Marie caught her breath. She hoped Jacque didn't notice. Lieutenant Pierre Gaston, who had trained Marie's Circuit, had by then gone home. She was expecting him back soon, along with her friend Josephine. The thought of Jacque being around when they arrived, and they could turn up at any time without warning, sent shivers up her back.

"Jacque dear," she said. "I'm not sure that's wise. The people have tolerated our friendship with General Scholtz, but they know you went to Germany of your free will and if they see you back here they're bound to be suspicious. They'll ask questions and put two and two together and nobody will convince them but that we're *all* working for the Germans."

"But mother we know that's not true," Jacque insisted.

"You've been out of France Jacque, and you don't know what it is like," Marie said. "The slightest suspicion's enough to turn, even our friends against us. It would make life unbearable and it wouldn't be safe even to walk the streets. And think of Andrea in the Hospital. She puts up with abuse as it is. It's better that you stay somewhere else."

Jacque was hurt but he didn't show it. "Very well," he said. "If that's how you feel, I'll find lodgings in Paris. Nobody will know me there and I can still visit you."

Marie was relieved, but not totally. "I think it's for the best, and of *course* you must visit often."

Nina came in with coffee and cakes. Marie excused herself saying. "I'll tell your father you're here."

Jacque sipped the coffee and admired Nina as she sat and smiled at him like a long lost brother. Marie returned. "Your father's sleeping Jacque," she said. "I didn't like to waken him."

"But I'd just brought him coffee," Nina spluttered and Marie gave her a withering look and she knew she'd spoken out of turn. "He must have been more tired than I thought after his exercises," she added quickly.

"Yes perhaps," Marie said.

Jacque finished his coffee. "I'll go to my room and clean up," he said. "And I take it you've no objection if I sleep here tonight?"

"Of course not," Marie said.

"I'll go to Paris in the morning and sort out accommodation," Jacque said and then with one last glance at Nina he left to go to his room.

"I'm sorry mam," Nina said. "I ... I didn't realise."

"It's not your fault Nina," Marie said. "You know Jacque's father hasn't been able to come to terms with his son working for the Germans, in fact I haven't either. Anyway it's probably better that they're kept apart."

"Of course," Nina said.

"And Nina," Marie said quietly. "We'll have to be very vigilant now that Jacque's back."

"I understand mam," Nina agreed.

Jacque's room was on the second floor but he hesitated at the second flight of stairs and changed his mind. With a quick backward glance he walked along the corridor to his father's room. The door was ajar and he looked through the gap between the door and the doorframe. He could see his father sitting in a chair with a paper on his knee and a cup of coffee in one hand. Jacque grimaced and shook his head and turned on his heel and went to his room.

In the very early hours of the morning Jacque was tossing and turning in bed, unable to sleep, with the vision of his father in the chair playing on his mind. At other times his mind drifted back to the

morning when the men from the Abwehr called at his flat. He
visualised the prostitute lying naked on his bed and her protests as he
dumped her outside the door. He'd liked her because she was almost
submissive. He enjoyed submissive women.

He remembered the Admiral's reference to his drinking and
whoring, as if questioning his commitment to the Führer. He knew
where his commitment lay, and his fondness for drink and women
didn't affect it, even if the Admiral thought it did! He rolled over for
the umpteenth time and then tossed the bedclothes aside and got out of
bed. He tiptoed downstairs to the wine cellar and took a bottle of wine
and two glasses. Then he made his way to Nina's room and knocked
on the door.

When there was no reply he opened the door quietly and slipped
inside. Nina smiled to herself and switched on the bedside lamp. She
propped herself up on one elbow as Jacque approached the bed, bottle
and glasses in his hands.

"Well," he whispered. "Are you going to move over, or keep me
standing here all night?"

Nina prepared his breakfast early in the morning before he set out
to catch the first train to Paris to search for accommodation. He left
without seeing his parents.

When Nina was sure that he was truly gone, she prepared another
breakfast and brought it to a secret hideout in the Château.

Chapter six

In the early hours of the previous morning a RAF pilot had been brought to the Château badly injured. He had been on a routine flight from England in a Lysander to drop off an SOE agent and to pick up highly sensitive documents to bring back to the Major.

All had gone according to plan. The agent was dropped off and the documents in a briefcase were left in the Lysander. The plane was taking off again after less than a minute on the ground when dark cloud obscured the almost full moon. The pilot didn't want to risk delaying his departure and proceeded to take off, even though he was unable to see ahead properly. The plane hit the top of a tree with its undercarriage and veered out of control to the right. As the pilot tried desperately to correct it, a wing tip struck another tree and the plane plunged towards the ground.

It crashed through the tops of the trees and then the sheer weight of it forced it close to the ground. The cockpit rested ten feet from the ground and the tail stuck high in the trees.   Fortunately the plane didn't go on fire but the pilot was knocked unconscious and he also fractured a number of ribs when the branch of a tree crashed through the cockpit. His left arm was also broken below the elbow.

The SOE agent had specific instructions to leave the area immediately, but knowing about the nature of the sensitive documents he'd left in the plane, he couldn't leave the scene. The members of the Résistance who'd met him with the documents ran with him to the crashed plane, hoping against hope that there wasn't a German patrol in the area. The plane had come down five hundred yards inside the wood but luck was on their side and they managed to get the pilot out of the aircraft and to retrieve the documents.

They made a makeshift stretcher by cutting down two branches and after lobbing off the twigs they inserted the branches through the arms of two of their jackets. They carried the pilot to their van and laid him out in the back and drove off on the same road taken by Josephine Butler and Pierre Gaston towards Chantilly. They knew they were taking a grave risk but none of them was prepared to leave the injured pilot behind. They discussed their options as they drove and then came to a collective decision.

It was 03:00 when they arrived at the Château Aveline. The SOE agent had been dropped off an hour earlier to make his own way to his destination. The documents were left in the hands of the Résistance. Henri was elected to ring the doorbell. It was Andrea who opened the door, after first looking out of the top window to see who was there at that hour of the morning.

"You've got to help us Andrea," he said. "We've an injured British pilot and we didn't know where else to turn."

"But you can't bring him here," Andrea protested. "We've nowhere to treat him."

"Your father saved the life of a Nazi so now he can save the life of a British airman," Henri said bitterly.

"Don't you know my father's paralysed?" Andrea said. "He couldn't help you, even if he wanted to."

"Your mother's a doctor."

"We've still nowhere to treat him," Andrea insisted. "And anyway how bad is he?"

"Come and see for yourself," Henri said.

Andrea pulled her dressing gown around her and followed Henri to the back of the van where the rear door was already opened. Charles, one of the others, shone a torch over the unconscious pilot. Andrea took the torch and crawled into the van. She felt his pulse, which was racing. She checked each eye and noticed that the pupils reacted to the light. The sleeve of his flying jacket was torn and blood stained and it was obvious to her that his arm was broken

She gently unbuttoned the flying jacket and pulled up his undergarments. When she saw the deep lacerations on his chest and gently felt his rib cage she turned to his rescuers. "I'm sorry," she said, sliding out of the van. "He'll have to go to a Hospital, there's nothing we can do for him here."

Henri took Charles to one side while Philip stood beside Andrea. They turned to Andrea. "He's about my size," Henri said. "We'll dress him in my clothes and then bring him to Hospital. We'll tell them we found him at the side of the road and they're bound to take him in. Without documents nobody will know who he is. When he regains consciousness, you must tell him to pretend that he can't remember who he is or what happened. When the time's right we'll collect him again and try and get him back to England. What do you say?"

"But he's English you young fool," Andrea said. "Have you forgotten you're in France?"

"Listen to her," Henri said. "He speaks better French than I do," he added. "So there's no problem."

"But why me," Andrea said. "How do you know I won't tell the Germans?"

"We don't," Henri said. "But if you do, we'll be waiting for your brother Jacque the next time he comes home!"

"That won't be necessary," Andrea said bitterly.

"I wouldn't have thought so," Henri agreed.

They removed the pilot's clothes and dressed him in Henri's, tearing them where appropriate, and smearing them with his blood. When he was dressed they looked at Andrea.

"Don't look at me," she said. "It would be far too suspicious if I went with you. Bring him to the Hospital yourselves and I'll see in the morning how bad he is. Then we'll take it from there."

They looked at her, uncertain. "You can trust me," she said.

The pilot was brought straight to the cottage Hospital at Chantilly and gently left on the ground at the entrance. The Staff were informed and the Résistance quickly left the scene. In the morning it was confirmed that his arm was fractured, as well as four ribs. His arm was put in a plaster and his chest strapped. His head wound didn't give any cause for concern but he was still unconscious.

The local Police were told and they took statements from those who had admitted him and a description to circulate in an attempt to identify him. They left instruction that they were to be informed immediately he regained consciousness.

It was forty-eight hours before he did. Andrea had told another nurse who she trusted, what had happened, and they arranged to be on different shifts so that one of them would always be on duty. Andrea and an elderly doctor, whom she wasn't sure about, and another member of staff were attending the pilot when he came too. He was confused and didn't remember what had happened. Andrea was standing behind the others and managed to get his attention. She pursed her lips and put her finger up with a silent shush. He made no response when he was spoken to.

Failing to get any information from him, the doctor went to inform the Police that he had regained consciousness. The other nurse went to check on another patient and Andrea was left alone with him for a few moments.

"You're in a Hospital in France," she told him in French. "The Résistance brought you here two days ago, and it's absolutely essential you don't speak English. They removed your flying gear and identification before you were admitted so it's assumed you're the victim of a road accident. Just pretend you can't remember who you are or what happened."

The pilot smiled slightly and nodded. "Mercie," he whispered.

"They're going to try and get you out of here when you're well enough, but that won't be for a while," Andrea said. "In the meantime try and relax. There's more than myself looking after you and we'll do our best to get you home in one piece."

The pilot smiled. "Mercie," he whispered again with an effort.

"Can you just tell me your name?" Andrea whispered. "We may be able to get word back that you're OK"

"Pilot Officer Gary Tucker," he replied without hesitation

The local Police visited the pilot every other day but always left disappointed when there was no sign of him regaining his memory. Their attempts to identify him from the missing persons files also failed so his case was put on hold until such times as it was decided what to do with him.

Chapter seven

Jacque left his parents' Château with mixed feelings. He was still disappointed that they didn't accept his point of view regarding the Germans and the war. He *was* hurt that his father didn't even want to see him. But as he walked to the Station he smiled when he remembered his night of passion with Nina. That in itself had made it worth his while going home. He pondered over how he was going to check on General Scholtz but put it to the back of his mind as he concentrated instead on lodgings in Paris.

Jacque found two things that had always been right working for the Adwehr, and that was money and authority, and he wasn't quite sure which he enjoyed most. As he walked to the Station he made a sudden decision. He wasn't going to stay in Paris after all. He would stay in Chantilly and walk into the local Police Station and lay his cards on the table. He would use their local knowledge to find the right lodgings and he would also insist that they kept him briefed on any Résistance activity in the area. Living in Chantilly would also allow him to go home whenever he wanted to see Nina. He was convinced his parents would eventually come round to his way of thinking

The local Police Station was small and mostly concerned with rural crime, but like all such Stations the Officers were remarkably well informed about what was going on in their area. As Jacque walked into the Station he was immediately recognised, but he was so sure of himself that he didn't notice the cool reception he received. Not even the French Police thought much of a fellow Frenchman who openly went over to the other side as Jacque had done.

Jacque smiled. "Good morning, I'd like to see the Officer in charge."

The Policeman looked up from his desk. "You're looking at him," he said gruffly.

"Right," Jacque said somewhat taken aback. Then he straightened himself in an effort to show an air of authority. "I'm Hauptsturmführer Jacque Aveline."

"I know," the Policeman sighed.

"You can't know that," Jacque said angrily. "And I don't appreciate your insolent attitude because I didn't inform you I was coming."

The Policeman looked straight at Jacque and smiled with resignation showing all over his face. "No," he said. "But General Hans Oster of the Abwehr said that you would probably call and make yourself known. We're instructed to assist you in every way possible. OK!"

Jacque stood dumbfounded for a moment. Then, lying in an attempt to regain his composure he said, "Yes I'd forgotten the General said he would be in touch with you. So here I am, and may I know your name and rank?"

"Inspector Marius Regnier," the Policeman replied with obvious pride.

"Thank you," Jacque said. "Now the first thing I'll need is suitable lodgings, preferably with someone who's sympathetic to the cause."

"Could be difficult," the Inspector muttered.

"Sorry?" Jacque said. "I didn't catch that."

"We don't *have* many Nazi sympathisers," the Inspector said tellingly.

"Do I take it you're not one then?"

"I do my job," the Inspector said. "You won't find any of your colleagues with a complaint about the Police in Chantilly."

"So can you recommend someone?" Jacque asked.

The Inspector rubbed his chin. "There's a widow who lives in the Rue d'Argenson. It's a quiet suburb so you shouldn't cause much of a stir." He hesitated. "You'll have to pay her of course."

"I don't think there should be any question of her agreeing to take me," Jacque said angrily. "I'll see to that. I am after all working for the best interests of the people of France, and I have the authority of the Abwehr behind me."

"Very well," the Inspector said. "She's in number 11 and her name's Madame Janine Cormeau. She'll be expecting you."

Jacque was looking around the Station as the Inspector spoke. His last remark made him jerk his head around, his mouth open in amazement. "Who had the effrontery to presume I'd require lodgings," Jacque demanded to know. "And to go so far as to arrange it? My family lives nearby, or didn't you know? I could just as easily have stayed there."

"Just following orders sir," the Inspector said.

"What?"

"General Oster?"

Having got off to a bad start Jacque lifted his case. "Would it be too much trouble to have a car bring me round?" he asked.

The Inspector raised his eyebrows. "Would that be wise sir; after all a Police Car will only cause a stir and start people talking? Might be better if you made your way round on foot, that way hardly anybody will notice and without a car they'll just assume you're another lodger."

"Very well," Jacque agreed. "I'll go and see this lady who's expecting me." He hesitated. "Later you can give me the benefit of your expert knowledge," he added somewhat sarcastically.

As Jacque left the Inspector shook his head and smiled.

Jacque remembered the quiet cul-de-sac and the three storey detached houses. Madame Cormeau was indeed expecting him. She brought him in and showed him to a bedroom on the top floor. He unpacked his few belongings and took brief stock of his position. Then he had a quick wash and went downstairs where Madame Cormeau poured him a freshly brewed coffee.

Afterwards he took himself for a walk around Chantilly, the town where he went to school. Everything appeared to be going on normally, almost as if there wasn't a War on. There was virtually no civilian traffic as practically nobody apart from the Germans was allowed petrol. There were quite a few military vehicles of one kind and another and also a few soldiers in uniform. They didn't appear to bother with anybody nor did the locals take much notice of them.

Jacque was quite happy relaxing and walking around for a while and was even beginning to enjoy it, when he noticed friends of his family coming towards him. He was ready to greet them but before they got to him they quite deliberately crossed the street, just to avoid him. He stood on the footpath and looked and was about to go after them and confront them, but then changed his mind. Instead he turned and went into a Café and took a seat at the window. There were four German soldiers, one of whom was an Officer. Jacque ignored them and when the proprietor came over he ordered coffee. While he was sitting there the Officer stood up and walked across to his table. He held out his hand.

"Your papers please," he demanded.

Jacque smiled pleasantly and handed him his papers. The Officer took them and gave them a quick glance and handed them back. "Have you just arrived?" he asked. "I don't remember seeing you here before."

"Yes," Jacque agreed. "I arrived this morning and I'm settling into lodgings."

"We come here every day," the Officer said. "While we have the chance. You may be back?"

"Yes quite likely," Jacque said.

As the Officer turned to rejoin his colleagues, Jacque called after him. "Excuse me," he said. "But do you by any chance know General Scholtz?"

The Officer stopped and turned. "Why yes," he said. "I know General Scholtz, and you?"

"I've met him," Jacque said truthfully.

The Officer nodded and returned to his table.

It was lunchtime when Jacque returned to the Police Station and he was determined this time to stamp his authority on the situation. The same Inspector was on duty. He looked up and made a half-hearted attempt at a smile when Jacque entered and then continued writing in a logbook.

Jacque waited a moment but the Inspector continued writing. Jacque coughed but to no effect and finally in exacerbation he burst out. "Has General Oster informed you as to why I'm here?"

The Inspector sighed. "As I said earlier we've been instructed to help you in any way we can. Other than that I have no idea why you're here." Then he continued to write.

Jacque had had enough. "Damn you," he said. "I have authority from General Oster to do whatever I consider necessary to achieve my objectives. If you continue to be obstinate and obstructive I'll see to it that you'll pay dearly for your attitude. Do I make myself clear?"

The Inspector was shocked at the outburst and realised he *had* taken too much of a liberty. He put his pen down and closed the logbook. "I apologise sir," he said. "My mind has been on other things. But now, what can I do for you? Can you tell me exactly why you're here?"

Jacque sighed. "That's better," he said. "Perhaps now we shall be able to get somewhere."

He looked around him and the Inspector read his mind. "A seat, of course," he said. "There's a room in the back we can go to. If anyone needs me they can ring the bell."

When they'd settled in the rather bare room Jacque turned to the Inspector. "We've information that an Allied escape route operates in the region of Chantilly," he said. "And I'm here under General Oster's orders to find out where it is, who operates it and to close it down."

"Where do you think we should start?" the Inspector asked.

"To start with I should see all your files of anybody suspected, for whatever reason, of aiding and abetting the enemy, and anybody who has been questioned about anything suspicious. And I want a list of everybody the Police suspect might be guilty but who has not been questioned. Nobody should be above suspicion, please don't leave anybody out. There's no doubt that somebody in the area is involved in this escape route. Also any suspicious activity reported to you and in what area and I want to know if any strangers have come into Chantilly."

"That's plenty to be going on with," the Inspector said. "I can let you see all the files we have on the kind of people you're looking for. I'll also consult my colleagues regarding any other activity in recent weeks that may be relevant. We'll also make a list of other possible suspects, though I must say there'll not be many on it and those who are will in all probability be innocent."

"Also," Jacque said. "I want somebody at the railway Station twenty-four hours a day, in plain clothes. And tell them to increase the number of random searches, paying particular attention to those who appear injured."

"Very well that can also be arranged."

"Right," Jacque said. "One last thing. How do you get along with the German army personnel, based in Chantilly?"

"They don't present us with many problems," the Inspector said. "They keep to themselves and don't generally bother the locals."

"And tell me about the young women of Chantilly? There must be some of them attracted to the handsome young German soldiers, because after all there can't be too many young French men around."

"We don't approve of that," the Inspector said. "You would understand it can lead to all sorts of problems. Not everyone's as pro-German as you might be. Young women liaising with German soldiers can create problems in the community. But of course it does go on. Some will do it for money and nothing else, whilst others, foolish girls can't help themselves and fall in love."

"I'd like the names of some of them," Jacque said. "It could be useful to me. And do you by any chance know General Scholtz?"

"Well yes as a matter of fact I do," the Inspector said. "He's one of the reasons the troops don't pose too many problems here, unlike other towns I could name. But then you'd probably know the reason for that," he added.

"Yes, maybe," Jacque said.

Jacque was given a number of files and other documents taken from a filing cabinet in another room and he settled down for a long afternoon and evening. He made copious notes as he went along.

Chapter eight

Over the next few days Jacque had various people brought in for questioning, but it was all to no avail because he drew a blank on every occasion. After one particularly fruitless interview he sat back in his chair looking at the ceiling. His fingers toyed with a cup of cold coffee. He hadn't expected any kind of a breakthrough so soon, and it didn't particularly concern him. What did concern him was how he was going to check on General Scholtz.

As he sat absent-mindedly, an idea came to him. He'd been trying to operate without transport or backup for too long. He didn't particularly want anyone else interfering but he realised he needed someone he could call on quickly and he wasn't impressed with the Inspector or his colleagues. His plan, simple as it was, would serve two purposes.

He decided to approach General Scholtz with his letter of authorisation from General Oster, and request transport and a driver from the army. He'd put off meeting him because he didn't quite know how he would react. With his letter from General Oster he didn't think there was any way General Scholtz could refuse. And he did believe that his family connections would help. He would also ask for a platoon of solders to be put at his disposal. Secondly, by so doing, he would have an opportunity to gauge the General's reaction. He might even get to know him because he'd only met him on a couple of occasions. He might be able to encourage him to reveal his true thoughts about the War and Hitler. He also decided to throw caution to the wind and let the people of Chantilly think what they liked. He would return to the Café where he'd been asked for his papers by the German Officer and fraternise with the soldiers there.

If anybody knew what the General was like, they would. And he had plenty of francs to get them drinking and talking!

Jacque telephoned the army camp, which was on the main road from Chantilly to Paris, and arranged a meeting with the General that afternoon.

The General was billeted in Chantilly Castle which was part of an Estate on the outskirts of Chantilly, and it was there that Jacque met him. Inspector Regnier had provided a driver and transport. Jacque sent the driver back fully expecting to have his own driver and transport for the return journey.

A young soldier led him to the General's quarters, where the soldier knocked on the door. The General told them to enter. The General looked up and gave a perfunctory nod towards the soldier, who then left. Jacque stood straight, saluted and said, "Heil Hitler."

The General smiled and gave a rather half-hearted "Heil Hitler" in reply. Jacque noted his apparent lack of enthusiasm. "Please sit down," the General said. "It's good to see the son of my friends Marie and Anton."

"And it's good to make your acquaintance again General Scholtz," Jacque said.

He gave General Oster's letter to the General, who read it slowly and then folded it neatly and handed it back to Jacque. "As well as your family connections," he said. "Your credentials are impeccable. But they don't tell me what I can do for you."

"It's really quite simple sir," Jacque said. "I'm instructed by General Oster to investigate a possible Allied escape route for downed airmen. I am, for operational reasons working alone, but as you'll appreciate, it *is* necessary for me to have backup and support and also to have transport at my disposal. General Oster is anxious, and I trust I don't speak out of turn, to keep this matter from the Gestapo and indeed the SS."

General Scholtz frowned.

"It's not that he's opposed to the Secret Police," Jacque hastened to add. "They have their job to do; it's just that the General believes any information gathered should in the first instance only be brought to the attention of the Abwehr."

"I see," the General said, as if his mind was elsewhere. "Your parents didn't tell me you were home!"

"They didn't know I was coming sir. Perhaps I should have warned them. But in any event I'd obviously not be in a position to discuss my movements with them, and perhaps it would be better if you did not tell them I had called with you."

"Of course," the General said. "I find it possible to engage in the niceties of friendship without it impinging on my duties to the Fatherland."

"To be honest Sir," Jacque said. "It's a difficult situation for me, especially because of my father whom I respect very highly. We still don't see eye to eye and I'm afraid I haven't seen him since I returned home."

"That's too bad," the General said. "Your father's a fine man and an honourable one." He laughed. "We don't see eye to eye either, but we still get along fine."

"The problem is," Jacque said. "You're the enemy without! I'm the enemy within."

"As bad as that is it?" the General said.

"So can you oblige me with transport?" Jacque asked, thinking it better to ignore the question. "I'm thinking of a car and a driver and a platoon of soldiers."

The General sighed. "What can I say?" the General asked. "You have your orders and you've your letter of authorisation from General Oster. You can have your driver and platoon of soldiers but I must insist that they remain under my command. I may call them back at any time."

"Of course," Jacque said. "That's understood."

"One other thing," the General said. "I'd caution you against driving around in a German army staff car in civilian clothes. You might be mistaken as Gestapo and draw unwarranted attention to yourself and the car. You could even be killed."

Jacque nodded. "I take the point sir. My uniform's in my lodgings."

The General nodded his approval and picked up the telephone and made arrangements to provide Jacque with the backup he'd requested.

Half an hour later, after sharing a cup of coffee and some small talk with the General, Jacque was driving out of the camp in a black Citroen staff car followed by an SdKfz 250 Light Armoured Personnel

Carrier. It had a driver and Commander and four full-equipped soldiers. A MG-42 'Spandau' light machine gun was mounted at the front behind an armour plated shield.

They drove to Jacque's lodgings where he changed into his Captain's uniform, and then to the favourite drinking place for the Germans. One soldier was left outside on guard and the rest filed in at Jacque's insistence, for drinks.

Jacque bought the first round, much to the appreciation of the soldiers. There were some civilians present huddled in a corner and they appeared apprehensive. After a short time they left and as the last one went through the door one of the soldiers laughed uproariously, slapping his nearest companion on the back. "These French," he growled. "They just can't stomach us Germans." Then he looked at the barman. "Let's have another round here barman," he ordered.

"Yes, let's have some service here," Jacque added.

The barman came over with the drinks and Jacque insisted on paying again. As the barman picked up the money he looked intensely at Jacque. He was going to speak but thought better of it. One of the soldiers turned to Jacque.

"He knows you sir," he said.

"Yes," Jacque agreed. "I'm a local."

"So you *are* French," the soldier asked.

"Of course," Jacque said. "But I'm also a Captain in the Wehrmacht!"

"I'll drink to that," the soldier said.

Jacque was careful not to drink too much and as time went by he noticed the others loosening up. He chose his moment carefully.

"I like your General Scholtz," he said.

The soldiers thought that amusing and almost as one they lifted their glasses and shouted. "To General Scholtz."

Jacque put his hand up to hush the soldiers and asked quietly. "Do you think the General is in favour of the war?"

A couple of them laughed at that but they weren't so drunk that they didn't know what they were saying. "The General's a good man," the Commander of the Personnel Carrier said. "He looks after his men."

One of the soldiers, Jacque's driver, Rottenführer (Corporal) Hans Kock, was a bit tipsier than the rest. "And his woman," he sniggered into the remains of his drink.

The Commander of the Personnel Carrier kicked the inebriated Hans on the shin and looked up at Jacque and laughed. "Pay no attention," he said.

But Jacque made a mental note.

Before the soldiers were too inebriated Jacque decided to call a halt. He didn't want the General getting a wrong opinion of him. Hans was incapable of driving and despite offers from the other soldiers Jacque insisted on driving himself. He ordered the Commander of the Personnel Carrier to return to the camp until the next day. He said he would look after the Corporal himself and sober him up before putting him in charge of the car again.

Jacque stood beside his black Citroen, unaffected by the drink he'd taken. Hans was slouched against the wall of the drinking house. When the Personnel Carrier had left, Jacque took Hans by the arm and placed him into the passenger seat. He went back to the bar and bought more drink and brought it with him. He was watched by a handful of curious onlookers.

He drove back to his lodgings and told Madame Cormeau that he had a friend back for drinks. He manhandled Hans up the two flights of stairs into his room and dropped him into a chair. No sooner was he in the chair than Hans reached out both hands and pulled himself up muttering. "The bathroom, where's the bathroom?"

When he'd finished being sick Jacque brought him back to the room. He poured him a drink and took a small one himself. Hans was feeling very much the worse for wear but that didn't bother Jacque. He held the drink in front of him, tantalisingly near but out of reach. Hans reached out for it.

"Tell me about the General's woman," Jacque said setting the drink down.

Hans reached out and Jacque didn't stop him. Hans belched and Jacque was almost on the point of throwing him out of the room but he contained himself. He despised men who couldn't hold their liquor.

"She's a fine woman," he slurred. "And I don't blame him myself."

Jacque reached across and slapped him on the back. "Why neither do I," he laughed. "I'd just like to know how he does it."

"It's easy," Hans said. "He gives her money and buys her gifts. I've seen them."

"Go on," Jacque said. "Are you serious?"

"Yes of course," he said. "I've driven him myself to see her and carried in presents sometimes."

"Has she got a sister?" Jacque asked laughing.

Hans took another drink. "Don't think so," he slurred. "But," and forgetting the difference in their ranks he pulled Jacque close to him. "I could introduce you to one if you like."

Jacque took the drink from Hans and set it down. "Right, that's what we'll do," he said. "I'll drive and you show me."

Hans staggered up reluctantly and Jacque helped him down the stairs and into the car. Once in the car he turned to him and said. "Show me where the General's girl lives first, and then bring me to mine."

He winked at Hans as he started the car and put it into gear. Hans was barely able to sit upright but he appeared to have sufficient command of his senses to know where to go. He directed Jacque to another part of Chantilly. It was a residential part of the town, well out of the centre. The houses were detached and most were surrounded by tall trees or hedges. Hans told Jacque to drive slowly and then he tugged at his sleeve.

"That's it," he said. "It's that one over there."

Jacque followed Hans's gaze and stopped outside a large well-to-do house. "You're sure that's it?" Jacque asked.

Hans nodded. Jacque made a mental note of the place and instructed Hans to bring him to the house 'of ill repute' he had referred to earlier in the car. It turned out that the house was in Paris but that suited Jacque far better. It was only forty kilometres. Hans slept until they were on the outskirts, when Jacque wakened him, whereupon he directed him to the brothel.

Paris was not new to Jacque, but the brothels were. There was no need of such establishments for students. Jacque was surprised when he found himself outside a respectable looking house. He looked at Hans, who was just about able to drag himself out of the car and ring the doorbell. He left the door of the car open. After a few moments a woman came to the door and Jacque watched as the two of them had a conversation. He saw her looking at him and she disappeared and Hans walked back to the car. He stood at the side of the car watching the house.

A woman in her early twenties appeared. A cigarette was hanging out of the corner of her mouth and she looked untidy, with a blouse and short skirt. As she came close Jacque had a sudden vision of Nina, and he wondered to himself what on earth he was doing there. He reached out of the door and pulled Hans in as the woman approached. Then with Hans's right foot dragging on the ground and the door of the car half open he accelerated away.

The bemused Hans managed to gather himself into the car and close the door. Jacque looked at him. "Last time I'll take *your* advice," he growled.

Jacque drove back to Chantilly and to his parent's Château. By then it was late and all the lights were out. Jacque instructed Hans to sleep in the car and told him he would return. He let himself in quietly, thankful that he had a key. All was quiet as he went to the cellar again for a bottle of wine and two glasses.

He knocked on Nina's door and didn't wait but walked in, as Nina switched on the light with a startled gasp. "Master Jacque," she whispered. "You scared the life out of me. What would your mother say, and what do you think you're doing?"

Jacque smiled and undressed. "I'll soon show you," he said smiling.

In the early hours of the morning he returned to his lodgings where he settled Hans on the chaise longue and threw himself on top of his bed without undressing. He lay for a while, wide-awake as he formulated a plan in his mind, and then he slept.

The next day he returned with Hans to the Police Station and then released him for that day, but arranged to be picked up again in the evening.

From 20:00 he sat with Hans up the road from the house, pointed out to him the night before as the house where the General's 'woman' lived. He'd identified her as Madeleine Boussine, a twenty-three year old whose husband had disappeared, presumed killed, during the German army's rapid advance into France. She lived with her invalid mother and young son.

Jacque decided there and then to take Hans into his confidence and told him he was working for German Military Intelligence. He also warned him that if he breathed a word of what they were doing he would answer to the Gestapo. That word struck terror into even the most loyal German, and he knew from the look in the man's face that he *would* remain silent.

At midnight he gave up waiting for anything to happen and they retired for the night.

For the next three days he did the same thing and on the third night he was rewarded. A German army staff car drove up to the house and a few moments later a woman came out and got into the car. As the car drove off Jacque ordered Hans to tail them.

They followed the car to a Hotel in Chantilly. After waiting a few minutes Jacque walked into reception. He rang the bell and a receptionist answered his call immediately.

"Has General Scholtz checked in yet?" he asked.

The receptionist appeared genuinely surprised. "I'm sorry," she said, as she glanced at the reception book. "I don't know General Scholtz."

"You're mistaken," Jacque insisted. "He came in here a few minutes ago. Perhaps it was just for a meal?"

"No," the receptionist said laughing lightly. "Pardon me, but *you're* the one who's mistaken. That wasn't General Scholtz. That was Standartenführer (Colonel) Klaus Richter."

"Colonel Richter, but of course," Jacque said feigning surprise. "That was stupid of me. I'm sorry to have bothered you."

He strolled into the hotel bar and looked around him at the few people who were there, and quickly identified the soldier he took to be the Colonel's driver. He was in the SS and that could mean only one thing. Colonel Richter was a Colonel in the SS! Then he called Hans and sent him into the bar with money for drinks, to 'get chatting' to the other driver, whilst he reclined in a corner out of sight, and waited.

Hans came over to him when the other driver left to go to the toilet. "He's the Colonel's driver all right," he said. "They come here every week for about three hours. He waits in the bar and then drives him home; the Colonel's billeted somewhere in Paris. He prefers to come here because there's less chance of him being known."

"You've done a good job," Jacque said. "And I'll not forget it, but I think we've accomplished enough for tonight. Let's go home."

The following morning Jacque telephoned Abwehr Headquarters from the Police Station and asked to be put through to General Oster. He informed the General of his progress, which he admitted on the face of it was not much, but insisted that he believed he'd found a way to get the information they wanted on General Scholtz. He then asked Oster for information on Colonel Klaus Richter and Oster agreed to get it for him.

The Monday after he'd followed Richter to the hotel in Chantilly, he sat in the car watching Madeleine Boussine's house. This time it was the General's car that arrived and again a young woman came to the car and got in. Keeping at a discrete distance Jacque followed the General's car.

They drove to a prestigious hotel, the Château Hotel Mont-Royal, just outside Chantilly. It was a splendid XV111 century style Château and despite the ravages of War it remained intact and accommodated many high ranking Nazi Officers on their off duty.

Largely because he'd nothing better to do that night, Jacque decided to wait for the General, however long it took. It was 03:00 when he finally appeared and Jacque and Hans followed him back to the woman's home. The General's car drove off as the young woman walked to the house without a backward glance. Jacque hadn't planned his next move for that night, but on the spur of the moment he decided to act.

He turned to Hans. "Go and bring her to me," he said. "Don't take no for an answer."

Hans walked up to the door and knocked hard. In a moment the woman opened the door. There was a discussion and then Jacque saw Hans drawing his pistol and the woman walked reluctantly towards the car. He opened the rear door and motioned to her to get in. She began to get in and then held back, protesting. Hans pressed his pistol in her back as Jacque moved over, and she huddled into the corner of the seat.

"Leave us alone," he said to Hans.

Hans walked a short distance up the road with a cigarette in his mouth.

The girl was frightened. Jacque smiled. "Madeleine Boussine," he said. "We haven't met."

Despite the fear in her eyes Jacque could see she was very beautiful. Madeleine looked at him, wide-eyed.

"How do you know my name?" she whispered.

"It's my business to know," he said. "But I know more than that about you!" he added threateningly.

"What do you want of me," she asked, wringing her hands in anguish.

Jacque reached out and held one hand in his. "Not much," he said. "I only want a little co-operation from you. That's all." And he smiled again and stroked her face with the other hand. She *was* attractive, very attractive, but he closed his mind off to the ideas that came flooding in.

"General Scholtz likes you for himself I suppose," he asked. And she nodded.

"Being a General do you think he'd mind if somebody else slept with you?"

"No, you can't," she cried. "He wouldn't permit it and I won't do it."

"That's what I thought," Jacque said. "So if he knew you also slept with Colonel Klaus Richter, he'd be *really* displeased I suppose."

Madeleine cringed in the corner. "He mustn't know," she cried in distress. "You don't understand."

"What don't I understand?"

"It's the Colonel. I ... I can't refuse him."

"Why can't you refuse him?"

"Please don't ask me."

"If we're to help each other, then I must know," Jacque insisted.

Her eyes brightened ever so slightly and Jacque let her hand go. "How can you help me?" she asked.

Jacque put his hand in his pocket and took out some money and gave her five thousand francs. "Perhaps that would do to start," he suggested.

Madeleine reached out her hand hesitatingly, but held back at the last. "It ... it's not just the money," she said.

"You must help me," Jacque insisted again. "If it's not the money, what is it?"

"I do need the money," she agreed, and took what Jacque had offered her. "What do you *really* want of me? What can *I* do for you? Is it to do with Jean?"

"Jean?"

"He's my husband." Then she began to cry and Jacque did his best to console her. "We married just before the War started," she continued eventually. "And Germany invaded France. Jean was called up, but he was captured. I thought that he was dead, because I heard nothing and nobody knew where he was. Then out of the blue Colonel Richter came to the hotel where I worked with a photograph of Jean. He told me he was in a Prisoner-of-War Camp. He looked terrible, but Colonel Richter said he could improve things for him if I helped *him*."

"I understand," Jacque said. "But I don't understand why he should be in a Prisoner-of War camp. If he was captured he would have been put to work along with thousands of other French soldiers."

Madeleine sobbed, covering her face with her hands. Jacque held her wrist gently and pulled her hands down. Her eyes were red and tears filled her eyes. He looked at Hans who was looking around him with the cigarette in his mouth.

"There's more, isn't there?" Jacque said.

Madeleine nodded and then looked up. "Jean is Jewish," she sobbed.

Jacque sighed. "So it wasn't a Prisoner-of-War camp after all, was it? It was a Concentration Camp."

Madeleine nodded again. "We've a son," she cried. "And because he's half Jewish the Colonel said he'd be taken away from me."

"So he's offered to protect your son and make things better for Jean, for a price? What have you to do for him Madeleine?"

"I work in the Hotel du Parc in Chantilly, that's where Colonel Richter first saw me."

"Yes I know the Hotel," Jacque said.

"General Scholtz comes there regularly to drink, or for a meal with other German Officers. The Colonel insisted that I was to seduce the General and sleep with him and get him to like me and trust me. I'm to tell the Colonel everything the General tells me. That's all, I promise."

"But you also sleep with the Colonel?"

"Yes," Madeleine agreed. "He insists."

"But you only see the General on Monday nights and the Colonel on Friday?"

"Sometimes if there's an emergency or something, one of them might not make it, but yes, that's usually what happens."

"Do they pay you?"

Madeleine nodded.

Jacque thought for a moment. "I'll tell you what I'm going to do. I'll help to protect your son and I might be able to do something for your husband Jean, I'm not sure. I'll not tell the General about Colonel Richter but you're going to have to meet me every Monday night, after you've seen the General and tell *me* everything he's said.

Furthermore I want you to find out some things about him just for me."

Madeleine was frightened and confused but she nodded in agreement.

He told her the information he wanted her to get and then said. "That's all then Madeleine. You've been very sensible. I'll see you again on Monday night, after you've been with the General. And don't let this worry you. Everything's going to be all right. I promise you'll keep your son.

Chapter nine

Jacque rose at the usual time the next morning. Hans arrived on time and they drove to the Police Station where Hans waited outside in the car. Jacque telephoned General Oster and told him about the further developments and asked him what information he had about Colonel Klaus Richter. He also asked him to do his best to trace Jean Boussine and find out how he was and if it would be possible to move him.

He was surprised by Oster's response. Rather than tell him what he wanted to know, he was ordered to return to Abwehr Headquarters immediately. He left the Police Station and packed his few belongings, ordering his landlady to keep his room for him. Then Hans drove him home where he told his mother briefly that he was returning to Germany, but hoped to be back soon. Finally he reported to General Scholtz that he'd been recalled but told him also that he would be back.

He was in Berlin in 48 hours and reported immediately to General Oster. The General was friendly and showed his appreciation of what Jacque had achieved. Then he told him about Colonel Richter.

"I want you to listen carefully Aveline," Oster said quietly. "This information's far too sensitive to talk about on the telephone. You need to be aware of the kind of man Richter is. In 1940 the British and French were fighting a rearguard action. Towards the end of May the Leibstandarte Division of the *SS* was advancing towards Dunkirk. Their Commander, Dietrich and his driver came under attack and their vehicle burst into flames. They survived, but it was some hours before their comrades realised that they were alive. Assuming Deitrich had been killed the Leibstandarte mounted a furious counter attack against the British. In one attack over 80 prisoners were taken. They were herded into a barn and hand grenades were thrown in. A few of the prisoners survived to tell the tale. In another instance 30 prisoners were taken. They were lined up against a wall and shot out of hand. None of them survived. The man who ordered that criminal act was none other Colonel Klaus Richter. Both he and a certain Captain Wilhelm Mohnke who ordered the other atrocity, went unpunished."

"That's truly terrible," Jacque said. "But don't these things happen in War?"

"You mean like Verberie?" the General said cuttingly and Jacque was sorry he'd spoken. Clearly the General wasn't going to allow him to forget Verberie.

Oster continued. "The *SS* have shown themselves to be a superior fighting force but we don't always approve of their methods. However we must do something about Colonel Richter. We have discovered that he's showing far too much interest in General Scholtz, and that he exerts more authority than his rank of Colonel would ordinarily allow him. It seems this man has connections in the very highest places, one of the reasons he was never court-martialled. So we, the Abwehr, are indebted to you for bringing this man to our attention."

"You don't mean he's connections with the Führer?" Aveleine asked in awe.

"Not quite," Oster reassured him. "But it might as well be. Richter was one of the original *SS,* the Schutz Staffel (Guard Detachment). They were the Führer's Personal Bodyguard and as such Heinrich Himmler got to know our friend Richter, and that might have been an end to it but for one other person. When we over-ran the Netherlands in 1940, a man by the name of Felix Kersten was 'persuaded' to become Himmler's personal physician. He'd previously treated the Dutch Royal Family. Now Kersten's not a bad man, unlike his psychotic patient Himmler. In fact we've come to know that he's been responsible for saving the lives of many people whom Himmler would otherwise have sent to the Gas Chambers. He's in a unique position, in that he can influence Himmler. But he went behind his back on one occasion, to stop one of Himmler's pet projects. Richter found out about it and he's been blackmailing Kersten ever since."

Aveleine sat almost mesmerised, as he listened to Oster. As Oster paused for breath Aveleine couldn't resist asking him how Richter could have blackmailed Kersten, Himmler's personal physician. "Surely," he said that was an incredibly foolhardy thing to do?"

"Foolhardy yes," Oster agreed. "But he took a calculated risk because he was playing for high stakes and it paid off. You see Himmler is determined to discover the secrets of Aryan origins and he set up the *SS* Institute of Anthropological Research. To further this 'important' research he's set himself the task of building up a collection of skulls of Jewish-Bolshevik Commissars. The whole thing is utterly appalling and only a lunatic like Himmler would think of it. Kersten found out about this research and was so sickened by it that he tried to put a stop to it without Himmler knowing. That was his big mistake."

"So what has Richter gained from this blackmail," Aveleine asked.

"Quite simply if Richter wants anything, he's only to put it to Kersten and he's no alternative but to persuade or encourage Himmler to accede to his request. It has given Richter cart Blanche to do virtually what he likes."

Aveleine sighed. "So he's a very powerful man, but have you something in mind Herr General to deal with him?"

"I have something in mind Aveline that will help you *and* the Abwehr," Oster said. "I hope you're up to it?"

"I believe I am, Herr General," Jacque said with confidence.

"It's Colonel Richter who holds the photographs of the Verberie incident!"

Jacque paled.

"Now if the Colonel was no longer there, no one else would have an interest in the photographs and General Scholtz would be free from interference from the SS."

"But why *should* Colonel Richter be interested in General Scholtz? Is it because the *SS* believes he's one of these traitors you talk about, and they're trying to get evidence? And if that's the case, should we not let them get on with it?" Jacque asked in an attempt to understand.

"All you're required to know Aveline is this," Oster said. "When Richter committed that atrocity by murdering British prisoners-of-war, a General in the Wehrmacht attempted to have him tried by court-

83

martial. That General was Scholtz and he was in command of the operation that led to the incident. We believe that's why Richter has it in for the General, not because he thinks the General's a traitor to the cause."

"So what's the course of action you propose Herr General?" Jacque asked.

General Oster held up his hand to silence Jacque as he remembered his conversation with Admiral Canaris and as he gathered his thoughts.

"I'm convinced Scholtz is loyal," the Admiral had said, after Oster had issued instructions for Jacque to report back. "And he carries enormous influence within the Wehrmacht so we've got to get him on our side, whatever it takes."

"And you still believe using Aveline is the best way to prove his loyalty?" Oster asked.

"Don't you Hans?"

"Yes I believe so Admiral, but I'm worried about Richter. He's a serious and unexpected complication and he'll have to be dealt with. I'm just not sure Aveline's up to it."

"Richter should have been court-martialled for that atrocity and put before a firing squad. Any lesser man would have been." He paused. "Only for Himmler's intervention and support Scholtz might have brought it off."

"Yes, but all he's done is to bring the wrath of the SS upon him."

"If anything goes wrong Hans, it'll be curtains for you and me."

"That's why I'm going to suggest something else Admiral," Oster said with a faint smile.

Jacque was feeling slightly on edge as Oster lowered his hand slowly and looked at Jacque. "Captain Jacque Aveline," he hesitated for effect. "I don't say this lightly. The Abwehr is investing what could potentially be the future of Germany, in your hands."

Jacque looked up startled. "I see," he said.

"You're going back to Chantilly to continue your investigation into General Scholtz, although we're fairly sure he's in the clear. But as you'll remember, we're aware of the presence of an Allied Escape route near Chantilly; one which so far you've failed to identify."

84

Jacque nodded.

"You'll give top priority to finding that escape route, still keeping an eye on General Scholtz of course. When you identify the escape route, instead of arresting those involved you're going to join them!"

"Herr General," Jacque exclaimed.

"You're going to join them and enlist their help in getting rid of Colonel Klaus Richter!"

"But Herr General!"

"That's an order Captain Aveline. I'd happily leave it to our assassin friend if we knew who he was, but Colonel Richter must go, and if you're in any doubt just remember the photographs. It's a job for the French Résistance now, so if anything goes wrong nobody can blame the Abwehr."

Then as an afterthought he added. "You may of course get lucky and find this assassin. Give him information about Richter, and who knows!"

"There's one last thing Herr General," Jacque said. "There is the husband of Madeleine Boussine. His name's Jean. It might be helpful if you could trace him and *perhaps improve his circumstances!*"

"I've already put someone onto it," the General said.

"Thank you Herr General. His wife has been a great help to me and I've no doubt I'll be able to use her again".

Jacque returned to Paris that night. Again it was an uneventful journey apart from one stop because of an air-raid warning, which proved to be a false alarm. Later, the following night, he arrived at the Train Station at Chantilly. Throughout the whole of the journey he agonised over Oster's instructions. He'd been left in no doubt that he was to infiltrate the French Résistance. He hadn't the faintest idea how he was going to do it because all the locals knew that he'd gone over to the Germans.

He was tempted to telephone Hans and arrange a lift from the Station. Instead he ordered him to be at the Police Station first thing in the morning with the car and the rest of the Platoon. Even though it was late he walked to his lodgings, deep in thought. Madame Cormeau greeted him and set him down to black coffee and cakes and then, exhausted from his journeys, he retired for the night and slept soundly until the morning.

Chapter ten

When Jacque left General Oster's office, the General telephoned Gruppenführer Karl Koch, the Commandant of Neuengamme Concentration Camp in Germany.

The camp had been built in 1938 by one hundred of its inmates. They had been transferred from Sachsenhausen Concentration Camp when Neuengamme was at that time one of its Sub-camps. The camp was on the river Elbe, near Hamburg. By 1940 it had become independent. From the very beginning it was hell on earth for its inmates.

Food was virtually non-existent and yet the inmates had to perform hard labour in all kinds of weather and with constant beatings by the *SS* guards. The mortality rate was incredibly high. Starvation, sleep depravation, total lack of hygiene and medical care and cruelty, killed hundreds on a regular basis. Then there were the thousands who were hung or shot or gassed or killed by lethal injection.

Perhaps the most appalling thing that went on at Neuengamme, were the experiments Dr. Heisskeyer carried out. He injected Jewish children with T.B., and watched them die.

Many of the inmates ended up being involved in armament production. Initially this was done in workshops in the camp but later they were transferred to armaments factories in the surrounding area.

The General took a friendly approach to the Commandant. "Karl, its Oster here. General Hans Oster, of the Abwehr. You remember one of my colleagues had a conversation with you recently about one of your inmates."

"I remember," the Commandant said. "The man you spoke about is still with us, unlike some I could mention." And he laughed with sickening gusto and then he broke into a fit of coughing caused by his chain-smoking.

Oster screwed his face up in disgust at having to deal with such a person. Like so many Germans, he knew about the Concentration Camps, but like so many of his fellows he tried to put the thought of them out of his mind. It was just another reason he was in the Black Orchestra.

The Commandant stopped coughing and looked up at the young Jewish boy standing half-naked in the corner of his office. He was fifteen and compared to other inmates in the camp he was fit and healthy. He was kept that way, fed and cleaned and pampered in his special quarters just for the Commandant's pleasure. The Commandant smiled and gestured with his hand to the boy to finish undressing.

"You were saying General," he said as he felt the desire stirring in his loins.

"The French soldier Jean Boussine, Commandant. He's the one my colleague spoke to you about. It would be very useful for the Abwehr if he could be moved. Shall we say to a slightly less rigorous environment? I trust that would be possible?"

"Anything's possible General, you know that," the Commandant said knowingly. "Given the right circumstances."

"I see," Oster said. He was aware of what the Commandant had in mind. "So perhaps we could exchange a case of Irish Whiskey and some gold nuggets for the French soldier in question?"

"That's exactly what I had in mind General. You know how these things are."

"I'll get on to it right away," Oster said. "One of my men will be with you shortly to affect the transfer."

The Commandant broke into another fit of coughing as he instructed the young Jew to light another cigarette. In between the coughing he tried to speak to Oster. "Better that you come yourself General," he said. "You know what security's like? The fewer know about our little arrangement the better for us both. You'll realise that if this got out I could be compromised."

Oster hesitated. It was the last thing he wanted to do. But he saw no option. "Very well," he agreed. "I shall be with you tomorrow and I'd be grateful if you could arrange for the man to be cleaned up for me. He must be as presentable as possible."

"I shall put someone onto that right away General, and I'll see you tomorrow," the Commandant said. "And you will of course be able to tell me where he's being transferred to, it's the paper work you know."

After the Commandant had allowed the young Jew to satisfy his passion he instructed him to bring Jean Boussine to his own quarters and to get him cleaned up and dressed.

Boussine was in one of the many large wooden huts. Everyone lived in appalling conditions. The stench alone caused the young Jew to wretch as he opened the door. None of the inmates stirred, they simply stared blankly, waiting the inevitable.

"Jean Boussine you have to come with me," the young Jew called out.

There was no protest and no refusal, just a blank acceptance. None of the others spoke, they simply watched. Boussine knew there was no point resisting. He would only be beaten again if he did. He climbed down from his wooden slatted bed and out of the hut, watched with idle curiosity by the others.

He stood looking around him, blinking in the bright light, and as he followed his fellow Jew a picture of his young wife flashed before his eyes. With a sinking feeling he believed he was going to his death. That he'd never be reunited with his wife and son. Then he realised he wasn't taking the same path he'd seen others take never to return. Instead he was going to a separate set of buildings. He dared to speak.

"Where …. Where are you taking me?"

"Just follow me," was all he got as he trailed behind the young Jew. His filthy clothes barely covered his emaciated body. His threadbare trousers trailed on the ground.

He was soon inside the young Jew's hut. It was a simple affair, but it was clean. It was just one room with a bed and a table. The window, with a slightly grubby curtain looked out into the Camp Compound. Its position was deliberate so that the young Jew could be reminded every day what would befall him if he displeased the Commandant.

The room had the luxury of a wash hand basin with a bar of soap and a towel. The bed had a mattress with a woollen blanket. There was a small cabinet above the wash hand basin. The young Jew opened the cabinet and took out a razor and left it down.

"You better wash and shave," the young Jew said. "And I'll bring you fresh clothes."

Boussine reached out and touched the young Jew on the arm. The young Jew pulled away, not wishing to be touched by his dirt. Boussine followed him but when he saw the look in the young man's face he held back.

"Just tell me why you're doing this?" he said.

"I'm only doing what I'm told," he said. Then he saw the look of bewilderment on Boussine's face and he felt sorry for him. "Somebody spoke to the Commandant on the telephone. You're being moved, but I don't know why or where."

He left Boussine who started to wash, and walked to a large building in the Compound. When he opened the door he was faced with a sickening sight, but one he's seen many times before. There were piles of clothes and shoes, which took up most of the space. There were also bales of human hair and a bench with hundreds of pairs of glasses and false teeth. Another bench had watches, bracelets and other jewellery.

The young Jew looked around him and then began to rummage among the clothes until he found all that he needed to dress Boussine. He left the building and returned to his hut. Boussine was washed and shaved and sitting naked and cold on the edge of the bed when the young Jew came in.

He threw the clothes on the bed and told Boussine to get dressed. Boussine dressed in silence and when he'd finished the young Jew told him he would have to spend the night in his hut, sleeping on the floor and that he'd be moving the next day.

Oster arrived at the Camp the following day and was brought to the Commandant's office. He was surprised that there were no inmates to see, just a few guards. It was almost as if the camp was deserted. In fact only those who were dead or near to death were left. The rest were employed making armaments.

"General Oster," the Commandant greeted him. "Heil Hitler."

"Heil Hitler," Oster said hoping the Commandant didn't notice his lack of enthusiasm.

They shook hands. "You've brought the merchandise!"

Oster turned to his driver who stood by the black Mercedes. He pointed to the boot and the driver went round and took out a case of Irish whiskey and brought it to the Commandant. Then he went back and brought a box of gold nuggets. The Commandant grinned as he lifted out a bottle of whiskey and then he felt the gold nuggets.

"The Abwehr's doing well then," the Commandant said.

Oster smiled. "We get by," he said.

The Commandant picked up the telephone and ordered Boussine to be brought to him.

"Shall we share a whiskey General?" he said smiling. "An Irish whiskey?"

"Perhaps another time Commandant, I'm anxious to be on my way."

"You don't like this place. I can tell."

"It's nothing," Oster said. "It just isn't soldiering."

"It's better than the Russian front, I can tell you that," the Commandant said opening one of the bottles. "I've been there, and I should know."

The young Jew brought Boussine to the Commandant. Oster could see immediately how emaciated he was and reckoned the clothes had made a big difference.

Boussine stood with his head bowed, fearful of what was going to happen. "You may take him away," the Commandant said to Oster. "I just need the papers."

Oster reached into his pocket and handed the Commandant some papers. "You'll see it's been authorised by Admiral Canaris," he said. "It's all perfectly in order. The prisoner will be going to Stalag X1-A. It's near the village of Schorstedt. He will become a farm labourer for Germany, working in the fields by day and in prison by night. A more profitable role than wasting out his time here, do you not think?"

"One less mouth to feed," the Commandant said.

Boussine felt his heart beating faster. 'He was going to a Labour Camp. Compared to Neuengamme that was heaven!'

Chapter eleven

Two weeks after Gary Tucker was brought to Hospital and on the night Jacque returned from his last trip to the Abwehr, Henri from the Résistance stood in the shadows outside the Cottage Hospital. He was waiting for Andrea to come off duty. She was later than usual, and Henri was beginning to get worried. For over a week now, he'd been coming at the same time, hiding in the shadows and waiting. Each time he went away disappointed. Now time was running out for Henri and the others. They'd only tonight left. Every night Andrea left the Hospital about the same time and each time she didn't hesitate at the gate but began walking home. Then he saw her stopping outside the Hospital gate, lighting a cigarette, and his heart missed a beat. That was the signal he'd been waiting for.

After a moment's hesitation and a quick look around her, Andrea began walking home. Henri turned and cycled away. He called with Charles and then they called at a small farm in the area, where they collected a horse and cart. The cart was loaded with hay and they set out for the Cottage Hospital, taking their time so as not to tire the horse. They were reasonably confident that there would be no German patrols at that time of the morning. The Germans preferred not to venture out during the hours of darkness for fear of ambush.

Henri and Charles went to an entrance at the rear of the Hospital, which had been left open. The pilot was in a side ward, at the end of a corridor near the rear entrance. They had left the horse tethered to a lamppost. The Hospital was in semi-darkness.

The door to the ward was open and the pilot was awake. He was wearing pyjamas and a dressing gown. Andrea had hidden a stretcher under his bed before she went off duty. Henri pulled it out as the pilot eased himself over to the side of the bed.

"I'm afraid I'll have to rely on you blokes to get me onto this thing," the pilot said. "I'm still not much use for anything."

"Our pleasure," Charles said. "That's what we're here for."

They lifted him as gently as possible onto the stretcher and left him on the floor. They found a couple of extra pillows and a blanket that Andrea had deliberately left for the purpose. They put them into the bed and covered them with the bedclothes to look like a body. They checked the corridor was clear and then carried him outside to the waiting horse and cart. He was covered quickly with hay and then they began the journey to the Château Aveline. The horse trotted most of the way.

Andrea and her mother were waiting anxiously for them. They brought the pilot into the Château and up two flights of stairs and along the corridor. There was a large bookcase at the end of the corridor. Andrea wheeled the bookcase across the floor to reveal a door.

She opened the door and switched on a light. The room was small and without a window, apart from a skylight. There was a single bed and a small table with a basin and a water jug and a chemical toilet in the corner.

"All right, put the stretcher on the bed," Andrea said. "Mother and I will manage the rest. It's better if you lot get off home."

"We've done it," Tucker said with a wide smile as Charles and Henri left the room. "Can't thank you enough boys. Take good care now."

"You too," Henri said.

Andrea and her mother rolled Tucker off the stretcher. "This is your home now Gary," Andrea said. "It's not much I'm afraid, but we'll help you make the best of it. Then when you're fit enough we'll try and get you back to England."

"England," Tucker said. "It seems an age since I left. Can't wait to see the boys again and get back in the air."

Marie raised her eyebrows. "I mean it," he said. "I'm going to fly again. If Douglas Bader can get back in the air after losing his legs, so can I."

"Who's Douglas Bader?" Andrea asked him.

Tucker smiled. "I'll tell you all about him another time Andrea."

It was 07:00 when the night staff was going off duty and they made a final check on the patient they called the mystery man. A nurse looked in, assumed he was asleep and closed the door behind her. An hour later the day staff came to his room and looking in assumed again that he was asleep and left him. It was a ward cleaner who came as she did every day, to talk to him and clean his room who realised he had gone.

She ran out of the room shouting at the top of her voice. "He's gone, he's gone. The mystery man's gone."

The Matron, an elderly lady of ample proportions and feared by all, heard the commotion and told the cleaner to, "Hush."

She went into the room, pulled back the bedclothes and then stormed out and telephoned the Police. She spoke immediately to Inspector Marius Regnier.

"Inspector," she said quite calmly. "He's gone. He's vanished into thin air and we don't know how or when."

The Inspector took a deep breath just as Jacque walked into the Police Station fresh from his trip to Abweher Headquarters and his night's sleep. He nodded to Jacque who stood and listened to the telephone conversation.

"Who has vanished Matron?" the Inspector asked.

"The man," she said. "The man who was brought in following a road accident. The one you've been trying to identify."

"I see," the Inspector said. "We'd better get up there."

He turned to Jacque. "Are you coming?"

The Inspector left the Sergeant in charge whilst Hans drove them to the Hospital. The platoon remained behind. The Matron met them at the door and told them to follow her. She pushed the door of the empty side ward open and pointed to the bed and exclaimed, "Look, he's absconded."

She took two strides across to the bed and pulled the bedclothes away to reveal the pillows and blanket left by Henri and Charles. "Gone," she said.

"Did anybody see or hear anything Matron?" the Inspector asked.

"Nothing," she said. "The night staff last saw him at midnight when he'd his night-time drink. Then in the morning when they looked in he was still asleep but they didn't disturb him."

"Only he wasn't asleep then," Jacque said. "He was long gone."

"We can't be expected to keep an eye on every patient every hour of the day and night," the Matron said in defence

"No of course not," the Inspector said. "But could he have walked out unaided? Had he recovered well enough?"

"I doubt it," the Matron said. "Somebody must have helped him."

The Inspector turned to Jacque. "I don't believe this man was involved in a road traffic accident," he said. "But perhaps we'll never know."

"If it wasn't an accident, then what was it?" Jacque asked.

"Could he have been an injured airman? I don't know. Anything's possible these days," the Inspector said."

He turned to the Matron. "There's nothing more we can do here," he said. "If you hear of anything let us know."

"Of course," the Matron said.

As they returned to the Police Station Jacque turned to the Inspector. "If this man wasn't involved in a road accident," he said. "Then as you suggested perhaps he was an injured airman, and that being the case he'll have been spirited away by the Résistance. We know there's an escape route here and that could be the answer."

"Well if you find your escape route in time, you might just solve the mystery as to who this man was."

Chapter twelve

They returned to the Police Station, as a train from Paris pulled in to the Station at Chantilly. There was a shrill whistle as it came to a stop. The passengers were German soldiers returning from a night in Paris, and men and women coming to Chantilly on various errands. The train stopped, with smoke billowing from it. High-pressure steam engulfed the area around the train and then drifted upwards to be lost in the canopy above. The Stationmaster came out of his office and blew his whistle and shouted, "Chantilly, Chantilly."

A small group of people waited on the platform to board the train.

There was a small Station Café serving coffee and sandwiches. It was a bleak place with half a dozen tables covered in white tablecloths. A young woman served behind the counter and she looked out wistfully as the passengers filed past the window. She had only one customer, a young woman, who was reading the morning paper and appeared to be waiting for someone. She was wearing dark glasses and a red beret. A silk scarf partially covered her face. She looked up as the passengers walked past the steamed up window of the Café. She got up and walked across to the window and wiped it to give herself a clear view.

As the passengers filed out of the Station they had to pass through a metal barrier. Two Policemen were standing there to check their identity papers. They selected individuals at random for more thorough interrogation. Soldiers in uniform were usually ushered through without any questions.

A few yards past the interrogation point three soldiers stood smoking, beside an SdKfx Kleine Kettenkraftrad (German army motorcycle half-track). It was mainly used by airborne troops but sometimes turned up in other circumstances.

A passenger stopped outside the Café window, looking around him. He was spotted immediately by the young woman with the paper. She left her paper on one of the tables and went to the door. As she opened it, the man from the train saw her and nodded and she walked towards the exit, followed by the man. They were the last to go out.

They walked in file through the barrier. "Papers please," one of the Policemen said.

They handed their papers for inspection and were waved through. They breathed a sigh of relief. Suddenly one of the Policemen called out, suspicious of something. The two turned and then panicked and ran straight for the three soldiers beside the motorcycle half-track.

There was no other way out, and before the soldiers could react the man who was in front felled one of the soldiers with a blow to the face. He grasped an MP-40 sub-machine gun that had been left carelessly in the half-track and turning it on the three soldiers fired a quick burst.

Without waiting to see the effect, they jumped into the half-track. It started immediately and they accelerated away from the Station. One soldier was dead and the other two were badly injured. Passengers ran for cover, women were screaming. The two fugitives kept their heads down as they cleared the outskirts of the town and headed out into the country.

The Police at the Train Station telephoned the Police Station and the duty Sergeant took the call and put it through to the Inspector who had just arrived back with Jacque from the Hospital. They were having coffee in the rest room.

"It's an army matter now," Jacque heard him saying to the caller.

The Inspector told Jacque what had happened and Jacque immediately ran to the car and ordered Hans to drive to the Train Station. He ordered the Commander of the Personnel Carrier to follow. Meanwhile the Inspector informed the Army Camp of what had happened and more troops were despatched towards the scene. A spotter plane was ordered up from the nearby airfield.

The black Citroen stopped briefly to allow Jacque to check the direction the fugitives had gone, and then ordered Hans to drive flat out in pursuit. The two fugitives had made good time in their motorcycle half-track, reaching 50 mph on straight stretches of road. The young woman drove while the other watched for the Germans.

It was the black Citroen with Jacque and Hans he saw first. "They're after us," he yelled above the roar of the half-track. "Can't you get anything more out of this thing?"

His companion gritted her teeth and shook her head. "When they're close enough give them a burst of that Schmeisser," she yelled.

The Citroen was closing fast and there was as yet no sign of the Personnel Carrier. The man in the back of the half-track knew the Citroen would catch them quickly. He had to spare his shots because he'd no idea how many he'd left. Then he saw Jacque's hand appear out of the passenger window with a pistol. He ducked and heard the bang but he knew they were still out of range, and not really close enough for *him* to return fire.

Again Jacque fired but he was still out of range. The half-track raced flat out whilst the Citroen closed fast. Again there was a pistol shot and this time the bullet ricocheted off the half-track. Then the man fired the Schmeisser. Hans and Jacque ducked as the windscreen shattered. He fired again. Hans swung the wheel to one side and lost control and the Citroen rolled over and crashed into the ditch, steam belching from the radiator.

The Half-track raced on, the two fugitives jubilant at the lucky shot. Jacque pulled himself out of the Citroen, badly shaken but otherwise unhurt. Hans was slumped across the steering wheel. Jacque watched as the half-track disappeared into the distance. He reached in and felt Hans's pulse, then he looked at his watch and stamped his feet in frustration.

The Personnel Carrier finally caught up with them and stopped. Jacque looked at one of the soldiers. "You," he ordered. "Get Hans out of there and look after him till someone else arrives."

Then he turned to the Commander. "Let's go, now," he said. "They won't have got far."

Further down the road, five Army Motorcycle Sidecar's caught up with the Personnel Carrier and they continued in convoy. Soon afterwards they came on the abandoned motorcycle half-track. There was no sign of the fugitives.

Jacque went over to the half-track and looked in the fuel tank. "Empty," he said.

He looked around him at open countryside criss-crossed with high hedges, small woods and copses. "They could be anywhere," he said.

A soldier from one of the motorcycle sidecar's spoke up. "Sir, General Scholtz has ordered out the dog handlers. They'll be here shortly."

"Thank you," Jacque said. "Perhaps it would be best to wait for them otherwise we'll confuse the trail for the dogs."

Three Dobermans arrived with their handlers and they picked up the trail almost immediately. They found the Schmeisser abandoned with its empty magazine. The trail led across the fields, through small woods and then it came to a dead end at the edge of a small stream. Undaunted the dogs and their handlers crossed the stream and very quickly picked up the scent again. It led them towards a much larger wood and then into it.

The dogs were getting excited, straining at their leashes. Their handlers were having trouble holding them back. They knew they were close to their quarry and they let the dogs lose and they bounded forward baying loudly.

The two fugitives had hoped to find refuge in the wood but their hopes were dashed. They'd nothing with which to protect themselves except their wits. They continued to run for their lives through the wood when they heard the baying of the hounds. In desperation they looked around them and then suddenly, just ahead of them they saw the wreckage of an aeroplane lying nose down in the wood. It was a RAF Lysander, painted black. It was the same Lysander, which had crashed after it had dropped of an SOE agent. It was Pilot Officer Gary Tucker' plane!

They ran towards it and first the man and then the young woman hauled themselves through the window of the smashed cockpit. The sound of the hounds was coming closer. Breathless they both knew the trail would still lead the hounds and the soldiers to them. But they'd nowhere else to hide.

Drawing breath the man gasped. "Listen to me. We've had it. We've come to the end of the road, but both of us needn't die. Pull yourself up into the tail section. I'll try and convince them that we split up when we dumped the half-track. And take this revolver, I'll not need it.

"No," the girl cried. "I can't leave you."

"You've got to," he said. "Now hurry before it's too late, you owe it to the others to survive if you can, and fight again. Go on, pull yourself up there and whatever you do don't make a sound."

She reached out her hand in desperation, tears of frustration and fear streaming down her face.

"NO," he cried again. "It's too late. You've got to survive. This is the only way. When I've tried to convince them you've gone another way, I won't let them take me alive."

The hounds appeared suddenly and reluctantly the girl scrambled through the wreckage up to the tail section of the plane, where she did her best to hide and remain quiet. The hounds were baying loudly and then she heard the voice of one of the handlers calling the dogs off. She heard her companion say he would come down and she bit her lip to hold back the cry of anguish welling up within her.

There was a scrambling noise and the sound of metal rubbing against metal and the plane moved precariously as her companion lowered himself to the ground. In seconds the dog-handlers covered him with their Schmeissers.

"Where's your friend?" One of them growled sarcastically, as he hit him in the left kidney with the butt of his gun.

The man doubled up in agony and fell to the ground. He was about to be kicked in the back by the same soldier when Jacque arrived. Jacque looked down at him as he squirmed in agony and then he looked up through the canopy above as he heard the spotter plane.

"Well," Jacque said. "Tell the man. Where's your companion?"

The man coughed and tried to get up. Jacque pulled out his Luger and held it to the back of the man's head. "Where did your companion go?"

The man kept silent and Jacque fired a shot past his ear. The shot startled the man. "We separated at the road," he said, and then he was promptly sick.

"Who are you and what were you doing?" Jacque demanded to know

Again the man tried to get up and this time Jacque helped him to get to his feet. "I'm saying nothing," he said.

Jacque hit him hard in the stomach and he doubled over in agony. "You'll talk," he said.

The man straightened himself as best he could and glared at Jacque. "Never," he said. "You'll never make me talk.

Then Jacque turned to the soldiers. "Bring him back to the road," he ordered.

But then Jacque saw the man's face contorted in agony as he bit on a cyanide capsule and he dropped dead at his feet.

"Damn," Jacque said.

He looked around him and told the soldiers to go on and wait for him back at the road.

They took the man's body away with them in the hope that by identifying him, they would find others. As they walked away a young woman's face peered out through a crack in the fuselage. She still wore her red beret and the scarf that now barely covered the lower part of her face. She saw her companion's body being dragged away and she gasped when she saw her brother Jacque looking up at the plane.

Andrea was huddled in the tail section with her hands clasping her knees and she wept silently, the Webley held firmly in her hand. She was determined to use it on herself if she was discovered.

Jacque hauled himself up and into the cockpit looking for anything that would indicate what the plane's mission was, or that would identify the pilot. He'd recognised the plane straight away as a Lysander and knew it was used by the SOE to drop off agents. He'd also realised that the missing patient from the cottage Hospital was almost certainly the pilot of the plane, or an SOE agent.

After searching the cockpit Jacque found nothing and he lowered himself to the ground and followed the others back to the road.

The dog handlers began a search on the other side of the road but the dogs failed to pick up a scent. Reluctantly Jacque called off the search and they returned to Chantilly.

When Andrea was sure Jacque and the others had gone, she left the plane and made her way through to the other side of the wood and then home.

Chapter thirteen

Later that morning, Colonel Klaus Richter of the *SS* called on General Scholtz.

"General," he said. "I understand there's been an incident at the Train Station."

"There has," the General said annoyed at the unwelcome intrusion. "And everything's under control."

"You've a dead soldier and a traitor committing suicide before you can even get him back here for interrogation. I wouldn't call that 'under control', General would you?" the Colonel said.

"The fact remains we acted and apprehended one of the culprits," the General said. "His death's unfortunate, but you above all people know how these things are. In any event Admiral Canaris has sent one of his agents to this area. He's the one who acted so promptly."

"Yes," the Colonel said. "I understand the Admiral has taken it upon himself to interfere in matters that don't concern him. I understand also that you've assisted the Admiral's agent in this matter. This will not go unnoticed General."

The General stood to his feet, his face ablaze with anger. "Is that a threat Colonel?" he demanded to know.

The Colonel smiled. "Not at all my dear General, it was simply an observation. And now I shall take my leave of you. The *SS* will investigate this matter. There's no need for you to concern yourself with it any further."

The Colonel turned to leave and then hesitated. "Oh yes," he said. "I knew there was something else. There's this annoying irritation of an apparent lone sniper whose activities haven't gone unnoticed at Headquarters. You'll know that he recently assassinated a good friend of mine, Otto Kramer, a sickening business, to lose one's friends in such a cowardly fashion. Now I did mean to ask you General, if you've any worthwhile leads in this matter or is that asking too much of you?"

"As you very well know Colonel, the Abwehr is also investigating that distasteful business," General Scholtz said, having calmed down. "Captain Jacque Aveline is also involved in that and I've every confidence in him, as has the Admiral."

"That may be," the Colonel said. "But in the meantime somebody is going to pay for that last episode *and* the SS will carry out its own investigations. Good day to you General Scholtz."

The Colonel left and General Scholtz sat down and lifted the telephone. "Get me Captain Jacque Aveline and bring him here," he said.

There was an animated conversation going on regarding the morning's incident when the General's message was delivered to Jacque. He'd been found in the Café in Chantilly, which was frequented by the soldiers. His driver Hans was recuperating from not too severe concussion following the shooting.

Jacque was driven to the General's quarters and directed to his office

"Captain Aveline," he said without asking him to sit down. "A word of warning!"

Jacque raised his eyebrows.

"Your action this morning was prompt and properly carried out."

"Thank you sir," Jacque responded with a smile.

"However not everyone would appear to agree. The SS, and Colonel Klaus Richter in particular, have for some unknown reason taken an interest in the incident this morning. You know there's rivalry, indeed suspicion and jealousy, between the Wehrmacht and the SS. Colonel Richter has taken it upon himself to investigate this morning's incident and he's aware that you've been despatched by the Abwehr. And believe you me there's no love lost between the SS and the Abwehr either."

"I understand sir," Jacque said in a subdued voice, as the spectre of Colonel Richter caused a sudden flashback to Verberie. "Are you advising me to pull out of this investigation?"

"I'm not saying that, but you may wish to consult your masters. If I know the Admiral he'll not countenance interference from anyone, especially the *SS* and a word from him may stop an ugly incident."

"I'll bear that in mind sir," Jacque said, willing to cling to anything to avoid a confrontation with the Colonel.

Hans had persuaded the Doctor in the sickbay to allow him to sign himself out. He had a slight headache but otherwise felt all right. Jacque had been pondering over what the General had told him. He also kept going over in his mind what General Oster had instructed him to do. Colonel Richter was to be eliminated, but why? Was there a connection between that and the Colonel taking over the investigation into the shooting at the Station? The more he thought about it, the more puzzled he was and the more alarmed he became at the thought of the Colonel using the photographs to compromise his already precarious situation.

He thought again and again about the shooting and the crashed Lysander and the woman who got away. The only description they had was that she appeared young and wore a red beret, dark glasses and a scarf. Then there was the mystery patient whom he was now convinced *was* the pilot of the crashed plane.

He gave up finally and knowing Hans had signed himself out he called him to bring him to his parent's Château. It was 01:00.

Chapter fourteen

Colonel Richter was displeased with his visit to General Scholtz. He resented the fact that he outranked him and he resented the fact that he had to call on him at all. But he resented most of all that he had tried to have him court-martialled. In fact he resented all Wehrmacht Officers and considered most of them to be inferior to their *SS* equivalent. The fact that he had to share Madeleine Boussine with him did not help matters either.

When he first met Madeleine it was her beauty that immediately struck him. She was tall and slim with a firm bust, and shapely legs. Her face was strikingly beautiful with bright hazel eyes and a small, perfectly formed nose. Her lips were full and slightly pouting. Her hair was a rich brown. Despite her looks Richter had no intention of falling in love with her, he just lusted after her, and then she became a means to an end, just another way of getting evidence of General Scholtz's suspected treason.

Scholtz was only one of a number of high-ranking Officers in the Wehrmacht whom Hitler suspected of treason. But the problem with Scholtz was that he was popular with his men and with the German people. He was also a hero from the Great War and had already shown his bravery and leadership qualities in the present war. Hitler himself had decorated him with oak leaves to his Knight's Cross and so even he recognised that without credible evidence he didn't dare touch him.

Richter was charged by his superiors, with getting that evidence and in the end if the evidence was not there he was perfectly happy to 'manufacture' it.

After his visit to Scholtz he returned to *SS* Headquarters in Avenue Foch in Paris. There he began a personal search for the lone sniper who had assassinated his friend Otto Kramer. He interviewed some of Kramer's fellow Officers and quickly established a link between Kramer's death and his last young boy associate.

The boy's mother, Charlene Cohen, was brought in for questioning. Richter questioned her personally and she quickly broke down after she was tortured. As a result Richter established that Charlene Cohen's family had sworn revenge on his friend Kramer and he discovered that her husband Andrée was not dead, as the SS had believed but was with the Maquis. So the Maquis were blamed for Kramer's death, whether by a lone sniper or not.

Richter's first act of revenge was to send Charlene and her young son Henri to a Concentration Camp. Normally Richter wouldn't have cared where she went; he would just as easily have had them shot out of hand. However in a twisted sort of way he felt he owed Karl Koch, the Commandant of Neuengamme a favour. He knew he 'enjoyed' boys for company and little Henri was particularly handsome.

When Richter first saw Medeleine Boussine at the Hotel du Parc in Chantilly and fell for her beauty, the first thing he did was to enquire about her family. That was when he found out about her husband Jean and the fact that he was a Jew. It was the ideal situation for Richter who wanted to be able to manipulate Madeleine to suit his own ends. He didn't particularly care whether Jean died in a Concentration Camp or not but in order to ingratiate himself to Madeleine he made it his business to see that Jean was at least kept alive. That was when Koch came into the picture. He agreed at Richter's request, to ensure that Jean did not go to the gas chamber.

So now Richter was able to return the favour. It also happened that he knew Koch's birthday was coming up soon. Charlene and her son Henri were escorted from Paris to the Concentration Camp by one of Richter's aids, Obersturmfürher Franz Vetter. He was given specific instructions to tell Koch that the boy Henri was a birthday present from his friend Colonel Richter and that it was by way of thanks for 'looking after' Jean Boussine.

When they arrived at Neuengamme, Henri and his mother were immediately separated on the instructions of one of the Camp Guards. Henri was taken along with Vetter to the Commandant's Office, and his mother to where she would later be taken to die in a Gas Chamber

Vetter introduced himself to Koch and explained the purpose of his visit. The young Jew who had looked after Jean Boussine before his transfer was in the office.

Koch stood up and laughed out loud and slapped his thigh. "Do you hear that Itzak," he said. "I've received a birthday present from my old friend Richter, and what a present! What a handsome boy! Do you like him?"

Itzak smiled. "Yes," he said.

"You'll be the best of friends," Koch said. "Now take him to your hut and I'll call you later."

He smiled malevolently as the two boys left. Then Koch turned to Vetter. "I haven't seen my friend for some time," he said to him. Then he went to a cupboard and took out a half empty bottle of Irish whiskey. "A drink," he said as he filled two glasses.

Vetter took the glass willingly. He'd never tasted Irish whiskey. "It's good," he said. "It's very good

Koch poured Vetter another glass. "It comes courtesy of Admiral Canaris of the Abwehr," he said proudly. They do very well for themselves there you know. It's a pity there won't be any more of this whiskey."

Vetter raised his eyebrows. "No," Koch said. "After today I don't think there'll be any more, because I want you to pass on a message to my friend Colonel Richter. I want you to tell him that I appreciate my birthday present very much. I also want you to tell him that the Abwehr requested that I agree to a certain Jew by the name of Jean Boussien being transferred from here to a forced Labour Camp, Stalag X1-A at Schorstedt. It may have some meaning for him."

Vetter returned to Paris to *SS* Headquarters on the Avenue Foch. When he reported to Richter it was as if a black cloud enveloped the Colonel, and he made Vetter repeat his message and asked him if he was sure.

Chapter fifteen

The Château was quiet as Jacque let himself in. Hans settled back in the car to sleep, not caring when Jacque would return.

Jacque crept quietly past the hallstand and he was about to go up the stairs when he stopped with a start, his heart beating madly. There on the hallstand was a red beret and a silk scarf! He stood transfixed for ages. Then he told himself it couldn't be, that hundreds of girls wore red berets. He put it to the back of his mind. There were other things more pressing on his mind. He slipped up stairs to Nina's room and opened the door. As he closed it behind him and switched the light on, a startled Nina sat bolt upright.

"Master Aveline," she cried. "You'll be the death of me."

He strode across the room and put his hand over her mouth and whispered, "Shush, we don't want to waken anybody."

He removed his hand as she smiled coyly and lay back in bed, pulling the bedclothes up to cover her nakedness.

Jacque undressed and got in beside her. He pulled her towards him and kissed her fiercely.

At 06:00 Nina wakened from a fitful sleep. She heard the clock in the corridor chime and knew it was time to get up. She turned to Jacque to waken him but he was sleeping soundly and she shrugged and rolled quietly out of bed and dressed. She knew she had plenty of time to get him away before the mistress of the house rose. She opened the door without making a sound and went into the bathroom, adjacent to her bedroom.

She flushed the toilet and as she walked back past her bedroom door, Jacque turned in bed. As he did, the sound of the toilet disturbed him. He stretched his arm across the bed and realised that Nina had gone. He got up quickly, pulling on his trousers and shirt and went to the bedroom door and opened it. He looked out along the corridor where Nina had gone, but there was no sign of her.

He knew that at the end of the corridor there was only a small box room and nothing else, apart from a large bookcase against the wall.

Mystified, he tiptoed along the corridor and in the dim light was surprised to see the bookcase pulled part of the way across the corridor. As he came closer he was aware of the faint sound of voices.

He listened intently, but he only heard whispering. He recognised Nina's voice, but the other was a man's which he didn't recognise! Then in case Nina walked out and saw him, he went back to the bedroom and closed the door. Nina came back into the bedroom, as Jacque was finishing dressing.

"Thank goodness you're up," she said. "You'd better hurry."

"I'm nearly ready," Jacque said. "Nip down to the kitchen and get me a coffee and then I'll be down in a minute."

Jacque gave her time to get downstairs and then he walked along the corridor. The bookcase was across the door of the box room and not against the wall where he'd always remembered it. His suspicions were confirmed. A stranger would never guess there was a room behind it.

He walked nonchalantly into the kitchen, his mind in a whirl, and sat at the table waiting for his coffee. "You're cutting it fine," Nina said. "If your mother knew you'd spent the night with me I'd lose my job and you wouldn't want that."

Jacque smiled as she handed him his coffee. "It won't happen," he said. "But why don't you meet me at the Café at lunch time and I'll make it up to you for all the trouble I've caused."

"I don't know Jacque. What if you mother or Andrea found out?"

"They won't. And anyway, who cares," he added.

"Well all right, but just this once. Now drink that coffee and be off with you."

Jacque had lots of time to think before he met Nina, and he'd already begun to formulate a plan. The Colonel and the photographs were uppermost in his mind. The thought of being blackmailed, not only by his colleagues in the Abwehr but especially by the SS really screwed him up. He was determined to remove that threat and the only way to do that was to get rid of Richter, and then confirm or deny the Abwehr's suspicions of General Scholtz.

After spending the night with Nina he was devastated to realise that the red beret and the scarf he'd seen at the Château had to be those worn by the young woman who'd evaded capture the previous morning. They had to belong to his sister Andrea. He was left with one explanation. Andrea, and perhaps even his mother, was in the French Résistance and they were harbouring the pilot of the crashed Lydsander. The same pilot who spent two weeks recuperating in the Hospital with everyone believing he was a road accident victim. Every time he thought of the implications it chilled his blood.

If the Germans found out, Andrea, his mother, Nina and even his ill father would be tortured and then executed. Not even General Scholtz could save them. And if Richter and the *SS* became involved he could even find himself in the same boat.

The more he thought about it, the more convinced he became that it was exactly the answer to his problem. He knew the pilot was being hidden in the Château. With that knowledge his sister Andrea *and* perhaps his mother would have no option but to assist him in getting rid of Richter! They were the key to infiltrating the Résistance!

Hans dropped Jacque off at the Café and he was sitting alone when Nina came in. The town was relatively quiet after all the excitement of the previous day. Nina smiled and sat down.

"I shouldn't really be here," she said. "People will talk and they'll have me branded as a collaborator."

"You mean like me," Jacque said.

Nina nodded. "Your mother gets it all the time, because of the General."

"And if they really knew about my mother," Jacque hesitated for effect. "Why they'd adore her."

"Yes but," Nina stopped mid-sentence suddenly suspecting a trap. "What do you mean exactly Jacque - if they really knew your mother?

Jacque smiled. "Let's get coffee."

Nina looked out of the window trying to hide her concern as Jacque went and brought two coffees to the table.

She looked up as he set them down. He looked at the door as two soldiers sauntered in. "I know about the pilot," he whispered menacingly.

Nina gasped and went pale. "The pilot?"

"The injured man, who was in Hospital," he said, knowing he was on the right track. "They brought him to the Château so that my mother could look after him. He's hidden in the box room and when he's well enough they'll get the Résistance to send him back to England."

Nina knew there was no point denying it because he knew too much. "Why are you telling *me* Jacque?"

Jacque smiled. "I had to be sure Nina."

"What are you going to do?" And there was an unmistakable tremor in her voice.

Jacque reached out his hand and put it over Nina's and squeezed it gently. "What's your involvement Nina?" he said, ignoring her question.

She tried to pull her hand away but he squeezed her hand so tightly she gasped. Jacque raised his eyebrows as he looked intently at her, waiting. Nina bit her lower lip and shook her head.

"Come now," he encouraged.

"I don't know anything," she said. "I only help to look after him."

Jacque took his hand away. "But you must know you're taking a dreadful risk. If the Germans found out they'd never accept that you were *only looking after him*. You would be shot."

Nina gasped. "I do it because of your father. He … he was very kind and good to my mother when she was dying of cancer. It's the only way I can repay him."

"Are you saying my father's involved in the Résistance, even though he's so ill?" Jacque asked.

Nina blushed. "I shouldn't be talking like this," she said. "And *you* shouldn't make me Jacque."

"Very well," Jacque agreed. "I'll not ask you anything more but now I want you to tell Andrea to meet me here at the same time tomorrow."

"She may be working, and anyway if I do she'll know I've been talking to you."

"Just tell her you met me in the town by chance. Now stop worrying. Tell her to be here in this Café, without fail at this time tomorrow. And tell her to make sure she comes alone, and not a word of what we've been talking about." He smiled again. "Now let's finish this coffee."

Chapter sixteen

That night Jacque called at the home of Madeleine Boussine. When she opened the door to him she felt a cold clammy fear and Jacque noticed. He invited himself in and Madeleine reluctantly stood back as he went into the sitting room. It was sparsely furnished. A woman in her fifties was asleep in a chair. Her mouth was pulled down at one side, the result of a severe stroke brought on by a blood clot.

"Where's the boy?" Jacque asked.

"Please no," Madeleine pleaded. "Don't touch him. I'll do anything you want, but please leave my boy alone. My poor mother, she needs me, but she's nothing. My boy is everything."

Jacque smiled. "It's all right," he said. "I just want to see him. Please, show me."

Madeleine walked out of the room and Jacque followed her to the boy's bedroom. He was asleep as Jacque went over and stroked his forehead. Madeleine was almost whimpering with fear and apprehension.

"Do you call him Jean, after his father?"

Madeleine shook her head. "No Louis, after Jean's father."

"I've spoken to someone about your husband. They'll get back to me, have no fear."

He bent over little Louis and lifted him up in his arms. He was warm and sweaty and his head flopped to one side but he didn't waken. "He's a fine boy," he said.

Madeleine was wringing her hands. Jacque laid the boy back in bed and pulled the clothes over him. "There's something you must do for me Madeleine. I know you won't let me down."

The next day he was sitting in the Café waiting for Andrea. Hans was given the morning off and Jacque was not in uniform in case it antagonised Andrea. A group of soldiers sat in a corner whilst Jacque sat at the window looking out across the street at a draper's shop. As he watched, a man cycled up and stopped outside the shop. He propped his bicycle against the wall, beside the shop, and then leaned against the wall himself.

Jacque studied him for a moment and was about to dismiss him when he saw Andrea arrive on *her* bicycle. He noticed an almost imperceptible nod between them and he smiled to himself.

He stood up as Andrea came in and pulled out a chair for her. He'd forgotten how beautiful his sister was.

Jacque smiled warmly but was rebuffed by Andrea's cold response. "This better be good," she said.

"Not much of a greeting for your only brother," Jacque said as Andrea sat down.

Jacque ordered coffee and then on an impulse he said. "Please don't leave; I'll be back in a moment."

He left the Café and crossed the street. He took out his Abwehr identification and showed it to the man with the bicycle. The man was obviously startled but retained his composure. He glanced across the street and saw Andrea watching him anxiously.

Jacque ordered him to turn around and spread-eagled him against the wall, with his arms above his head. He frisked him expertly and immediately found a pistol in his coat pocket and took it out and put it in his own.

"You're taking quite a chance," he said.

The man said nothing as he suddenly felt the barrel of Jacque's pistol in his ribs.

"It's *your* lucky day," Jacque said. "If I'd been somebody else you wouldn't *be* so lucky; so take yourself off and leave me and my sister in peace, before I have you arrested."

Jacque stepped back and the man lowered his arms and glowering at Jacque took his bicycle and wheeled it away. Jacque returned to the Café.

"What was that all about?" Andrea demanded to know as Jacque sat down and gestured to the waiter to bring the coffee over.

He smiled. "Just something to let you see you can trust me," he said and placed the young man's pistol on the table in front of her.

Andrea scowled at him fingering her cup of coffee the waiter had left.

"You can stop the pretence Andrea," he said. "That pistol belonged to your friend with the bicycle, from across the road."

He lifted the pistol again to hide it from the soldiers, but he was too late. One of them saw it and he jumped to his feet followed by the others. He strode across the Café and held a Luger pistol against the back of Jacque's neck and relieved him of the pistol. Another soldier grabbed him by the collar and pulled him roughly to his feet.

Before he had time to protest, another soldier moved round the table and grabbed Andrea and hauled *her* to her feet. He put his left arm around her neck and then forced his hand into her blouse. She screamed, and at that Jacque flew into a rage.

He swung round in a fury, grabbing the Luger off the unsuspecting soldier. A fraction of a second later his elbow shot out in an almost lethal blow that felled another soldier. Then he head-butted the one he'd relieved of the Luger and he too fell to the floor with blood pouring from his nose. The coffee cups were sent flying. The soldier who'd grabbed Andrea now found himself staring into the front end of the Luger.

"Let her go," Jacque growled.

The soldier withdrew his hand from Andrea's blouse and released his arm from around her neck. Jacque withdrew his Abwehr identification with his free hand and shoved it in front of the soldier.

The soldier stared in disbelief and began to mutter an apology but Jacque cut him short. "Take your friends out of my sight," he ordered. "And tell General Scholtz that *I'll* report to him personally about your appalling behaviour."

The soldier gathered his companions together and managed to bundle them outside and down the road towards their camp. Jacque apologised to the Café owner for the debacle and then asked him politely for more coffee.

When things had settled down and fresh coffee arrived Jacque sat down again at the table and Andrea reluctantly joined him. "I hope we'll not be disturbed again," he said.

"So what exactly are you trying to prove big brother?" Andrea asked. "That you're *not* hand in gloves with the Germans after all!"

Jacque produced his letter of authorisation from General Oster and handed it to Andrea without comment. "So you *do* work for the Germans," Andrea said with a hint of sarcasm. "For a moment back there I thought you *might* be on the side of France."

"I'm here for France *and* Germany, and I want *your* help," Jacque said patiently.

Andrea raised her eyebrows.

"Yes I mean it Andrea," Jacque said. "You see as I was going to say before we were so rudely interrupted, I know about your Allied airman."

He could see Andrea was startled. "It's all right," he went on. "Don't bother trying to talk your way out of it. You'd be wasting your time and mine. And there's no need to worry. Nobody else knows - yet! I now know he was the mystery patient in the Hospital whom nobody could identify. What I don't know is who caused him to mysteriously vanish."

"Well if you think that just because you rescued me from that German scum, because of an incident *you* created, that I'm going to have anything to do with you, you can think again."

Jacque smiled again. "You don't get it Andrea. I'm not interested; though I'd hazard a guess your friend with the bicycle was involved. But forget about that, there are much more important things to worry about."

"Yes there are, such as how did you come to know of my involvement in the Résistance? Where did we slip up Jacque?"

Jacque smiled, determined to retain an air of mystery around the discovery of his sister's involvement.

"That would be telling sister. All you need to know is that nobody else knows or suspects, and if you're co-operative it can stay that way. So now I'll endeavour, as far as I can to put you in the picture. I didn't know until recently that you were in the Résistance and whatever you might think of me; I'm not going to pass on what I know to the Gestapo or the *SS*. Neither am I going to ask you who is involved with you. I'm not even going to ask you whom the man was you met at the Station and who shot dead one of General Scholtz's men. When you escaped on that motorcycle I didn't realise *you* were in the driving seat and I'd love to know where you learned to drive like that. You know you could have been killed!"

Andrea sighed. "So get to the point Jacque. Why did you bring me here and what exactly do you want?"

"You know your friend poisoned himself?"

Andrea looked up. There was fierce anger in her eyes.

"If he was a friend of yours then I'm sorry Andrea, truly I am," Jacque said. "But if he hadn't, he'd have been made to talk and we wouldn't be sitting here having this conversation now."

"You've made your point Jacque. Get on with it."

"One other thing Andrea, I'd dearly love to know how *you* managed to escape. But I'm sure you're not about to tell me. So to business and there's no mystery. I want your Circuit to kill an *SS* Colonel."

"I'm sorry, but assuming I'm involved with the Résistance, which I'm not admitting to you, why should they? The Germans have shown themselves to be quite capable of carrying out their own dirty work, so why Jacque? What's so special about this Colonel? And why use the Résistance to do *your* dirty work?"

"I can only tell you a little Andrea, and I shouldn't even tell you that. This Colonel, his name's Klaus Richter, is in a position to compromise an Officer in the Wehrmacht. If he were successful that Officer would almost certainly be court-martialled. He would then either be shot or sent to the Russian Front, and I don't know which is worse. The Officer's very important to the Wehrmacht but the *SS* are unscrupulous, cruel and vindictive and unless Colonel Richter's removed the Wehrmacht and Germany will lose one of its best Generals."

"So what has this Officer done, that the *SS* are so determined to destroy him?"

"Colonel Richter committed an atrocity on British prisoners of war. The Wehrmacht Officer tried to expose Richter but the *SS* covered it up. They've not forgotten and have sworn revenge."

He'd decided not to mention his involvement with the Colonel.

"And what do you call this Wehrmacht Officer?" Andrea asked.

"It doesn't matter Andrea," Jacque said trying to put her off.

"It matters to me Jacque," Andrea said angrily. "If somebody I knew was about to risk their life for someone, I think they'd be entitled to know who it was; don't you!"

"I suppose," Jacque said reluctantly. He paused as he tried to work out the implications if he told her. "All right Andrea," he went on. "You win, but the fact is you already know him!"

"Me, I couldn't," Andrea said. Then as Jacque remained silent the realisation dawned on her. "Not ... not General Scholtz!"

"It *is* General Scholtz Andrea. So not only would you be doing Germany a favour but yourself and mother and father as well. I know all of you secretly like the General."

"I'm still not convinced and I'm still not saying I've anything to do with the Résistance."

"Think what life could be like for you, mother *and* father if anything happened to the General. With our family being a friend of the General, everyone, me included, would feel the wrath of the Colonel and the *SS*."

"Is that what this is all about Jacque?" Is it really about you?"

"Believe me Andrea, it's not about me. It's about getting rid of Colonel Richter *and* saving my family."

Then he reached into his inside pocket and took out General Oster's letter and showed it to Andrea. She read it quietly and handed it back.

"You still haven't told me why the Résistance should do your dirty work for you."

"Simply because, unlike the *SS* or the Gestapo, the Abwehr doesn't have a 'dirty tricks' Department; and we simply don't have an assassin we can send in to do the job, at least not one we can trust."

"I see," Andrea said. "And if the Abwehr did attempt it and things went badly wrong and you were found out, it just simply would not do, would it!"

"I couldn't have put it better myself," Jacque said dryly.

"Well," Andrea said. "I can't give you a decision now. There are people I'll have to discuss it with so you'll have to meet me again."

"Shall I see you at home?"

Andrea looked up startled. "I don't think that would be a good idea just at the moment," she said quickly. "I'll meet you here at the same time tomorrow." Then she thought of her friend who'd come to try and protect her. "And have I your word that no action will be taken against my friend?"

"You have my word."

They parted company and Jacque paid for the coffee and walked to the Police Station. There was an envelope waiting for him. He opened it and inside was a letter from Jean Boussine to his wife Madeleine. A photograph of Jean accompanied it. The letter explained that he - Jean - had been in what he called a Prisoner-of-War camp but that he'd been transferred to a forced Labour Camp instead. The conditions were much better for him now and he was with other French soldiers. He also said that he was in good health and that he was grateful to the German authorities for what they had done for him. He closed by telling Madeleine he loved her very much and that he hoped the War would be over soon and that he could come home. He finally sent his love to his son.

Jacque took the letter and the photograph to Madeleine Boussine's home. As always she appeared frightened and startled when she opened the door but Jacque reassured her and told her not to worry. He showed her the letter and the photograph and she cried with joy, clasping them to her bosom.

"I'm afraid I'm not going to be able to let you keep them," Jacque said. "If it ever came to Colonel Richter's attention that I'd arranged for your husband to be moved, then we'd both be in grave danger."

He held out his hand and waited whilst Madeleine read the letter again. Then reluctantly she handed it back with the photograph. "I'll try and make sure he writes again," Jacque said. "Now have you done what I asked you?"

Madeleine nodded. "You'd better come in."

She looked anxiously up and down the street before closing the door. Then she showed him into the room where her mother was sitting in the same chair, oblivious to anything going on around her.

"So," Jacque enquired. "You've been in touch with Richter like I told you?"

Madeleine nodded.

"Well come on girl," Jacque said impatiently. "When's he coming to see you? Is it Friday as usual?"

"Yes, this Friday night," Madeleine whispered. "But why do you need to know about him? What's happening?"

"You don't need to know that Madeleine."

"But if anything happens to the Colonel what will become of Jean?"

"I told you I'd look after him, didn't I?" Jacque said angrily. "Did the Colonel bring you a letter or a photograph? No, of course he didn't, but I did. I have the full weight of the Abwehr behind me don't forget."

Madeleine tried to fight back the tears but her eyes filled up. She walked up to Jacque and looked him straight in the eye. She reached out and her fingers just touched him. He could see the pleading look in her eyes. "Please," she whispered. "I must know Jean and my boy will be all right."

"All right," Jacque said. "After Friday, the Colonel won't be in a position to do anything about your husband or your boy. I promise you, they'll be safe then. We'll look after them so just don't do anything foolish."

When Andrea returned to the Château she sat down with her mother. "There's bad news mother," she said.

Her mother looked up. "How bad?"

"I met Jacque today like I told you; in fact I've just left him. He knows about us!"

"Knows?"

"He found out about Gary and I suppose as a consequence he put two and two together and got the right answer. I don't think he knows about any of the others but he wouldn't tell me how he knew, except to say that he's the only one knows."

"Then there's only one way he can have found out and it's my fault because I should have warned Nina."

"But mother Nina would never talk."

"I know she wouldn't, at least not knowingly, but I saw the way he looked at her that day he came back from Germany. You know what he's like about women, especially one as good looking as Nina."

"But she still wouldn't have said anything. She knows how Jacque turned out, where his loyalties lie."

"Yes Andrea, but you're forgetting. It was Nina who told *you* that Jacque wanted to see you, so he must have been in touch with her. Ask Nina to come and see me. We've got to know, because this could mean the Circuit will be disbanded."

Chapter seventeen

The next day Jacque was waiting for Andrea in the Café. She was punctual and appeared cautious. Jacque ordered coffee. "No minder this time!" he said smiling at her.

"Very funny," Andrea said. "So what's the plan?"

Jacque looked around the Café and leaned forward. "I can tell you where Colonel Richter will be next Friday. He'll be in a German staff car accompanied only by his driver. I can provide you with his route and the approximate time he'll arrive at his destination. The Résistance can ambush him anywhere along the route. It's up to them where they chose, but it has to be before he reaches his destination, otherwise innocent lives will be lost."

He looked at Andrea waiting for a response. "If the Résistance is successful, innocent lives will be lost anyway. There'll be reprisals, or hadn't you thought of that?"

"Yes I've thought of that," Jacque said. "But it doesn't stop the Résistance any other time, so why make an issue of it now."

"Because brother, we've to know it's worth it," Andrea said. "The Germans might throw away innocent lives for nothing, but not the Résistance."

"I'm acting under orders," Jacque said. "My superiors have considered this operation and they believe it's in the best interests of France and Germany. I can't say more than that, except of course that as long as Richter's alive you're all in danger."

"How do I know it's not a trap?" Andrea asked. "How do I know you're not being blackmailed? How do I know that you're not being forced by this Colonel to set us up? We know the Gestapo have been trying to find our Circuit. What better way than this?"

"Have you really such a low opinion of me, Andrea?" Jacque said, and Andrea heard the genuine hurt in his voice.

"I suppose not," she said. "But maybe your superiors are using you, and you don't realise it."

"General Oster of the Abwehr is not in the Gestapo and he's *not* in the *SS*.

"I still have to ask the others, and London."

"London!"

"You must know the British are helping the Résistance. How else do you think we get arms and explosives?"

"I hadn't realised you were in so deeply, that's all."

Andrea looked at her watch. "I'll have to go," she said and got up from the table. Then she turned to Jacque who was still sitting. "Oh and by the way, have you been seeing Nina?"

"Me? Why of course not. What ever makes you think that?" Jacque protested.

"It's nothing," Andrea said. "Just leave her out of it. I don't want to see her getting hurt. So if you're here tomorrow someone will bring you a message."

That night Andrea cycled to a deserted farmhouse some ten miles from Chanilly. Darkness was falling as she dismounted from her cycle and walked the hundred yards up a rough path to the house. The door was open and as she went in Inspector Marius Regnier was lighting an oil lamp. He set it on a wooden table in the centre of the stone floor. He looked up and smiled.

"It's always an anxious time waiting for you and the others Andrea," he said.

"I know Marius," Andrea agreed. "But they'll be along in good time."

"So I take it you met with Jacque?"

"Yes I did."

"And?"

"I don't know him the way I used to Marius. He's changed."

"Haven't we all?"

"Yes but with Jacque it's different. Father won't even speak to him and mother finds it nearly as difficult. There's just something about him."

"So do you trust him or not? That's the question."

Andrea went over to the fireplace and raked out the old ashes and proceeded to put paper and sticks in to light another fire. She was on her hunkers when she turned round and looked up into Marius's intense face. "I believe I do," she said.

"But how did he find out about *you* Andrea? I thought our Circuit was watertight. There must have been a slip up somewhere."

"It was Nina," Andrea said standing up.

"She wouldn't say anything Andrea."

"She didn't mean to, but it seems she fell for Jacque's charms. He was coming back to the Château in the early hours of the morning and sleeping with her. And he slept with her the morning after the Germans nearly caught us at the Station. The morning poor Edward took his own life."

Andrea stopped then, overcome with emotion. Marius came over and put his arms around her. She looked up into his face and he wiped the tears away with his sleeve.

"It was awful," she whispered. "There I was hiding in the tail-end of the aeroplane from Jacque and the other Germans, when I should have been with Edward. He shouldn't have died like that Marius. If I'd been with him I might have been able to make Jacque let us both go."

"You know that's not likely Andrea, not in front of the other Germans."

Andrea turned away from Marius as he lowered his arms. "Anyway all that Nina knows is that Jacque was asleep when she wakened. She dressed and went to check on Gary. When she returned to the bedroom Jacque was getting dressed. She says she can only presume that he followed her when she left the bedroom and heard her talking to Gary. He must have put two and two together."

Suddenly she put her hand to her mouth. "Oh gosh," she said. "Maybe it was my fault after all. I was wearing a red beret and scarf when we escaped from the Station. I left them on the hallstand when I returned home. Jacque would have seen them and remembered I'd been wearing them on the motorbike."

126

"He'd never have guessed without Nina," Marius said. "And anyway so long as we know how he found out, that's all that matters."

Andrea knelt down again and put a match to the paper and watched it take light. "I don't quite know why I say I trust him," she said as she stood up and stared at the flames leaping into life. "I don't believe he'd deliberately put his whole family in danger. I just don't think he would."

"What about London? Have they said yet what they think of this operation?"

"Mother made contact by radio. She's waiting for a response."

"So can we start to plan or do we have to wait for London?"

"We don't require London's permission, Marius, but they may be able to throw some light on what Jacque has asked us to do." She stood up and looked into the fire. "It's all so scary. I believe Jacque but I'm not certain about his motive."

"We could refuse Andrea," Marius said. "Tell him the Résistance discussed it and decided it was too close to home and far too risky."

"That's what my instinct tells me to do, but Jacque implied that if Colonel Richter isn't killed then General Scholtz is doomed, and you know as well as I do that the General's the best cover we have. As long as our family has the General as a friend, we're probably safer than any other Circuit in France."

"I know that Andrea, but now that Jacque knows about you, your mother and Nina, where does that leave the rest of the Circuit? He might feel a sense of loyalty to you, but there's no guarantee it would be extended to the rest of us."

"He doesn't know about the rest of you, only that there's a Circuit somewhere, and after all we're not the only Circuit in the area." Andrea piled some logs on the fire and then two more of the Doctor's Circuit came in.

They were Charles and Roger Bayard who also made their way on bicycles. Charles and Roger were twins, aged twenty-three. They escaped the round up of young men to Germany because they worked on the land. Their farm, like many in France, was relatively small but it did provide enough work to support themselves and their widowed mother. It was they who provided the horse and cart to transport Pilot Officer Gary Tucker to the Château Aveline.

Their father had been called up during the First World War and he died two years after the war's end from War wounds. Their mother, with local help, had kept the farm running during the war. When her husband came home from the War as an invalid she carried on the best she could. Then when the twins' schooling was over they began working full time on the farm.

When the Second World War started they were exempt from military service in the French army. The Germans took a different view and ordered one of them to be deported to Germany, whilst the other was to remain on the farm.

Their mother, Josiane, had heard of what Anton Aveline had done for the 'German General'. She was so desperate to keep her two sons at home that she pleaded with Anton to ask the General to intervene. Anton was only too happy to oblige but the spin off was that once his wife Marie heard, she made enquiries about Charles and Roger and their mother. She approached the twins and asked them to join the Résistance.

Charles and Roger were big, strong men. They were identical twins and both had an irrepressible sense of humour. A huge smile broke on their weather beaten faces as they came into the farmhouse. Charles walked over to Andrea and putting his two hands around her waist he lifted her bodily off the floor so that she was left kicking helplessly in mid air. Then he set her down on the table and turned to his brother.

He laughed out loud. "And that's what we're supposed to fight the Germans with."

Andrea glared at him and then laughed along with the rest of them as she jumped nimbly from the table.

"Great big ox," she said.

Marius smiled to himself because he secretly admired their strength and sense of fun, even in the midst of danger. "Good to see you two," he said.

"Is there any coffee going?" Roger asked, taking an enamel mug from a shelf.

"Fire's just lit," Marius said. "So it won't be long; just waiting for coffee. Simone said he'd bring some."

"And it's right here," a voice called out as Simone de Beauvoir, one of Chantilly's schoolmasters, walked in.

They all turned to see the man who planned their operations with masterly precision. "I've left Father Michael at the end of the road to keep guard and I've told him we'll send coffee when it's ready. You know what he's like about coffee."

They all smiled.

Father Michael de Bourbon was the Aveline's priest and confessor, but he was also a trusted family friend. He'd been in the Circuit from the beginning.

"What about your mother, Andrea?" Simone asked. "Is she able to come?"

Andrea checked the percolator, hung precariously over the fire. "She's waiting to hear from London, Simone," she said.

The Doctor Circuit, as Josephine Butler had named it, comprised twelve individuals. Each one had been carefully selected for their individual skill and had undergone the same intense training devised by Lieutenant Pier Gaston. Andrea's mother was still the recognised leader, but she was happy to leave the planning of operations in the capable hands of Simone. Only those who met that night in the deserted farmhouse to plan the assassination of Colonel Richter, would know the plans.

The priest, Father Michael de Bourbon was the Circuit's Chaplain and he also acted as lookout. Simone de Beauvoir was the Planner and Director of Operations. Charles and Roger Bayard were in charge of the arms and explosives and also the procurement of transport - a very difficult commodity. Marie Aveline was the Radio Operator. Her daughter Andrea was the Medical Officer who also had responsibility for Allied personnel on the run. Father Michael assisted her in that duty by hiding Allied airmen at great personal risk. Inspector Marius Regnier was responsible for intelligence gathering and the spreading of mis-information.

Andrea poured coffee and asked Charles to bring some to Father Michael. When he returned, Nina was with him.

"Is there a message from London Nina?" Simone asked her straight away.

"Yes sir," Nina said, never able to forget that she'd once been his pupil! "Madam Aveline says that London has given the green light. The Colonel must be killed at all costs."

"Thank you Nina," Simone said, and she left again immediately.

"Well that's it," Simone said. "Let's gather round and get this show on the road."

When the plans had been agreed Simone looked around him. "It appears this is important, not only to us but also to London," he said. "They will have *their* reasons which we may find out about later. But there's one other matter must be decided upon and I feel it falls to me to bring it before you."

He looked directly at Andrea. "I'm sorry Andrea," he continued in a subdued voice. "But this needs to be dealt with. It's your brother Jacque."

Andrea was about to protest but Simone continued. "It's a grave matter Andrea. However much you trust him, he knows too much. I know he's your brother, and that's why I'm proposing a controversial solution.

"Simone you can't even think of it," Andrea cried.

"Hear me out," he said as the others look on Andrea with compassion. "In any other circumstances Jacque would be shot, but as far as I'm concerned that's out of the question. I propose instead that Jacque be taken prisoner immediately this operation's over. He will be held until we can send him to England in one of the Lysanders. We can arrange it with London."

There was silence and Simone looked around the sombre faces. Then Andrea spoke out. "But Simone the British would treat him as a collaborator and shoot him instead. We can't send him to London."

"Not if we explained the situation Andrea. After all, your mother's influential friend in London could surely arrange something. And with the right persuasion he might be persuaded to become a double agent for the British."

Marius moved over beside Andrea and put his arm around her. "We do know what you're going through Andrea, and you're not the only family with this problem. But surely in your heart you know it has to be done. If Jacque isn't silenced not one of us will sleep soundly again. It's far too grave a risk. Simone's right."

He turned his head and looked directly at Andrea. She avoided his gaze and then nodded reluctantly. "I suppose you *are* right," she said.

"I'll tell your parents," Simone said. "I know they'll understand."

"No I'll do it," Andrea said. "I'll tell them tonight."

The Circuit split up, and for security they left the building at ten-minute intervals. Simone de Beauvoir was the last to leave.

When Andrea arrived at the Château her mother knew instinctively that something was wrong. She was unable to discuss anything because General Scholtz had arrived unexpectedly an hour earlier. The General appeared to enjoy the opportunity to talk to Andrea's father Anton. Andrea didn't dislike the General but she had a sneaking suspicion that the real reason he called was because of her mother. He never behaved improperly or said anything to indicate he had feelings towards her. There was just something in the way he looked at her.

Her mother was still a very beautiful woman and Andrea mentioned it to her on one occasion but she blushed and dismissed it out of hand. They laughed about it afterwards. The General waited longer than usual but the minute he was gone Marie turned to Andrea.

"There's something wrong Andrea. What is it," she asked. "Can they not agree a plan for the operation?"

Andrea shook her head. "No mother, that's all sorted, Nina can bring Jacque a message tomorrow. It's Simone. He says that Jacque will have to be abducted and sent to England the minute this operation's over. I believe the rest agree."

Marie was silent for a moment, and then she said. "We'd better tell your father."

Anton was smoking a cigar when they came into his room. He appeared deep in thought. "Anton dear," Marie said. "They want to send Jacque to England, out of the way."

Anton looked up sharply. "Who does?"

"Simone and the others, because they believe it's too big a risk not too. We don't know what he might do. I think they're right." Then she turned to Andrea. "My dear I'm so sorry, I didn't ask you what you thought."

"Simone said if it was anyone else they'd be shot," Andrea said with a slight tremble in her voice. "I think it might be safer for everyone, especially Jacque."

Anton drew deeply on his cigar and blew the smoke towards the ceiling. "Did they suggest *how* we would send him to England?"

"In one of the Lysanders, father."

"Hmm," Anton said. "Do they think it's as simple as that?"

"Where's the problem Anton?" Marie asked.

"Well to start with a Lysander will only come in one week at most, on either side of a full moon. By my reckoning that means we've to imprison our son for two weeks. If we abduct him, where do we hide him? What would happen if he escaped? If we hide him here, this is probably the first place the Germans will come and ask questions. They might search the place from top to bottom and where does that leave Gary? He can't be moved yet."

"Couldn't we ask Father Michael to hide him?" Andrea asked.

"It's not fair to burden Father Michael with what is in effect *our* problem."

"But it's everybody's problem father and it's not our fault Jacque became a collaborator. We owe it to the others to make sure Jacque doesn't give their names to the Germans." Andrea insisted. "I didn't like it when Simone suggested it at first, but what's the alternative, really? If we do nothing Jacque will have a free rein and who knows *what* he might ask us to do next time. He might blackmail us if we refuse and threaten to expose us."

"I know," Anton said. "I know, and I'm not surprised it's come to this." He paused for a moment. "When do you ambush this Colonel?"

"It has to be this Friday, which only gives us three days," Andrea told him.

Anton rubbed his chin with his free hand and then drew slowly on the cigar again. "Marie," he said. "This is my last cigar. Tell that friend of yours in London there'll be no more Lysanders landing in this region unless she sends a box of these cigars. I can't live without them."

"Anton how you can be so frivolous at a time like this I don't know," Marie said angrily.

He gave a half-hearted grin and reached out his hand and Marie smiled back and walked over and put her arm around him. "I'm sorry," he said. "I know this business of Jacque is killing you, and I didn't intend to appear frivolous. I feel gutted about it as well remember."

"Well that's all right then," Marie said. "And remember those cigars are from Winston Churchill's own supply. You should count yourself jolly fortunate to have them."

"I do," Anton said. "Really I do." He paused. "Marie, Andrea, I've decided. If we're sending Jacque to England then we don't wait 'til this operation's over."

"What will we do with him until we get him out?" Andrea asked. "He can't stay here and you say Father Michael can't hide him, so where does he go?"

"As a Circuit we've kept ourselves isolated, that's what London wanted and it's paid off until now," Anton said. "But that doesn't mean I don't know about other Circuits, so I'm going to call in a favour from someone. You remember the lad we treated some months back with the gunshot wound to the leg?"

Marie and Andrea both nodded. "We didn't ask questions at the time, well you don't do you? But I learned that the Germans shot him after an abortive attempt to blow up a railway line. He was lucky to be alive; two others weren't so lucky. That same lad was with a Circuit called 'The Baker's Dozen'. There were thirteen when they started, hence the code name, and that's the way they want to keep it. Inevitably some fell by the wayside. They were *very* selective, like us, as to who joined them. I believe there are nine of the originals left and they'd recently brought their numbers back up to twelve and now it's back to thirteen again. The thirteenth member's a young man from near Verberie. His code name's 'Lucky thirteen!' Quiet lad who saw his family tortured to death and his home burned to the ground. Anyway I know their leader. He's an English agent sent by the SOE by the name of Balfour and as you'd expect he's totally reliable. He hides out in the forest, but I'll get word to him and he'll take care of Jacque and hold him until we can organise a Lysander. He'll understand, and won't ask questions. Neither will he tell Jacque what's going on."

Marie looked worried. "It'll *be* all right dear," Anton said. "It's better this way and when the war's over, if we all survive, Jacque can return to France, unless he becomes a double agent and maybe nobody will know about the part he played in the war. Or perhaps we will even be able to sing his praises when it's all over. In the meantime Marie you'd better let Jay Bee know what's happening."

Marie sighed, "I suppose you're right."

"Father how will we get word to this man in the Baker's Dozen, because we don't have long?" Andrea asked her father.

"Tell Marius I want to see him. He knows the man's whereabouts; it's safer that way and the fewer who are involved the better."

"But what about Jacque, Anton?" Marie said. "I'm worried something will go wrong. It's so dangerous."

"Jacque won't be suspecting anything, and I think Nina owes us one, don't you?"

Inspector Marius Regnier called to see Anton the following morning. As well as getting a message to the leader of the Baker's Dozen, he was also able to give Anton information about his son's whereabouts.

Anton also told Regnier to get Balfour to inform London when the operation was completed.

Nina went into Chantilly in the morning and walked past the Café that Jacque usually frequented and casually looked in. It was made easy for her when Jacque saw her and waved her in.

"You'll stay for coffee," he said.

134

"No I can't," Nina retorted. "I just came to give you a message. Your mother will be expecting me back."

Jacque didn't heed her and went to order a coffee anyway but Nina protested, feeling in some way that she was betraying the man she slept with. "I can't stay," she said. "Not now Jacque, but why don't you come and see me later like you did before, after midnight when everybody's in bed."

Jacque smiled. "I'd like that," he agreed. "After midnight it is. But weren't you going to give me a message from someone?"

"Yes of course," she said. "I'm just to tell you that it will be taken care of on Friday."

At about the same time Regnier was talking to Roger Balfour, the SOE leader of the Baker's Dozen.

"You know our friend Anton Aveline, the doctor?" Regnier said.

Balfour nodded. "A good man, he lives in the Château Aveline outside Chantilly. He's got a beautiful wife."

"He wants to call in a favour."

"He's only too ask, Marius. What is it?"

"No questions asked, you'll understand. And you'll wonder when you hear, but believe me it's necessary."

"Go on."

"It's his son Jacque. He wants you to abduct him tonight and to hold him prisoner, treat him well of course, and when a flight's arranged he's to be sent to England, probably in about two weeks time, for the duration of the war."

"And that's it?"

"Unless you hear from me again Jacque will be calling at the Château Aveline tonight around midnight or shortly after. He'll almost certainly be driven there. His driver usually parks the car on the road and waits for him. He'll be alone apart from the driver. Oh and one other thing. Anton wants *you* to inform London when the Operation's over. I believe the poor man finds the whole thing quite distasteful."

Chapter eighteen

Jacque left the Café feeling somewhat elated. Some things were falling into place. Colonel Richter who threatened his well being was going to be taken care of, and that was a relief. Strangely, he thought to himself, he had no qualms about it. Then he had discovered, purely by accident, the Résistance that General Oster had spoken about. That was presenting him with a problem, about how to eliminate a Circuit that was at least partly made up by members of his family. It wasn't something he felt he could divulge to the General! Yet he had to report to the General that day.

He went back to the Police Station where he intended to contact the General. At the same time he was tossing over in his mind what he'd do about his family's involvement in the Résistance. His only solution was to offer them an ultimatum. Either they disbanded completely after they dealt with the Colonel or he would have to have them arrested. That way he felt he was absolving himself of any blame, and he was sure they'd agree. He knew they would have no other option.

Roger Balfour met with three members of the Baker's Dozen to draw up a plan of action. He had been in the game long enough, never to accept anything at face value. That was how he survived where many of his associates in the Résistance failed. In the past he had known of similar operations where Résistance fighters had gone to set up an ambush, only to find that they themselves were the ones being ambushed.

Anton Aveline's credentials were impeccable, but Balfour was of the belief that virtually anybody could be bribed, including himself, and the doctor *was* very friendly with a German General. It just depended on the circumstances, and the circumstances surrounding Anton Aveline's request were unusual, to say the least.

Of the three members of the Baker's Dozen whom Balfour met with to discuss the Operation, two were experienced and dependable fighters. The third, though less experienced, had other qualities that Balfour thought were appropriate for the occasion.

They discussed the situation calmly and logically and agreed a plan of action that they trusted took care of any eventuality. Then they went their separate ways.

Anton and Marie Aveline were uneasy as they retired for the night. Andrea did a night shift in the Hospital because she knew she could not have settled at home. Nina went to bed early, blaming tiredness and the emotional drain of the last two days. She lay on top of the bed, fully dressed and uneasy. She was torn between loyalty to her employers and her growing infatuation with Jacque.

As darkness fell a lone figure cycled slowly down the road towards the Château. He did not appear to be paying heed to anything. But in fact he was taking in every movement and noting everything. He cycled for two miles past the entrance to the Château, stopped and began to cycle back again, two miles past the entrance in the other direction. He stopped and returned yet again and then when he was within a hundred yards of the entrance he dismounted and hid his bicycle behind a wall and proceeded slowly on foot.

A tall hedge and mature trees lined the road on one side, and on the other side there was a stone wall. Every so often there was an iron gate. The man climbed over one of the gates and walked along the hedge in the direction of the Château until another hedge running at right angles to the road barred his way. He walked along that hedge until he was able to make his way through and then he continued until he was well past the entrance to the Château. Then he made his way across the road and over the stone wall. He walked back along the length of the wall to where it joined the boundary of the Château.

He made his way around the boundary and rejoined the stone wall again and followed it to where he had hidden his bicycle. At that point he was satisfied that there wasn't a trap, but he knew the night was early. He remained hidden and watching.

Debré was used to waiting and watching. Ever since his family were murdered and the farm destroyed by fire, he'd been doing just that. He learned how to remain concealed for hours at a time, even under the very noses of the Germans. He learned how to survive on his own and provide for his every need, often at the expense of his fellow countrymen. When he needed money or food he stole it, and the same applied to clothes and shoes.

He'd moved around the countryside, never staying in one place for long. As the weeks went by he began to be more and more confident. He overheard conversations, witnessed things he shouldn't have witnessed. He observed the comings and going of the Germans and his fellow countrymen and women. He watched their interactions. He was soon confident enough to go into villages or towns where he had previously established there was no permanent German presence.

He came out of himself a bit and talked to people, all the time learning and amassing information about what was going on. He made up a story to explain why he was at a particular place but he never revealed what had driven him from home. Always at the back of his mind was the fear that if it became known that he had witnessed his brothers' murder he too would die at the hands of the invader.

Then he got his first opportunity to acquire a gun. A group of soldiers had been drinking in a village Inn, just a few miles from camp. He had observed them driving to the village and from his experience he knew where they were going. After a couple of hours, when it was getting dark they emerged from the pub because it was normal practice to return to camp before dark in case of an ambush.

Three of the soldiers came out singing and laughing and walked to their half-track where they waited. Then the fourth and last soldier, a Sergeant, came out with a girl on his arm. They too were laughing and the soldier was swaying from side to side as the girl tried to steady him. Instead of following his colleagues who were waiting, he took the girl behind the village hall. He left his sub-machine gun against the wall and began to fondle her. She made a half- hearted attempt to protest.

Debré had seen where they went and in the semidarkness he crept round the side of the hall and watched. The soldier's mind was taken up with other things when Debré picked up a large boulder as if it was a pebble. He walked up quietly behind the Sergeant and crushed his skull. As he fell to the ground the girl opened her mouth to scream but he grabbed her and forced his hand over her mouth.

"Shut up," he hissed. Then he saw her coat and bag on the ground. Still holding her tight against him, with his hand over her mouth he bent down and picked her belongings up. He shoved them at her. "Disappear," he hissed again. "And don't worry about him or his friends."

The girl was terrified and as he released her she stumbled away into the gathering darkness clutching her coat and handbag. Debré had no experience of sub-machine guns or indeed of hand grenades but his blood was up and nothing was going to stop him. In the dim light he looked at the gun in his hand, and then at the hand grenades in the dead soldier's belt. He left the hand grenades and pulled back a lever in the sub-machine gun and began walking towards the half-track.

The three soldiers were leaning against the vehicle, enjoying the effects of the drink they had consumed. They did not see him as he walked slowly and deliberately towards them from the blind side. He came at them from the rear of the half-track. One soldier was looking his way as he suddenly appeared in the gloom as if from nowhere. There was a look of utter surprise and astonishment on the soldier's face. As if he couldn't believe what he was seeing. Debré was going to kill or be killed. He didn't care any more.

He levelled the sub-machine gun on the three soldiers and pulled the trigger, just as the one who had seen him started to dive for cover. He was too late. At point blank range they were at his mercy and they collapsed like puppets on a string when he mowed them down.

One soldier didn't die instantly and struggled to move. Debré kicked him over on his back with his foot. The soldier looked up at him, his eyes pleading for mercy. Debré looked at the agony in the soldier's eyes. The face he saw transformed itself before his very eyes into the faces of his brothers as they hung upside down and choked to death. He bent down and removed a knife from the soldier and without hesitation drove it through his heart.

He manhandled the three soldiers into the half-track and then as an after thought retrieved the knife he used to kill the injured man. He climbed into the driving seat and put the knife down beside him. It wasn't the first time he had been in a half-track! A soldier had shown him the workings of one the first time the Germans came to question his brothers at the farm. Now it all came back to him like it was yesterday. He started the engine and put the half-track into gear and manoeuvred it around and drove it to the side of the village hall. He picked the Sergeant up like a sack of potatoes and put him in with the others.

As he drove away a few villagers heard the roar of the engine and the rattle of the tracks on the tarmac. They came out of the pub and when they saw the half-track moving off they went inside again. They'd heard the shooting but were afraid to investigate and didn't notice one of their own driving the half-track.

Debré had no idea where he was going, but something told him to get as far away from the village as possible. He had seen and heard enough of reprisals to be aware of their consequences and he didn't want that responsibility on his head.

His experience told him that it was unlikely he would meet other Germans at that time of the night, but he was prepared for that eventuality. He would simply dump the vehicle and vanish into the night. As it was he met nothing on the road and he drove as fast and as far away as he could.

He kept looking at the fuel gauge because he desperately wanted to be able to hide or dispose of the half-track so that the Germans would never know what happened. He had driven for an hour without incident and in that time had not passed another village. The darkness of the night was relieved at times when the broken cloud revealed a half moon. It was in that half-light that Debré saw the trees that soon gave way to a forest.

He slowed the half-track as he searched for an entrance into the forest. After more than a mile he found it. It was nothing more than a cart track but it suited his purposes. He turned into the forest and then for the first time switched on the blacked out headlamps. They only gave a dim shaft of light but it was sufficient. He drove along the track until he came to a fork. On impulse he turned right and followed that until he came to another fork when he turned left, going deeper and deeper into the forest. Finally he saw a break in the trees and he forced the half-track up a steep bank of earth covered in moss and into the heart of the forest itself.

He stopped before he finally ran out of fuel. By then it was late and Debré was beginning to feel the emotional and physical effects of the night's events. He found a groundsheet in the half-track and he put it under the vehicle to lie on. There were a couple of army greatcoats and he took them as well. Finally he took one of the sub-machine guns and checked it had a full magazine.

He crawled under the half-track and pulled the greatcoats over him and laid the gun by his side with his hand around it. In the morning he intended to dispose of the bodies and cover the half-track with leaves and branches. He quickly fell asleep.

The raucous call of a cock pheasant wakened him at first light. For a moment he lay in the stillness that followed. Then there was the sudden flapping of wings and his hand tightened around the gun and he rolled over on his side and looked out from underneath the half-track. He could see figures in the distance. He couldn't understand how the Germans could have tracked him down so quickly. Then he heard the sound of voices, but they were French!

He held his breath as the men came closer. They were talking among themselves and then they were only feet from him and they were unaware he was underneath.

One of them, whom he assumed to be the leader, spoke. "You were right," he said. "You did hear something. But how the blazes did it get here and where are the Germans?"

Debré was certain he heard an English accent. One of them looked into the half-track. "They're here," he said excitedly. "And they're dead. They've been shot."

It was at that point that Debré decided he had better show himself. "Don't shoot," he called out from under the half-track as he rolled out. "I can explain."

It was his first meeting with Roger Balfour. He quickly acquired the code name, Lucky Thirteen.

Now he remained hidden and watching. He didn't expect any traffic on the roads, because virtually nobody, except the army had access to petrol. If there was to be an ambush he knew it would be set up with great stealth and cunning. But Debré could move like a shadow in the darkness, without making a sound. He moved around constantly, listening for the slightest sound that might indicate enemy activity, but there was none.

At 23:00 he returned to the spot he had already selected for the Baker's Dozen ambush. From the information they had received from Nina, Jacque would be dropped off at the entrance to the Château. This was to avoid wakening anyone in the house. At exactly 23:30 Roger Balfour arrived and ten minutes later the last member of the Baker's Dozen.

At midnight Nina could stand the tension no longer. She rolled off her bed, still fully clothed and walked out of the bedroom. Her mind was made up. It was her fault entirely that Jacque had got into trouble and she was determined to get him out of it. She tiptoed quietly down to the kitchen and took out an oil lamp and matches and went to the front door and opened it, and slipped out into the night.

She knew where the ambush was going to take place and realised that if she walked down the driveway she might be heard. Instead she made her way quietly through the grounds to the boundary wall, the same wall that Debré had walked around. She opened a wooden gate and walked through it towards the stone wall that ran alongside the main road.

There was another gate in the wall that allowed her onto the road. On the road she hurried in the direction of Chantilly, listening for the sound of a car, and trying to get as far away from the Château as possible. When she was well away, she stopped and lit the oil lamp and waited, shivering in the cool night air.

She was beginning to think Jacque was not going to come when in the distance she heard the unmistakable sound of a car engine. She prayed it was Jacque. As the car approached she stood on the grass verge and held out the lamp, swinging it from side to side.

A short distance away Debré was hidden in a ditch waiting for the car. He saw the dim light of the oil lamp. As the car passed him he stood out on the road and watched the taillight of the car and the car was stopping!

Jacque was in a happy frame of mind as Hans drove him to his lover's bed. He was happy that his immediate problems would soon be solved and he was looking forward to reporting to General Oster that the Colonel was dead. He had put the thoughts of his own family out of his mind for the time being.

It was Hans who saw the light first.

"There's a light," he said looking across at Jacque. "They're waving us down."

"Stop," Jacque shouted to him. "It could be a trap."

Hans stepped on the brakes and the car slued to a halt. "They're coming towards us," Hans called out as he reached into the back seat for his machine pistol.

Hans drew his Luger and stepped onto the road using the car as a shield to protect him from gunfire. "Halt, whoever you are. Don't move, or we'll shoot."

Jacque was also out of the car now, peering into the night.

"Jacque it's me, Nina, don't shoot," Nina called at the top of her voice.

"Are you alone?" Hans called.

"Yes."

"Then come here quickly, and keep that light up so that I can see you," Jacque shouted.

Nina ran towards them, holding the light so that Jacque was able to see her face. She was breathless when she reached them. "Thank heavens," she gasped. "There's a trap ahead of you. They want to send you to England."

Jacque lowered his pistol. "Who wants to send me to England?"

"Everybody does." Then she corrected herself. "The Résistance, your parents, all of them want to. They're afraid you'll have them arrested."

"Where is the ambush and how many of them are there?"

"Two men I think. I don't know them. They don't belong to." Then she realised she was making an admission she'd never made to Jacque.

143

"It's somebody from outside."

"You mean another Circuit?"

"Yes .... No, I don't know Jacque. I'm only told what to do."

"But you told them I was coming? You set me up Nina," Jacque said. "Damn you," he said slapping her hard across the face. "They'd never have known if you hadn't told them."

"It wasn't my fault," she cried. "Your mother found out you'd been visiting me at night."

Jacque turned to Hans. "Hans we've got to handle this ourselves. There's no time to get backup but there's only two of them, and they want me alive so they won't shoot."

He turned to Nina who was sobbing quietly with the oil lamp hanging limply in her hand. "Do they know Hans drives me here?"

"Yes," Nina sobbed.

"We'll play them at their own game Hans. I'll drive and you lie down on the back seat, and be ready the minute I get out of the car, but don't shoot them. I *want* them alive because they're going to talk."

Jacque got into the driving seat and Hans lay on the back seat with his machine pistol ready. As Jacque was closing the door Nina cried out to him. "What about me Jacque, what about me?"

He held the door open briefly. "If I ever see you again I'll have *you* arrested." And he slammed the door shut and accelerated away.

Debré heard the animated conversation but couldn't make out anything, but his instinct told him something was wrong, very wrong. He ran after the car, and then he heard the smash as Nina threw the oil lamp on the road and ran crying towards him but not seeing him, "I hate you, I hate you," he heard her cry.

He came on her quickly stopping her in her tracks and startling her. She cried out, frightened in the darkness. "What's going on?" Debré demanded, ignoring her fear and grabbing her by the shoulders.

She shook herself free. "Leave me alone," she cried.

Debré knew instinctively that there wasn't time to argue so he left her and ran back to the Château.

Roger Balfour was concealed on the right-hand side of the road just before the entrance. His companion René Monnet was with him.

144

"I'm beginning to think he's not coming," Balfour whispered.

"There's time yet," Monnet said. "We'll get him."

Then they heard the car, and soon afterwards the slits of orange light that were the headlights. "That's it," Balfour said. "It has to be him."

Jacque slowed down and as he did so Hans opened the back door ever so slightly. The car stopped only feet from where Balfour and Monnet were hidden. "Remember Hans," he whispered. "Don't show yourself until they appear. I'll feign surprise and I won't put up a fight. That'll put them off their guard. I'm getting out now."

Jacque turned the engine off but left the lights on. He opened the door in a leisurely manner and stepped out into the night. He closed the door quietly, his heart thumping madly as he waited. Even though he was expecting it, he was still taken by surprise when seemingly out of nowhere Balfour pressed a pistol into his back. He felt the hair on the back of his neck crawl and he cursed himself for sweating.

"Jacque Aveline," Balfour said calmly. "Put you hands up and turn around."

Jacque tried to remain calm. "You scared the life out of me," he said. "Who the blazes are you?"

Monnet appeared by his side. "The Résistance. Just get back into the car, we're taking you somewhere."

Jacque turned as if to comply with their request when Hans silently opened the back door and slid out. "I don't think so," he said menacingly, the machine pistol still in his hands. "One wrong move and you'll both be dead. Now lie face down on the road."

Balfour and Monnet drew a quick breath. "Damn it," Balfour said, somebody *has* set us up.

They hesitated and Hans turned the butt of his machine pistol round and rammed it hard into Balfour's back. "Now," he growled. "Lie down on the road, on your faces."

Balfour cried out, and again Hans went to hit him but he bent down and lay on the road, face down. Hans put his boot on the middle of Balfour's back as Monnet, with Jacque's pistol in his ribs was also forced to lie face down.

"What a pretty picture," Jacque said. "You people will never learn." And he kicked Balfour in the ribs and he cried out in pain.

"You'll wish you were never born," he Jacque said.

Debré watched the light of the car and the faint shadows on the road as he ran like the wind and silent as night. He closed in fast on the unsuspecting Hans and Jacque. Jacque had no sooner uttered the last words than Debré unsheathed his German soldier's knife and sprang like a panther. He sank the knife deep into Hans's rib cage and gave it a twist before pulling it out.

It happened so quickly that Jacque was taken completely by surprise. As Debré withdrew the knife and Hans crumpled in a heap, Monnet threw his arms around Jacque's ankles and pulled him to the ground. Balfour rolled over and grabbed the pistol but already Debré's foot held Jacque's gun hand pinned to the road.

He reached down and relieved Jacque of the pistol, keeping his foot on his hand. "Can't leave you two for a minute," he said, slightly out of breath.

Balfour pulled himself up gingerly and Monnet gathered himself. "How did you know to come back François?" Balfour asked him.

"It was the girl," Debré said. "She must have come from the house to warn them. There wasn't time to stop and ask why, but we'll probably see her on the way back."

Jacque was hauled to his feet and his hands tied behind his back and as he started to protest they put a gag in his mouth. He was forced into the back of the car. Debré then lifted Hans's lifeless body and deposited it unceremoniously into the boot. Then with Monnet at the wheel they turned around and drove away.

Nina attempted to hide at the side of the road when she saw the car coming. But they were looking out for her and saw her half hearted attempt to hide. Monnet pulled the car up beside her and waited at the wheel while Balfour got out.

"Who are you?" he asked. "What's your name?"

"Nina," the frightened girl muttered. "Nina Péri."

"And what have you been up to?"

146

"Nothing," she said. Then she saw Jacque face gagged, through the car window. "What are you doing with him?" she cried.

"What's it to you what we do with him?"

Nina stepped up to Balfour and pummelled his chest with her fists. "I loved him," she cried. "All I did was try to warn him. I didn't want him to die." Then she looked again at Jacque peering out at her. "Now I don't know any more," she cried. "Do what you like but just leave me alone."

Balfour turned to Monnnet. "What do you think René? Do we take her or let her go?"

"She's more trouble than she's worth Roger," René said. "But we'd better not leave her, she knows too much."

"You heard that," Balfour said. "Get into the back of the car, we might even send you to England with lover boy here. Give you a chance to patch up your differences.

Chapter nineteen

Just over an hour later they arrived at their camp deep in the forest. Debré took the car and concealed it and then disposed of the body. Jacque's gag was removed and then he and Nina were securely bound, hand and foot inside a rough corrugated tin shelter and a guard set over them for the night.

In the morning a message was passed to Anton and Marie Aveline to let them know their son was safe but imprisoned, pending his departure to England. They were also told of the part Nina played in the previous night's events and that a decision had been taken for her own good to send her to England as well.

Marie took it badly when she heard the news, even though she'd been expecting it. She was torn between loyalty to her son, and the safety of her fellow Résistance workers. Anton did his best to console her and managed to convince her that it was all for the best in the long run. However they both knew they had, along with Andrea, to get on with their lives the best they could.

Debré had left the camp early without looking at the prisoners to make sure Jacque's car was properly hidden. He was meticulous about such things and it was two hours before he returned. When he did, breakfast was being prepared on an open fire. He arrived as a plate of beans and coffee was ready for the two prisoners.

Balfour and Monnet were sitting by the fire as he walked back into the camp.

"François," Balfour said. "Will you take this plate of beans and coffee into our two prisoners for me? My back's killing me after that bastard hit me with the butt of his gun."

Debré, always a man of few words simply shrugged and said, "Sure."

He took the beans and coffee and strode over to the shelter, slightly curious to see what the two of them looked like in daylight. It was dull inside with the door partially closed over. Debré set the plate and coffee on the ground and opened the door fully to let the light in. He bent down and lifted the plate first and without saying anything reached it out to Jacque.

Jacque had had his head bent down. Now he lifted it up and said. "My hands are tied. How do you expect me to eat?"

Debré felt a chill crawl up his spine. He froze on the spot, staring at Jacque. Jacque stared back blankly and shrugged his shoulders and then he looked at Nina. "What's got into him?" he said.

Debré backed out of the hut, trying to clear his mind. He set the plate of beans down on the ground and by this time Monnet had come over, curious to know what was happening. Balfour watched from beside the fire.

Then slowly and deliberately Debré drew his soldier's knife and advanced again into the hut. Jacque saw the look in his eyes and he called out. "This nut case is going to kill me," he yelled. "Somebody get him off me." There was terror in Jacque's voice.

Monnet grasped Debré's arm but he shook him off. Debré moved like lightening, but instead of slitting Jacque's throat, which is what Jacque thought he was going to do, he cut the rope free from around his wrists. Then he hoisted him up on his feet and dragged him outside and threw him to the ground.

Bidault and Billoux came running over from a Kubelwagen they were working on and stood looking puzzled beside Monnet and Balfour. Debré, with a look of unimaginable hate on his face, looked at them as he pointed the knife at Jacque. "You see that bastard we risked our lives to capture and send to England. You see him," he yelled. "Well *he's* the Butcher of Verberie."

There was stunned silence because they had all heard about the Butcher of Verberie though not all they heard was true. Many other atrocities, in which he hadn't taken part, had also been attributed to him. It had always been assumed that he was a German and the Germans used the rumours to fuel fear among the French.

Here was a man, the son of Resisters, being accused by Debré of being one of the most hated men in France. It took seconds for the accusation to sink in and it was Jacque who eventually broke the silence.

149

"He's mad," he shouted struggling in vain to get to his feet. "I'm Jacque Aveline. My father's Doctor Anton Aveline. My own sister's in the Résistance for heaven's sake."

Balfour turned to Debré whose eyes blazed with fury. He put his hand out to him in an attempt to calm him. "Are you sure about this François? And if you are, how do you know?"

"He killed my brothers, and shot my parents and burned our home to the ground."

"But how do your know this?" Gaston Bidault said raising his fists in the air. "It's strange that nobody else was able to say who this Butcher was. You came to us out of the blue and we accepted the story you told us about your self, but you never mentioned any of this."

"You need to prove this," Billoux said. "Some of us know this man's family, and those who *really* know them hold them in high esteem. You must give us evidence because everybody knows the family's name was Desjardine, not Debré which is your surname, and that all the family died in that fire."

"He's right," Balfour said. "So come on François, where's the evidence?"

François looked thoughtfully at the knife in his hand. He turned it over and held it carefully by the tip. Jacque was sitting up, leaning with one hand on the ground supporting him. Suddenly François flexed his hand and threw the knife with such force that it went through the back of Jacque's hand pinning it to the ground.

Jacque cried out in shock and pain. He reached over in agony with his other hand to pull the knife out but like lightening François stepped on his impaled hand and he screamed even louder.

It happened so fast that the others were taken by surprise. Suddenly they rushed as one man to pull François away but something in his eyes held them back at the last minute.

Jacque moaned in agony. "I'll tell you," François said finally as he looked at the others gathered around. "My name's not François Debré, it is François Desjardine."

He looked down at Jacque, whose face was contorted in agony. "You didn't kill us all," he said. "I watched from the top of the hay loft as you hung my two brothers upside down until they choked on their own vomit."

There were tears in François's eyes as he recounted the awful story. "I lay there in the hayloft, biting my hand in case I cried out to you to stop and gave myself away. And I knew that if I did, you'd have killed me as well. You can't even imagine how I've hated myself ever since. How many times I've wished I'd died there as well."

"Why didn't you tell us this?" Balfour asked him.

Debré hesitated for a moment. "Because I've lived with the fear that if my true identity was revealed to anyone, then I might suffer the same fate as by brothers. If I had told any of you and you'd been captured and tortured by the Gestapo what would have happened?"

Debré's pain and suffering was almost palpable as Balfour touched him lightly on the arm. "François how can you be sure it was him?" he asked gently.

Debré lifted his foot off Jacque's hand and stepped back. Monnet knelt down and holding Jacque's arm with his left hand, he grasped the handle of the knife and pulled it free. Jacque screamed in pain.

Debré ignored his cries of pain and turned to Balfour. "Turn out his pockets."

"He's not armed François," Balfour said. "We've already searched him."

"Turn his pockets out anyway," Debré said.

Balfour shrugged his shoulders and knelt down beside Jacque who was moaning in agony as he nursed his injured hand. Monnet and the others stood and watched with puzzlement as Jacque pockets were emptied.

Jacque was past protesting. The search revealed little. There was a pencil and some scraps of paper in one pocket. In another pocket there was some loose change and a comb and a handkerchief. Balfour stood up when he'd finished.

"That's it François," he said. "What were you hoping I'd find?"

François looked at the various bits and pieces. He knelt down and picked up the handkerchief and then stood up with a look of satisfaction on his face.

Again he looked around him. "My older brother Gerard was the last to die," he said. "This Butcher had wiped the perspiration off his forehead with his handkerchief. He'd taken it from his back pocket. I can still see it. Gerard somehow gathered the strength to swear at him. He told him to 'shut up and die quietly – that he was giving him a headache'. Gerard swore louder. I … I think he was hoping one of them would shoot him and put him out of his agony. But instead this Butcher rammed his handkerchief into Gerard's mouth to keep him quiet. The handkerchief eventually fell to the ground. After Aveleine and the *SS* soldiers left, I went down and picked up the handkerchief. I used it to wipe the vomit from both my brothers' faces. I wanted to cut them down but I was afraid in case those brutes came back. So without thinking I put the handkerchief in my pocket. They just left them hanging there. When I knew they'd gone for certain I went back to the house. They'd shot my parents. But my mother … my mother."

François stopped, overcome with grief.

"It's all right François," Balfour said. "You don't need to go over it again. You've said enough to convince us."

François stopped sobbing. "NO," he said. "There's more. I need you to know. They didn't only shoot my mother. They RAPED her," he shouted as he glared at Jacque.

"No, no," Jacque cried out in panic. "Not that. I'd nothing to do with that."

"You were part of them," François said. "You're every bit as guilty."

He turned away from him in disgust and looked at Balfour again. "After that I just ran for my life. I was ashamed I'd done nothing to stop them."

"But there was nothing you could do François," Balfour said.

"But there was," he retorted. "I could have died with them don't you see. Then I wouldn't have this guilt living with me day and night. Anyway a few days later I remembered the handkerchief and took it and washed it and I saw the initials J. A. and so I kept it for an occasion such as this."

He put his hand in his pocket and pulled out the white handkerchief he'd kept. "There you are," he said. "That's the handkerchief, exactly the same as the one you've just pulled out of his pocket. Now do you believe me, all of you?"

"We believe you," Monnet said. "We all do."

Georges Bégué, a member of the Résistance from its beginning and a hard, sometimes cruel young man in his early twenties had pulled out a pistol and cocked it. He pointed it at Jacque, who was lying on his back again with sheer naked fear in his eyes.

"No don't do that Georges," Bidault interrupted. "It's not for us to act as judge, jury and executioner. We've done what we had to do. Leave it at that."

Balfour looked directly at Bégué. "It's not your business Georges. Gaston's right. Put your gun away."

Bégué looked sheepish but reluctantly put his gun away. "If anybody has the right it's François," Balfour added.

Balfour asked Bidault to bandage Jacque's hand and then he took François and Monnet to one side. "I'm obliged to tell his family," he said. He looked directly at François. "We owe it to them François. I know you've had one hell of a cross to bear, but I promise you'll get your revenge one day."

Debré turned and walked away with tears in his eyes.

Jacque and Nina were kept in the shelter and given food and water and allowed out one at a time to answer the call of nature. One man remained on guard and occasionally another checked that all was well. The rest slept as well as they could, which at the best of times was poorly, though after a number of bad nights sleep it came like the sleep of death for some of them.

It was not like that for Debré. He tossed and turned as he tried to get the image of his brothers choking to death at the end of a rope, out of his mind. Every time he closed his eyes he saw the Germans grab his brothers and tie the rope around their ankles as they laughed and spat at them. Tears formed in his eyes as he cursed Jacque for bringing it all back to him. He even remembered one of the Germans taking photographs.

Bidault did not sleep either. The sight of Jacque lying there, cringing with fear, and the agony of the pain in Jacque's hand, only served to remind him of what he himself had gone through. Of how it was only because of Jacque's father that he was alive, and how it was no thanks to Bégué.

The Operation had gone according to plan. It was simple enough, and there should not have been any complications. Blowing a railway line was, by that time, all in a days work. There were four of them detailed for the job, including Bégué. Two men waited a couple of hundred yards from the railway line to keep guard. Bidault and Bégué went as far as the line to set the explosive. Then as Bidault waited Bégué unwound the wire back as far as the plunger a hundred yards from the railway line.

Bidault shouted to Bégué to go ahead and catch up with the other two, while he detonated the charge. As Bégué ran towards the others, there was a cry of Warning from them. Bidault looked behind him as five German soldiers raced up the line towards the explosives. He rammed the plunger home and there was a loud bang. It was too far from the Germans to harm them but it slowed them down momentarily and Bégué tried to make good his escape. Bidault had no chance to hide and he ran as the Germans climbed the wire along the line. They raced towards him across a ploughed field, firing as they did.

Suddenly Bidault felt a sharp blow to his leg and a searing pain shot through his body. He fell headlong, crying in agony. He doubled up grasping his upper leg. The Germans came on him and stopped briefly to look. Realising he could not get away they raced on after the others, knowing they could deal with him later.

Bégué and the others had nearly cleared the field, where on the other side a short strip of land led to a narrow bridge and their car, on the road below. But the Germans were gaining quickly. Two of them stopped and got down on one knee and steadied their aim as they fired at the fleeing French. The other three Germans ran on. A French man stopped and kneeling down returned fire and two of the Germans fell, critically wounded.

The third stopped in his tracks, but by now his colleagues were on their feet and firing from the hip as they ran towards the French. The French knew it was hopeless to run so they stood their ground but they were no match for the German firepower and soon only Bégué was left standing with his weapon.

Almost recklessly he raced for the ditch and jumped over to the other side. Grasping his rifle he glanced desperately behind him. The Germans were firing and closing fast. He knew he couldn't make it to the car and his only choice was to shoot it out. He dropped down behind a small mound and quickly levelled his rifle at the fast approaching Germans. A short burst of gunfire rang out and one of the Germans fell.

Unknown to the Germans, Bidault had pulled himself up and dragged himself towards the Germans who'd been shot. They were in no condition to do anything as Bidault grasped one of their guns and levelled it at their comrades and opened fire. They were taken completely by surprise, and fearing an attack from another source spun round. As they did Bégué shot one of them dead. The other died from the last rounds from the machine pistol fired by Bidault.

Bidault fell to the ground again. He was white, shaken and in agony. He saw Bégué look at him as he fell and he waited for him to come and get him. He felt very weak as he lay on his back. Then he heard a sound. At first he though his mind was playing tricks on him but the sound became louder and louder. He realised it was a German spotter plane.

It circled and then flew down low, as the pilot took a closer look. Then he circled again, sweeping low over the countryside and then along the railway track. Using the gun as a crutch Bidault cried out in agony as he raised himself up again.

Bégué on the other hand was still free. He'd seen Bidault fall and he told himself he'd been hit, probably dead. For only a moment he hesitated and then ran across the short stretch of ground towards the bridge. He looked back and saw Bidault trying desperately to get away, but he ignored him and slid quickly down the grassy bank and into the car as the spotter plane swooped low over him.

Balfour was waiting anxiously at the camp, as he always did when anyone was away on an Operation. When he saw Bégué get out of the car alone, he felt even more despondent.

"What went wrong Bégué?" he called as he rushed over to the car. "Where are the others?"

"Ambushed," Bégué said. "Bidault detonated the explosive just as the Germans appeared. He was behind us and the last to leave. He'd no chance. They took us completely by surprise. I was lucky to get away."

"What about the Germans? How many were there?"

"There were five of them but I, or we, managed to get them all, though I didn't wait around to see if they were all dead."

"We'll have to go back and get the bodies," Balfour said. "If we don't, the Germans will find them, and if they identify them, their families and their villages will pay a heavy price."

Balfour hesitated. "Bégué, you'd better rest. Some of us will go back and get them before it's too late."

"But it's already too late. It's not safe," Bégué explained. "As I left, a German spotter plane flew over. He'll have seen the bodies."

Balfour hesitated. "Are you *sure* they were all dead Bégué?"

"I'm," he hesitated. "Yes," he said. "I'm certain."

Balfour noticed the hesitation. "There's not a moment to lose," he shouted to the rest of the men. "Take the motorbike and sidecar and the other car. It's full of petrol. We've got to get there before the Germans."

They drove off at speed through the forest path to the road. Balfour had thrown all caution to the wind. He knew what the Gestapo and the *SS* did to the families of Resistance fighters and sometimes to the villages as well if any of them were caught and identified. And he knew what they'd do to any of them; if per chance they *were* still alive. He'd always had a niggling doubt about Bégué, but he could never actually pinpoint anything. But of all the men he was always the

156

most outspoken and the most vehement in his hatred for the Germans. His words were not *always* met with actions.

They arrived at the bridge without incident and quickly climbed the grassy bank with stretchers and made it across the patch of grass to the ploughed field. A quick glance of the field revealed the bodies.

Balfour beckoned to the men to follow him. They found two of their own men and there was no doubt that they were dead. Without ceremony they were put on stretchers and brought back to the car.

René Monnet ran on to where they had seen the other bodies. Two German soldiers lay close beside each other. Their faces fixed in the cold grimace of sudden death. Bidault lay still beside them.

Monnet didn't touch him but stood up and waved his hand towards Balfour. "Over here," he shouted.

Balfour walked across the field as Georges Billoux came back from the car with a stretcher and followed him.

Monnet stood solemnly as Balfour rolled Bidault over on his back. He was glancing at Billoux when he heard a groan and looked down at Bidault. "He's alive," Balfour said. "Quickly, get him on the stretched and let's get out of here."

Without taking time to check how Bidault was they put him on the stretcher and hurried back to the car. One of the bodies was put into the sidecar and the other in the boot of the car. Bidault, who was unconscious, was put as gently as possible onto the back seat. Everyone else fitted in as best they could.

It was an uneventful journey back to camp. Bidault was taken out gently and Balfour immediately examined him. He quickly established that he was suffering from severe blood loss. His leg was red and badly swollen. His breathing was shallow and his pulse was rapid and erratic.

"We can do nothing for him," Balfour said. "And if we don't get him help he'll surely die."

"I could have sworn he was dead," Bégué said rather sheepishly.

"Could you now," Balfour said sarcastically. "Pity you didn't wait to check."

"I couldn't have done anything anyway because I couldn't have got him back on my own."

"No," Balfour said. "But if he was still conscious you could have told him you were going for help. As it is he'll have thought he was abandoned."

"I only know one man who can help us and there's no time to lose," Balfour said. "Anton Aveline lives outside Chantilly. He's a surgeon and his wife's a Doctor. The problem is that he's paralysed, but between himself and his wife I'm sure they'll do something."

He looked at Bidault. "There's no way we can move him. They will have to come to us."

Balfour looked at the rest of the men. "Do your best for him," he said. "Keep him warm and I'll be back as quickly as possible with help."

Anton and Marie were reluctant to leave the comparative security of the Château on what was potentially a perilous journey, but they could not resist Balfour's plea. So with Anton Aveline's help and guidance, and his wife Marie carrying out his instructions Bidault's life was saved. It was many weeks before he was fully active again.

As he lay tossing and turning and unable to sleep, he kept seeing Bégué, running to save his own life while he left him to die in the ploughed field. And he remembered the Doctor and his wife from Chantilly who had risked their lives to save his.

Chapter twenty

Jacque and Nina were kept in the shelter. They were provided with food and water to keep them going and allowed out one at a time to the toilet. One man remained on guard and occasionally another looked in to check that everything was all right.

Jacque's mind was in turmoil. He had no answers to François's accusations and no excuses. As he lay against the wall of the shelter nursing his hand and frequently grimacing with the pain, he became more and more convinced that he was going to die.

Every time he looked at Nina, she avoided his gaze. He tried to open up a conversation but she ignored him. He heard Balfour return and knew that he was discussing the situation with the others. After a while there was silence. The guard changed and the new man looked in on the prisoners and then lit a cigarette and settled for his period of watch. Nina dozed off.

Jacque manoeuvred himself over beside her and nudged her with his elbow. He had come up with an almost hopeless plan, but he believed it was his only chance. He was c

Nina opened her eyes. "Did you hear them?" he whispered.

"Hear what?" Nina said sleepily.

"Ssh," Jacque whispered. "Did you hear what they said?"

"No," Nina hissed.

"They're going to shoot both of us in the morning," Jacque lied.

Nina drew a sharp breath. "No," she gasped.

"I heard that English man say that my family has washed their hands of me. They've disowned me, and don't care if I die," he continued lying.

"But not me," Nina said, holding back the tears.

"Yes, you as well," Jacque said convincingly. "They said you know too much and can't be trusted any more."

"But I did nothing."

"You fell in love at the wrong time Nina. Now listen carefully. We've got to help each other if we're going to survive. You must try and untie my hands."

"How can I? My own are tied."

"At least try. It's our only chance. It's impossible for me with this hand. It hurts like blazes."

Jacque manoeuvred himself again so that he and Nina were back to back and Nina reluctantly began to try and untie Jacque's wrists. She struggled desperately, believing as Jacque had said that she was going to be shot.

Bidault could stand it no longer. The resentment he felt towards Bégué simply got the better of him and he saw a way of dealing with that and repaying the Avelines for risking their lives to save his.

He crept out of bed and looking around him saw that he was alone. A short distance away Bégué was hunched over on a wooded seat as he guarded the two prisoners. He whittling away at a piece of wood to pass the time. Bidault crept closer, a Luger pistol in his right hand. As he was about to crack Bégué on the head with the pistol, Bégué suddenly stood up to stretch and as he turned he saw Bidault with his pistol drawn.

Instinctively he believed Bidault was about to shoot him and he lunged at him with his knife, but Bidault dropped his gun and grasped Bégué's arm and twisted it viciously so that he was forced to drop the knife. In an instant Bidault had thrown him to the ground and as they wrestled Bidault grasped the knife and as Bégué struggled to get free Bidault killed him.

Checking instantly that nobody had been disturbed by the struggle, Bidault picked himself up and crept towards the captives.

Nina was making little progress when Jacque whispered. "Hold on, I think somebody's coming."

They turned again so that they were both facing the same direction and they listened intently. Then the door of the shelter opened and someone crept in. In the darkness their features were hidden.

The figure moved around behind the two captives and cut the ropes binding them with a knife. Jacque groaned as he accidentally rolled the wrong way on his injured hand. Their rescuer took a Luger pistol and gave it to Jacque and without a word left them.

Jacque and Nina struggled to their feet. They glanced quickly at the open door as the figure vanished, but in the darkness they saw nothing and couldn't make out who it was.

They hurried out of the shelter and saw the still figure of Bégué lying on his side. Without stopping, Jacque and Nina walked quickly and quietly out of the camp to freedom.

François arrived at 06:00 to take over guard. He stood transfixed when he saw Bégué's lifeless body lying in front of the shelter. He spun on his heel and yelled at the top of his voice. "He's gone. The Butcher of Verberie's gone and he's killed Bégué. The girl's gone as well. We *should* have let Bégué shoot him when he wanted too."

There was sudden pandemonium in the camp. Balfour was first out, pulling his clothes on as best he could as he ran to the shelter. "I don't believe it," he cried. "How *could* he have got free?"

"They must have managed to untie themselves and surprise poor Bégué and get his knife. He was killed with own knife," François said. "But it doesn't matter now because he's free and now we'll probably never get him. I'll never avenge my parents and brothers death."

"We'll worry about that later," Balfour said, as he walked over to Bégué's lifeless body.

He looked at the rest of the men as they gathered around. "Right," he said. "We'll have to move back into the forest to our base camp, just in case. I don't believe the Germans would dare to venture out here without a regiment of soldiers. They know they'd lose too many men, but no point taking a chance. Pack up everything and let's get moving."

Monnet approached Balfour. "What about Aveline's family Roger? If he spills the beans on them they've had it. They'll all have to go into hiding. Their son might not know all the members of their Network but that girl does."

"Would he really betray his own kith and kin?" Gaston asked.

"He'd betray his own grandmother if it suited his purposes," Debré said bitterly.

161

"Enough of this debate," Balfour said finally. "We'll waste no more time here."

He turned to Monnet. "Monnet, tell the family for me. They'll know what to do, but for goodness sake be careful, and somebody take Bégué and bury him where it won't be too obvious. We'll mark his grave when this War's over"

François had already walked away and without anyone noticing had taken their German Army motorcycle and filled it with petrol. He kicked it into life and accelerated towards Balfour and Monnet, who were taken completely by surprise. He halted briefly a few yards away from them. "I'll tell the family," he said as he accelerated away from them.

Balfour called after him but Monnet told him it was pointless and they set about the task of moving out of their camp.

François had already made up his mind what he was going to do. When the camp had settled for the night and the last guard was set over the prisoners François found it impossible to sleep. The events of the night had brought back everything so vividly. He could not get the image of his brothers out of his mind. At 02:00 he left his camp bed to walk in the woods in an attempt to clear his mind. When he returned he walked past the shelter where the prisoners were held and spoke briefly to Bégué before he returned to bed.

He knew that if Bégué had been knifed to death by Jacque, even just after that, they would not have been able to get more than about sixteen miles from the camp, and possibly less. They had no chance of getting a lift from anyone and the nearest village, which was a small mining community, was twenty miles away. He believed he had a fair chance of apprehending the two of them before they reached the village.

He raced down the road at full throttle, knowing that even a minute could make all the difference. The darkness of night had given way to the light of dawn. The road, like most of the roads in occupied France, was quiet. François knew that timing was vital. If he judged it wrongly, they would hear the motorcycle, and hide in the ditch and he'd

He slowed as he approached the brow of a hill fifteen miles further on. He knew the village was only another five miles away. He was fit and could easily run that distance but he knew he might be cutting it fine. He came over the brow of the hill and the road stretched away before him and there in the distance he saw two figures. His heart leapt within him as he stopped the motorcycle but he was too late and he cursed to himself.

It was Nina who heard it first, even before François came into view, but Jacque told her she was imagining it. Now he saw motorcycle for himself. He grasped Nina by the arm and they turned up a dirt track into the hills.

As François saw them disappear he raced away down the road after them.

Nina was not as fit as Jacque was and she struggled to keep up with him. He was impatient and goaded her on and she did her best. Jacque believed he had a better chance off the main road and as he ran for his life he looked for a place where he could ambush the motorcyclist.

François found the track they had taken and drove up it searching for them, watchful for an ambush. Then he caught a glimpse of them in the distance, as Jacque pulled Nina off the track. He abandoned the motorbike and ran after them on foot. The track ran through bracken and trees and the ground was littered with rocks and boulders. As François looked for the spot they had run through he heard them ahead of him. He was now in terrain that he was used to and he closed in fast.

"It's no use Aveline," he called out. "It doesn't matter where you run I'll still get you. There's no getting away from me."

Jacque ignored the taunt and concentrated on where he was going but he had no idea where he was heading and Nina was beginning to hold him back. He started to leave her behind. "Wait for me Jacque," she called out breathlessly. "I can't keep up with you."

Jacque ignored her and ran on. His heart was thumping and the pain in his hand was like a red-hot knife but fear caused the adrenaline to surge through his pain wracked body and it kept him going. He broke clear of the bracken and trees and found himself in a clearing, strewn with boulders.

François caught up with Nina, but he ignored her in his determination to catch Jacque. Then he too broke clear of the trees but there was no sign of Aveleine. He stood perfectly still. Nina had stopped running and he could hear her panting and sobbing. Suddenly a shot rang out to François's right. He ducked and looked in the direction of the shot and just caught a glimpse of Jacque as he ducked behind a boulder. He was holding the Walther in his left hand and he was a crack shot with a pistol, but *not* with his left hand. François guessed as much and relaxed and watched and waited his eyes darting everywhere.

Then he heard Nina running again and she was panting and out of breath, as she stumbled up to him and grabbed him by the arm. "Please don't hurt him," she cried.

François shook her off and suddenly Jacque appeared from behind another boulder. He held the pistol in his left hand, pointing it at François. Nina called out. "No Jacque, don't shoot." And she ran towards him.

"Nina, get out of the way," Jacque shouted as he fired again but Nina stumbled and instead took the bullet in her chest. She fell dead instantly.

François leapt towards Jacque in a blind fury. Jacque was so taken by surprise that he fired another wild shot and then he turned to run but François was quickly onto him. He knocked him to the ground and the pistol flew from Jacque's hand. They rolled over in a frenzied embrace. Jacque was screaming in agony. His right hand was useless to him and he knew he'd no hope against François but he fought like a wild cat.

Somehow he broke free from François and rolled over, but he had not noticed that they had come to the edge of the quarry, whereas François had seen it. Suddenly he looked around in panic for something to hold on to. His left hand found the trunk of a sapling just as he found himself rolling over the edge of the quarry. He looked down at what appeared to be a sheer drop beneath him. His legs were dangling in mid-air. He held on for dear life as François stood over him. His face was contorted with fear and agony.

François looked at him without pity. "I've waited a long time for this, you bastard," he said.

He took a knife from his belt and knelt down and proceeded to cut the sapling through. He took his time as it slowly bent over. Jacque tried desperately to grasp the remaining stump but it was no good. His right hand was useless and he disappeared down the sheer quarry face with a piercing scream.

François stood still for a moment and then as if a huge weight had been lifted off his shoulders, he heaved a sigh of relief. He turned away from the edge of the quarry and went back and picked up Nina's lifeless body and dropped it into the quarry after Jacque.

When he arrived back at the camp in the forest, there was no trace of the Baker's Dozen. François followed the path he knew they would have taken.

Chapter twenty one

When Jacque's parents Marie and Anton had become aware of how much their son knew they were alarmed, and Marie radioed London as soon as she could to let Josephine Butler know. When Josephine received the coded message she reported it immediately to the Major and he in turn arranged an urgent meeting with Churchill.

He met with Churchill early in the morning at the same time the Baker's Dozen was moving camp in case of a German attack.

"Now what's this meeting all about Major?" Churchill asked. "Not more trouble from your end I hope. Not the inner circle. I sometimes believe they're the only friends I've got."

"I'm afraid it is' Prime Minister," the Major said. "Bit of a set back really. Jay Bee's Network has been rumbled. It's a nasty one actually. Marie and Anton Aveline's son Jacque, the one who works for Canaris, found out they were involved in the Résistance and were hiding an airman, Flight Lieutenant Gary Tucker, one of my best pilots. He flies Jay Bee every time she goes to France and now he's the only one she'll fly with. Anyway as far as we know Jacque didn't tell anybody what he knew and the Résistance is going to abduct him and send him to us for debriefing and to keep 'till the War's over."

"Damn nuisance Jack, so how does that affect our plans?"

"They *can* go ahead Prime Minister, but *your* safety is absolutely paramount. So if the Doctor Network *has* been compromised and you still insist on going ahead we shall have to make other arrangements."

Just then there was a knock on the door. A young woman from SOE stood calmly to attention as the Major opened it.

"An urgent message for you sir," she said and handed the Major an envelope.

He dismissed the Officer and opened the letter, reading it as he closed the door again. He looked at Churchill. "Better news this time Prime Minister provided Jacque Aveline really didn't tell anybody else, it looks as if we're in the clear. It seems he was killed in an attempt to escape from the Résistance. Another young woman, an accomplice is also dead."

"And who's that message from Jack?" Churchill enquired.

"It's the same contact again sir, Aveline's mother Marie. Must be devilishly difficult for her," the Major said.

"Those people in France show the greatest of courage," Churchill said. "And there's little we can do for them but carry on, but I'm as determined as ever. I'll still go to France when Canaris and Oster have confirmed it's the right time, but we've still to get confirmation from our own agents. I'm not chancing this neck of mine for nothing Jack."

"I still believe it's foolhardy sir," the Major said. "If anything should happen to you there's nobody to lead us. We could lose the War if that happens."

"Damn it Jack, don't you see," Churchill said getting up from the chair. "The way things are going hundreds of thousands more will die if this War doesn't end soon. I've got to meet these German Generals and assure them by my presence in occupied France that I mean business. That they can trust the British to give them all the backing they need when the time comes. Hess *did* risk all and if this meeting doesn't go ahead he *will* have lost all because I'll deny any knowledge of any collusion with a damned Nazi and he'll be hung or he'll rot in gaol. But Jack, if we pull this one out of the hat, we'll shorten the War. Damned if we don't."

"If this escapade fails and you survive Prime Minister, the country will crucify you if word gets out, after you yourself refused to compromise with the Germans or discuss mutually agreeable terms with Hitler."

"We'll cross that bridge when we come to it Jack. I'm depending on you to cover my back. When the time comes, nobody, and I mean nobody, only those *directly* involved must know. I'll be out of the country and into France and back again before anybody misses me. Damn it Jack, I'll have one of my bad days. They can tell whoever's looking for me that I'm in one of my foulest moods and I've locked myself away with instructions I'm not to be disturbed."

The Major laughed. "And you think that will do it Prime Minister?"

"You'd better see it does Jack."

"And if you succeed Prime Minister," the Major asked. "Will you make Hess the new Chancellor of Germany as he has insisted?"

Churchill chuckled. "The Germans will have him for breakfast as soon as they get their hands on him and good luck to them. I'll hand him over myself. I can't stand the little Nazi rat. Chancellor of the new Germany Jack! Never."

After his meeting with Churchill the Major called Josephine Butler to his office.

"Have a seat Jay Bee," he said. "You look tired."

Jay Bee smiled. "Isn't everybody tired these days, Major?"

"You're right Jay Bee. I suppose they are. It's the War you know."

They laughed together. "Everybody blames the War for everything," Jay Bee said.

The Major looked serious. "I've just left the PM," he said. "He's concerned about your Doctor Network." He put his hand in his pocket and looked at the note he'd received from the young SOE agent and handed it to Jay Bee. "That's the latest," he said. "Just came in as I was speaking to the PM. What do you think?"

Jay Bee took the note and read it. "That's terrible," she said. "Terrible. Marie and Anton will be devastated to lose their only son like that. It was bad enough that he went to work for the Germans, but this. I'll have to go to them, sir."

"I know," the Major said. "I was going to ask you anyway. The PM is very concerned about this Network and you know that I can't tell you why, but believe me this is vital. We've to know beyond any shadow of a doubt that the Network is still secure."

"I'll do my best sir."

"You'll have to do better than that Jay Bee. How soon can you go?"

"Well you know Gary Tucker's not available to fly me, but there are others I suppose I can use in an emergency. In fact Marie was suggesting that Gary should be moved. They were going to use the

168

usual route through Switzerland but it's always risky, so I'll arrange for them to send him back with me. Much safer that way."

"Can you fix it in time?"

"I'll have to. If the Germans caught Gary, he'd be tortured and forced to talk. Then the Network would be useless, so we've got to move him now."

The Major stood up. "Keep me informed, Jay Bee. Things are moving to a head and there's not much time."

"There's one other thing sir before you go. What's going to happen to Richter, now that Jacque Aveline's dead? You did say that some high-ranking Nazis were using Jacque to influence the Résistance to kill Richter."

"You're quiet right Jay Bee. In fact it's vital, and with a bit of luck this time tomorrow Richter will be no more, because Aveline had all the arrangements made before he died. Your friends in the Doctor's Network have agreed to kill him."

Chapter twenty two

The assassination of Colonel Richter had been planned in meticulous detail. Jacque Aveline had given his movements, on the night on which he was to be killed, to his sister Andrea. There were however still some misgivings within the Doctor's Network. There was communication from London confirming the urgency of the matter. But there was no information forthcoming regarding the reason, other than that General Scholtz's life was in danger from the Nazis. Why that should concern the British, no one knew. Even Marie Aveline, whom everyone knew had a special relationship with London, had been unable to throw any light on the situation.

It was simply accepted that the Colonel was to be killed, even though it would mean renewed reprisals from the Germans, maybe even from General Scholtz himself, whom they were protecting. When Jacque's death was subsequently reported there were more misgivings amongst everyone involved.

The night before the ambush, Father Michael de Bourbon, dressed as a labourer, had driven an old van up the side road that led to Madeleine Boussine's house. He stopped after two hundred yards and jacked the van up and removed the rear wheel and put it in the back of the van. Then for good measure he opened the bonnet and removed the rotor arm and put it in his pocket. Two Sten Guns had been carefully concealed in a hidden compartment under the floor. The floor was covered with a thin layer of hay and a couple of hessian sacks. When he was satisfied with his work he went into the back of the van and changed into his clerical clothes. He discarded the labourer's outfit in the process. After checking that nobody was watching, he climbed out of the van and made his was to Chapel to celebrate Mass and hear Confessions.

Madeleine Boussine had confirmed with Jacque Aveline that Colonel Richter was to call with her on the Friday night. She said he always came alone, except for his driver, and that he was always punctual, though for security reasons he didn't always follow the same route.

The ambush was planned to take place before the Colonel reached Madeleine's house. Charles and Roger Bayard went over the plan again with Simone de Beauvoir late on the Friday afternoon.

That night Charles and Roger Bayard met again in the old farmhouse with Simone de Beauvoir and Inspector Marius Regnier. Nothing had happened since their last meeting to change their plans, and so Charles and Roger set out separately for their destination.

To reduce the possibility of being caught in an impromptu search of the van by German soldiers they waited until 19:50 before going to it. Charles went first on a bicycle. He drove past the van checking that all was clear and then parked the bicycle against the kerb and walked back to the van. Nobody was on the street as he opened the back door and climbed in. Roger followed him quickly.

"I'm always nervous when it's this easy," Charles said.

"It's because we're so careful brother," Roger said as he pulled aside the floor covering to reveal the hidden compartment containing the guns.

He opened the lid and removed two Sten Guns and handed one to Charles. They checked their weapons quickly and then waited. Charles looked at his watch. "A minute to go," he said calmly. "It's time Simone was here."

The rear window of the van was steaming up and he wiped it, and then gave Roger a nudge. "He's here," he said with satisfaction.

Roger looked out and saw that de Beauvoir had pulled up in another van a hundred yards from them, and got out, leaving the engine running. He watched as he closed the door and walked to the front of the house, where he had parked, and turned and looked down the road and waited. His only role was to provide transport for Charles and Roger after the ambush.

Then they saw the car. "It's Richter," Roger said. "He's on time."

They crouched in the van ready to throw the back door open and jump out as the Colonel's car passed them. Down the road from them, de Beauvoir turned his back to the approaching car and knocked on the door of a house to give the impression he was visiting. The car passed him without slowing down, and he turned as it drove past, watching as it drew level with the van.

The back door of the van burst open suddenly and the two brothers jumped out as the car drew level. They levelled their Sten Guns as it sped past and opened fire. The driver hadn't a chance as the windows in the car shattered and he slumped across the steering wheel and the car careered across the road and crashed into the front of a house. Empty shell cases littered the road. There was a deathly silence and then steam hissed from the punctured radiator and de Beauvoir jumped into his van and raced towards the two brothers.

He braked violently and shouted through the open side window. "Quickly you two, let's get out of here."

As he shouted, German *SS* soldiers appeared as if from nowhere. Charles and Roger looked around them, surprised and startled. The soldiers had emerged through the front doors of the houses along the road and they paid no heed to the occupants of the crashed car.

An Officer barked out an order. "Throw you weapons down and put your hands up."

They lowered their guns as soldiers converged on de Beauvoir's van, guns menacing him. Without a word from them he got out of the van and looked at the brothers. There was a look of resignation on his face. "Stand over there with the others," he ordered and de Beauvoir walked warily towards his friends and stood beside them, his hands in the air.

"We've been set up," de Beauvoir said. "Somebody's set us up."

"Shut up," the Officer said.

Then they heard the sound of a car approaching. It was obviously a high-ranking Officer. The car stopped a short distance away. The driver got out and opened the rear passenger door and the Officer appeared. The *SS* soldiers clicked their heels as they came to attention. The Officer acknowledged their presence with a "Heil Hitler", and then walked over to the three captives.

He looked them up and down, with disdain. "You'll all regret the day you were born," he said. "As will the rest of your Network. I am Colonel Klaus Richter. What are your names?"

They stared blankly at him, disbelieving.

"Yes," he said. "You find it hard to believe because you came here to kill *me,* but as you can see you didn't succeed. Instead you may have most probably killed General Scholtz."

"Now your names," he demanded. But they remained silent.

Richter looked at the *SS* Officer commanding the soldiers, and nodded to him. Without a word the Officer reversed his machine pistol and rammed the butt brutally into Charles's midriff. He doubled over and gasped with pain, and then the Officer brought the machine pistol upward in a violet uppercut that broke Charles's jaw and he fell to the ground unconscious.

Roger lost all reason and swearing blindly he lashed out at the Officer, but Richter had by this time drawn his pistol and he shot him through the head.

De Beauvoir was stunned and helpless with his mouth wide open, as blood poured from Roger's head. Charles lay unconscious close to his brother.

Richter glared at de Beauvoir, threatening him also with his pistol and furious for allowing his temper to get the better of him. He'd shot a member of the French Résistance, when he should have kept him alive for questioning. He knew that some of them could be persuaded to talk, and sometimes it was those who appeared to be the toughest that talked the most.

"All right," Richter said as he continued to stare menacingly at de Beauvoir. "Your time to talk will come later believe me, but there's one thing you're going to tell me right now or so help me I blow your head off right now. Captain Jacque Aveline, of the Abwehr. I know he was behind this botched attempt to kill me, but where has he bolted to? You won't mind telling me that!"

De Beauvoir looked at Richter who pointed the pistol menacingly right between his eyes. "You're right," he grimaced. "Why should I mind telling you where he's gone, because he's gone to hell where he belongs?"

Richter moved his head involuntarily and slowly lowered the pistol, surprised at what de Beauvoir had said.

"That's right," de Beauvoir continued. "He was a disgrace to France and a disgrace to his family. So there'll be no more rumours about the Butcher of Verberie. Justice has finally been done."

"How did you people know he was the Butcher?" Richter asked slowly.

"Scum like that are always found out," de Beauvoir said determined to give nothing else away.

Richter replaced his pistol in its holster and turned to the Officer. "Take these two to the Castle," he said. "And dispose of the other one."

Then he walked calmly over to the crashed car where the soldiers had forced the rear passenger door open. Richter pushed them impatiently to one side and felt for a pulse in the General's carotid artery. He saw a bullet hole in his left arm and another in his leg and blood coming from a head wound, seeping down inside his cap and onto his collar. He looked at the driver and knew immediately he was dead.

"The General's alive," he said turning to the Officer. "But the driver's dead. So you'd better get the Doctor from camp, and an ambulance. We must keep the General alive!"

Charles, who was still unconscious, and de Beauvoir were taken away. Richter waited for the Army Doctor to arrive. The Doctor who arrived was attached to the Wehrmacht and he knew General Scholtz, but not Richter.

Soldiers helped the Doctor and his medical orderlies to pull Scholtz out of the car and lay him on a blanket on the road. The Doctor examined him quickly and expertly, concentrating on the wound in his head.

He looked up at Richter who was standing with a look of almost disdain on his face. "He should really go to Paris," he said to him. "But he'd never survive the journey. There's a bullet lodged in his

174

head. Too much movement could move it and kill him. His only hope is the Cottage Hospital at Chantilly, but we'll have to hurry."

"Very well Major," Richter said. "But I'll hold *you* responsible whether the General lives or dies. Keep me informed, every day."

With that Richter walked away and Scholtz was lifted carefully into the Army field ambulance and driven to Chantilly Cottage Hospital, accompanied by the Doctor.

Richter watched as the ambulance drove away, and then he ordered his driver to bring him up the road to Madeleine Boussine's house. The driver waited in the car as Richter walked to the front door and knocked.

Madeleine answered the door and she looked stunning but she trembled when she saw Richter and then her pale face broke into a faint smile as she tried to appear welcoming. Richter smiled back benevolently, and walked past her into the house. She followed him in timidly, wringing her hands in agitation.

"You're sorry it's not Scholz," he stated, and then without waiting for an answer he said. "I'm so glad you kept me informed my dear. It's just unfortunate for the General; because I'm sure he was looking forward to a good night."

"Is ... is General Scholtz all right?" Madeleine asked quietly.

Richter walked into the front room ignoring her question. Madeleine's mother was sitting in her usual chair, staring blankly in front of her. "Not much change in the old lady," he said without even the hint of empathy.

"There's never any change," Madeleine said quietly.

"Then she'd probably be better off if she were dead," Richter said.

"NO!" Madeleine gasped.

Richter shrugged his shoulders. "And your son?"

"He's well enough."

"And he's not with you tonight?"

"I can't leave him alone with mother. A friend is looking after him."

"And who was going to look after your mother? Because I presume the good General would have taken you somewhere. Paris perhaps?"

Madeleine sighed. "Mother won't come to any harm on her own," she said struggling to contain the tremor in her voice. "Hardly anybody will help me," she said. "You know what they call me Karl?"

"I can imagine," Richter said smiling.

"I hear them," she said. "Behind my back, wherever I go in the town. It's always in a whisper when I walk past them, but loud enough for me to hear. 'There's that Nazi loving whore', they say."

Richter looked around him as if he hadn't heard. "Scholtz won't bother you any more my dear. You're all mine now. No more sharing. And as for these people who seem to annoy you." He hesitated. "Point them out to me, give me their names and it won't happen again."

Madeleine gasped. "No, no it's all right, but is … is he dead?"

"Not quite," Richter said. "But don't give Scholtz a second thought," he added coldly. "That's an order. He was a traitor to Germany so forget him. He's history now. And as for the scum that taunts you, their day will come, believe me."

Madeleine walked quietly over to her mother and pulled the black shawl up around her shoulders and patted her gently on the hand.

"I just need to get her to bed," she said quietly. "She'll be all right there."

"In a minute," Richter said, pulling Madeleine towards him. "Tell me what's been happening behind my back?"

"Nothing Karl; honestly. I … I saw General Scholtz at the Hotel du Parc where I work. I asked *him* to come and see me tonight just like you told me to."

The words spilled out of her as she tried to understand what was happening and why Richter was questioning her.

"You haven't quite told me everything Madeleine," Richter said threateningly. "There's the little matter of Captain Jacque Aveline, of the Abwehr."

He put his black-gloved hand out, cupping Madeleine's chin, gripping her tightly. "Why didn't you tell me about Aveline before?"

Madeleine tried to speak and then he released his grip on her. "I couldn't," she said with tears in her eyes. "He threatened me, and said he would tell General Scholtz that I was seeing you, and I knew that would displease you."

"And what had you to do in return?"

"Nothing. He just wanted to know when I would see you and General Scholtz. I've told you that already Karl. And … and he promised to help Jean, and he did. He brought me a letter from him and a photograph, and Jean looked happy and … and I was happy as well. Karl I hate this War."

"And didn't *I* say I would look after your husband?"

"Yes you did, but I wasn't sure what to do and Jacque promised to help Jean as well and I believed him. I thought he could do more and Jean was moved to another camp, a better one. That was good wasn't it?"

"Did you sleep with *him* Madeleine?" Richter demanded to know. There was suppressed anger in his voice. "Is that how you paid him for looking after your husband?"

"No I swear I didn't, it wasn't like that." She stopped and sighed. "He came in and asked where my son was. I didn't want to tell him, but he saw him anyway and picked him up when he was sleeping. I just knew by him. He was threatening to do something to him if I didn't co-operate. He was evil. And he gave me money"

"Very well," Richter said. "You should have told me nonetheless. But what's done is done. Now why did you suddenly decide to tell me Aveline was asking questions about my movements?"

Madeleine quivered involuntarily. She was terrified of saying the wrong thing and putting her son or her husband's life in even more danger than they were already in. It didn't occur to her that her own life might be in danger.

"The truth," Richter said. "Tell me the truth and I promise nothing will happen to you, but if you lie …!"

"He told me that you wouldn't be here after tonight, and that you wouldn't be able to touch Jean or my boy ever again. I … I believed him, but when I thought about it I was worried. What if something happened to you and he *didn't* look after Jean? I trusted you Karl, that's why I told you."

"Hmm," Richter mumbled. "Perhaps you're telling the truth, we'll see. But you'll be glad to know that not only will you not see Scholtz again, you'll not see Aveline either."

"Has ... has something happened to him Karl?" Madeleine whispered.

"Yes," Richter said. "As a matter of fact it has. The Résistance have done me a favour in a way. They've killed him. Pity really, I did so want to question him."

Then Richter shrugged his shoulders. "Enough of this, it's beginning to bore me my dear. Why don't you get the old lady off to bed, then as you were going to give the General a good time, you can give me a good time instead?

Chapter twenty three

Although it was only a small Cottage Hospital the staff there, were used to serious casualties, most of whom victims of the War. The Hospital's theatre was a fairly basic affair, but adequate for emergencies. Nurses and orderlies were drawn from wherever they could be spared and local Doctors operated a rota system, doubling up as anaesthetists or surgeons whenever the need arose.

Scholtz was taken from the ambulance and transferred to a stretcher and wheeled to theatre, where Andrea Aveline stood with some others at the door, waiting to see the casualty arrive. The German Army Doctor and his orderly rushed ahead of the stretcher. Scholtz was unconscious and his uniform was covered in blood.

"Make way," the Doctor called out. "Give us room."

The orderly brushed past the onlookers, as they stood back at the Doctor's command, and followed him. The stretcher was then wheeled into theatre without anyone knowing that the casualty was Scholtz. Then Andrea noticed the uniform and recognised it was that of a General. She peered after the stretcher and just as the door closed she caught a glimpse of Scholtz's face, grey and blood stained.

Andrea turned away and she felt the blood draining from her face. "Are *you* all right?" A colleague asked.

Andrea shook her head. "I'm feeling faint," she said. "I'd better go and sit down."

She left the theatre, her mind in turmoil, not knowing what to believe. Then on a sudden impulse she contacted a senior member of staff not involved with the casualty, and told them she was sick and had to go home.

Although she had walked to work, she borrowed a bicycle and cycled home. She was breathless when she arrived and her mother looked at her anxiously when she walked into the room.

"Andrea what's happened?" her mother asked. What's wrong? I wasn't expecting you."

Andrea pulled the scarf off her head. "I don't know," she said. "Maybe nothing, but we've got to contact Simone."

"But you can't, not now Andrea. The Germans will be everywhere and Simone won't go home, at least not tonight. He'll stay at the farm with Charles and Roger."

"Then I'll have to go there and wait for them," Andrea said. "I'll be back when I can."

Her mother put out her hand and stopped her. "Not until you tell me what's going on."

Andrea sighed. "It's maybe nothing mother, but General Scholtz has been ambushed and shot. He's critically ill in Hospital."

"But it should have been Colonel Richter," her mother said. Then they looked at each other as if the sudden realisation of something had dawned on them at the same time.

"It must have been Jacque," they said in unison.

"He convinced us he was telling the truth," Andrea's mother said. "He told us Richter would be going to see that woman in Chantilly tonight. But why? What had he to gain by having the General killed instead of Richter?"

"We don't know mother," Andrea said. "Maybe we'll never know. That's why I've got to see Simone immediately. They may have fallen into a trap."

"Andrea dear, please be careful," her mother said.

"I'll be all right," she said. "Tell father for me."

Andrea left immediately and cycled to the farmhouse. When she got there it was deserted. She thrust her hands into her pockets and paced about the farm kitchen, deep in thought. Every now and then she peered out into the night. She listened at the door for the faintest sound of someone coming. As time went by an awful feeling of dread came over her. When two hours had passed she left the farmhouse and cycled home.

As she approached the driveway to the Château she heard unfamiliar sounds and slowed down. She dismounted and hid the bicycle in the ditch and approached the house from over the boundary wall. She heard voices in German and the sound of vehicles. Then

180

she was able to see through the trees, just in time to watch her mother being dragged out of the house. She could see she was bleeding from a wound to her head. Then her father was dragged out, his feet trailing on the ground. He appeared to be unconscious.

Andrea bit on her hand to stop herself from crying out. She had to force herself to stop running forward screaming at them to leave her parents alone. Her mother was forced to climb into the back of an Army truck and her father was dragged to it and thrown in by two soldiers.

Andrea watched with horror as the scene they'd always dreaded unfolded before them. The Network had suddenly and unexpectedly been torn apart. She stood transfixed as the soldiers climbed into their vehicles and drove away.

She stood for ages in the dark of the night, shivering in the cold, waiting to see if there was any movement from the house but it was deadly quiet. Then she gasped as she remembered Gary Tucker. Dread filled her mind as she realised that he must be either dead or by some miracle have avoided detection.

Eventually she made her way cautiously to the house with a pistol in her hand. The front door had been left lying open and she stepped inside. Her heart was pounding as she stood inside listening for the faintest sound. There was nothing but an eerie silence. She realised straight away that the house had been ransacked.

Tables and chairs had been overturned and pictures torn from the walls. The grandfather clock, a favourite of her father's, lay smashed on the ground. Drawers were pulled out everywhere and the contents scattered on the floor. As she looked around her at the devastation she blamed her brother Jacque, and wished above anything that he were still alive so that one day he would face true justice.

Fearful of what she would find, she made her way up the stairs, careful not to make a sound. She looked down the corridor, dreading what she might find, and expecting to see Gary Tucker's body lying dead in his room or lying in the corridor. As her eyes became accustomed to the darkness she could see the bookcase at the end of the corridor had been pulled away. The door to the secret hideaway was lying open and the room was bare.

It was then that she realised Tucker must have been brought down before her mother. That he'd been put in one of the vehicles first. Suddenly she felt dreadfully alone and fearful. In one fell swoop her family had been wiped out. She was now destitute with nowhere to go. She held out no hope at all for their rescue because she knew only too well what the Gestapo would do. She prayed they would not suffer but knew from all the stories she's heard that that was a forlorn hope.

She came down the stairs slowly, deep in thought, and praying for her family. Then she remembered the radio. It was just possible it had not have been found. The radio above everything else was well hidden. She made her way in the darkness down into the wine cellar. There she found a candle and lit it. She heaved a sigh of relief when she saw the crate of wine bottles exactly where it always was.

She pulled it to one side and using the iron bar hidden in the cellar she lifted up the stone slab to reveal the radio. She breathed another sigh of relief as she lifted it out and brought it upstairs. She used the candle for light to switch it on to contact London.

Chapter twenty four

A radio operator was standing by waiting for a call from the Doctor's Network to confirm that Operation 'Midnight' had been successfully completed. The Major was in his room smoking a cigar. He tried to appear calm but Jay Bee, sitting opposite him, could see he was anxious. She was getting worried herself because the call should have come through hours ago. Even though they knew full well that Operations like 'Midnight' didn't always go to plan, both the Major and Jay Bee had a feeling things were not right.

The Major got up from his desk, paced up and down a couple of times and then went into the radio room. Jay Bee shook her head slowly. She was getting really worried. The Major looked across at the radio operator. He shook his head, looking as glum as the Major, who turned around to walk away when the operator called out. "There's something coming, sir."

He began taking down the message. "It's not coded sir. There's something wrong."

Slowly the message came to life as the Major and now Jay Bee peered down at what the operator was writing. The message read.

Scholtz ambushed and shot. Repeat. Scholtz ambushed and shot. Critically ill. Richter presumed alive. Marie and Anton Aveline arrested. Pilot Officer Gary Tucker presumed arrested. Whereabouts of others unknown, presumed arrested or shot. End of message.

"Damn," the Major said. "What an appalling tragedy. The Prime Minister will be furious. After all the planning and everything was just about ready. This is an unmitigated disaster. If this had gone right we could have shortened the War by months. Who knows? Now it's all for nothing."

He had barely finished when the operator said. "There's more sir."

The Major and Jay Bee bent down eagerly to get the next message. The operator wrote again.

Message for Jay Bee. Other half of French Franc note available.
Await instructions. End of message.

"What the blazes is that Jay Bee?" the Major asked.

Jay Bee's face lit up. "It's Andrea, the Aveline's daughter. She's OK. The Germans haven't caught her."

"Have they not by jove?" the Major said. "What do you make of that Jay Bee?"

"Andrea was obviously not involved or in the vicinity of the ambush, and somehow she's got to their radio. We can only assume anything else."

The Major turned to the radio operator. "Send this." 'Message received and understood. Stand by one hour from now for instructions.' End of message. Jay Bee.'

He turned to Jay Bee. "My office; now Jay Bee."

Jay Bee followed the Major as he strode quickly to his office. He closed the door behind her and shut it. "Take a seat Jay Bee."

Jay Bee sat down. "Can we help sir?" she asked. "And can I still go over?"

The Major took a cigar - one of Churchill's - and lit it and blew a cloud of smoke into the air. After a long pause he put the cigar down.

"That's something I'll need to think on Jay Bee, at the minute I believe it's far too dangerous. But there's something you had better know," he said. "Winston forbade me to tell anyone, so damned dangerous you understand. If anybody got wind of it they'd hang Winston for treason and we could lose the War over the head of it. Goodness knows who would take over from him."

He paused. "You understand Jay Bee. If Winston mentions this to you, you know nothing. He's paranoid about it, and he's probably right, but he's going to need you."

"I understand sir."

"Now I know full well he gives you instructions when you're going to France, which I know nothing about. And I know you're sworn to secrecy, but if you get anything from him that impinges directly on

184

this affair it's vital you tell me. He plays his cards far too close to his chest for his own good. This secret circle's all very well, but it has its limits."

"But sir, with all due respect, the Prime Minister couldn't run it without *you*. He knows that. We all report to you, so why does he not trust you with everything?"

The Major smiled. "He always likes to keep something up his sleeve. He likes to surprise me now and again." He paused again, looking very serious.

"When Hess took that seemingly crazy flight to Britain, nobody took him seriously. The German high command said he was mad. Point of fact we were all just glad to have one Nazi nut case out of the way. What we didn't know was that Winston knew all about it before it happened. Admiral Canaris decided at the outbreak of the War not to have all his eggs in one basket. He knew Hess and realised he had serious ambitions for himself, but he also knew Hess had grave misgivings about Hitler and the Nazi's ability to win a World War. Canaris had the same misgivings. The upshot was that both Canaris and Hess were conniving under Hitler's very nose. It was Canaris who persuaded Hess to embark on his crazy flight to Britain. Winston had agreed to meet Hess if he arrived safely, which of course he did. Winston kept his side of the bargain and met him. Of course nobody, and I mean nobody, but two other people know of that meeting. I'm one of them. We believe Hess knows the names of high-ranking Officers in the Wehrmacht who would be willing to support a revolt against Hitler and his henchmen. But the only name Hess gave us is General Scholtz and we are convinced he holds the whole thing together. Now the idea was that Scholtz was to be given an absolute assurance that Britain would support other Officers, in the event of such a revolt. There would have been diversionary raids and all manner of things, to create the right environment for the Officers to bring it off. However, quite naturally the Germans were not willing to put their own necks on the line, without a pretty good idea that it *would* come off. That's where Winston really stuck his neck out. He gave an assurance to Canaris and Scholtz that if Hess travelled to

Britain to prove his credibility, then Winston would travel, when the time was considered right, to France, and meet the German Officers in person to prove *he* was serious."

"That's a desperate plan sir. Could he have pulled it off? I mean would the Prime Minister *really* have gone to France?" Jay Bee asked.

"Would he by jove? He jolly well would and guess who'd have gone with him?"

"You sir?"

"The point is Jay Bee, it could still happen. A lot depends on your friend Andrea. We've got to know if Scholtz is alive, and if he's critically ill. Somebody must have suspected him, or else Richter is settling an old score, but we need to know. And if Scholtz is alive and capable of recovering we have either to rescue him or kill him. Can't have him talking or they'd get the names of the other Officers involved and we might have a use for them yet. If Scholtz dies there just might be another to take his place. And there's also Gary Tucker. He knows too much about our Operation here. We've got to get him out or …"

"Make sure he doesn't talk sir!"

"Exactly Jay Bee, and there are some friends of yours as well if any of them are alive. They were a good bunch."

"What do you suggest sir?"

"Radio your friend Andrea, and tell her it's imperative she finds out about Scholtz and also where Gary Tucker is being held, along with any others. And she must find out who survived. Tell her we must get that information quickly. In the mean time I'll try one or two other contacts to see what we can find out. We might even be able to get a message to Canaris. He'll be gutted if this thing goes up in the air, especially when Scholtz could implicate him."

The Major paused, deep in thought. He picked up his cigar and drawing heavily on it blew another cloud of smoke into the air. "If we can find out where these people are there's someone who just might be able to pull of a daring raid and release them."

"Might I ask who you have in mind sir?"

"Of course; Lieutenant Colonel Blair 'Paddy' Mayne. 1 Special Air Service Regiment."

"Don't know him sir.

"You will Jay Bee. I've a funny feeling you will. Now there's one other thing for you to do. When you've radioed Andrea, get in touch with your French Lieutenant. We might need him as well. I'll go and talk to Winston and tell him the bad news. And keep me informed."

Jay Bee returned to the radio room where she whiled away the time until she was ready to send another message to Andrea.

Chapter twenty five

After she had sent her last message from the darkness of her own home, Andrea switched the radio off to conserve the battery, and blew the candle out and sat very still. Beads of sweat had broken out on her forehead and she had an aching feeling in the pit of her stomach. She wasn't sure where to turn, and just hoped against hope that something positive would come out of her message to London.

She checked the time and then made a snap decision. She packed the radio in a case and then gathered a few clothes and other necessities including food, all of which, apart from the radio she put into a rucksack. She also brought candles and matches. She put the case on the carrier of her bicycle and with the rucksack on her shoulder she cycled off towards the old farmhouse.

It took her longer than she expected to get there and it was past the time for her radio message from London. She was not overly anxious as she quickly unpacked the radio, knowing that London would keep trying for a reasonable length of time until they made contact.

She lit a candle and put the radio on the kitchen table and switched it on and waited.

Back in London Jay Bee stood anxiously beside the radio operator as she tried for the fourth time to make contact. When she got through, Andrea acknowledged her call and prepared to take the message.

As always the message was as short as possible.

Andrea scribbled the message on a scrap of paper.

Keep money safe. Further deposit may be imminent. Essential inform whereabouts and condition of General, Doctors and pilot. Most urgent. Jay Bee.

Andrea acknowledged the message and then looked at the notes she had scribbled and she was cheered slightly. The money could only refer to the torn French Franc note Josephine had given to her on her first meeting, and a further deposit could only mean Josephine, or somebody else was going to make contact, and possibly soon. She did not know how she was going to get the information London wanted, but she was determined to get it.

She packed the radio away and hid it. Then she uncorked a bottle of wine and drank it with bread and cheese. She thought hard as she munched her way through the bread.

The Major was by then having a private audience with Winston Churchill. He had informed Churchill of the recent developments, and he watched as Churchill descended into one of his black moods. He had said very little, and then he lifted a bottle of whiskey and poured some into a glass. He lit a cigar but he was preoccupied as he stared into space and forgot the Major was in the room with him.

After a while he turned to the Major. "I'd high hopes for this mission Jack," he said gruffly. "Is it dead in the water?"

"Not yet sir," the Major said. "If Scholtz is dead or unconscious he can't tell the Germans anything. A lot will depend on his condition."

"So what's the plan?"

"It depends on Scholtz. We either rescue him, or kill him. No point risking lives on a man who may never recover. Once we've established how he is then we can act, but if he's out of action, we'll contact Canaris and see if he's willing and able to carry on without Scholtz."

Churchill looked glum. "And is this Aveline girl the only contact we have, now that the Network's been rumbled?"

"Not quite sir. We still have Roger Balfour, I mentioned him to you before. He heads up quite a successful Network not far from Chantilly. They call themselves the Baker's Dozen. He's SOE, a good man and reliable, and been there almost from the beginning. He's lost some volunteers, not many, and the last time we were in touch he was back up to strength again. If Andrea Aveline can't get the information we want, he could be the right man."

"Better get on to it then," Churchill said. "In case this Aveline girl is rumbled. And you'd better let her know we're involving the Baker's Dozen."

The Major returned to the Radio Operations room and left instructions for Balfour to be contacted as a matter of urgency, whilst he snatched a few hours sleep.

The Baker's Dozen had retired well into the forest where they waited until they knew what had become of Jacque and Nina. There was relief and no recrimination when Debré appeared and explained what had happened. The group relaxed their vigil, when it was clear there was no reason to expect the Germans to come looking for them.

A fire was lit and the men settled down for the rest of the night. Roger Balfour lay awake, wondering to himself about the events that had happened. He was still awake when the radio came alive. He moved away from the others so as not to disturb their much-needed rest and noted the message from London.

The message read:

Most urgent you establish whereabouts and condition of General Scholtz ambushed near Chantilly. Also Anton Aveline and wife Marie and British pilot Gary Tucker. Aveline's daughter has also been contacted. Repeat most urgent. Major.

Balfour replied:

Message understood.

Andrea was also sent a message letting her know that the Baker's Dozen had been contacted. Despite several attempts she did not receive the message.

Balfour looked around him, conscious of the cool night air. Everyone, including Debré, was sleeping, but when London said 'most urgent', he knew it meant immediately. He stepped quietly over to Debré and shook his shoulder. Debré wakened immediately. Balfour motioned to him to get up and follow him to where no one would hear him if they wakened. He explained the situation to Debré and then scribbled a short note and left it where the others would see it.

They walked through the trees to where Debré had left the motorcycle, and after pushing it out of hearing, Debré kick-started it and they rode through the forest and into the clearing, where Jacque and Nina had been held. Debré then followed the same route to the main road.

They drove without lights towards the Château Aveline.

Andrea had meanwhile found blankets in the deserted farmhouse, and wrapped them around her. She lay down to sleep before she acted on Jay Bee's instructions. She only dozed lightly because her mind was in turmoil, and she couldn't stop going over everything that had happened, again and again. Suddenly she sat bolt upright. She remembered the torn French Franc note. She'd left it in the Château, and without it, whoever came across from England, might not trust her. She knew she would have to retrieve it before daylight because after that she wouldn't dare return to the Château.

She shook blankets off and went out into the cold night air, and rode off on her bicycle to the Château. Everything was as she had left it a short while ago, but there was an eerie feel about the place. It felt violated, that as if it had a heart it would cry out that it had been raped. Andrea shivered as she left her bicycle against the wall and walked into the hallway. Her heart was racing and a cold sweat broke out on her forehead as she walked quietly up the stairs to her room.

She felt the cold more than she did outside. She pushed the door of her bedroom open and walked to her bedside locker and pulled out a drawer. She turned the drawer over. The torn French Franc note was fastened to the bottom of the drawer with a drawing pin. She removed it and put it in her bag.

Then breathing a sigh of relief she made her way down stairs again and outside. She was careful to leave the door open; the way the Germans had left it. She was certain they would take the Château over and billet Officers in it. Maybe, she thought, even Richter. The thought of it sent shivers up her spine.

She reached for her bicycle, when suddenly from nowhere, a hand grasped her arm and another hand fastened over her mouth. She tried to scream and kick but Debré held her firmly.

Balfour then appeared. He saw the terrified look in Andrea's eyes and reached out his hand and grasping Debré's wrist, pulled it forcibly from Andrea's mouth. "It's OK," he said, at the same time. "I'm a friend of your father; we're from the Baker's Dozen."

The fear left her eyes as Debré relaxed his grip. "Sorry," Debré muttered

"Who are you then," Andrea asked, gasping for breath as she looked at Balfour.

"I'm Roger Balfour," he said. "And this is Francois Debré; his real name's Desjardine."

Debré nodded.

"Are you anything to the Desjardines of Verberie?"

Debré looked at Balfour who shook his head. "Another time Andrea," he said. "We've business to attend to and I'm not sure this is a safe place to discuss it."

He began to move away but then turned to Andrea. "You must have food, coffee and wine in the house? Will you gather up what you can and put it in a bag or something? Every little helps."

"Of course," Andrea said and she went back into the house. She returned a short while later with two pillowcases stuffed with food and wine.

Balfour led the way down the driveway where the motorbike was hidden behind the wall. "We'll have to double up on this thing," Balfour said. "It's the only way."

Andrea didn't ask questions as she climbed on the motorbike between Debré and Balfour. Debré had one pillowcase resting on the petrol tank and Balfour hung onto the other one. It was a cold and uncomfortable ride back to the Baker's Dozen camp. Before they reached the camp they had to push the motorbike the last mile because they ran out of petrol. Andrea walked behind carrying one of the pillowcases while the other two pushed.

Nobody had stirred since they left and there were still red embers glowing from the fire. Debré threw some sticks on it and then a few logs. He put a can of water on the fire for coffee and sat poking the fire with his knife to bring it quickly to life. Andrea stood watching for a moment and then sat down and warmed herself. Balfour went into the trees to relieve himself.

She looked at Debré who seemed lost in thought. "You *are* connected to that family," she said.

Debré nodded. "I'm the only survivor; everyone thought I'd been killed. But no, I survived. I've been on the run, hiding from the Germans ever since."

"That's been tough for you, but how did you come to join the Baker's Dozen?"

"It was just by accident. I chose to hide here after stealing a German half-track. These people came on me when I was asleep." He gave a slight laugh. "Thankfully it was them and not the Germans or you wouldn't be talking to me now."

"So were you involved in abducting my brother Jacque?"

"He was your brother? Roger never said." Debré looked around frantically for Balfour.

"What's wrong?" Andrea asked.

Debré ignored her. "Where's Roger?" he half whispered, trying not to waken the others.

Andrea reached out and grasped Debré's arm and forced him to look at her. "Why don't you answer me Francois? What's to hide?"

Just then, much to Debré's relief, Balfour came out of the trees, still adjusting his trousers. Debré stood up and walked towards him, and Andrea followed.

"She doesn't know," Debré said. "She doesn't know about her brother."

"What don't I know? Will somebody please tell me?"

Balfour took her by the arm and they sat by the fire again. Debré poured coffee and handed each of them a mug.

"You know your father asked us to abduct your brother?"

Andrea nodded.

"We didn't ask why. It was enough that your father asked, but there was a slight problem because your brother's girl friend warned him we were coming."

"That was Nina," Andrea said. "Foolish girl; and after all my parents did for her."

"Well only for Francois I doubt we'd be talking now because she very nearly succeeded. However your brother's driver was killed and we took you brother back here to keep him out of harm's way, until arrangements were made to fly him to London. During the night he appears to have overcome the guard and killed him, and he and the girl escaped."

"But that's terrible," Andrea said. "He knows too much. We stay here; we've got to leave."

Balfour looked at Andrea and even in the dim light she could see he was trying to tell her something without speaking.

"Are you trying to tell me you've caught Jacque again? Is that what it is?"

Balfour shook his head. "There's no easy way to tell you this. Your brother and the girl got clean away, but they were on foot, and when it was realised what had happened, Francois went after them on the motorbike. Your brother put up a fight. The girl was accidentally shot dead and your brother fell over the edge of a quarry. I'm afraid he's dead."

Andrea was quiet for a moment. She looked up at Debré. "Couldn't you have saved him?"

Debré looked at Balfour and then walked away, holding his head in his hands.

"I'm afraid there's more Andrea," Balfour said.

Andrea looked puzzled. "More?"

Balfour took a deep breath. "You've heard of the Butcher of Verberie?"

"Who hasn't? He's an animal."

Balfour put his hand on Andrea's arm and squeezed it. "Andrea," he said quietly. "I'm afraid your brother was the Butcher of Verberie."

Andrea gasped. "NO, he wouldn't."

"Francois was there Andrea. He witnessed the whole thing, and it's a miracle he escaped. He has the proof. I'm so sorry."

194

"You mean Francois saw his own family butchered, and it was my brother who did it?"

"I'm afraid so. We'd still have sent him to London if we could, but in the end perhaps what happened was for the best."

Andrea felt numb but in a strange way she also felt relief. "If my parents come out of this I don't want them to know. Is that possible?"

"It must have been awful for you," Andrea said. "I'm so sorry it had to be my brother."

"There would be nothing to gain," Debre said. "It's best forgotten. Debré nodded.

"Listen," Balfour said. "I've had a message from London. I don't know what it's about but your people have got themselves into a bit of a mess, and they need information urgently."

"Yes I know," Andrea said. "They've been in touch with me also. I don't know where to turn and I don't know whom the Germans have caught, except I saw them taking my parents and I think they must have taken a British airman as well."

"What happened?"

"The Doctor's Network, were told by my brother Jacque that we'd to assassinate a German Colonel by the name of Richter. He said he was following orders from the Abwehr whom he worked for as a special agent or something. He implied that a friend of our family, a General Scholtz was in grave danger from Richter, and that if Richter wasn't killed, then Scholtz's life was in danger."

"This General Scholtz; who's he?"

"My father saved his life and he's been indebted to him ever since. He visits us and of course the locals know that. As a result they tend to shun us. I believe they think we're collaborators, but that suits because it means neither the Germans nor the locals would ever imagine we were involved in the Résistance. So naturally we wanted to protect him because by so doing we were also protecting ourselves.

"Go on."

"We were concerned at Jacque,s involvement and the fact that he'd found out about our connection with the Résistance, so we contacted London. It was a strange twist of fate, because London knew about

General Scholtz through one of their agents whom I've met, but they insisted we kill Richter."

"And you don't have any idea why London was behind this as well as the Abwehr?"

"Absolutely none."

"We set up an ambush based on information my brother gave us about Richter's movements. I'm convinced my brother told us the truth, but something went wrong, and instead of Richter being killed, it was General Scholtz who was caught up in the ambush. He's in Chantilly Cottage Hospital but I don't know if he's badly injured."

Balfour sighed. "That's one of the things London needs to know, as well as the whereabouts of your parents."

"They'll have taken my parents to the Army camp at Chantilly and maybe later to Paris."

Andrea caught her breath. "I can't bear to think about it. They do terrible things to people. We've got to do something. Can you help?"

Balfour looked at Andrea, catching her beauty in the flickering light of the fire. He felt sorry for her and the plight of her family. He knew it had happened so many times to other families. He sipped the coffee that had gone cold.

"I'm so sorry this has happened to your family?" he said.

"Thank you," Andrea replied quietly. "Someone must have talked and ...." Unable to control the tears any longer Andrea collapsed into Balfour's arms.

He held her for a while as she cried bitterly with great sobs that wracked her body. After what seemed like ages she began to calm down and Balfour slowly released his hold on her.

"Who else was involved in the ambush?" He asked her then. "And do you know what has happened to them?" Balfour asked.

"There were three people. We thought it was a simple enough Operation. Charles and Roger Bayard, they're farmers, and they were to carry out the gun attack and Simone de Beauvoir, the schoolmaster was to provide transport. One of our other members had left a van at the scene the night before. But he was not supposed to be there at the time of the attack. There shouldn't have been anybody else. If they were able, they'd have come to the farmhouse afterwards, but they didn't show up, so the Germans must have shot them or captured them."

"And the farmhouse?"

"It's where we meet to discuss Operations. It's derelict," Andrea assured him.

"Could your brother have known who all was in your Circuit Andrea?" Balfour asked.

"That's not possible," Andrea said. "He got some information from Nina, but she didn't know the names of everyone."

"I take it that it's reasonable to assume Inspector Marius Regnier is part of your Circuit," Balfour asked.

"Yes he is," Andrea confirmed.

"In that case, if he's still in the clear, he might be our best way of getting the information we need. But it's essential he be warned of what has happened in case he doesn't know. If anyone in your Circuit gives the Germans the names of the others the Gestapo will arrest them. That is if they haven't gone into hiding. They must be informed immediately."

Andrea shook her head. "No they wouldn't," she said.

Balfour looked kindly into Andrea's face. "Andrea very few people can survive what the Gestapo do without breaking. We've to assume it's possible, even likely."

"But it's not Roger," Andrea insisted. "All of us carry suicide pills, you know that. Every one of us would take one rather than tell the Germans anything."

Balfour looked up at Debré and gave a half nod of his head. Debré circled around behind Andrea as she looked with faint surprise in her eyes. Suddenly Debré crouched behind her and pinned her arms by her side. She cried out. "What are you doing?"

"Take your pill now Andrea!" Balfour said.

Andrea bowed her head and sobbed.

"I know it's a harsh fact Andrea," Balfour said. "But it's not always possible; the Gestapo know that many of us carry suicide pills, including myself."

"He's right," Debré said. "We've to assume that somebody will talk, and that means we must warn the rest."

"Somebody has to contact Marius, and if he's not there Andrea, who would you suggest?" Balfour asked.

Andrea stood up. "The best person then would be Father Michael," she said slowly. He's incredibly brave, and very careful."

"I know Father Michael," Balfour said. "He's a good man. But I didn't know he was in the Resistance. We'll try and contact both of them and ask them to get whatever information they can, and also warn them of the danger they're in. Now," and he turned to Debré. "They've slept long enough. Get the rest of them up Francois and then put petrol in that motorbike. We'll have to move quickly before daylight."

Chapter twenty six

Daylight was just breaking when Debré left two men on the outskirts of Chantilly. One of them made his way to Father Michael de Bourbon's Chapel. The Chapel door was never closed and he walked in quietly.

A candle was flickering inside the door, and an old lady sat hunched up on a pew at the front. She'd pulled a shawl tightly round her for warmth, in the clammy coldness of the Chapel. The old woman fidgeted with her rosary beads as the man took a candle and lit it and placed it beside the other. He put some coins into a collection box, crossed himself and walked down the side isle.

The confessional was dark and foreboding and set against the right hand side of the Chapel, near the front. The man walked slowly towards it, hesitated and then opened the door and stepped in. He pulled his coat around him and sat on the wooden bench and waited.

The other man had taken a lift with a farmer and his horse and cart as it wound its way into the market area of Chantilly. The farmer didn't ask any questions as the man simply jumped up beside him. It didn't do to ask question at that time in France. Near the market place the man nodded his thanks and slipped off the cart, to make his way to the Police Station.

The centre of town was quiet and just beginning to come to life. In the distance a train whistle shrilled loudly as the train pulled into the Station. A small convoy of German Army vehicles made its way through the town. The man picked a paper up from a corner shop. It was days out of date but he tucked it under his arm as he walked to the Police Station.

Although the door was ajar there was nobody at the counter, so he opened the paper, and leaning against the counter he began to read. It was full of German propaganda with fanciful claims of how the Germans were winning the War. The man hardly took in what he was reading, but was all the time watching.

Then he heard someone cough and he knocked on the counter and Inspector Marius Regnier appeared. He looked tired, and there was a worried frown on his pale face.

"Yes," he said. "Can I help you?"

The man looked around him quickly. "Are we alone?"

The Inspector nodded.

"The Operation last night was not a success," the man said.

"Operation?" The Inspector said cautiously.

"I've come from Andrea Aveline," the man said. "Colonel Richter's still alive. Scholtz was ambushed instead and he's in Hospital. Charles and Roger Bayard and Simone de Beauvoir are either dead or captured. Andrea's parents and possibly a British pilot have also been taken."

The Inspector appeared unconcerned. "I know some of the people you mentioned," he said. "But why are you telling me? The Germans will deal with any incident such as you describe, it's not a Police matter."

"Listen to me," the man said. "I'm telling you for your own good. I know you're part of the Doctor Network and there's no time for this pretence. Right now my colleague is informing Father Michael, and we need your help and the Father's."

The Inspector appeared to relax. "One can't be too careful," he said.

"I'm aware of that," the man retorted. "But London urgently needs information. They must know the condition of General Scholtz and who of the others are alive, and where they are being held. As for yourself and the Father, you don't need me to tell you what will happen if one of them talks. It won't be safe for you here. And if you're taken alive you'll talk also, as will the Father."

The Inspector smiled, "Not everybody breaks under the Gestapo."

"That's as may be," the man retorted. "But which of us knows who'll break? You must leave Inspector, for everybody's sake while you have the chance, and bring Father Michael with you."

"Father Michael will not leave his flock."

"But don't you realise he may be taken and tortured and then other's lives will be put at risk?"

The Inspector smiled again. "Yes I do," he said. "And I'll try to persuade him, but he'll not go, and he'll not talk."

"Very well then," the man said finally. "You must look out for yourself. But can you get that information before it's too late?"

"Can you meet me at the Chapel then in, say one hour's time?"

"I'll do my best," the Inspector said. "Father Michael has somewhere he can hide you in case there's a search. If I'm delayed don't be alarmed."

The man nodded. "Thanks," he said. "I'd better go."

He walked a mile to the Chapel, taking care to stick to the side roads. There was more activity on them as people gathered for market day. The man came to the end of a narrow side road, which led onto the main road leading to the Chapel. It was only a short distance from there, and he waited until a group of people passed in the right direction and then he joined them. He broke away from them as they passed the Chapel and walked briskly into it.

Like his colleague he took a candle and lit it and then walked up the isle, and sat on a pew at the front and waited.

Father Michael came out of the Sacristy. He was in his early thirties, tall and well built. His face was rugged and he had melancholy blue eyes and bushy eyebrows. He looked at the man in the front pew, who sat with his head bowed in an attitude of prayer.

Father Michael looked around him and then spoke to the man in a quiet authoritative voice. "You must be Gaston Bidault?"

Bidault stood up and nodded. "Your friend Georges is through here," he said. "Please follow me."

Bidault followed the priest, looking cautiously behind him as he did. The priest led the way into the Sacristy where a stone slab had been removed from the floor.

"Georges is waiting down there," the priest said. "If the Germans arrest me I've told him how to get out. But if you have to escape that way, you must wait until darkness."

"We don't have that long," Bidault said.

"It's all I can offer," the Priest said. "I can't risk this escape route being discovered by the Germans. If I'm taken there's someone else can make use of it."

"But what about you?" Bidault asked. "We can't risk your being captured. I told the Inspector that."

The Priest smiled. "And what did he say?"

"That you wouldn't go into hiding."

"He's right. I've a flock to look after. A shepherd can't look after his sheep if he's not with them."

"But if the Germans arrest you, you won't be with them."

The Priest smiled again. "If I go into hiding, they'll say I've deserted them in their hour of need. If I'm arrested they'll band together even more to fight the Germans. I won't let them down."

"But Father," Bidault protested.

The priest shrugged his shoulders. "Please wait down there. I'll come to you as soon as I can. But in the mean time I must replace the slab. You'll have light enough."

"Very well," Bidault said. "The Inspector said he would try and get here within the hour."

"I shall look out for him," the Priest said.

Bidault walked down the stone steps into an underground passageway. An oil lamp on the wall gave enough light as he heard the stone slab being replaced. He followed the passageway for a short distance and then he heard Georges Billoux call his name.

"Down here," Billoux called in a low voice.

Billoux was in a small room, which had been carved out of solid rock. There was nothing in it except a light on the wall.

"Damn cold," Billoux said as he smiled at Bidault.

"You can say that again Gaston; still better safe than sorry."

Bidault pulled the collar of his coat around his neck and put his hands into his pockets, his shoulders hunched. "So did the Priest know anything Georges?"

Billoux shivered. "He knows the ambush went wrong, but nothing else. He was waiting to hear."

"So it's down to the Inspector then," Bidault said.

"Afraid so,"

They waited in the cold underground cavern for over an hour and a half before they sighed with relief when they heard the sound of the stone slab being dragged away. A dim shaft of light penetrated the semi-darkness as they walked towards it.

"You can come up now," the Priest said.

The Inspector was standing alone in the Sacristy. "Father Michael is attending to things in the Chapel," he said.

"What have you found out?" Bidault asked.

"Enough," the Inspector said. "General Scholtz is critically ill and he may not regain consciousness. He certainly won't be moved from the Cottage Hospital, unless someone wants to finish him off in the process."

"But nevertheless he may regain consciousness?" Billoux asked, seeking some confirmation.

"He may indeed; you know how these things are. It's not an exact science, but the German Doctor attending him is apparently under instructions to do everything possible to aid his recovery."

"And have you more news?" Billoux continued.

"Yes but it's not good. Anton and Marie Aveline have been arrested; so has Charles Bayard and his brother Roger was shot and killed. Simone de Beauvoir the teacher has also been arrested."

"And that's it?" Bidault asked.

"Yes, but equally importantly the captives are being held in the German Army camp outside Chantilly. And if anybody has ideas of releasing them, they can forget it. Even if you'd the whole of the Résistance behind you, they'd never get in there and out again in one piece."

"Nevertheless it seems that London needs to know," Bidault said. "Perhaps they'll carry out a bombing raid on the camp in an attempt to kill the captives and stop them talking."

"Thank you Inspector," Bidault said. "Now we must make our way back again."

"My family's in Vichy France," the Inspector said. "So they're out of harms way, and until I see how things work out here I'll stick around."

"And the Priest?" Billoux asked.

"He won't leave either," the Inspector said. "But there's a tractor and trailer with a load of hay going in your direction. It'll be here in a few minutes, though it can't bring you all the way, just enough to get you out of the town."

"In that case we'll be happy to go along. Francois Debré brought us in and he's waiting for us about three miles out of town," Billoux said.

The news they brought back to Balfour was not what Andrea had wanted to hear. However Balfour passed the information to London and they waited for London's response.

Chapter twenty seven

The Major was sitting asleep in his office when Balfour's message came through. He immediately sent for Jay Bee, who was also wakened.

"They've worked wonders in the time they had," he said as he tossed the transcript of Balfour's message to her.

Jay Bee was still shaking the sleep from her eyes as she studied the message. "Anton and Marie prisoners," she whispered quietly. "At least they're alive, but what will they do to them? And Gary as well?"

"Gary may be lucky," the Major said. "If the Germans accept that he's a British pilot. But Charles was also taken prisoner with Simone, and they'll certainly not be so lucky, that's for sure."

Jay Bee shook her head slowly. "I don't need to ask what they'll do to them."

The Major sat up suddenly in his chair and reached out for one of Churchill's cigars. He struck a match, lit it, and drew heavily on it. "That's the wrong attitude Jay Bee," he said. "We're not going to let it come to that."

"But sir, I know where the camp is. It's impregnable without an Army," Jay Bee insisted.

"We'll see about that," the Major said. "What do we know about this camp?"

"It's the Army base for the Wehrmacht outside Paris," Jay Bee said. "The main building is an old castle. It was lived in before the War until the Germans requisitioned it. It's part of a large estate, surrounded by an eight-foot stonewall covered with rolls of barbed wire. Inside the wall are high wooden fences, which again have barbed wire all over them. The perimeter inside and out is patrolled constantly, and there are watch towers at regular intervals."

"And what about the rest of the camp?"

"There are Cottages on the estate and apparently they are lived in by Officers and their families. Then there are wooden huts for the soldiers, and of course they have several compounds where they keep their vehicles with repair facilities."

"And presumably there's ammunition and explosives dump?"

"I'm sure there is sir, but I'm not certain."

The Major scribbled a note on a piece of paper and signed it. "Get that to the Photo Reconnaissance boys immediately Jay Bee. Tell them it's of the utmost importance. I want the report yesterday. Understood?"

Jay Bee jumped enthusiastically to her feet. "Yes *sir!*" she said. "Right away sir."

She left the Major's office with a bounce to her step, believing in her heart that the situation was dire, but the Major's determination gave her hope. She didn't know what he could possibly do, but nevertheless she was clinging to that glimmer of hope.

Chapter twenty eight

Klaus Richter sat behind the large oak desk in what had been General Scholtz's office in the Castle in the German Army camp at Chantilly. He had gone there after spending two hours with Madeleine Boussine following what was his attempted assassination. Although he didn't at that time have the authority, nobody dared to question him, and soon after his arrival a 'phone call to Himmler gave him all the authority he required.

He left orders not to be disturbed as he thought about Scholtz and the captured French Resisters and the British airman. As long as Scholtz was still unconscious he was in no hurry, and his other captives could rot in the cellars beneath him until he was ready for them. He would decide later about the airman.

More than anything he wanted Scholtz alive; because he was convinced he was one of the main men behind a plot against Hitler. He smiled to himself as he thought of how he would have Scholtz tortured to reveal the names of the other conspirators. He was also motivated by a profound hatred for the man, because he was instrumental in trying to have him court-martialled. Then his smile changed to a worried frown, because he knew the General was a hard man, not necessarily the kind who would break under torture, even after all the Gestapo could do to him.

He nodded to himself as he realised he might have to try and find another way to get the information from Scholtz. But how, that was the question?

Richter believed that if Hitler knew he was responsible for exposing Scholtz, and as a consequence the whole cowardly plot to assassinate him, then his position would be enormously improved. He stretched out in Scholtz's leather chair and allowed himself a smile. He could just see himself as SS-Obergruppenführer Karl Richter! Not a mere Colonel anymore.

But Richter was also a shrewd man and he knew the way the War was going, and it did not look good. So if the worst came to the worst, he was determined to ensure an easy passage for himself into post-War Germany. To do that he had to remove the suspicion that *he* was responsible for the murder of allied prisoners of War! His solution was to torture General Scholtz and make *him* confess to the atrocity. He also had it in the back of his mind that the British airman, if he sent him to a prisoner of War camp, might remember his good will gesture!

He was concerned that the Résistance had tried to assassinate him, and that he appeared to have been singled out. He realised however that any Officer in the German Army, especially the *SS,* was a target and that he was fortunate to have been warned. But he wondered why him? And above all, what exactly had Captain Jacque Aveline been up to?

A French man working for the Abwehr! Could it possibly be that *he* knew he had the copies of the photographs from Verberie, and he'd tried to have him killed to destroy the evidence? If that was so, then Richter realised that only the Abwehr could have told him that, and that would implicate the Abwehr in his attempted assassination.

Then he thought of Aveline's parents. Had Aveline enlisted their help in having him assassinated to protect their son from the damning evidence of Verberie? He was aware of the association there was, between General Scholtz, and Jacque's parents. The locals looked on the Doctor and his wife as German sympathisers because of that relationship. But Richter wondered if there was more to it than that. If that was the case, why was a British airman being hidden in their Château? Was their relation with Scholtz a cover for something else; an escape route perhaps?

He had never trusted Canaris and his bunch of spies, but he couldn't understand what they had to gain by his death. Then he suddenly sat up in his chair and thumped the desk with his fist.

"Of course," he said out loud. "How stupid of me. I've been suspicious of Scholtz and his cronies for months. It's no secret, and Canaris must know it. So if Scholtz *was* implicated in a plot to kill the Führer then so is Canaris and Canaris must have used Aveline to have me assassinated, before I stumbled on the truth."

The enormity of what Richter had suddenly realised made him sink back in his chair. Then he sat up again and picked up the phone. Outside the stately room, a corporal of the Wehrmacht took the call. He left his desk and came in to Richter.

He came to attention and saluted and waited.

Richter looked up. "I need a whiskey," he said. "Get me some of the General's best."

The corporal was about to protest, but he saw the look on Richter's face and changed his mind. He went to a cupboard and took out a bottle of whiskey and a glass and poured Richter a large one.

"That will be all," Richter said.

'Now,' he thought to himself as the corporal left. 'All I've to do is to prove it. If only the Résistance hadn't killed Aveline."

He sipped the whiskey and smiled as he thought of his two hours of passion with Madeleine. Because it was so good and because she was the one who warned him, he was determined to make it up to her. He would find her a room in the castle for herself and her son and to really show his gratitude he would tell Koch not to do anything about her husband after all.

He smiled again when he thought of the pleasure his news would give Madeleine. He called the corporal again and told him to find Obersturmfürher Franz Vetter and to send him in to him.

Vetter arrived shortly.

"Franz," Richter said. "I want you to contact Gruppenfürher Karl Koch again. Tell him to do nothing about the Jew, Jean Boussine. Then I want *you* to go and see that French Jew yourself, and I know it's distasteful for you, tell him to write a loving letter to his wife and get a photograph of the Jewish bastard looking well dressed and smiling."

"Very good sir," Vetter said. "If you insist." He saluted and turned to leave. "And Vetter," Richter called out. "I'm not finished yet. When you've done that, I want him transferred to Chantilly and kept in safe custody until I tell you otherwise. You Vetter will be solely responsible for him. Now, send that corporal in here again."

Chapter twenty nine

Official records make no reference to the fact that Lt-Col Blair 'Paddy' Mayne met Churchill. But then there's very little in the way of official recognition that Churchill's 'Secret Circle' ever existed either.

From the early part of the War the SAS was under the leadership of David Stirling. After his capture by the Germans, it came under the superb leadership of Paddy Mayne. Throughout that time they performed some amazing feats. The credit for what they did often did not go to them, but to the Long Range Desert Group, or some other faction within the British Army. The SAS however became such a thorn in the side of the German forces that Hitler decreed they should not be taken alive.

The SAS left Italy for Great Britain in the early part of 1944 to prepare for Operation 'Overlord' – the invasion of Europe by the Allies.

Back home the men of the SAS and new recruits were sent to Darvel in Ayrshire to train and prepare for the invasion. Paddy Mayne was the Officer commanding 1 SAS and at Darvel, whilst involved in training the men, he met the SAS'S new Padre, Fraser McLuskey and they became firm friends.

Training took place on and around the Lanfine Estate at Darvel and the Officers would meet at the Turf Hotel to eat and drink. Every morning from eleven it was filled to almost overflowing. It was there that Jay Bee first met Paddy Mayne and Fraser McLuskey. She had arrived on the first available train from London.

A number of Officers were sitting around the bar area relaxing. Some were leaning against the bar drinking, whilst others were at a table having a snack. Here and there amidst the smoke laden atmosphere men in and out of uniform were sleeping. Jay Bee walked into the bar room, confronted by the stale smell of smoke and drink and the din of people engaged in animated conversations.

She stood in the doorway, holding the door open as she hesitated and took in the scene before her. She only carried a handbag and was dressed in civvies and didn't in any way look remarkable. Her previous training had led her to always dress and appear in a manner that would not draw attention. However it was clear that however she had dressed, her appearance in the bar at the Turf Hotel in Wartime was bound to attract attention. Having said that, the men were used to seeing wives and sweethearts of the soldiers coming and staying over at the Turf and the landlady Mrs McLelland and her daughters, did everything in their power to accommodate them.

A few of the men looked up, turned to one another, and then went on with their conversations. Jay Bee hesitated and then stepped in and closed the door behind her. A tall well built man stood up and left a group of men who were having an animated conversation.

He walked across the room towards her.

"You look as if you're lost," he said in a kindly voice, with more than a hint of a Scottish accent. "Are you sure you're in the right place?"

Jay Bee smiled. "This is the Turf Hotel isn't it?"

The man smiled and nodded.

"Then I'm in the right place," she said.

"Are you looking for someone?" the man asked.

"Yes I am actually," Jay Bee said. "I'm looking for Colonel Blair Mayne."

The man stopped smiling and took a deep breath. He brought Jay Bee by the arm to a quiet part of the bar.

"Do you know the Colonel?"

"No," Jay Bee said. "I've never met him. But if you know where he is I'd appreciate you telling me; it's rather urgent."

The man coughed nervously. "I'm afraid it's really not a good time, you see, well with the War and everything, things aren't quite normal, if you know what I mean."

"No," Jay Bee said sarcastically. "I don't know what you mean. I've come from London expressly to see Colonel Mayne. It's a matter of national importance, now will you kindly bring me to the Colonel."

The man recognised the exasperation in Jay Bee's voice, but he was uncertain what to do. "But my dear lady," he said.

"Don't 'dear lady' me, my good man," Jay Bee said raising her voice above the din.

There was a sudden silence for a moment, and then someone called out. "Hey Padre, what are you up? Are you molesting that young lady?"

The man smiled as he saw Jay Bee blush. "You're a Padre," she said. "I didn't realise, your scarf obscured your clerical collar."

"My fault," he confessed. "I should have introduced myself. I'm Fraser McLuskey. And yes I'm the recently appointed Padre of this rum lot."

"Well Padre," Jay Bee said quietly, and the hubbub of noise picked up again. "I'm not quite sure why you're hesitating but it's vital I see the Colonel right away."

McLuskey sighed. "Very well, I'll get him for you. But I'm warning you; he's not at his best with women, especially when he's been drinking. Very fond of his mother and sister I believe, but a man's man for all that. Just be careful how you handle him."

The Padre moved quickly over to a small table in the corner of the bar. There were two men, with full beer glasses on the table in front of them. The Padre bent down and spoke to one of the men. He looked across the room at Jay Bee. "Who let that bloody woman in here?" he bellowed. Then he looked accusingly at the Padre. "YOU?"

Again there was silence and nobody dared breath. There was a room full of some of the bravest men in the British Army and they cowered before this man. Some of them had faced death many times but nobody dared to speak and the Padre simply shook his head. They all knew the Colonel was completely unpredictable when he had been drinking. Some of them knew he was even more unpredictable when women were involved.

Jay Bee hesitated for a moment. She opened her handbag and removed an envelope, and then ignoring the looks of the men around her, she walked purposefully towards the table where the two men watched her approach. She was conscious of her footsteps on the bare wooden floor and the silence around her.

At the small table she looked directly at the larger of the two men and addressed him directly. "Colonel Blair Mayne I presume," she said confidently.

Paddy Mayne lifted his glass and downed the pint of beer. "Who wants to know?" he said gruffly.

Jay Bee said nothing but handed him the envelope. Paddy Mayne looked at it and then nodded to his companion to take it. As his companion reached out for the envelope Jay Bee withdrew it.

"Colonel it's for you alone," Jay Bee said as she looked him up and down.

Paddy Mayne reluctantly took the envelope. He drew his Fairbairn Sykes commando knife from its leather sheath and slit the envelope open and took out the letter and read it, and then stood up quietly.

He was a tall man, six foot four and broad shouldered. He was sporting a neatly trimmed beard on a finely chiselled chin. His eyes were narrow and piercing. He reached the letter back to Jay Bee and she immediately noticed the strength in his wrists and strong powerful hands.

His manner had changed as he looked around the room. "Right, everybody out," he shouted. "Now, everyone, make it sharp."

There was a grumble of discontent but everybody did as Paddy Mayne ordered. The last to go was the Padre and the proprietor and Mrs McLelland.

"Not you Fraser," Paddy Mayne said quietly. "I'd like you to wait. And you," he said to the proprietor.

Jay Bee looked slightly puzzled at the Colonel. There he was, a man who was well over six feet and according to the Major incredibly strong. In an instant her well-trained eye sized up the man they were depending on to rescue their colleagues in France.

He beckoned to Jay Bee and McLuskey to join him at another table. "Three coffees here Mrs McLelland," he said. "And make mine strong and black."

213

They sat down at the table. "This is our Padre, Fraser McLuskey," he said to Jay Bee. "May he see the letter?

Jay Bee hesitated but when she saw the challenging look in Paddy Mayne's eyes she showed the letter to McLuskey. He read it and nodded his appreciation at being allowed to read it.

"So what do we call you and what's this all about?" Paddy Mayne asked. "I'm sure Churchill doesn't send women such as you around the countryside with letters of introduction like that without a good reason?"

"Just call me Joe, that's short for Josephine," Jay Bee said. "It goes without saying that what I'm about to tell you is top secret."

The two men nodded.

"The Prime Minister has a plan, which could shorten the War my months and save the lives of thousands of people. Only a handful of people are aware of this, but it carries with it very considerable risks for the Prime Minister and the others involved. The problem is that the Germans have captured key French Résistance fighters. A German General, who also plays a pivotal role in the plan, is seriously wounded and in Hospital. If the Germans torture any of these people, and they talk, everything will be lost and the Germans would gain a very considerable propaganda advantage, and they would make the most of it."

Paddy Mayne rubbed his chin slowly. "And it doesn't take a genius to know what you want the SAS to do."

"No it doesn't," Jay Bee said. "We know where these people are being held, and the Prime Minister wants the SAS to either aid their escape or I'm afraid silence them before they have a chance to talk."

"You mean kill them," Paddy Mayne said.

Jay Bee bit her lip and nodded.

"And do you have a plan?" McLuskey asked.

"You can bet they do," Paddy Mayne said.

"We understand Colonel that you have been making clandestine visits to France, prior to the invasion of Europe," Jay Bee said.

McLuskey looked at Paddy Mayne with a puzzled look in his eyes. He smiled. "The fewer people knew about that the better Fraser, sorry." Then he looked at Jay Bee. "But how did you people know about our visits to France?"

"It's our business to know these things Colonel, but don't worry we'll not interfere," Jay Bee said.

"So what's your plan," Paddy Mayne asked, as Mrs McLelland brought three coffees.

"My superior, we know him only as the Major, is very impressed with the way you operated in the desert against the German airfields. Quite an impressive number of German aircraft destroyed. He wondered if the same tactics could be employed in France on this Operation." Jay Bee suggested.

Paddy Mayne sat staring at his cup of coffee. Then he looked up at Jay Bee. "I'll require detailed plans of where these people are being held. That includes accurate information about enemy strength, both at the scene and the surrounding area. I'll need to know if I can call on the French Résistance, and they need to be reliable. I'm not risking my men with a bunch of amateurs and not a word about anything to anybody, without my express permission. There've been far too many traitors in France, especially among the Maquis."

"You're going ahead then Paddy?" McLuskey asked.

"Before you answer that Colonel," Jay Bee said. "I should tell you that you're not being ordered to carry out this mission. I was expressly asked to tell you that. It's entirely voluntary and that's from the Prime Minister himself."

"If it's feasible we'll do it, won't we Fraser?" Paddy Mayne said with a smile.

"You're the boss Paddy," McLuskey agreed. "If you say it's OK then it's OK."

"What about equipment over there Joe? We'll need a lot of gear including Jeeps fitted with two twin Lewis machine guns. Explosives, ammunition, radios, you name it we'll need it. And how long have we got anyway?" Paddy Mayne asked.

"There isn't much time Colonel. If we don't act quickly we'll be too late, that's why I'm hoping you'll join me on the next train to London."

"Right," Paddy Mayne said without further hesitation. "I'll go to London."

He turned to McLuskey.

"Fraser you'll come with me on this one because I've a feeling we might just require your particular expertise. I know it'll be your first trip to France and your first sight of the enemy, but it'll give you a foretaste of things to come."

"Delighted to have the opportunity sir," McLuskey said.

"OK Fraser, if you'd be good enough to fetch Bob Holmes for me and I'll brief him. And when he's selected the men for this mission will you ensure that every man, including yourself, has made a will. I've a feeling we may not all be coming home from this one."

Major Bob Holmes was an explosives expert. He was five foot ten and weighed thirteen stone. He looked younger than his twenty-six years and carried himself with a boyish enthusiasm. He had already proved himself in battle winning the MC in Sicily. He arrived at the bar in the Turf Hotel and walked casually over to his Colonel who introduced him to Jay Bee. She hid her surprise at one who appeared so young being a Major.

Paddy Mayne filled him in briefly on the task ahead and then gave him his instructions.

"I want you to get together twenty of our best Bob," he said. "That means we need two explosives experts, as well as yourself, two on navigation, one medic, two of our best mechanics, two radio men, one cook to make sure we don't starve and at least three with fluent German and say two with fluent French. No inexperienced hands on this show, apart from Fraser whom I've asked to come along. We'll wire you from London as soon as we can, but have everybody ready, with all their equipment to leave at a moments notice. We'll parachute in with a full payload each and with all the ammunition we can carry plus all the usual gear. Don't tell them where they're going but tell them we don't plan to stay longer than we have to."

Holmes nodded as Paddy Mayne stood up, and followed by Jay Bee he walked to the door. "And pass the word around Bob," he said smiling. "That the Turf is open to all customers again."

"And thank you Colonel," Mrs McLelland called out cheerfully as they left.

With that Paddy Mayne walked out followed by Jay Bee and Holmes. "Listen Joe," he said, turning to Jay Bee. "Why don't you wait here till I get my things together? The Major here, that is my Major, will start to round up the boys, and I'll be with you shortly."

Paddy Mayne and Jay Bee took the next train back to London. Paddy Mayne slept most of the way and they only talked about the Operation briefly. They took a taxi from the railway Station to Storey's gate.

Chapter thirty

Winston Churchill referred to Storey's Gate as 'The Secret Place', and some others referred to it as 'The Hole in the Ground'. Other service personnel called it 'The Annex.' In fact it comprised a series of cellars forty feet under the Ministry buildings. All together there were six acres of bombproof rooms. Churchill's 'Secret Place' was the seat of War. The Operations room and the map room indicated how the War was progressing. High-ranking personnel from the three services worked together to plot Operations. Different coloured telephones gave direct access to bases around the country. There was also a direct line between Churchill and President Roosevelt in its own telephone booth.

Jay Bee led the way into Storey's Gate and down into the Secret Place forty feet below. Paddy Mayne followed her as she led him along a corridor. There were various military and civilians walking around. As she continued purposefully down a corridor she well remembered her first visit there and her personal interview with Churchill. She stopped at a door, which had a large M on the front. Jay Bee knocked and a voice called out, "Enter".

The Major stood up and reached out a hand to Jay Bee and then to Paddy Mayne. "Good of you to come Colonel," he said. "I'm afraid for security reason I'm simply referred to as the Major. Believe me it's no reflection on the present company. Please take a seat."

Only Churchill knew the Major's real name, not even Jay Bee knew it was Major Holland.

He looked at Jay Bee. "Jay Bee, would you do the honours?"

Jay Bee smiled as Paddy Mayne looked sideways at her. She turned to the Major. "I asked the Colonel to call me Joe!"

The Major smiled as Jay Bee got up and poured two coffees. "Jay Bee is her code name. Best stick to Joe as she suggests."

Paddy Mayne relaxed in the leather padded seat and stifled a yawn. "You've had a long journey Colonel," the Major said apologetically.

"Both of you in fact, and unfortunately there's little time for you to recuperate before this Operation gets off the ground."

"One becomes accustomed to lack of sleep in War," Paddy Mayne said

If you'll excuse me Major," Jay Bee said, turning to the Major. "I must go sir, there's a lot to do in a very short time. I'm very conscious that if I hadn't brought Marie into this we wouldn't be in this mess now." She paused.

The Major nodded. "Very well then Jay Bee, and you mustn't blame yourself. It's the War. "

Jay Bee turned towards Paddy Mayne as she was about to leave, and reached into her handbag. She pulled out an envelope and opened it, and withdrew the torn half of a French Franc note. "I'd like you to take this," she said to a mystified Paddy Mayne. "Guard it well because it could save your life."

Paddy Mayne hesitated for a moment and then reached out his hand to take the torn note. "A courageous young French Résistance fighter has the other half of this note," she said. "Her name is Andrea and if I can't make it myself, she'll lead the party that'll meet you when you land in France. If whoever meets you *doesn't* have the other half of that note you'll have been betrayed!"

Paddy Mayne took the note and after examining it he put it carefully into an inside pocket for safekeeping.

"So if you'll excuse me," Jay Bee said, as the left the room.

Both men stood for a moment and Paddy Mayne smiled and nodded. "Be careful Jay Bee," the Major said.

When Jay Bee had gone the Major appeared momentarily dejected. "So much depends on her," he said to Paddy Mayne. "It worries me at times."

Then he appeared to brighten up. "Look at this map Colonel," he said pointing to a map of France that hung on the wall. "That's where you're headed," he said.

He took a crayon from his pocket and drew a ring around Chantilly. "Right there. There's a heavily guarded Army camp with an old castle as the main building. The people we want released are being held there, apart from one. He's a German General who's critically ill in the local Cottage Hospital."

Paddy Mayne looked closely at the map. "Have we photographs of this camp Major?

"They've been ordered Colonel. The Photoreconnaissance boys might already have one, but if not they've been ordered to get one right away."

Paddy Mayne pursed his lips and then faced the Major. "It seems to me Major that you're expecting an awful lot from us. You want us to go right into the heart of occupied France and attack a heavily fortified Wehrmacht base with only a handful of men, and to come out alive with your prisoners intact."

"That's the general idea Colonel," the Major smiled. "Can you do it?"

"I never commit my men to a battle unless I know the prize is worth the risk Major," Paddy Mayne countered. "Can you justify it?"

The Major reached into a drawer and removed one of the cigars he received on a regular basis from Churchill. He offered one to Paddy Mayne, but he declined it. The Major thoughtfully lit his cigar and drew heavily on it. Suddenly the room was filled with the smell of cigar smoke.

The Major picked up one of the three telephones on his desk and dialled a number. It was answered immediately. "He's here sir," the Major said. Then he nodded and replaced the receiver.

"If you'd be good enough to come with me Colonel," the Major said. "I'd like you to meet someone who may be able to convince you."

Paddy Mayne followed the Major down two corridors and half way down the second one, the Major stopped at a door. Two Marines stood one on either side. They saluted as the Major stopped. One of them knocked the door and a gruff voice was heard to say, "Come in."

The Major opened the door and ushered Paddy Mayne into the room. Churchill sat alone behind a large oak desk. A smoking cigar rested on the table and Churchill had a glass of whiskey in one hand. Paddy Mayne came to attention and saluted. Churchill set the glass of whiskey down and lifting the cigar in his left hand he stood up and sticking the cigar in his mouth drew on it and set it down again.

He looked Paddy Mayne up and down for a moment before saying anything. Then he smiled broadly and reached out his hand and shook Paddy Mayne's. "Colonel, Wellington would never have won the Battle of Waterloo without the Irish Regiments, especially the Inniskillings. And by all that's mighty, we need good Irish men in on this one, and they tell me you're the best, Colonel. Won't you sit down and have a taste of this Irish whiskey. They tell me you're fond of a drop!"

Paddy Mayne smiled broadly and took the seat that was offered. Churchill poured him a whiskey and Paddy Mayne raised his glass. "Your good health sir," he toasted, and then he drank the whiskey.

"A man after my own heart Major," Churchill said. Then he turned to Paddy Mayne. "Colonel, I've heard a lot about you and your exploits. Damned impressive, I don't mind saying. Damned impressive."

"Thank you sir," Paddy Mayne said.

"Wouldn't want you to think it has all gone unnoticed and if there was time I'd love to hear your first hand account, especially those desert raids. But there's so little time, you understand?"

"Yes sir," Paddy Mayne said. "I'm led to believe there's very little time."

"I want you to understand something Colonel," Churchill said as he blew a cloud of smoke towards the ceiling. "This mission you've volunteered for. It's vital to our War effort; we wouldn't ask you otherwise. If you're successful it could shorten the War by months and save the lives of thousands of our men. The problem is, it's so damned secret, I can't tell you what it's all about. I wish I could, and then you'd really see how important it is."

Paddy Mayne smiled. "Your word is good enough sir; for me and my men. I've heard all I need to."

"Well done Colonel," Churchill said. "And the lady we sent to see you in Scotland. She's very important to me. If you come across her in France, look after her."

"I'll do that sir," Paddy Mayne said as he stood to his feet, realising that he was being dismissed without the words being spoken.

Churchill stood up again, dwarfed by the giant Irish man. "Something else Colonel before you go. Nobody must know about this meeting and you must never speak of Jay Bee to anyone. Apart from looking out for her in France, you never met her."

Paddy Mayne nodded as the Major opened the door. "And it goes without saying Colonel that whatever you need, the Major will see you get it – anything!"

"Thank you sir," Paddy Mayne said, and as he turned to go Churchill held out his hand again. "It's been an honour to shake your hand Colonel."

Paddy Mayne shook Churchill's hand. "May the luck of the Irish go with you sir," he said.

Churchill laughed. "And with you Colonel." Then he turned and reached into a cupboard and took out a bottle of Bushmills Malt Whiskey. "With my blessing."

"Thank you sir," Paddy Mayne said as he followed the Major out of the room.

"Now that you're definitely on board," the Major said as they walked towards his office. "I take it I've your permission to order your men down here without delay?"

"Yes of course Major," Paddy Mayne agreed.

Back in the Major's room, Paddy Mayne took a chair whilst the Major made the necessary phone call.

Chapter thirty one

The conditions that Charles and Simone were held in were bleak. They were in almost complete darkness in two cellars in the castle's dungeon. The doors were wooden with a small iron grill.

They were far enough apart so that they could not communicate and there was no heat. The walls and floor were damp and they had neither bed nor chair, not even a table. There was a bucket for a toilet. Charles never regained consciousness and died shortly after being thrown into the cell. When the guards realised, they took his body unceremoniously and disposed of it in the grounds. Simone was not allowed to sleep and was doused with cold water every time he showed signs of dozing off.

He was only given a bowl of soup and a crust of bread each day.

Marie and Anton were treated in a similar manner. Their cell was on an outside wall and there was a small window with a metal grill that allowed in some light. It was too high up for them to see out.

Their cell was dry initially and cold, and it was unfurnished apart from a rough mattress on the floor and a bucket in the corner. Their food was the same as the others except the soup had been warmed slightly. They were also kept awake but not with cold water but by the guards constantly shouting at them. But after a short while that changed. They had both been trying to doze, huddled together on the mattress, when suddenly the iron grill of their cell was opened and a hose was pushed through and cold water sprayed over them.

Anton shouted at the guard in protest but it only made things worse. Marie pulled him back and they huddled together again to try and keep each other warm but it was useless.

Gary Tucker was treated slightly better. His cell was the same as Marie and Anton's and he also had a mattress to lie on. His food was similar but he was allowed to sleep undisturbed. Neither was he able to communicate with anyone.

Richter had decided to let them all sweat for a while, leaving them cold and hungry and deprived of sleep. He was in no great hurry to interrogate them and when he did, he expected they would break easily. His main concern was still General Scholtz who remained critically ill but stable.

Chapter thirty two

It was some minutes after the 'phone call, before the Major finally appeared to relax. He turned to Paddy Mayne who had taken a seat and was drumming his fingers impatiently on the table.

"I understand your frustration Colonel," he said. "But it's no worse than ours. It's one thing dropping off one of our agents, but it's a darned different matter when it comes to twenty or more of your blokes."

"I know it is," Paddy Mayne said with sympathy. "So how do you plan to do it?"

"I want you to go in on your own Colonel," the Major said. "We've a tried and trusted way that's safer than most. You'll be flown over in a Lysander. The pilot will just touch down very briefly. In fact he won't actually stop but he will slow enough to ensure you 'disembark' with your kit safely."

"Why me Major? I prefer to travel with the men," Paddy Mayne said.

"There's always a risk with parachuting in Colonel, you know that. A broken leg or shoulder and you'd only be a liability. If it happens to one of the men, well that's different. We can still operate with one less, but we need you to lead this one."

"And there'll be someone to meet me, Jay Bee for instance?

"Yes there will, but hopefully it'll be the daughter of two of the people we want released. Her name's Andrea and I know Jay Bee has mentioned her to you."

Paddy Mayne reached into an inside pocket and took out the torn French Franc note and held it up for the Major to see. "I was told this could save my life," he said.

The Major smiled. "Simple but effective," he said.

"So what about the men?" Paddy Mayne asked.

"I thought of a beach landing from a submarine but time is against us, and anyway it would be almost impossible to make your objective without being caught. The only alternative is to drop the men in from a Douglas C-47 Skytrain, we call them Dakotas as you know; don't ask me why."

"And is there suitable terrain near to our objective?"

"There's a forest a few kilometres from Chantilly where a French Résistance circuit, led by an SOE agent called Roger Balfour operates. It's safe and there's a large enough clearing for your men to parachute in. Into the bargain we're in regular contact with the French in that sector."

"The more people who know about this the less happy I am Major. If we're to pull this off then surprise is the key and if there's a traitor in this Circuit we could lose that element of surprise and the Operation, and some of my men as well."

"I understand your concern Colonel," the Major argued. "But Roger Balfour and his Circuit, the Baker's Dozen, have proved themselves over and over again. They're reliable and resilient."

"This isn't my field Major, espionage and all that sort of thing I mean, but in regular contact with the French surely gives the Germans a better than even chance of tracking down a radio. And if they intercept a message ..."

Paddy Mayne didn't finish the sentence and the Major could see he was not happy.

"Colonel," the Major said slowly and deliberately. "The Operation you're going on is our last chance to save a mission that's been in the planning for almost two years. The invasion of Europe's not far away and it'll go ahead whatever happens, but if this Operation's successful, thousands of Allied lives will be saved and the War will be shortened by months. Certainly there are risks but we'll do everything within our power to minimise them."

"So what next Major?"

"If you'd be so kind as to take yourself off to the canteen," the Major said. "I'll call you when the Photoreconnaissance boys come up with the photographs I've ordered. Then you'll be in a position to work on a plan of attack, because I'll also have details of the equipment we can supply you with, courtesy of the French Résistance."

When the Major went to the canteen some time later, he looked around him searching for Paddy Mayne. He found him eventually, slumped in a chair in a corner fast asleep. His peaked cap with the winged dagger of the SAS clearly visible, rested precariously on his head. Various personnel, civilian and military were seated around the canteen and the Major was conscious of curious glances as he wended his way between the tables towards the big Irish man.

He looked at Paddy Mayne for a moment with sympathy in his kind eyes and then gently shook him by the shoulder. Paddy Mayne wakened instantly and sat up with a huge grin on his face and righted the cap on his head.

"You're back Major?" Paddy Mayne said as he stood up and stretched.

"Yes," the Major said. "And I'm sorry to disturb you Colonel but time marches on. Your men are on their way right now in a Dakota. They'll be landing at Fairford where they'll wait at a Sealed Camp in the airfield until we join them prior to takeoff. We might even get there before them."

"Well let's see what you have for us then Major, 'til we get this show on the road."

Paddy Mayne followed the Major back to his office where they went in and closed the door.

The Major opened a folder on his desk and removed a number of photographs. "There've been a huge number of photographs taken over the whole of Europe prior to the invasion," he said. "Took a bit of time to single out the area we needed but I think you'll agree that what we have are pretty good. Those on the top are the most recent, taken especially for us by a low flying Spitfire. They've just been developed in fact. Then there are these."

He showed Paddy Mayne a number of post cards. "The Inter-Services Topographical Unit appealed to the public through the BBC for holiday snaps and postcards from all over the world. They were inundated with the blessed things, so much so that they actually flew in 50 American servicewomen to sort hundreds of thousands of them.

We're fortunate to have some of the Castle at Chantilly before the War."

Paddy Mayne smiled as he lifted the photographs and postcards and looked through them. He selected close ups and photographs taken at a distance of the Army camp at Chantilly and of the forest clearing where the Baker's Dozen were based.

"Detail's good," Paddy Mayne said as he looked at the close up of the camp. Then he returned to the photographs taken at a distance. "Power lines, roads and railway line are clear enough on this," he muttered to himself.

"And if you look at the close up," the Major said. "You can see the fuel dump and the area where we know from intelligence the ammunition and explosives are kept in an underground bomb proof store. It's been clearly marked for you."

Then the Major opened another folder. "Here's a map drawn to scale of the camp and the approaches to it. They've covered everything they can think of, and this is the approach road from the forest area where the Bakers Dozen are holed up."

"If all of this is accurate Major, you've given us a head start," Paddy Mayne said.

"That's the general idea Colonel, always to be one step ahead," the Major said.

"So what about transport, and armaments in France? We'll need to be able to move swiftly," Paddy Mayne said.

The Major looked slightly crest fallen and for once a worried frown crossed his brow.

"You're not going to tell me that we'll have to requisition the stuff ourselves from the Jerries," Paddy Mayne said with a veiled threat in his voice.

"You must understand Colonel," the Major said quickly to reassure Paddy Mayne. "It's not easy but we're working on it, even as we talk. I'm going on the assumption that you'll want to employ the same kind of tactics you used in the desert. Now the right vehicles are not in ready supply, but I'm confident we'll have something in time."

"We can't go unless something's put in place," Paddy Mayne insisted. "Have you thought of parachuting jeeps in before we land?"

"It crossed my mind Colonel, believe me, but it's too uncertain. Those things can fall apart or be damaged beyond repair on landing. No we need something more definite than that, and we'll get it. I've left word for me to be contacted at Fairford as soon as we have something."

"Well then I suggest we head for Fairford," Paddy Mayne said. "And we'll brief the lads and work out our plan of action on the assumption that transport is available."

RAF Fairford, in Gloucestershire, had been built south of the town of Fairford in 1940. The Major and Paddy Mayne arrived there by car. At the far end of the airfield was what was referred to as a 'Sealed Camp'. It was there to provide absolute security for military personnel who were about to embark on special or secret missions. Military Police patrolled the perimeter of the camp and covered security at the entrance. Once ensconced in the camp it was normal that no one should leave it prior to their mission. In some circumstances that ruling was relaxed, but it was only in exceptional circumstances.

As they were driven past security at the entrance to the airfield a Dakota circled overhead and then flew in and landed. The Major instructed the driver to drive towards the plane as it taxied to a halt. They drew up a hundred yards from the plane and waited and watched.

The door opened and the men of 1 SAS selected for the mission jumped out with their gear. The Major looked at Paddy Mayne and saw a smile of satisfaction. The men were laughing and joking as Paddy Mayne and the Major got out of the car and walked towards them. They were a mixed bunch of men and all of them, apart from the padre, had already seen plenty of action. Major Bob Holmes led them across the tarmac and onto the grass area where Paddy Mayne and the Major met them.

"All present and correct sir," Holmes said to Paddy Mayne.

"Well done Bob," Paddy Mayne said. "We've some serious planning to do before we get this show on the road, so let's get settled in somewhere."

The Major led the men towards the 'Sealed Camp' where he showed his pass and they were admitted. Paddy Mayne then took Bob Holmes to one side along with his four troop leaders. He turned to the rest of the men. "You'd better bed yourselves down lads. Once we're on the move there'll not be much sleep for any of us. Bob and I and the troop leaders have some planning to do and then we'll be in a position to fill the rest of you in on the details. Then you'll finally know what this is all about, but at this stage I can tell you it's vital to the War effort."

The men went off in search of their billet for the rest of their stay at Fairford, whilst the Major led Paddy Mayne and the others to a wooden hut. The hut was sparsely furnished, with one large window looking out towards the runway. There was a table in the centre of the room and half a dozen chairs. A lamp hung from the ceiling over the centre of the table. One wall had a large map of Europe with various markers and flags pinned on it. There was a blackboard and some chalk on another wall. A telephone rested on a small table in a corner of the room.

The men sat down around the table as Paddy Mayne set out the photographs and maps they'd brought with them. The Major picked up the telephone and made a call. The men glanced towards him and saw him smile.

He turned to the men seated around the table, looking directly at Paddy Mayne. "I believe we've our transport sorted Colonel," he said, with more than a hint of satisfaction in his voice. "It may not be the same as the jeeps you were used to in the desert but I believe they'll suffice. You can count on a half-track and four Kubelwagens and an ambulance, all courtesy of the French Résistance and all ready to go. The ambulance is useful because it's one of the newer armoured half-track ones. It will take two stretcher cases and four walking wounded. The Résistance has done a good job and it's all down to that SOE leader I told you about. A young farmhand apparently took the half-track single-handed from the Germans and killed four of them in the process."

"That's great Major," Paddy Mayne said. "Now we can really get down to business, but there's one more thing. We'll need two twin Vickers machine-guns for each Kubelwagen and the half-track and I want a .50in Browning heavy machine gun for each vehicle as well and a Bren gun for the drivers. And I want a searchlight fitted to each vehicle. All of that will have to be dropped along with ammunition and explosive at the same time as the men, together with the necessary mounts to attach the twin Vickers and searchlights to the vehicles. The vehicles are useless without the firepower."

"I'll get on to that right away Colonel, and in the mean time I'll leave you and your men to sort out your plan of action."

Chapter thirty three

Madeleine Boussine hated herself, but more than the self-abhorrence that ate away at her every day of her life, she loathed what she ended up doing to protect her family. Time and again she found herself on the brink of taking her own life to end her misery, only to be stopped by the thought of what would happen to her son.

She had started work in the hotel in very low spirits. Her mother had taken a stroke, and her husband Jean was missing, presumed dead, and she was fighting to scrape a living to provide for what was left of her family. Colonel Richter at first seemed like an angel from heaven. The news he brought about Jean thrilled her, and she really believed he was going to look out for him. It soon became clear that anything the Colonel promised would be at a price.

He had been quite persuasive and left Madeleine in no doubt that she would never see her husband again unless she did his bidding. Even then she hesitated, but when Richter threatened her son she gave in immediately.

General Scholtz on the other hand had turned out to be not nearly as bad. Of course she felt she was betraying Jean but she easily persuaded herself that what she had to do was easily the lesser of two evils. Shortly after she began her affair with him, Scholtz gave her a Luger pistol for her own protection, because he knew that by associating with him, she was open to all kinds of abuse and even the threat of death from the locals.

The General was thoughtful and generous and Madeleine even began to like him. But when Richter began pressing her to get information out of him she felt she was being disloyal and actually said the same to Richter. He was quick to remind her of the consequences if she didn't comply

It was not long before Richter began to make other demands of Madeleine and there was always the threat of what would happen to her family. It was then that she began to feel so desperate. She was hardly surviving in the midst of it all when Jacque Aveline suddenly appeared and she felt as if she was being pulled in every direction at once. She just could not understand how one German Officer was spying on another and then a third Officer, even though he was a Frenchman in German uniform, seemed to be spying on both of them.

She was in turmoil when Jacque asked her to confirm Richter's movements and implied that very soon Richter would be no more. She had no guarantee that Jacque would keep his promise about Jean if anything happened to Richter, even though she would have loved to have seen an end to him. Although Schotlz knew about Jean and her son he had never offered her any reassurance about their welfare.

When she weighted up the possibilities she decided she had to look out for herself and her family, and so she told Richter about Jacque. She knew something awful was going to happen when Richter told her to arrange for Scholtz to meet her on Friday night.

When Richter came to her door that evening she had a dreadful sinking feeling as if everything was getting out of control. Then when he insisted on having two hours of sordid sex, after implying that she would not see Scholtz again, she could barely keep herself from being sick. Luckily Richter drank so much that he didn't notice.

She dreaded her next encounter with Richter and was almost sorry she had warned him about Jacque. Somehow the prospect of only seeing him without the support of Scholtz filled her with dread, but when she thought of Jacque a shiver ran up her spine. Even more than Richter, there seemed to be something decidedly sinister and evil about him.

Madeleine had checked on her son, and looked in on her mother for the last time before she went to bed, when she was startled by a knock on the door. It was nearing midnight and she was in her nightdress. She hesitated and then went to her bedroom where she and Richter had spent those two dreadful hours. Reaching under the mattress she took out the Luger pistol Scholtz had given her. Her hand shook as she flipped off the safety catch the way Scholtz had instructed her and tiptoed quietly down stairs with her heart racing. Her fierce motherly instinct carried her forward, determined that if there were any threat outside, she would kill if necessary to protect her family.

She hesitated at the front door and then walked quietly into the living room and almost cried out in terror when there was another loud and impatient knocking on the door. Trembling with fear and dread and expecting either the Gestapo or some drunken locals determined to take out their revenge on her; she moved the curtain ever so slightly and looked out.

She gasped and became almost rigid with fear when she saw the unmistakable figure of Jacque Aveline. In a panic, she looked around the darkened room, not knowing what to do or where to turn. Again he knocked loudly on the door and then she heard him cry out. "Madeleine for pities sake help me."

He banged on the door and then in desperation put his shoulder to it in an attempt to force it open. Madeleine cringed in the corner of the room and then as if he knew she was there he banged on the window. "You've got to help me … please … I beg of you!"

She grasped the pistol firmly in her hand and switched on the hall light, and then slowly opened the door.

Aveline stood in the doorway swaying from side to side. He was dirty and unshaved and thoroughly dishevelled. Drunkenly he took one step forward and then fell on his face in the hallway. Madeleine set the pistol down and grabbing him by the coat collar pulled him further into the hallway and closed the door.

She rolled him over on his back. His face was covered in cuts and scratches and there was a large cut on his forehead and dried blood congealed on his face. His right hand was badly swollen, and with a ghastly looking wound. As she stared unbelievingly at him he opened his eyes, blinking in the unaccustomed light.

He rolled over and shook his head and managed to sit up. "Get me a drink," he said.

Madeleine hesitated. "P l e a s e," he implored. "I'm desperate."

It was one thing Madeleine had plenty of. She brought him a large brandy and he took it in one swallow.

"Please, another one."

She fetched another and after he had taken it he struggled to his feet. "I need to sit down," he said.

Madeleine went into the front room and pulled the curtains before putting on the light. She helped him into the room where he sat down on the first chair he saw. Then she went to her bedroom and put on a dressing gown before coming back down and standing in front of Aveline, waiting for him to speak.

He looked at her with bloodshot eyes. "They left me for dead," he said.

"I thought you were dead," she whispered. "What has happened?"

Aveline looked at the empty glass and Madeleine poured yet another brandy, smaller this time and he sipped it more slowly. "It was the Résistance," he said. "I'd gone to see my girl friend at the Château Aveline but she'd tipped off the Résistance that I was coming. Then she'd a change of heart and tried to warn me, but it was too late. They killed my German driver and drove me to their camp in the forest and were going to send me to England because I'm a collaborator."

"But how did you manage to escape?"

"We were kept under armed guard but during the night somebody killed the guard and gave me a gun and told us to run for our lives."

Madeleine looked sceptical. "But who'd do such a thing? Who'd help you to escape?"

"I don't know," he said impatiently. "I have no idea who it was. But they did it, and we ran towards the nearest village. Eventually one of them came after us on a motorbike. We'd almost made it but we were forced to run across country, near to a disused quarry, in an attempt to get away. It was there my girlfriend Nina was shot as she tried to escape. I'd a tussle with the man who came after us and I fell into the quarry. He must have assumed I'd fallen to my death but a tree and some boulders finally broke my fall. I was left unconscious and I've just managed to make it here now under cover of darkness."

"But why come here?" Madeleine queried. "I can't do anything for you."

"Look at me," he said. "I must look wretched. I've no papers, no identification and if I'm arrested I could fall into the hands of the Gestapo, and you know what that means."

"But I still don't see what I can do for you."

Aveline took another sip of Brandy. "I must get in contact with my parents, or General Scholtz or even the Abwehr. You *must* help me Madeleine."

Madeleine was quiet for a moment, crossing her arms over her breasts as if to comfort herself. "Things have changed since you saw me last," she said slowly. "Colonel Richter's been here."

"Richter!" Aveline gasped. "When?"

"Friday night," Madeleine said. "The night you told me to ask the Colonel to come, instead of General Scholtz."

"But what happened?"

"I don't know," Madeleine lied. "The Colonel came and said that I'd never see the General again and that you'd been killed."

"And General Scholtz?" Aveline asked quietly.

"I've heard rumours," Madeleine said. "There was an ambush but the Germans were waiting and members of the Résistance were shot or captured and I believe the General's critically ill in Hospital."

Aveline blinked as Madeleine looked at him with something akin to pity. "There's more, isn't there?" he said.

"It's all around Chantilly," Madeleine said. "Your parents have been arrested also."

Aveline groaned. "But how could that have happened?" he cried, looking at Madeleine with anguish in his eyes. "Nobody but my sister and the Résistance knew about the ambush."

There was something in the way Madeleine looked at him that touched a raw nerve. He stood up slowly, swaying slightly and then staggered towards Madeleine. She realised he suspected and turned towards the door to retrieve the pistol. He let out a roar of rage and before Madeleine could reach the door he had grabbed her by the throat.

"You traitorous bitch," he yelled. "It was you."

Overcome by anger and fury Aveline tightened his grip around her throat. Blinded by hatred and consumed with rage he yelled abuse at her, until she finally collapsed. No sooner had she fallen to the floor when there was an almighty crash and the front door burst open and three Germans in *SS* uniform stormed into the hallway.

Two of them grabbed Aveline by the arms from behind whilst the other one bent down to Madeleine. Aveline tried to wrestle free but he was no match for the two soldiers. They held him firmly and then the other one looked up. "She's still alive," he said.

Chapter thirty four

There was a half moon as Paddy Mayne and the Padre Fraser McLuskey walked across the grass towards the Lysander, which stood alone on the runway at Fairford. The rest of the men were sleeping because they were not flying for another four hours. The conditions were far from ideal and introduced an additional risk. However there was no time to wait for a full moon and Paddy Mayne understood the risk he and his men were taking.

Both men were fully laden and carried as much gear as they could. Neither of them spoke as they loaded their gear into the plane and then McLuskey climbed in first. Paddy Mayne checked again that he had the torn French Franc note safely in his pocket and then he too climbed in.

The pilot looked back and Paddy Mayne gave the thumbs up. A lone figure had followed from a distance and the Major now stood, with his hands in his pockets watching, as the Lysander taxied and took off into the night.

Paddy Mayne had decided to take the Padre with him, as it was his first experience of going into battle, but he also wanted someone else with him in case of unforeseen circumstances. The two men huddled up side by side in the cramped and cold conditions. Paddy Mayne looked at McLuskey who smiled and nodded and then Paddy Mayne closed his eyes and McLuskey prayed with his New Testament Bible held to his lips.

As they left the English coast behind them three Spitfires from 242 Squadron based at Devon followed them. It was not usual for this kind of air support to be given and their mission was considered so important that air cover was provided for the whole of the flight. They experienced only light flack as they crossed the French coast but it wasn't really a threat

As they approached their destination a red light came on, which if McLuskey hadn't been awake, Paddy Mayne would not have noticed. McLuskey shook Paddy Mayne by the shoulder and when he looked up he pointed to the light. Paddy Mayne smiled slightly and then pushed his pack in front of the door with McLuskey's right behind it. Then he positioned himself opposite the door with his back against the fuselage and his feet firmly against the two packs.

An orange light came on and McLuskey stood up and opened the door. A draught of cold air rushed in. The pilot had seen the prearranged signal of lights from the ground and Paddy Mayne and McLuskey could see that they were very low. They were depending entirely on the pilot as to when they should leave the aircraft. Any mistake on his part could mean instant death or serious injury.

The plane touched down and shuddered and shook as the pilot brought it under control and slowed as quickly as possible. Then a green light came on and Paddy Mayne instantly jerked his feet forward and the two packs flew out of the aircraft. Paddy Mayne immediately followed, rolling himself up in a ball as he threw himself out. McLuskey was right behind him. They hit the ground, rolling over and over. Paddy Mayne finally rested on his back and as he looked up he saw the Lysander disappear into the night sky.

The noise of the plane quickly faded into the distance. Paddy Mayne stood to his feet and looked around him. McLuskey was dazed but not hurt and had come to rest a hundred yards from Paddy Mayne. He gathered himself together and half stumbled, half ran towards Paddy Mayne. They located their packs and Paddy Mayne immediately armed himself with a Sten Gun and put his .45in Colt Browning pistol back in its holster from where he'd taken it, in case it caused injury when he fell.

Neither man spoke as they heaved their heavy packs on their backs, and walked briskly from the centre of the field towards the hedgerow. They used the cover of the hedge and listened and watched intently for the slightest sound. Then in the distance, across the field on the other side, they glimpsed the dim light of a torch.

Paddy Mayne looked at McLuskey. "That could be our reception committee Fraser," he whispered. "But let's just wait here a minute and see what happens."

They hugged the hedgerow, watching and waiting and then the light from the torch went out. After a short while McLuskey spotted another light, but this time it was on their side of the field, to the left of them and moving slowly towards them.

"It's someone else," McLuskey whispered. "They couldn't have crossed the field that fast, and we'd have heard them."

"I know," Paddy Mayne said. "And we're to be met by only one person, most likely a girl."

The light moved slowly towards them, but they didn't hear a sound. Then from the far side of the field a searchlight lit up the hedgerow. A lone figure was silhouetted against the hedge. Paddy Mayne and McLuskey immediately fell to the ground and slid backwards into the ditch. Paddy Mayne raised his head slightly and saw the figure of a young woman standing motionless.

A German voice called out in French through a megaphone. "Stay absolutely still or you'll be shot. Don't move."

The woman stood still, the torch now switched off and hanging limp in her hand. There was the sound of a vehicle as the searchlight suddenly drew closer. Paddy Mayne watched intently as a half-track with the searchlight mounted on the front came to within fifty yards of the woman.

Andrea stood motionless, blinded by the light and uncertain whether to run or brazen it out. She was perplexed because nobody but the people in London and Jay Bee were supposed to know the arrangements for the drop.

Paddy Mayne turned to McLuskey. "Stay here Fraser," he whispered. "You're on your own if anything happens to me." And with that he slipped off his pack and with his Sten Gun in his hands he melted into the darkness.

The Germans on the half-track scanned the whole length of the hedgerow, the bright searchlight skimming over McLuskey's head as he hid in the ditch. As the light swayed back towards the woman he looked up again wondering what his Commanding Officer was up to.

Paddy Mayne had moved stealthily behind the half-track, his eyes searching the darkness as he watched for any Germans following the vehicle on foot. He saw none and only heard the deep throbbing of the diesel engine. He watched from a safe distance as Andrea stood, fearful of what was going to happen.

A soldier climbed down from the half-track with a 9mm Schmeisser Sub-machine gun and walked towards Andrea, motioning with the gun for her to raise her hands. She raised them slowly with her heart thumping. There was a guttural laugh from one of the soldiers in the half-track and then he jumped down and walked after the other soldier. The driver of the half-track sat smiling towards his other companion.

Paddy Mayne crept stealthily up the side of the half-track, on the driver's side. He'd left the Sten Gun on the ground and was holding his Fairbairn Sykes Commando knife in his right hand. As he came level with the driver he suddenly reached across with his left hand and pulled the driver forward as he drove the knife into his heart.

The driver slumped over the steering wheel as Paddy Mayne leapt into the cab and despatched the other soldier in like manner. The noise of the diesel engine drowned out any noise. Paddy Mayne fumbled around quickly and found the switch for the searchlight and turned it off. Instantly one of the soldiers shouted out. "Otto put that damned light back on."

But Paddy Mayne was already circling around the two soldiers having pulled out his Colt pistol. He knew the bright light would have dazed them momentarily when they turned around, but he could still see their shadowy outline. At twenty yards he fired four shots in quick succession and the first soldier fell dead. He swung round quickly but before he could fire again at the other German, a single shot rang out and the second soldier stumbled and fell.

Slightly taken aback Paddy Mayne watched as the woman who had been in the searchlight walked towards him with a Luger pistol in her hand.

Paddy Mayne shouted out. "Over here," Fraser. And then he walked over to the body of the other soldier and confirmed that he was dead.

McLuskey ran towards them and Paddy Mayne still held his pistol at the ready when Andrea spoke for the first time.

"Sorry about the reception committee," she said apologetically.

"Hm," Paddy Mayne said. "And who might you be."

Andrea put her hand in the pocket of her jacket and took out the other half of the torn French Franc note. Paddy Mayne smiled to himself as he retrieved his own half of the note and held it out. Andrea switched on her torch briefly and Paddy Mayne saw instantly that the two halves matched.

"So you're Andrea," Paddy Mayne said, and there's no Joe!"

"Yes I'm Andrea," she said. "And you must be Colonel Paddy Mayne. And no Joe's still in England I'm afraid."

"Right," Paddy Mayne said, and turning to McLuskey. "And this is my Padre, Fraser McLuskey"

McLuskey smiled. "Pleased to meet you Andrea," he said. "What went wrong here?"

"I don't know," Andrea said. "It must have been a casual patrol, because otherwise there'd have been more of them."

"Hope you're right," Paddy Mayne said. "So I take it *you're* alone."

Andrea nodded. "It's safer that way," she said

"Right we'd better get these bodies into the ditch before anybody else comes along," Paddy Mayne said. "And what about transport Andrea?"

"I've a motorcycle and sidecar combination," she said. "Might be a bit crowded but I'm sure we'll manage."

"Aren't you afraid of being stopped by the Germans?" McLuskey asked her.

"No the Germans tend to stay off the roads at night. This one must have been a one off because they're generally afraid of ambushes, so it's relatively safe at night."

"In that case," Paddy Mayne said. "Fraser you drive the motorcycle and Andrea and I'll take the half-track. It might come in useful."

They manhandled the bodies of the Germans into the ditch, taking their weapons first of all, and then Andrea led the way out of the field and onto the road. The motorcycle and sidecar combination was

242

partially hidden in a gateway. Andrea drove the half-track to leave Paddy Mayne free in case they were stopped by a German patrol. McLuskey followed behind on the motorcycle and sidecar.

The sound of the half-track made talking difficult but Paddy Mayne was happy to remain quiet with his own thoughts. He was never at his best where women were concerned but he was reasonably happy because they had landed safely and on balance believed that the German patrol was, as Andrea suggested a chance happening. However he was conscious of what Andrea had said about German patrols usually keeping in at night.

It took them two hours to arrive at the camp in the woods were the Baker's Dozen were. That left them almost two hours before the rest of the men parachuted in and with six hours to daylight.

Andrea introduced Paddy Mayne and McLuskey to the men and then Balfour took them to one side.

"We don't have much time to lose," he said. "We've a large area right in the centre of the forest where your men will land. Did you bring the 'S' phone Colonel?"

Paddy Mayne looked at McLuskey. "Your pack I believe Fraser," he said.

"What's an 'S' phone," Andrea asked.

"It's a small portable radio telephone developed by the SOE for people like you," Paddy Mayne said. "I'm surprised you haven't got one. We can use it, if we're fortunate; to talk to the pilot as he comes in and let him know that all's well. The great thing about it is that if the pilot and the agent know each other they can recognise each other's voice. That way if the Germans happen to have captured a code, it may be no use to them."

"So why don't we have one?" Andrea asked.

"Ask Joe when you see her," Paddy Mayne said. "But don't worry; you can have ours with my compliments when this show's over?"

Andrea smiled and Paddy Mayne winked at her.

"It'll take us all of the two hours to get into the drop zone," Balfour said. "The good thing about it is that the Germans won't venture anything like that far into the woods, so there's no fear of an ambush."

"In that case we'd better get going," Paddy Mayne said. "The men will expect us to be there, and it's a great night for the drop, hardly a breeze."

"I'll lead the way," Balfour said. "And we'll bring Francois and Gaston as well."

He turned to Andrea. "You'd better stay in camp," he said.

Andrea looked at the tall figure of Paddy Mayne, who was glancing at her with a strange questioning look in his eyes. He looked as if he was maybe ten years older than she was and suddenly she felt butterflies in her stomach and she was thankful for the darkness because she knew she was blushing. Paddy Mayne too, for the first time in his life, felt a strange attraction to the young and stunningly beautiful, member of the French Résistance.

He looked away quickly and Andrea said. "I'm going as well and you needn't try and stop me."

Paddy Mayne smiled to himself thinking this was a different breed of woman to what he was used to. He was accustomed to the men, when the opportunity arose – and that wasn't all that often - of seeking out women for only one thing. He didn't blame the men or indeed the women, but he couldn't compete on their level, because he knew he would have to feel deeply for a woman before he could make love to her. He never before felt that way about a woman.

Jay Bee had also taken him by surprise, but only because he recognised her bravery and knew that she had put her life at risk many times. But it seemed to Paddy Mayne that as far as Jay Bee was concerned it was just a job to do, even though it was a very dangerous one. Whereas in the brief time he'd known Andrea, and the little Jay Bee had told him about her and her family, there was something different. He sensed a strong willed passion for justice for her family and it was that passion that drove her to take the chances that she was taking. He felt strangely drawn to her.

The way through the forest was not obvious to the casual observer. Tall oak, beech and sycamore trees stretched high up to the night sky, and every here and there thickets of thorn and bramble and fallen trees appeared to block the way. There was no path as such and there was very little light to see by, but Balfour led the small party unerringly towards their goal, easily avoiding the obstacles. Occasionally they came across a clearing in the forest when they could look up and see the sky and the broken cloud and scattered moonlight.

Every now and then a deer bolted in front of them, and the screech of an owl broke the otherwise eerie silence. Desjardine and Bidault followed Balfour, with Andrea walking just in front of Paddy Mayne, and McLuskey taking up the rear. There was very little talk between them, each taken up with their own thoughts.

McLuskey was far away in his beloved Scotland, thinking of his lovely wife and baby daughter Joan and wondering to himself was he mad to volunteer for such things. Paddy Mayne's thoughts were in the deserts of North Africa and then Sicily and Italy and the many friends he had left behind. He thought of home in Newtownards, and the mother he loved dearly, of a girl he once knew, and then his thoughts turned again to Andrea.

He wondered what drove a beautiful young woman like that to risk her life with the French Résistance, and what made him suddenly feel so powerfully drawn towards her. Then he quickened his pace ever so slightly until he was walking beside her. He looked down at her as she smiled warmly at him, and his face broke into a huge grin.

McLuskey smiled to himself and wondered what all the men still training hard back in Scotland would think of their Colonel right then. There appeared to be more to this commanding Officer than met the eye, he was sure of that.

Then Balfour stopped and waited for Paddy Mayne to catch up.

"I've been checking the time," he said. "And I'm afraid we might be running a bit late so I'm sending Francois on ahead just in case they're early and we're late."

"Good thinking," Paddy Mayne said. "We'll quicken our own pace anyway."

Balfour resumed his place at the front and Desjardine ran ahead.

When they arrived at the drop zone it was obvious they were on time, and Desjardine had already lit bonfires at the four corners of the clearing. They stood together at the edge of the trees farthest from the direction the approaching aircraft would take, and listened for the drone of the engines. Somewhere in the distance they could hear the crump of artillery shells or bombs or explosions of some kind. There in the middle of Chantilly forest it all seemed so far away. And then there was the unmistakable drone of an aircraft.

They stood silently as Paddy Mayne held the 'S' phone and waited to get a line of sight between the phone and the aircraft. He kept sending a message to assure the pilot that the reception committee was waiting and that all was well. It was only when the aircraft, high in the sky, had a clear line of contact with the phone that Paddy Mayne heard the voice of the pilot loud and clear. Desjardine ran around the four bonfires to stoke them up so that the pilot would have a clear view of them.

It all seemed so different to Andrea as the aircraft began to descent to its Operational height to allow the men to jump. She had waited for many drops and there was always the awful dread, as had happened such a short time ago, that the Germans would be waiting. But here in the forest everything was so relaxed. There were no Germans, only the approaching aircraft and themselves waiting for it to disgorge its cargo of fighting men and equipment.

Then the signal came from the pilot and Andrea felt her heart beat faster. Paddy Mayne watched anxiously, knowing that there was always a risk when men were jumping in the dark. The sound of the aircraft began to die away and everybody searched the night sky for the first sign of a parachute, of the white billowing silk, against the night sky.

"I see one," Andrea shouted as a parachute suddenly appeared as if from nowhere.

The men had jumped with only their parachutes on their backs. Each man's equipment, including his personal gear, was in a large 'leg-bag' equivalent to a regulation Army kit bag. It was attached to his right leg by two straps and it could weigh up to ninety pounds. When a man jumped he pulled a quick-release cord that allowed the leg-bag to swing from his belt at the end of a twenty-foot length of rope.

The leg-bag had the advantage on a dark night of letting the parachutist know when he was about to hit the ground. As the leg-bag touched down, the parachute, released from the extra weight billowed, giving a lighter landing. It also meant the parachutist didn't have to scramble about in the dark looking for his equipment.

Suddenly another parachutist descended. He landed perfectly, rolling over as he hit the ground. In seconds he was on his feet and getting rid of his parachute. Andrea let out a shout of glee and ran out to meet him. She didn't notice another parachutist who had almost overshot the drop zone and was dropping right in her path with his leg-bag dangling beneath him. Paddy Mayne ran after her and swept her off the ground a second before the bag would have struck her.

He set her down as he glanced around him and recognised one of his men. Andrea clung to him for support and Paddy Mayne put his strong arms around her and held her as they watched other parachutists land.

In that instant, as men and equipment thudded to the ground before them, Paddy Mayne had a strange and unfamiliar feeling, as he felt fiercely protective of Andrea

"Are you crazy?" he said to her. "If one of those bags or the men landed on you, your War would have been over quicker than you could blink your eye."

She pushed herself away from him. "Sorry," she said coyly. "But does that mean you care?" she added with a wicked grin.

Paddy Mayne smiled and gave her a squeeze and then set her free, as the men released their parachutes and gathered them into a bundle. Major Bob Holmes called out an order and the parachutes were gathered together and thrown onto one of the bonfires.

Then he called the men together and did a roll call and then ran across to Paddy Mayne. "All present and correct sir," he said. "No casualties and all the equipment seems to have made it." He glanced briefly at Andrea, showing mild surprise and returned to the men.

Paddy Mayne turned around to Balfour who'd been watching Paddy Mayne and Andrea. "Roger," he said. "We'll need every man to get this equipment back to the camp. My men are already fully loaded with equipment so it may take another trip."

"We'll bring what we can now Colonel," Balfour said. "I'll send the others for the rest of the gear when we get back to camp."

Paddy Mayne then called Holmes. "Bob," he said. "We can't bring everything this time round but I want the Lewis guns and the mounts for them now. Have to get those fitted as a priority.

"We're already onto that sir," Holmes said. "Some of the men will leave their own gear and pick it up later."

In an amazingly short space of time everyone was loaded with as much equipment as they could carry. The rest had been taken into the forest edge and left for collection later. A good-humoured band made its way back through the forest to the Baker's Dozen's camp.

Chapter thirty five

Aveline was held firmly by the two *SS* soldiers, whilst the third one did his best to revive Madeleine. As they waited, Aveline tried desperately to extricate himself from the grip of the two men. He cursed and swore but it was hopeless and soon he almost slumped to the ground tired out by his exertions.

Madeleine began to stir and the third soldier put his arm around her shoulder and helped her to sit up on the floor. He saw the bottle of brandy and gave her a sip from it and that seemed to help. When she was able she sat on a chair and then stood shakily to her feet.

"I'm all right now," she said. "I think you must have come just in time."

"Colonel Richter sent us," one of the men said. "You're to come to the castle."

"But why?" she asked, feeling aggravated. "I can't leave my child or my mother. They need me, both of them."

"That's taken care of," one of the soldiers said. "You can take your child with you, and there's someone outside in an ambulance to see to your mother."

"But why would the Colonel do this?" Madeleine asked.

"Let's just say you're a fortunate woman."

"And what about him?"

"We'll bring him along too. The Colonel will know how to deal with him."

Madeleine lifted her son from his bed and brought him down stairs. Aveleine was escorted to a waiting car. He was put in the back seat between the two soldiers, and the car drove off. Madeleine came out with her son wrapped up and still asleep. A medical orderly and a driver then went into the house and came out with Madeleine's mother on a stretcher. Madeleine sat in the back of the ambulance with her mother and the third soldier.

The ambulance drove past the sentries at the camp without stopping and pulled up outside the castle where the soldier let Madeleine and her child out. The driver and the orderly took her mother on the stretcher and they all went together through the castle's magnificent entrance, where a woman bade them follow her.

Aveline had arrived a short time earlier, and was brought straight down to a cell in the base of the castle. By this time Richter was asleep in his own stately room having left orders that he was not to be disturbed until first thing in the morning, unless it was absolutely necessary

Early in the morning Richter was told by the corporal that a man had been found in Madeleine's home, and that he had almost strangled her. Richter sat up in bed and shook the sleep from his eyes as he tried to take in what he'd been told.

The questions spilled out. "Who is he? Why was he there? Who are his friends?"

The corporal shrugged his shoulders. "We don't know sir?"

To which Richter shouted. "Am I surrounded by imbeciles? Find out who he is and report back to me immediately."

"But sir?" The corporal said.

"Whatever it takes," Richter said rolling out of bed. "Just get that information and get it now."

The corporal left and Richter reached for a glass of brandy and a cigar and sat down at his desk drumming his fingers impatiently.

Aveline was in a sorry state. He was dirty, dishevelled and unshaved. He hadn't washed and he smelt to high heaven. He was lying in the foetal position in the corner of the cell and there was nothing between him and the cold stone floor. He was shivering uncontrollably when two *SS* soldiers came in. They shone a light in his face and then dragged him up from the floor and sat him on a chair.

"Your name?"

He blinked and said nothing and a soldier hit hard across the mouth. He cried out in pain and put his hand up to protect himself. The soldier pulled his hand down and shone the torch in his face again. "Your name?" he demanded. "Or things will get so bad you'll wish you'd never been born."

Aveline looked up and blinked as blood trickled from the corner of his mouth. "You'll be sorry for this," he said. "When you find out who I am."

The soldiers laughed. "So surprise us then," one of them he said.

Aveline wiped the corner of his mouth. "There was no need to be violent," he spluttered. "I'm not afraid to say who I am." He paused. "My name's Hauptscharführer Jacque Aveline of the Abwehr and I'm acting under the direct orders of Admiral Canaris." He paused again as he drew a deep breath to try and keep his voice calm. "So I'd be careful what I did if I were you," he added threateningly.

The soldiers laughed again and one of them drew his hand back once more to strike him on the mouth when his colleague grabbed his sleeve.

"Wait a minute Kurt," he said.

He grabbed Aveline roughly by the chin forcing him to look up, and he shone the torch directly on his face. "He's telling the truth," he said. "His name is Aveline."

He relaxed his grip on Aveline and then directed the torch on his own face. "Look closely Aveline," he said. "Remember me?"

Aveline took a deep breath and looked up at the soldiers face. "Franz Ernst," he gasped.

"This," Ernst said, turning to his colleague. "Is the Butcher of Verberie."

As the two *SS* soldiers prepared to report back to Richter, who was smoking the remains of his cigar, the SAS were back in the camp in Chantilly forest. Paddy Mayne put one of his own men on guard. He still did not trust the Résistance, and gave orders for the rest to bed down for what remained of the night. Men from the Baker's Dozen began the task of attaching the Lewis guns to the Kubelwagens and Half-Tracks, whilst others were sent to retrieve the remaining equipment from the forest clearing.

A portable generator was used to provide lighting for the work that had to be done to the Kubelwagens. Paddy Mayne gave strict instructions on where and how they were to be fitted, along with a

Bren gun for quick access by each driver. The .50in Browning heavy machine guns were not mounted.

Paddy Mayne then settled down to sleep; leaving instructions that he was to be wakened in two hours.

SS Obersturmführer Franz Ernst knocked timidly on Richter's bedroom door. Richter stood up naked, and stubbed out the remains of his cigar. The smoke floated lazily to the ceiling. He threw back the last drop of brandy and pulling a dressing gown around him called out for Ernst to enter.

Ernst came in and stood to attention. "It's Aveline sir," he said with gratification. "Jacque Aveline, the Butcher of Verberie. He's the one who nearly strangled Mrs Boussine."

Richter paled visibly and stood motionless for a moment. "What condition is he in?"

"He's filthy sir. Hasn't shaved I'd say for at least two days and he smells to high heaven and looks wretched."

"Did he tell you what he's been doing? Why he's in that state?"

"We didn't ask sir because we believed you might rather do that yourself."

Richter was about to roar at Ernst, when he added. "We thought there might be things you'd rather nobody else knew sir. We were being cautious."

Richter calmed down and gave a grudging nod of approval. "Very well Ernst," he said. "You've done well. I won't forget it."

He turned his back on Ernst for a moment and then turned and faced him again. "Take him out of that cell," he said. "Get him washed, shaved and cleaned up, and get the Camp doctor to see him as well. Find him an *SS* Captain's uniform and give him a decent meal and then bring him to me in my office."

Ernst blinked in disbelief and then turned to leave and Richter added "And treat him well Ernst. Remember he's a Captain in the *SS* now!"

Ernst looked at Richter but he could read nothing into his Colonel's icy cold blue eyes.

Aveline couldn't believe what was happening when he was taken from the cell, and allowed a bath and a shave and was given a hearty breakfast. Then when the uniform of an Officer of the *SS* was laid out for him he believed that his veiled threat to the two soldiers had really paid off. But an *SS* uniform! He dressed slowly, relishing every moment. When he looked at himself in the mirror he thought that despite his ordeal of the last few days he wasn't looking too bad at all.

He patted the empty holster on his black leather belt and shrugged. Then Ernst came and asked him to follow him and he brought him to the doctor. The doctor didn't bother much about the rest of him, but paid particular attention to his hand. He cleaned the wound thoroughly and put on some sulphonamide powder and a dressing.

Then Ernst brought him to Richter's office, and after knocking showed him in. Richter stood resplendent in his *SS* Colonel's uniform with his back to Aveline.

"Captain Jacque Aveline, Colonel," Ernst said.

Richter stood still for effect and then spun around and glared at Aveline, whose heart was pounding. He tried to remain calm, and pretend he was not concerned. But he knew he had broken into a cold sweat and his hand hurt abominably, even after the doctor had worked on it

Richter said nothing and reached down and took a Walther P38 pistol out of a drawer and pointed it at Aveline. Aveline's mount went dry. Then Richter held the pistol in his other hand by the barrel and smiled as he handed it to Aveline.

Aveline hesitated and took the pistol. "You may put it in your holster," Richter said. "It's loaded. And take a seat."

Ernst left the office and shut the door.

Aveline fidgeted, waiting for Richter to speak.

"You must wonder why your fortunes have changed Aveline," Richter said.

Aveline nodded.

"Never forget they could change back just as quickly."

"I understand," Aveline muttered.

Richter looked him up and down. "You've two options Aveline," Richter said. "Either you cooperate fully, and I mean fully or I hand you over to the Gestapo."

Aveline suddenly felt cold all over. His heart was thumping again and his mouth was dry.

"I can see you realise what that would mean," Richter said and Aveline sat motionless.

"I want to know what you're doing here in France; whose orders you're under and what those orders are. I want to know everything that's happened that you've had a part in, whom you've met and what they told you. I want to know everything Aveline. Is that clear?"

Aveline nodded.

"Then let me hear it then."

An hour later Aveline sat at a desk. His hand hung over the telephone as he hesitated. Richter sat on the other side of the desk watching and listening. Aveline took a deep breath and dialled.

He got through eventually to Abwehr headquarters and asked to speak to General Oster. He was asked for his name, which he gave as Captain Jacque Aveline and he was eventually put through to Oster.

"Aveline, is that you?" Oster said with obvious surprise in his voice.

"Why yes sir," Aveline said. "I'm speaking to you from Chantilly."

There was silence for a moment. Then Oster spoke slowly, almost whispering. "I understood you were dead Aveline. Revenge for Verberie from a member of the family you thought you'd wiped out."

Aveline couldn't help gasping and he looked at Richter, who was listening to the conversation.

"That's right sir," Aveline said slowly after a pause. "I was left for dead in a disused quarry. But I don't understand. How could you possibly know?"

"Don't be a fool Aveline," Oster said. "Do you really think you are the only agent we have?"

Again there was a sharp intake of breath as Aveline was once more dumbfounded by the extent of Oster's knowledge of events. Richter couldn't conceal his anger either, at the Abwehr's infiltration of the Résistance without his knowing.

"I'd no idea sir," Aveline confessed. "I don't know who set me free, except I thought it must be a member of the Résistance, but why he'd have done it I don't know."

"So what else has happened that I'm not aware of?"

"There have been developments sir. I'm afraid General Scholtz is critically ill in Hospital in Chantilly."

"Yes," Oster said. "I know that. I understand things didn't go as planned!"

"You know that also sir?"

"Of course, and there have been arrests, including your parents, but what did you find out about Scholtz?"

Aveline looked at Richter who nodded slightly. "I'm afraid it's not good news sir. General Scholtz *was* planning a revolt against the Führer."

"You're sure of that?" Oster asked excitedly. "How can you be certain?"

"The General was having a meal with my parents and they were hiding a British pilot who'd been shot down and injured. I'm afraid my own parents were the ones involved in operating the Allied escape route, and now they're in custody. The pilot had the run of the house unless my parents expected visitors. The rest of the time he hid in a secret room. They forgot to tell him that the General was coming and he walked in on them in the middle of the meal."

"Go on," Oster said.

"My sister told me this, because she was there to make arrangements for the pilot to be moved out of the country. They tried to bluff it out, but it was difficult because the pilot simply walked into the room and spoke English before he saw the General. It was useless of course, but it seems the General only laughed and told them not to worry about it, but to get the pilot away as quickly as possible."

"So did the General tell them what he was involved in, or did he mention any other names?"

"No other names sir, but yes, apparently he did confide in them and that he might even be asking for their help."

"To the best of your knowledge did the General ever discuss your allegiance with Germany with your parents?"

"I know they told him they were not happy about it, but I don't believe it went further than that."

"I want you to listen carefully Aveline. I told you before that what you were doing was for the good of the Fatherland, and you must never forget that. And what I'm going to tell you to do now is no less vital to Germany's future."

"I understand sir," Aveline said.

"It's essential you persuade the General to confide in you. We must know the names of the other Officers who were in league with him. I know the General was critically ill, but my information is that he's recovering, though he's kept it hidden from the German Doctor."

"But sir, how am I going to do that?"

"He trusted your parents, that is obvious from what he said after he saw the pilot. He already knows you work for the Abwehr, so you must tell him that your sister told you about the incident with the pilot. Convince him that he must confide in you Aveline. We must know the names of those other Officers."

"But sir," Aveline said with disbelief. "If he's involved in a plot to kill Hitler, he's never going to reveal the names of the other conspirators; certainly not to me and the Abwehr."

"He is, if you tell him you already know the name of one other Officer."

"But I don't know the name of another Officer Sir. How could I?"

"Quite simple Aveline; because I'm going to tell you."

Aveline looked at Richter who was sitting on the edge of his chair. His knuckles were white as the tension caused him to grip the arms of the chair in a vice like grip. There was a look of utter disbelief on his face at his apparent good fortune. Aveline paused, uncertain what to do next. Richter relaxed his grip of the chair and waved his hand towards Aveline, encouraging him to keep talking.

Aveline tried to remain calm. "Very good sir," he said. "I'm listening."

"The Officer's name is General Hans Oster. Tell him that he's instructed you to memorise and bring back the names of the other Generals to him at Abwehr Headquarters."

"But General," Aveline gasped. "I *can't* do that."

"Listen carefully," Oster said patiently. "General Scholtz has always suspected my allegiance to this cause and when he's aware that I've spoken to you, he'll do as you ask."

"Sir that means," Aveline started to speak; his mouth was dry. "You're involved sir!"

Oster was silent and Aveline continued. "But I don't understand sir. If you're involved and you knew General Scholtz was also, why did you send me to check on the General? It doesn't make sense to me."

Oster grimaced at the other end of the line because he disliked having to explain to Aveline. "When we instructed you about this Operation you're on, you were reminded that we live in dangerous times," he said. "So it's very necessary for me to cover my back. Who's going to accuse me of being involved in a plot to kill Hitler when I'm doing my utmost to find those who are plotting?"

"I understand Herr General," Aveline said. "And I'll of course do as you've instructed me."

As Aveline replaced the handset Richter stood up and looked directly at him. "And you'll do exactly as he told you to do," he said threateningly. "Only you will report to me, and not to that traitor Oster, who will certainly face the consequences of his betrayal of the Fatherland." And he sat back with a smug look on his face.

257

Chapter thirty six

Breakfast was served at the Baker's Dozen camp deep in Chantilly forest. Everybody, except those working on the Kubelwagens, sat around in good-natured groups sharing stories and experiences with the Maquis. Andrea moved among them with the coffee pot listening intently as Paddy Mayne recounted stories from the deserts of North Africa. Every now and then she would cry out with a laugh, 'You didn't, you couldn't have.' And always somebody would retort, 'Oh but he did.'

Meanwhile work continued on the Kubelwagens and Half-tracks and when Paddy Mayne grew tired of telling stories he called for his small portable gramophone. He often brought one with him on his Operations, parachuting with it attached to his waist, and much to everyone's delight he started singing old Irish Ballads as the tunes were played on the gramophone.

The men had heard and learned them all off by heart and joined heartily in the singing. Andrea came and sat herself close to Paddy Mayne, as the coffee grew cold in the pot beside her. She looked up into his handsome rugged face, oblivious to everything else around her. McLuskey enjoyed the singing as much as anyone but couldn't help studying the expression on Andrea's face.

Then the tune for the Mountains of Mourne began as one of the men wound the gramophone again and Paddy Mayne started singing and the rest followed. Over a third of the SAS were Ulstermen and their voices rose loud and cheerful in the midst of the forest as they sang the Ballads. Andrea laughed suddenly and stood up and then reached down her hand to Paddy Mayne, beckoning him to stand beside her. He looked up at her as McLuskey watched, fascinated by the look on his face. Then Paddy Mayne's voice tailed off, whilst the music played on. The men singing along with him followed his lead and soon there wasn't a sound but the noise of the men working on the vehicles and the tune playing on the gramophone.

Paddy Mayne's face opened up into a huge grin and he jumped to his feet as Andrea took his outstretched hand. He towered above her and as the music played on; Paddy Mayne opened his mouth in amazement as Andrea picked up the tune and in a beautifully rich and velvety voice sang the rest of the song. The work on the vehicles stopped and the men sat enraptured and then the song ended and almost as one the men cheered and applauded.

Paddy Mayne let out a great laugh. "Where did you learn to sing like that?" he asked. "And how do you know our songs?"

Andrea laughed along with him. "My Grandmother was English," she said. "And she had lots of friends from Ireland. We sang all the old Irish songs. Sure I love them.

One of the men called out. "Give us another one Andrea." And a cheer went up from the men.

She looked at Paddy Mayne and all the men around her, marvelling that some of them were not much older than she was. He nodded and Andrea looked serious for a moment, and then composing herself she began to sing, 'Oh Danny boy, the pipes, the pipes are calling.'

There wasn't a sound from the men as they sat enraptured. Suddenly thoughts of home, sweethearts, wives and sisters and mothers flooded into their minds as never before on active service. As Andrea's voice trailed off and the song finished, many battle hardened soldiers had tears in their eyes.

It was Bob Holmes who broke the silence as he unashamedly wiped a tear from his eye. "Sure that was marvellous," he said. "Absolutely blooming marvellous, but with all due respects sir," he continued as he looked at Paddy Mayne. "We'd better get a move on."

Paddy Mayne nodded. "Quite right Bob," he said. "Let's check these Kubelwagens and then we'll sit down and finalise our plan of attack."

The men working on the vehicles had made good progress and Paddy Mayne was pleased with the work. Each Kubelwagen had a single twin Lewis machine-gun mounted on the front instead of the two originally planned. Two twin Lewis machine guns were mounted on the rear. A .303 Bren gun rested in a cradle on the driver's side where he had ready access to it and the .50 calibre heavy machine-gun was simply propped up in the back. Additional fuel cans were not being taken because of the added risk from enemy fire.

The half-tracks were similarly fitted out and all the vehicles were given a final check over before Paddy Mayne declared himself satisfied.

A few square yards of ground were cleared of moss and grass, leaving the bare soil. Bob Holmes then took a map from his pocket and using his knife as a marker, began to transfer the details of the map unto the bare soil. He marked out the perimeter of the Army camp at Chantilly and then the roads leading to it, and the railway line.

Then he drew in the details of the camp itself, whilst Roger Balfour and Gaston Bidault looked on and confirmed each location within the camp. When he was satisfied he left a white card on each location stating what it was. His job completed he told the men to familiarise themselves with the map until they had it firmly imprinted on their minds.

Meanwhile Paddy Mayne was conferring with Balfour. "We're clear about our objective as regards your friends held by the Nazis in the camp," he said. "My orders are to release them or if that proves impossible, then to kill them."

"Yes I'm aware of that Colonel," Balfour said. "And I don't like it any more than I'm sure you do, but I understand the powers that be consider this to be an absolutely vital mission as regards the War effort."

"So I believe," Paddy Mayne said. "I'm aware of some of the reasoning behind this Operation."

"So the same order applies to this German General they call Scholtz," Balfour added. "We must try to get him out of Hospital alive if possible, but if not!" And Balfour drew his hand across his throat.

"And that depends on whether or not he's fit to travel," Paddy Mayne said. "Our information is that he was critically ill, but he can't be left to the Germans in case he talks!"

"Hm," Balfour muttered. "Talks about what? I'd have a lot more enthusiasm for that side of things if I knew why we'd to save the neck of a German general. The boys aren't too happy risking their necks for a Nazi."

"If it's any consolation the General isn't a Nazi," Paddy Mayne said. "Anyway it has to be done and that's all that matters. Now my medic will have to examine Scholtz to decide if he's fit to travel. If he's not, one of your men will have to despatch him; we can't expect a medic to do that. So how do we arrange this?"

"Andrea knows the Hospital inside out. She was a nurse there until her family was arrested, and she knows whom she can trust. I suggest we disguise your medic as a patient with bandages and a crutch, that sort of thing. Andrea can select the right time during the hours of darkness and get your medic in to examine the General."

"He'll have an armed guard of course," Paddy Mayne added.

"Indeed," Balfour agreed. "Andrea will have to assess the situation first and the others can act accordingly."

"So with the help of my medic you're confident you can get the General out, provided he's fit to travel."

"We'll do our bit," Balfour said. "They'll go in the ambulance and with any luck the Germans will have the sense to keep off the roads at that time of the night. Then we'll use the ambulance to bring the General out, if he's fit to travel."

"That's settled then," Paddy Mayne said. "I'll allow you two hours from the time you leave here, to complete the Operation. If they're not back in that time our other attack goes ahead as planned, is that clear?"

"Very clear," Balfour agreed. "Two hours should give them ample time, so with or without the General they'll report back here."

"I'm still not at all happy with Andrea getting involved," Paddy Mayne argued. "She must stay here out of harm's way. Surely there's somebody else knows their way around the Hospital."

"She's the best one for the job," Balfour insisted. "Anyway you try telling her to keep out of it and see how far you get."

"Very well," Paddy Mayne agreed. "But I still don't like it." And he had an uneasy feeling in the pit of his stomach that he wasn't used

261

to. Going into battle was one thing that he was used to, but having a beautiful your French Résistance fighter to worry about as well was another thing all together!

As preparations were made to visit the Hospital; Paddy Mayne made brief contact with Fairford. He confirmed that three bombers were on stand-by and scheduled for take off once he gave the word. Flying conditions were good and the RAF did not expect any problems. Flying time to Chantilly was estimated as three hours.

When darkness had enveloped the camp, Andrea and Captain Phil Graham, a Doctor recently qualified at the Royal Victoria Hospital in Belfast and a native of County Antrim, sat side by side in the back of the ambulance. It had been commandeered months previously by the Résistance. Graham had been chosen for the Operation to Chantilly, not only because he was medically qualified, but he also spoke fluent German.

He was dressed in a French peasant's nightgown. His head was bandaged and his right eye covered. His left arm was in a sling and he had a crutch with him. Andrea wore a nurse's uniform and she'd borrowed a pair of glasses to disguise her appearance.

Desjardine drove the ambulance and Bidault acted as his attendant. Both men wore the appropriate uniform. The drive to the Hospital was uneventful, though they stopped a mile short of it just in case there was an Army checkpoint in the town. They parked in a field, where a hedge hid the ambulance.

Using the cover of darkness they made their way along the road towards the Hospital. A short distance from it Desjardine and Bidault hid in a doorway while Graham and Andrea walked on.

Andrea led the way to the rear entrance. She told Graham to wait for her outside while she tried to contact another member of staff. The corridor was dimly lit and the familiar smell of the Hospital hit her immediately she entered the corridor, and walked past the single ward where Gary Tucker had been.

Things appeared to be relatively quiet, but she could hear subdued talking from behind doors. She was conscious of her heart beating faster because she had no idea whom she was going to meet. She knew that some of the nurses were sympathetic to the Germans but most couldn't stand them, but if she met the wrong one she knew she would be in trouble. She was startled at the sudden sound of a telephone ringing in the distance.

It was eerie walking along the corridor in semi-darkness, every sound causing her to stop and catch her breath. She came on the staff room. A light was on and the door was slightly ajar. She moved closer and peered in. To her delight and amazement she could just see a former colleague through a haze of smoke.

Andrea looked quickly around her and pushed the door open. Her colleague, who was a nurse, waved a thick cloud of smoke away from her eyes and gasped with amazement when she saw Andrea. She stood up and greeted her warmly.

"Where have you come from?" she gasped.

Andrea shrugged. "Please don't ask Yvonne," she said.

Yvonne smiled and shook her head as she took a long draw on the cigarette and blew the smoke to the ceiling. "I should have known better," she said. "France, this damned War, it's all such a mess. But are you back?

Andrea shook her head. "No," she said. "I can't, but I need your help."

Yvonne drew on the last of the cigarette. "Look Andrea," she said. "I heard about your family and it was a terrible business, but I can't get involved with what you're doing. I mean you no harm, indeed I wish you well, but please leave me out of it. I promise you nobody will know I saw you."

Andrea nodded. "It's Ok," she sighed. "I understand. But just tell me one thing. Where's the German General. He's called Scholtz? That's all I need to know."

Yvonne made to leave the room and Andrea put out her hand to stop her. She brushed past her and then stopped in the doorway. "Same room the British pilot was in," she whispered, and then she was gone.

Andrew breathed a sigh of relief as she left the room and retraced her steps back the way she came. She met nobody as she made it quickly to the side ward, close to the rear door she came in by. Taking a deep breath she opened the door.

There was a dim bedside light at the head of the bed where Scholtz lay motionless. A wooden trolley was at the foot of the bed. His head was still bandaged and his eyes were closed. Andrea moved over quickly beside him and shook her head and turned to leave the room. The General opened his eyes and looked after her as she walked out leaving the door open.

Graham was standing nervously in the shadows, finding it difficult to deal with the inactivity and not knowing what was going on. "Thank goodness you're back," he said. "Did you find him?"

"Yes," Andrea said. "And he's not far away, but I'm not sure I like the look of him."

"Let me be the judge of that," Graham said, not unkindly. "And bring me to him quickly because I can't stand this waiting around."

"Follow me then," Andrea said and she went back in through the rear door of the Hospital with Graham close behind her, making a poor attempt at using the crutch.

They went into the side ward and Graham hobbled over to the side of the bed on the crutch. He felt the General's pulse. Then he took the bedside lamp and asked Andrea to hold it over his face as he opened his eyelids and peered into his eyes. He grunted slightly and then pulled the bedclothes back and checked the General for broken bones.

He looked around the room and his eyes rested on the trolley where he saw a pair of scissors. He took the scissors and stuck them sharply into the Generals thigh. The General winced, but didn't open his eyes. Graham smiled and took Andrea outside the room.

"I believe he's conscious," he said. "But I don't think he wants us to know. You'd better go in and convince him who you are so that I can ask him some questions."

Andrea went over to the General as Graham watched. She shook him gently by the shoulder and whispered. "General Scholtz, it's Andrea Aveline, please tell me if you can hear me? General please, it's important. We're here to help you."

Graham stood leaning on the crutch beside her and noticed the General's eyes flicker. He nodded to Andrea who shook the General's shoulder again and whispered. "It's all right. We mean you no harm. We are here to help."

Neither of them had noticed the *SS* Captain who'd appeared quietly at the door of the ward. He stood silently without moving. His eyes never flinched. Andrea whispered again. "It's urgent General, please, if you can speak tell me. We need to know. We must know the names of the other Officers involved with you."

Graham watched intently. Then the General opened his eyes and looked up at Andrea. He gave a week smile and nodded. "I can hear you," he said. And Andrea was about to speak when he reached out his hand and grasped hers in a firm grip. He raised himself up slightly from the pillow and pulled Andrea towards him.

"It's your brother Jacque," he whispered. "He's been to see me and he's coming back, but I've told him nothing. You mustn't stay."

Andrea gasped and turned and looked at Graham. "But my brother's dead," she said as Scholtz fell back on the bed again with a sigh.

"They'll try and make me talk," he whispered, struggling for breath. Then he turned his head slightly and looked towards the door as the *SS* Captain walked quietly in. At the far end of the corridor Yvonne, Andrea's erstwhile friend and colleague turned and walked away. Scholtz opened his mouth to speak as he stared at the Captain, but no words came out.

Andrea turned. "Jacque," she cried. "They told me you were dead."

Her brother gave a week smile. "But as you can see I'm not. In fact I'm very much alive."

"But, but I don't understand," Andrea said.

"What I don't understand," Aveline said. "Is what this..." He paused. "What this patient is doing here."

Andrea felt her heart beat as she looked briefly at Graham. He stood stiffly to attention and saluted. "Unterscharführer Schwarz, sir," he said in German. "I'm attached to General Scholtz's regiment."

"That doesn't tell me what you're doing here Sergeant," Aveline said threateningly.

"Accident at the camp sir," Graham said. "I hope to be discharged shortly, but I always look in on the General. He was a good man and none of us understand what's happened sir."

"Then I suggest you take yourself off," Aveline ordered.

"Very good sir," Graham said and he made his way to the door where he paused briefly.

He turned as he went to walk out and managed to draw his finger across his throat as he caught Andrea's eye whilst Jacque was looking at the General. Andrea shook her head and he left.

He hobbled out of the Hospital through the rear door and ran to where the other two were waiting impatiently. He told them what had happened.

Back in the Hospital, Aveline had closed the door of the ward. Andrea stood defiantly at the foot of the bed whilst her brother hovered around close to the General. "You've put me in quite a dilemma," he said to the General. "Both you and my sister that is. I've been trying all day to get you to talk and low and behold the minute you see the lovely Andrea, would you believe it, you can talk after all."

The General was speechless and Andrea looked at her brother with daggers in her eyes. "Nothing to say, either of you," Aveline said. "Well I know some people who might be able to fix that. Now we know you've got your speech back General, there's nothing to stop us moving you to the camp, is there? But what to do with my little sister? That's the problem. Can't leave you here that's for sure, so there's only one solution, you'll have to join our parents in the camp."

"Even you wouldn't sink so low," Andrea said scathingly.

"Oh but I would dear sister," he said. "And one day soon, when Germany's victorious and the Allies are defeated, you'll thank me. Believe me you will. But as for you General, your War's over and your evil plot to overthrow the Führer has been rumbled. Colonel Richter's onto you, and as soon as we get the names of the other traitors from you, you'll be executed along with them."

266

The General smiled faintly. "What would your poor parents think if they saw you now?"

"They'll come to thank me too," Aveline said.

"And if Germany loses the War?" The General suggested. "But I'll not be here to see that now, thankfully. The Germany I know and love is gone for ever, whatever happens."

Aveline turned on his heel and opened the door. Two soldiers in *SS* uniform were standing on either side. He turned to one of them. "Get a theatre trolley for the General and bring it here. And bring that nurse and the Doctor."

The soldier left and then Aveline turned to the other one. "Bring this woman to the ambulance at the front. If she escapes or you lay a finger on her you'll be shot."

"Yes sir," the soldier said as he walked into the room. He drew his pistol and led Andrea by the arm out of the room.

"Jacque," the General whispered.

Aveline turned and looked disdainfully at the General. "While we're alone just listen to me for a moment," Scholtz pleaded.

Aveline remained silent. "I know my days are numbered," he said. "That I'll never recover properly from my injuries anyway, so I've nothing to lose. But for the sake of your parents, for the sake of Germany, for France, think what you're doing."

"I'm doing what I'm convinced is best for Germany, and for France," Aveline said. "I don't know how you could turn traitor on your Fürher; after all he's done for Germany."

"I can see I'm wasting what time I've left," Scholtz said. "But everything you said during the day when you thought I was unconscious. It means nothing to me. General Oster of the Abwehr said he was in league with me! I'd be careful whom I'd believe if I were you, because if you really want to know what this is about, ask Richter about the atrocities near Dunkirk. It's revenge he's after, because I tried to have him court-martialled. He's terrified of the truth getting out if Germany loses the War."

"Germany won't lose the War," Aveline growled, but talking was making the General tired and he said nothing more.

Aveline was left with a twinge of doubt in his mind but he shook it off as the soldier arrived with Yvonne and the duty Doctor. The General was examined briefly by the Doctor and then lifted onto the trolley and wheeled out of the ward towards the waiting Wehrmacht ambulance. A medical orderly sat beside him. Andrea was already sitting in the ambulance with the soldier, who had a pistol pointing at her stomach. Aveline got in beside the driver and then as the ambulance was about to drive off Yvonne appeared at the rear door as it was being closed. Andrea saw her and their eyes met briefly. Yvonne gave a half-hearted shrug and said. "I had to." And then she closed the door. Andrea held back her tears and shook her head in disbelief at her friend's treachery.

Chapter thirty seven

Desjardine had watched from a distance as Andrea and the General were put into the ambulance. Then a short time after the ambulance was driven away from the Hospital the others followed

The ambulance was driven to the Army camp, and as it entered the camp gates Desjardine slowed down and veered off towards Chantilly forest. He turned to Graham who was sitting next to him. "That Colonel of yours is not going to like this," he said.

"And if I know Colonel Paddy Mayne, whoever's taken that girl is going to rue the day," Graham said.

Aveline instructed the driver to stop outside the front entrance of the castle. The General was lifted out gently and brought inside to a bedroom in the staff living quarters. A guard was left inside with him and another one stood outside the door. Aveline then gave instructions for the Wehrmacht Doctor on duty to come and examine the General.

The Doctor was in a small anti-room off Madeline Boussine's bedroom where he had just finished attending to Madeleine's son Louis, who had an ear infection. There was a knock on the door and Madeleine opened it. A corporal begged her pardon, and asked to speak to the Doctor who had just come out from Louis's small bedroom. "Yes what is it?" the Doctor asked.

"You're requested to attend immediately to General Scholtz sir," he said. "He has just been transferred from the Hospital."

Madeline gasped and the Doctor looked at her. She lowered her head and said quietly. "I ... I am acquainted with General Scholtz."

The Doctor nodded.

"I'd appreciate it very much if you could let me know how he is," Madeline asked.

The Doctor turned to the corporal first. "Very well corporal," he said. "Let them know I'll be there directly."

As the corporal left, the Doctor looked at Madeline. "I'd like to help," he said kindly. "But you'll understand it's more than my life's worth."

"Please, just let me know how he is!" Madeline pleaded.

"I'll see what I can do," the Doctor agreed. "But I'm not promising anything." And with that he left

Madeline Boussine's bedroom was on the floor above Richter's office. She was now established as his lover and as the Doctor walked out she left her bedroom, and strolled over to the balcony where she could look down at the office.

She watched as Andrea was taken there under guard with Aveline following close behind. Madeline watched, puzzled as an armed guard outside Richter's office knocked and opened the door as they approached. Aveline dismissed the guard who had accompanied them and pushed Andrea into the room in front of him.

Madeline pulled back from the balcony. She couldn't believe what she'd just seen. The woman looked vaguely familiar, but she'd only caught a quick glimpse of her face. But the man she'd let into her house out of pity and who then almost strangled her, was now dressed as an Officer in *SS* uniform, and with the apparent freedom to roam at will around the castle, and even enter Richter's office. She slipped back to the balcony again and waited.

Richter was sitting behind Scholtz's desk, with a cigarette in his mouth and a glass of whiskey in front of him. He removed the cigarette slowly and stubbed it out and stood to his feet. His jacket was unbuttoned, and he immediately buttoned it and straightened it around him and then walked out from behind the desk.

Andrea stood defiantly in front of him. She was still in her nurse's uniform. The top two buttons of her dress were undone. Her hair was cut short and brushed back.

"This is my sister Andrea," Aveline said proudly. Then lowering his head slightly and with a hint of regret in his voice he added. "She also works for the Résistance, I apprehended her while she was visiting the General."

Richter nodded as he came and stood in front of Andrea. "I'm certain that now she's in custody, and if she cooperates," Aveline suggested, feeling a little uneasy. "You'll ensure that she comes to no harm Colonel."

"You didn't tell me you'd such a beautiful sister Aveline," Richter said ignoring Aveline's assertion as he moved around Andrea and looked her up and down with greedy eyes. "That was very remiss of you."

Aveline managed a half-hearted smile. "My apologies sir," he said. "That *was* an oversight on my part. My sister is very like her mother."

Richter turned away suddenly. "Very well Aveline," he said. "That will be all. I'll call you when I'm ready."

"Very good sir," Aveline said. Then he turned to Andrea. "Come with me Andrea," he ordered.

"No, no," Richter said. "I'm finished with you Aveline, but not with your sister. *You* may go, she'll stay."

Aveline was about to protest but he saw the look in Richter's eye and decided against it. Reluctantly he saluted and then left the room, closing the door behind him. He was beginning to wonder if he'd done the right thing bringing his sister to the castle.

As Aveline closed the door Richter moved behind Andrea and put his hands on her shoulders. She stood like stone, unflinching. "Come, come," Richter said. "You can relax. As your brother says, despite having joined the Résistance, I'll make sure no harm comes to you."

He forced her to turn and face him. Then he started to unbutton the rest of her dress and at that point something snapped in Andrea and she slapped him hard across the face. Richter was completely taken by surprise and drew back, and Andrea ran to the door and threw it open. She had only made a few paces when a guard outside caught up with her and pulled her back struggling and shouting.

Richter strode to the door in a fury and glared at her. "Take her away and lock her up," he ordered. "I'll deal with her myself personally, and see that no one interferes with her."

As the soldier took her away, Richter called after him. "And send Aveline to me now."

Madeline felt anger and resentment building up in her as she saw the girl trying to flee and then being caught. She noticed the partly unbuttoned dress, but she couldn't understand her feelings. It was plain that Richter had tried to molest the woman whom Madeline now recognised as a nurse from the Hospital. She didn't notice Richter glancing in her direction, as she turned and went back into her room fighting back her tears.

She closed the door and sat on the side of the bed trying to make sense of how she felt. She was jealous, but why? She'd been forced through blackmail to be a mistress to someone who cared nothing about her. To be mistress to a man who'd taken away from her someone who showed her love and respect. To a man who sought sexual gratification for himself and who cared nothing about her feelings. So why should she care if he took a fancy to someone else?

Then there was a sound from Louis's small bedroom. Madeline looked up as her young son toddled out to her with an innocent smile and with his arms raised up for her to pick him up. At that moment she knew why she felt as she did. If Richter's attention was drawn elsewhere, and he became infatuated with the nurse from the Hospital, she would lose the protection Richter gave her.

She realised that her only worthwhile attribute was her beauty, and her sexual appeal to a man she loathed. If she fell out of favour with Richter, she knew she'd never see her husband Jean again. And because her son was half Jewish the Nazis would take him from her as well.

Tears flooded her eyes as she bent down and took Louis into her arms and nearly crushed him to death. How, she wondered, was she going to keep the affections of a man she despised but without whom her whole life would fall down around her? And why was Jacque Aveline who tried to kill her, allowed to walk around the castle at will.

Chapter thirty eight

Desjardine, Bidault and Graham arrived back at base camp in Chantilly forest. As they drove into the clearing the SAS and the Résistance were engaged in final preparations for the raid on the German Army camp. A handful of them walked over to meet Graham as he jumped out of the ambulance and headed towards Paddy Mayne to report.

Paddy Mayne stood dreadfully still as he listened. Balfour and McLuskey watched his expression closely, and when Andrea's name was mentioned it was as if a dark cloud had descended over him.

"I damn well knew it," he said when Graham had finished. "I told you she shouldn't have been allowed to go."

"We'd no other option," Balfour said. "But I'm not any happier than you are about it."

"It's just one more we've to rescue," Bob Holmes, ever the optimist said cheerfully. "It doesn't alter anything. If we get the others we'll get the girl as well. The men will see to that." And there was a rumble of consent from the men.

"Don't you understand," Paddy Mayne said. "The others were expendable and our orders were very clear. We were to rescue them or silence them, but that didn't apply to Andrea."

"What's done is done Colonel," Balfour said. "The Baker's Dozen's ready if you are."

Paddy Mayne looked around the men, indistinct in the darkness. He had left Bob Holmes to select his own men for the Operation and he knew each one personally. They were all dressed in their British Army uniforms. Despite the edict from High Command that all Air borne forces should wear the maroon beret they all wore their traditional SAS beret with the SAS cap badge. The Maquis as always were dressed in their every day working clothes.

"Now men," Paddy Mayne said. "You know I'm not one for great speeches, so I'll make this short. You've not been told much about this Operation except that our aim is to rescue key French Résistance fighters from a castle inside a Wehrmacht Army camp. I'm not in a position to tell you more than that, but you know me well enough to know I'm not one to send you on a fruitless Operation. You can take my word for it that this Operation, if it's successful, will have a significant impact on the Allied War effort. We've gone over the plan of Operation and when we get there I'll expect each unit to carry out their objective as quickly as possible. We expect to take the Bosh by surprise, but in this War nothing is certain, so don't you be taken by surprise. Remember finally, we don't leave anybody behind, alive or dead. Now any questions?"

There was silence for a moment and then McLuskey spoke up. "With your permission sir I'd like to offer a prayer for God's blessing on the men and yourself."

"That's appreciated Padre," Paddy Mayne said immediately. "Gather round men."

The men, both SAS and the Maquis came closer together in a circle. The Maquis looked at one another, not used to hearing someone ask God's blessing on their varied activities. But they closed their eyes and bowed their heads.

McLuskey stood at ease and with a New Testament in his left hand he raised his right hand heavenwards. "Heavenly Father," he prayed. "We humbly ask your blessing upon each one gathered here as we go out into the darkness against an enemy who may show no mercy. We ask for the light of the guidance of your Spirit, and may His protection be upon us, so that as we boldly go to do our duty, we may go in the knowledge that we go to uphold right and honour and justice, and that we do so for all men. Amen."

Every one, to a man repeated the 'Amen'.

Then Paddy Mayne took command again. "That's it lads. To your vehicles and good luck to every one of you."

They walked quickly to the Kubelwagens and the two half-tracks; Captain Phil Graham and McLuskey went in the ambulance with one of the Baker's Dozen as driver. The SAS took the Kubelwagens and the Baker's Dozen the two half-tracks.

Paddy Mayne was in the lead Kubelwagen driven by Corporal Redmond O'Hanlon, a South Armagh man. He was nicknamed 'Red' because of his shockingly red hair and he'd a temper to match. But in battle he was as cool as they come. Privates George Ruddell and Robert Kelland, both Ulstermen, were in the back manning the twin Vickers machine guns.

Beauford was to lead the column in the half-track, along the forest path to the road, and then to Chantilly. There were six heavily armed Baker's Dozen with him. The second half-track followed the last Kubelwagen with another six men. Bob Holmes commanded the last Kubelwagen and they also brought the ladder to help them scale the wall surrounding the castle. The ambulance brought up the rear. When all the men were in their vehicles Paddy Mayne walked quickly to the rear and then to the head of the column making sure everything was in order. Then he returned to his vehicle and shouted to Beauford ahead of him to move off.

Paddy Mayne's left hand rested on the round magazine of the front Lewis gun. He touched O'Hanlon on the shoulder as the half-track in front of them roared into life and moved forward. Paddy Mayne looked behind him briefly as the rest of the column followed. The forest reverberated with the roar of the engines as the men settled in for the journey to Chantilly. The night was mild with scattered cloud and the light from the half-moon helped to light the way.

The journey through the forest was slower then planned because the moonlight didn't penetrate everywhere. But Paddy Mayne had issued instructions to take it slower if necessary rather than risk an accident in the dark.

The SAS were tense but excited at the prospect of battle. Every one of them had trained hard at Darvel after returning from months of action in Sicily and Italy. They knew what was ahead of them because they'd seen it all before. They'd seen friends and colleagues die, shot or blown to pieces. They'd held colleagues in their arms as they had died and they'd seen the enemy fall dead at their feet from bullets from their guns. Paddy Mayne had himself dispatched many Germans and Italians silently with a knife.

They were aware that the chances of them all returning home alive were slim but each man was convinced that he would be among the lucky ones.

Once on the main road they began to make better time. Only Beaufort's half-track at the front of the column had headlights. All of the others had their headlights covered and only displayed their tail lights for the vehicle behind to follow.

Beaufort knew the road well and had told Paddy Mayne that he'd be surprised if they met any German vehicles. Because it was dark and they knew the last thing the Germans would expect would be Allied troops, they had decided to drive past them if they did happen to meet them.

As they approached the camp Beaufort slowed down and stopped, and the rest fell in behind him. Paddy Mayne jumped out of the Kubelwagen and walked up to meet him.

"We're half a mile from the camp now sir," Beaufort said. "Which means the searchlights on the perimeter wall will be able to spot us fairly soon. We'll ease forward slowly until we see them and then stop."

"Right," Paddy Mayne agreed looking at his watch. "The RAF is due overhead in thirty minutes. Remember they'll only be around for about fifteen minutes, so we've got to work fast."

Beaufort returned to his vehicle and eased forward again for another two hundred yards until he saw the searchlight. He stopped and the other vehicles drew up close behind. The night was silent and the moon was still coming and going from behind the scattered cloud. Bob Holmes and the men from the last Kubelwagen walked to the front of the column. One man from each of the other vehicles joined them. Paddy Mayne was searching the night sky and praying for darkness as he listened for the sound of the RAF bombers.

Everyone found the waiting to be the worst. The four men from the front vehicles had divested themselves of everything but what was necessary for the Operation. Each one carried a knife and a Browning pistol and spare magazines and they'd two wire cutters between them.

They'd packets of plastic explosive and time delay fuses. For the rest they depended on their wits.

Bob Holmes and his men carried a knapsack with explosive and fuses, a knife and Browning pistol, and two wire cutters and the ladder. Time passed slowly and there were many anxious glances at watches. The radio operator listened intently for a signal from the bombers. Everyone kept looking to the sky, listening for the familiar sound of the Lancaster's' four Merlin engines.

Then suddenly, away in the distance they hear the sound of anti-aircraft fire. They looked at one another and smiled with relief and then to the radio operator who nodded to Paddy Mayne. "ETA ten minutes," he said. "Everything's on schedule."

"Right," Paddy Mayne said. "You've ten minutes to get to the perimeter wall and fifteen minutes from then until the bombers take their leave. Make the most of every minute. Twenty-five minutes from now you must be back here or we go on in without you. Got that everyone?"

"Yes sir," Holmes answered for the men. "We're on our way."

The eight men ran down the road towards the wall surrounding the camp. As the searchlight swung round they fell to the ground and then picked themselves up again as it swung away.

The wall ran parallel with the road. There were searchlights, on tall wooden towers positioned at each end. A hedge and a small ditch separated the men from the wall, which was twenty yards across open ground from the ditch.

They kept low, pressed in against the hedge as they waited and listened for the bombers, and then they heard the satisfying drone as they approached their position. As the bombers flew closer, the pattern of the searchlights changed as the intense beams began probing the sky above the camp.

It was the sign they'd been waiting for and at a signal from Holmes they raced to the wall and quickly threw the ladder against it. The wall was topped with a roll of barbed wire and they cut through a section of it and pulled it to the ground.

They waited as the sound of the bombers came closer and the searchlights sought to pick them out as they approached. Then the bombers were almost overhead and flying so low that the sound of their engines reverberated across the countryside. In a second they were past the camp and banking fast to circle round again and then the air was filled with the sound of a siren inside the camp, followed by gunfire as anti-aircraft guns opened up.

The two teams of two men waited no longer and quickly scaled the ladder and were over the wall and then dropped to the ground below. The last man over brought the ladder with him and propped it against the wall on the other side ready for their escape. Their next objectives were the wooden towers, two men to each one, climbing fast towards the upper platform. One German operated the searchlight whilst another stood and gazed into the night sky searching for the aircraft. Speedily the attackers inched their way to the platforms, until they were able to reach them with their hands outstretched.

Then they pulled themselves up and onto the platforms in one smooth silent movement. The Germans were so intent on trying to fasten a beam of light on the bombers that they neither heard nor saw anything. Before they realised what was happening, the attackers had drawn their knives and killed the soldiers instantly, keeping one hand over their mouths to stop they crying out.

The two men on each tower then took control of the searchlights and continued the sweep of the night sky. Again the bombers roared overhead and the gunfire was almost deafening. Meanwhile Holmes and the rest of his men had run two hundred yards along the inside of the back wall, which ran at right angles to the wall with the searchlights.

Then they followed the faint outline of the electric power lines just visible against the night sky, which led them to a massive steel electricity pylon. They quickly unpacked a quantity of plastic explosive and attached some to the bottom of two of the steel supports and then attached time delay fuses to them.

Chapter thirty nine

Richter turned around in a fury after he'd ordered Andrea to be taken and locked up. He was not the sort of man who was used to being turned down by women. And because Andrea had spurned his advances it made him all the more determined to have her. But he was annoyed at himself also for losing control, as he remembered he had done immediately after the ambush. He prided himself in his ability to remain calm in even the most trying of circumstances.

He had been passed by for promotion three times since the War started, and each time he had given the appearance of graciously accepting the decision. This, despite the fact, that on each occasion it was younger men who succeeded. Time was passing however, and he was certain the War was coming to an end and he was eager to rise at least to *SS* Obergruppenführer – Lieutenant General - before that happened. He still saw the plot he had discovered, to assassinate Hitler, as his passport to success and General Scholtz was his key witness.

He sat down behind his desk and waited for Aveline to return. He was convinced that the time had come to get the information he needed from Scholtz and from the other captives. He had left explicit instructions that they were to be deprived of sleep and kept cold by spraying them constantly with water. The meagre diet they were to get had been cut to nothing so that the only water they had was from that which was sprayed over them.

Aveline returned to Richter's office. He was surprised to be called back so soon and found Richter quiet and subdued.

"Ah, Aveline," Richter said. "Come in and take a seat."

Aveline sat down and Richter handed him a cigarette packet. "Cigarette? They're Russian. If the War doesn't kill you these will."

Aveline smiled.

Richter lent back in his chair, resting a leg on the desk. His black leather-riding boot gleamed. "It's time we had some answers

Aveline," he said as he lit himself a cigar. "Tell me all you know about Scholtz and what he's told you?"

Aveline coughed nervously. "I believe it's clear the General's involved in something," he said.

"Go on."

"Well as I reported to you earlier in the day from the Hospital, I was unable to rouse him. He was unresponsive and appeared to be unconscious. The Doctor said that he had on occasions opened his eyes but he didn't respond to questions from him. As a matter of fact I was going to tell you that for the time being it was hopeless trying to question him."

"So what changed your mind?"

"I was deliberating what to do, when a nurse told me that my sister had returned to the Hospital and was asking after the General."

"This nurse; who was she?"

"She's just someone I used to keep a look out for me. Her brother's in Germany doing forced labour. He was in the Army and no doubt if Germany hadn't taken him to the Fatherland he would have joined the Maquis, like so many other misguided Frenchmen. I know this because I come from Chantilly. Anyway I told her that I could bring some influence to bear on her brother's welfare if she cooperated."

Richter nodded and continued to blow clouds of smoke towards the ceiling.

"I returned to the General's ward, and as the nurse had told me, my sister was there with him."

"Alone?"

"No there was another patient, a soldier wounded in an accident here in the camp. Apparently he came round regularly to see how the General was. I told him to leave after I'd heard my sister say to the General quite distinctly, 'If you can speak tell me. We need to know. We must know the names of the other Officers involved.' Then the General opened his eyes and said. 'I can hear you.' And he told her that I'd been to see him and then I'm afraid at that point they became aware that I was listening. But obviously my sister's aware of the General's involvement in some conspiracy, because he didn't say, 'I

280

don't know what you're talking about,' which convinces *me* he's involved."

"This other patient; did he hear this brief conversation?"

Aveline swallowed nervously. "Why yes I suppose so," he muttered. "But it was all in French so I don't imagine he understood."

"And did you check his story? Or did you simply ask him to leave?"

"I *told* him to leave," Aveline said indignantly.

"But you didn't check his story!" Richter rolled his eyes and sighed. "No wonder the Abwehr is helping us to lose this War. Get to the Hospital immediately and check if that soldier is really there. And report back to me immediately."

Aveline left and Richter stood up and started to pace about the room. He faced a dilemma over how to question Scholtz and the other prisoners. He was all too aware that the Gestapo were the recognised experts. He knew all about their ingenious methods of extracting information from enemies of the Fatherland, and that many died under torture rather than reveal anything to their tormentors. That was the last thing he wanted to happen. He desperately needed Scholtz to sign a confession of his involvement in a conspiracy against Hitler, and also to absolve him from his part in the massacre of the Allied soldiers. If the General died afterwards that would be of no consequence; he would be executed anyway.

So far he had managed to keep what he knew about Scholtz to himself, but he knew that if the Gestapo got to hear of it they would simply step in and take over and claim the credit for themselves. Richter had no intention of allowing that to happen. He began to hatch a plot and he thought of Madeline.

When Andrea had darted from Richter's office he had followed after her as far as the door, and he'd noticed Madeline turning away. He caught the look of jealousy on her face. He didn't imagine that Madeline was pleased to be the centre of his attention, being well aware that she only pleased him because of the hold he had over her. But that was the way he preferred it, because it gave him satisfaction to have a woman as his slave. He lost the feeling of power that he thrived on when a woman showed him affection of her own accord. That was why the thought of Andrea sent his blood racing. But she would have to wait.

He picked up the telephone and ordered a staff car and then he went up to Madeline's room. When he went in she still looked upset and he could see she had been crying.

"Now," Richter said. "We can't have this, can we?"

Madeline looked up at him and wiped her eyes with the silk handkerchief he handed her. She shook her head and forced a half-hearted smile.

"That's better," he said. "Now I've a little surprise for you, so tidy yourself up quickly, there's a car waiting for you and the boy. I'm bringing you to see somebody!"

Madeline stood up. "But Louis is asleep," she said quietly.

"None the less waken him. I'll wait for you downstairs."

Madeline looked after Richter and then went into Louis's small bedroom and lifted him out of bed. She hugged his warm body as he slowly wakened and then she dressed him. She tidied herself quickly and went down to where Richter was waiting for her. He brought her to the car, where she sat in the back beside him.

Two motorcycle outriders led the car down the long tree lined avenue, and a half-track Armoured Personnel Carrier with two 7.92 MG42 machine guns followed.

Madeline held Louis on her knee whilst Richter, sitting stiff and erect, rested his hand on her thigh. Madeline was anxious, knowing that Richter was capable of anything. They drove from the castle into Chantilly without speaking and stopped outside the Police Station.

Every day Jean Boussine had spent in the forced labour camp Stalag X-1 A at Schorstedt, he expected to be returned to the concentration camp at Neuengamme, where he knew he would die by gassing or some other cause. And so he was constantly baffled as to why he had been singled out and given special treatment, and when once again an *SS* Officer had him removed from Stalag X-1 A, he expected the worst.

He was told nothing and simply did as he was told without questioning. He was ordered to wash and shave and he was given a clean set of clothing and a modest meal. Then he was transferred by car to the railway Station and so began his journey back to Paris.

When they arrived in Paris he was taken by car to The Drancy camp. The Drancy camp was situated in the north-eastern suburb of Paris from which it took its name. It was a multi-storey complex, and it served as a transit camp, from where the Majority of French Jews deported from France were held, prior to their deportation to concentration camps in Germany and Poland. Barbed wire surrounded the U shaped building and its courtyard, and it had a capacity for 5000 prisoners.

French Police staffed it after the Germans had established it in 1941. Then in 1943 the German Security Police took direct control. An *SS* Officer Alois Brunner became the camp commandant. Brunner was another personal friend of Richter.

It was from the Drancy camp that Jean Boussine had been deported to Germany and he could hardly believe what was happening when he realised he was being returned there. It was almost as if he was going to relive that part of his life all over again.

He was brought to a single cell in the camp, given a light meal and told he would have to wait there. Later in the day he was taken from Drancy camp and again without being told anything he was brought to the Police Station at Chantilly and locked in a cell.

Richter's driver opened the door of the car and motioned to Madeleine to follow him. She looked at Richter who smiled and said. "I can let you have ten minutes my love. Make the most of it. And tell nobody about our special relationship or anything else that has happened."

Madeleine took Louis by the hand and followed the driver, who walked with authority into the Police Station. A Constable was writing at a desk and he stood up when the driver came in. Inspector Marius Regnier was at another desk. He looked pale and worn and he felt apprehensive, but he kept his seat. After the Avelines had been arrested along with the others, he had been living on a knife-edge, expecting every minute to see a Gestapo car drive up to the Station or to his home. But he and Father Michael de Bourbon had tried to keep out of the public gaze. They knew from information gathered from civilian workers in the camp, that the survivors from the Doctor's Network, who had been arrested, had not yet been questioned. Unless and until that happened they felt relatively safe.

The driver ignored the Constable and looked directly at Regnier. "I believe you've been expecting us," he said.

Regnier nodded and stood up looking questioningly at Madeleine. He knew her from the reputation that the locals put out about her. They called her a slut and a prostitute, a Nazi lover and a collaborator and he knew she had no friends left in Chantilly. If the opportunity had presented itself they would have shaved her hair off and dragged through the town as an example to others. But nobody was that brave or foolish enough yet to do that.

Regnier knew the other side to the story, the all too common human side, of a woman desperately fighting to save her husband and her child. Prostituting herself rather than see them killed. He knew that other women would rather have died than do what she did, and he wondered which took the most courage. He had seen so many Jews dragged off to camps in Germany, having himself been forced to work for a while in the Drancy camp. He could only imagine what their fate was, though he had heard rumours. But he knew that some of those who scorned Madeleine would almost certainly have done the same thing in similar circumstances.

As he led the way to the prison cells, normally used for common criminals, he felt a great deal of sympathy for Madeleine. At the back of the prison Madeleine saw the doors of three cells. An armed *SS* guard stood outside one of them. Like the others it had a stout wooden door with a small iron grill.

"Why have I been brought here," Madeleine asked Regnier as she held Louis firmly by the hand.

Regnier looked at the guard. "Your husband's here," he said kindly. "He was transferred on Colonel Richter's orders from Stalag X1-A, at Schorstedt."

Madeleine looked at Regnier and gasped and then almost collapsed in tears. Regnier put his arm around her. "Come now," he said. "You don't want him to see you like this."

"But why?" Madeleine asked, and Regnier shook his head.

Then he looked at Louis, quiet and too young too understand anything of what was happening. He wondered if he would even get to know his father. He reached out his hand to touch him on the head but was conscious of the guard watching and he drew back. He nodded to the guard who held the keys of the cell and he opened the door, and as it swung open Madeleine with Louis behind her walked into the arms of her husband.

The door was closed and locked and Regnier looked at his watch and returned to his desk.

Madeleine and Jean held each other. Tears rolled down their faces and neither of them could speak. Finally Louis pulled at his father's trouser leg and Jean loosened his hold of Madeleine and reached down and lifted his son into his arms and almost hugged him to death.

It seemed like a lifetime before Jean set his young son down and looked at his wife whom he thought he would never see again. There were still tears in his eyes. "I don't understand," he said. "Why are we here Madeleine, what's happening? Ever since I was arrested I expected to go the way of the others, but I'm singled out and treated differently. I just don't understand."

Madeleine put a finger against his lips, hating herself for not being able to tell him the truth, for she knew it would kill him. "I don't know either, my love," she whispered. "But little Louis and myself, we're well treated, and you're not to worry. But how are you? Are they treating you all right?"

Jean managed a smile that hid the horrors of his recent imprisonment. Images of corpses, men and women and children, naked or scantily clad flashed before his eyes but he tried to forget them. He didn't want Madeleine to worry and he said. "It's OK. We've to work hard, but we're fed and clothed and there's somewhere to sleep. I keep myself to myself and the War will soon be over and then we'll be a family again. God will look after us, you'll see."

They stood and held each other close and Louis clung to his father's legs and before they knew it they heard the rattle of the key in the lock. Regnier opened the cell door and motioned to Madeleine that it was time to go. They gave each other a final hug and then kissed passionately so that Regnier had to pull her away.

Jean stood pale faced and forlorn, believing he would probably never see his wife and son again. As Madeleine backed away from the open gaol door, she held Louis firmly by the hand. But then the *SS* guard reached out his hand and shaking his head with a sinister smile pulled Louis away from his mother.

Madeleine gasped and looked around her. She suddenly felt terribly alone, and afraid. She was filled with a terrible foreboding. Jean started walking towards her but the guard raised his machine pistol and shook his head. Then the guard looked at Madeleine.

"The boy stays with his father," the guard ordered. "Colonel's Richter's orders."

Madeleine gasped. "No, please no. He never said that. He wouldn't."

The guard pulled Louis towards him and then pushed him roughly towards Jean. "Take the boy," he said.

Jean reached out with tears in his eyes as the guard forced him to take Louis into the cell with him. He only had time to call out to Madeleine. "He'll be all right with me," he said. And he held his son close as the prison door slammed shut.

Madeleine was dragged back to the waiting car crying bitterly. Richter ignored her tears and smiled sweetly at her as she was forced to get in beside him. He ordered the driver to bring them back to the castle, where Richter told Madeleine to follow him to his office.

He sat behind his desk and Madeleine fully expected the usual harsh groping and the smell of his stale breath that nearly made her vomit, followed by the brutal sex, but this time was different.

He smiled instead. "You enjoyed my little surprise?" he asked.

"Yes," she muttered under her breath. And then almost afraid to speak the words she asked. "When will Louis be coming back?"

Richter motioned with his hand to Madeleine to sit down. "I'm sure you're wondering why I've gone to so much bother to reunite you and your son with your husband," he said, ignoring her question.

Madeleine was about to speak but again Richter held up his hand to silence her. "It's all right," he said. "I knew what it would mean to you, and I wanted to prove that so long as you do as I ask, your husband will continue to be well cared for and that's all. As for your son, don't you think it's time he spend some time with his father, after all he hasn't seen him in ages?"

Madeleine's heart sank because she knew he wasn't answering her question, and now she expected Richter to start making more frequent or even worse physical demands of her. Despite Jean's imprisonment with their son in Chantilly, she was beginning to think that she couldn't take much more. Again the thought of suicide crossed her mind.

"Now I want you to listen carefully," he continued. "I know you're aware that General Scholtz has been transferred from the Hospital to be under my direct protection and there's a reason for that. You see the General knows the names of other Officers in the German Army who have been disloyal to the Fürher and I need to know the names of those Officers."

He looked keenly at Madeleine. "I want you to get those names for me my dear."

Madeleine bit her lip. "But he'd never tell me those names. Why should he?"

"Why indeed?" Richter said. "Why indeed?"

He looked to the ceiling and then reached out for a cigar and lit it. "You liked Scholtz, didn't you?" he said and then without waiting he went on. "No, don't answer me my dear, because I know these things. You see he was a gentleman, misguided but a gentleman none the less, and you enjoy the company of gentlemen. He treated you well and you respected him, and the funny thing is I believe he respected you. And we're going to use that, or at least you are. You see I've come to believe that the Résistance as well as myself, wants the names of the Generals who are conspiring to kill the Führer. I'm not sure what the

287

Résistance's motives are, but I'll find that out as well; and that brings me to how you're going to get me those names."

Madeleine left Richter's office knowing that if she did not succeed her chances of seeing Jean and Louis again were slim. She felt forlorn and hopeless as she approached the room were Scholtz was being held but determined to do her best to follow the plan Richter had presented to her. She stood at the door of Scholtz's room as the guard stood aside to allow her in.

Madeleine was left alone with Scholtz. The Doctor had been to see him earlier. He reported to Richter that there was no change in his condition, but that he was thinking clearly and able to talk. She looked down at the man she *had* come to look up to and even like. He had always been kind to her and showed her the kind of respect she imagined Richter didn't even know about.

She decided to waken the General, which she managed to do quite easily. He was obviously weak but when he opened his eyes there was an immediate sign of recognition and a smile. Madeleine smiled in return. "General, it *is* Madeleine. You must be surprised to see me?"

The General nodded.

"I don't have much time," she said. "I shouldn't really *be* here."

"It's good to see you," Scholtz whispered. "But how did you manage it?"

"I'm working here now and I'm going to have to trust you with my life. You see it was getting too difficult for me in Chantilly because of your relationship with me. You know what people called me, and they had started to threaten us so I didn't feel safe anywhere."

"But how did you get a job here? We never had many French civilians working in this camp," Scholtz said.

"This is where I've to trust you. You see I'm in the French Résistance and before you say anything, I never spied on *you*. Believe me I wouldn't have done that, even for the Résistance and I know this will hurt you, but I had to do this." Madeleine paused. "I've been Colonel Richter's mistress."

Scholtz rolled his eyes and his breathing suddenly became laboured. Madeleine reached out a hand and held his as she stroked his forehead with the other. "Don't fret," she said. "He meant nothing to me, but I had to do it. He threatened to make sure I'd never see Jean again if I didn't agree, and to have little Louis taken away."

A worried frown crossed Scholtz's brow.

"You knew my husband Jean was in the French Army and that because he's a Jew he was deported. Somehow Colonel Richter got to know and promised to protect Jean provided I became his mistress."

"You should have told me this," Scholtz whispered. "I've influence you know, he's only a mere Colonel." And he gave a half-hearted smile.

Madeleine shook her head as she tried to keep her mind focused on what Richter had told her to do. "I couldn't," she said. "I'd have lost Jean and my son Louis. Anyway the Résistance got me this job, in order that I could pass on information about troop movements as the threat of the Allied invasion approaches."

Scholtz closed his eyes briefly and then opened them again and looked at Madeleine. "So why have you come to see me? What do you want from me?"

"The Résistance knows you're involved in a plot to overthrow Hitler and they must have the names of the other Generals to warn them, in case you're tortured and talk. Please General you've got to trust me. We both know that Doctor Aveleine and his wife and daughter are in the Résistance also. I know they're close friends of yours and I know they're prisoners here. But please hurry I don't have much time."

Scholtz shook his head. "How can I Madeleine?" he said. "Even if what you say is true and even if I did know the names of these Generals you speak of. I couldn't in all conscience tell you."

"But General," Madeleine pleaded.

Scholtz shook his head again. "For all you know the Gestapo might be on to you even as you speak. If I told you the names you speak of and the Gestapo tortured you, you'd tell them everything."

"But so might you."

Scholtz smiled. "Sometimes the Gestapo treat people like me as if we're fools. You see I've known for a long time that I'm under suspicion, and if it comes to the bit the Gestapo will never get to torture me."

"General?"

"It's all right Madeleine. I knew this could happen and I've taken precautions. I'm afraid my War's over."

Madeleine was at a loss what to do. She recognised that Scholtz was determined to take his own life rather than reveal the names of the other Generals and she couldn't see how she would persuade him otherwise. Reluctantly she shook her head as the General smiled and closed his eyes. "I'm tired now," he whispered.

She kissed him on the forehead and left the room dreading what Richter would say to her. As the guard closed the door she thought of trying to make a run for it, but instead she began to make her way back to Richter.

As she did so, she saw Jacque Aveleine entering Richter's office ahead of her. She had no desire to see or meet the man who had tried to kill her and so she held back, but then curiosity got the better of her, and she walked faster to the office and stood outside the partially open door.

Aveleine had just returned from the Hospital, forlorn because once again he had failed where he should have been much more astute. When he made enquiries from Nurse Yvonne it became clear that there was no soldier from the camp who had an accident. This meant that the other 'patient' in the room at the same time as his sister must have been a member of the Résistance.

He stood before Richter and told him what he had found out.

"Just as I thought," Richter said. "And you know what that means Aveline? Thanks to your incompetence the Résistance knows where Scholtz is and they'll do anything to rescue him or to get that information from him. If he's in league with other Generals and the Résistance find out who they are, they'll warn them so that they can go into hiding. Then when this invasion comes they'll throw in their lot with the Résistance against the Fatherland."

He thumped the desk with his fist. "They'll never get that information Aveleine, but I will, as well as Scholtz's confession on another little matter."

He looked at his watch. "It's getting late. I've sent Madeleine Boussine to the General's room with instructions to persuade him to give her the names of the others involved with him, on the pretext that she's been working for the Résistance all the time. It probably won't succeed but it's worth a try. If she fails then it's down to you Aveleine, I don't want anybody else involved in this. Do what you have to do, but get that information."

Aveleine's heart missed a beat. "It's the only way you can redeem yourself," Richter added. "It will test your loyalty to the Führer and prove your worth to me. But Madeleine might have saved you the bother, if you're lucky."

Aveleine couldn't contain his anxiety at Richter's expectations, knowing he'd almost certainly fail. "But Colonel," he almost whimpered. "The General was a family friend. I … I can't go in and torture a family friend. Surely even you wouldn't expect that of me!" And his voice tailed off as he saw the look on Richter's face.

Richter glared at him. "Your father and mother, and your sister are here Aveleine. I suggest you bring your problem to them. They were great friends of Scholtz. If he won't listen to you, perhaps he'll listen to them. After all it could save their lives and yours. You can even tell them if they'll believe you, that I'll spare the General's life as well as their own."

Madeleine stood outside the door listening to the conversation between Aveleine and Richter. She was conscious of the curious looks from soldiers working in the castle as they hurried about their business. She was well able to know the thoughts that would be running through their minds.

The castle was like every Inn and eating-place in France, alive with rumours and innuendoes. Then suddenly her mind went numb as she heard Richter say to Aveleine. "And see to it when you're finished, that Madeleine's husband that Jew, Jean Boussein in the Police cells in Chantilly is removed to the Drancy camp immediately with his brat of a son. I want them deported to Poland without delay because I've no further use for them."

"Yes Colonel," she heard Aveleine agree as he turned to leave the office.

Then Aveleine hesitated and turned and looked at Richter, who in turn frowned and looked around him.

Madeleine, who was still outside, began to panic. She'd heard it herself, how her husband Jean's fate was sealed along with her little boy Louis. She dared not think what would become of them. She'd heard the rumours about the Jews and what happened to them. She turned to run back towards her room, desperate to do something to protect Jean and Louis. Then she stopped, as did others around her, and like them she looked up as if the vast ceilings of the castle would open up and reveal the cause of the sudden noise.

It was a deep roar like thunder, coming ever closer. Richter stepped across the office and threw back the huge drapes that covered the windows and looked outside into the inky blackness. He saw the searchlights on the distant perimeter wall, searching the night sky. The sound came even closer and suddenly it was all around them and the sound of gunfire startled him.

Holmes checked his bearings and then he and another man ran towards the ammunition store. The other two ran to the fuel depot where they placed plastic explosive with time delay fuses and then they ran on towards a transport area where they placed explosives where it would have the maximum impact.

There was bedlam in the camp with soldiers running everywhere. Aveleine stepped across to the window of Richter's office and reached out to pull the drapes across. "The light, Colonel," he said and without waiting pulled the drapes back across the windows.

Chapter forty

All the lights in the camp, apart from the searchlights had been switched off and the whole area was in darkness. At the ammunition and explosives store Holmes found a heavy metal door barred their way. They put plastic explosive around the lock and hinges with a time delay fuse of sixty seconds and then ran for cover.

The explosive went off in forty seconds and they wasted no time in running back to find the door lying at a grotesque angle. They made their way into the underground store using torchlight. They placed the rest of the explosive in strategic points and set the time delay fuses again and retired as quickly as they'd come.

Holmes and his companion then made their way back to the perimeter wall and waited for the others. They arrived beaming from ear to ear, and together they returned to the wooden towers and called to the men there who'd captured them. When they'd got their attention above the siren and the gunfire they placed plastic explosive with a fuse at the base of each searchlight.

The men who had captured the searchlights joined the rest and as they all made it back to the convoy in safety with minutes to spare, there was pandemonium in the camp with the Germans believing the explosions were bombs. The bombers were then on their last run, flying low over the camp when suddenly there was a flash in the sky. The raiders looked up and saw the outline of a Lancaster silhouetted against a dim moonlit sky. Smoke and flames were billowing from an engine and the plane was obviously stricken.

They watched in anguish while the plane descended lower and lower, praying that the crew managed to bale out. As they jumped into their vehicles they heard the explosion and saw the burst of flame as the Lancaster crashed on the far side of the camp.

The other two bombers had started their homeward journey as the anti-aircraft fire subsided and the siren stopped. Lights came back on around the camp as the convoy began its final run to the camp entrance.

Inside the camp, vehicles were hurriedly started and soldiers climbed in as they were ordered to race out to the crashed Lancaster and also to search the surrounding area for any crewmembers that managed to bale out.

Paddy Mayne's convoy reached the camp entrance just as the first vehicle roared out through the camp gates. Balfour, in the first half-track, was taken unawares and he stopped suddenly, uncertain what to do. Paddy Mayne swore loudly and shouted at O'Hanlon to drive around the half-track.

Ruddell and Kelland, in the back of Paddy Mayne's Kubelwagen, were already ahead of their commander. O'Hanlon accelerated after the German vehicle. It was a Maultier – Mule – that was a German truck with the rear wheels removed, bolted unto the tracked assembly of a Panzer 11 light tank. Paddy Mayne was eager for the attack as they caught up with it. The unsuspecting Germans didn't even look at who was following them, assuming the Kubelwagen to be one of their own. O'Hanlon let a whoop out of him as he drew level with the Mule. Paddy Mayne and Ruddell opened fire with the twin Lewis guns and Kelland was able to throw a grenade, which landed in the middle of the vehicle, because the Germans had driven off without the canvas top. It was a massacre and the German vehicle careered across the road and burst into flames.

O'Hanlon braked and turned the Kubelwagen around in the direction of the camp. He drove back furiously past the burning vehicle as two survivors tumbled out, one with his tunic in flames. "Back to the camp Red," Paddy Mayne shouted. "We don't want to lose the initiative and allow those Krauts time to gather their wits."

One of the soldiers tried to get up and staggered to his feet. He was bewildered and badly shaken. Ruddell fired a short burst from the Lewis gun and he tumbled over and fell dead.

Balfour had already gathered himself in the short time it took Paddy Mayne's Kubelwagen to return, because his men had strafed a second vehicle, a Hanomag with eight soldiers on board, as it raced from the camp. When it also crashed they finished off the survivors without mercy.

Balfour then positioned his men, armed with Bren guns, on either side of the camp entrance. There were two men on either side shielded by the massive stone pillars that supported the iron gates. The rest lay prostrate on the grass verge armed with sub-machine guns and hand-grenades.

O'Hanlon drove up to the huge Iron Gates and on Paddy Mayne's command paused briefly. Paddy Mayne jumped out and ran back down the convoy that had stopped to see what was happening. He shouted at the top of his voice. "Nothing's changed lads. Plan stays the same, everybody follow us, and make it sharp. Anything moves, shoot it."

He leapt into the Kubelwagen beside O'Hanlon who was sitting with a huge grin on his face. "Off you go Red, you Southern rebel," he shouted. "We might have lost some of the element of surprise, but not it all. Those Krauts still won't know what's hit them."

Madeleine heard the distant explosions amidst the turmoil around her. She didn't wait any longer, and like others, believing the explosions were bombs, she ran to her room. For a while she sat cowering in the corner, covering her ears with her hands, almost willing a bomb to end her misery.

Richter stood transfixed for a moment in his office. He felt no fear, but was perplexed as to why the Chantilly camp had apparently been singled out by the Allies. He strode out of his office as the sound of the planes faded into the distance, but he was unaware that one had been shot down.

Then the ammunition dump went up with an almighty bang, followed by explosions from the transport depot. He immediately assumed that bombs with some sort of delay fuse to catch unwary soldiers had exploded.

When Madeleine heard those explosions she began to sob bitterly.

Richter raced down the great stairway of the castle towards the front door to find out what was happening. He called across to an Officer of the Wehrmacht and demanded an immediate report only to be told that Gruppenführer Franz Hössler was in charge.

He swore and turned around just as he became aware of distant gunfire and then he ran back to his office. Madeleine had since forced herself to leave her room. She walked over to the balcony from where she had seen Andrea try to flee, trying to hold back the tears. She saw Richter return to his office and then saw Aveleine walk out of it in a great hurry.

People ran everywhere and in the ensuing pandemonium, Madeleine, knowing she could do nothing about her invalid mother, raced down the stairway towards the front entrance. Ahead of her she just managed to see Aveleine rush out through the front door. She nearly tripped as she turned desperately in case Richter had seen her, but nobody paid any attention as she followed Aveleine and slipped out into the night.

The convoy of Kubelwagens and Half-tracks was racing up the tree lined gravel path towards the castle. After the confrontation at the front gate they met no further opposition.

Paddy Mayne was still in the lead Kubelwagen with O'Hanlon driving flat out. With trees on either side they could not see any movement, and the castle itself was still half a mile ahead of them. Paddy Mayne had issued instructions not to use the searchlights until absolutely necessary. Flames from the distant fuel dump were just about visible through the trees. Then they came to a fork in the road. The castle was straight ahead, and the fork to the right led to the fuel store and transport depot. The ammunition silo was further away again. Other roads then led towards accommodation blocks, various offices and miscellaneous stores.

Paddy Mayne stopped briefly at the fork in the road. He jumped out and ran back to the Kubelwagen behind him, ignoring the radio beside him. Corporal Trevor Bell was the driver, with Privates McIntyre, Weir and Burke.

"This is it Dinger," he said to Bell. "You drive off to the right and Tim will follow. You're on your own now and give them hell and get back to the front entrance of the castle as quickly as you can. We need maximum confusion out there. Don't let them know what's hit them. Keep on the move, firing all the time as you do."

He stood back and waved Bell on. Private Tim Anderson followed them, with Johnston, Wilson and Teggart. Major Bob Holmes had moved up in the last Kubelwagen and Paddy Mayne ran back briefly to the last Half-track with six of the Baker's Dozen eager to get into the fight. Most of them had old scores to settle and couldn't wait.

"Wait here," Paddy Mayne said. "I'm depending on you to hold this junction at all costs for our getaway and be ready to move up to the castle. If we need you I'll call you, and if you come under serious attack call us on the radio or bring up our friends guarding the entrance. We'll be as fast as we can."

Then as an after thought he shouted. "And look after that ambulance, we may need it."

Phil Graham looked up with a wry smile. "We'll be here," he yelled back.

Bell drove off at speed followed immediately by Anderson. Their hearts were racing but they knew they still had the major advantage of surprise. There was still no way the Germans could possibly know what was about to hit them. The German Officers still believed they had been subjected to an Allied air raid. They waited to hear from the two vehicles they'd sent out to search for any aircrew that managed to bale out of the stricken Lancaster, and they had sent troops to the areas where the explosions had been heard to check for casualties and damage.

Meanwhile Paddy Mayne settled back grimly in his Kubelwagen, both hands firmly grasping the Twin Vickers machine-gun. Inside he was experiencing emotions he had never had to contend with before. He couldn't get the image of Andrea out of his mind, nor was he able to shut out the sound of her beautiful voice singing 'Oh Danny Boy'. And he felt the velvety touch of her hand in his. He closed his eyes briefly and grimaced to concentrate on the mission in hand and then turned and nodded to Red O'Hanlon, who grinned with glee as he accelerated towards the castle. Ruddell and Kelland checked their guns yet again, and gave a wave to Major Bob Holmes and his men as they followed them.

The castle had been in virtual darkness during the air raid, but when it was over lights came on again. Paddy Mayne saw them through the trees as they drove the short distance towards the front of the castle.

Then a German Staff car raced towards them. The driver obviously did not realise the Kubelwagens he was approaching were manned by British SAS soldiers. Paddy Mayne held his fire rather than give advance warning to Germans at the castle, whom he was still expecting to take by surprise. And in any event he expected the French at the gate would deal with the Staff car and its occupants appropriately.

Aveleine had been glad of the excuse to leave the castle. The last thing he wanted was to die as the result of an aerial bombardment. The very thought of being blown to bits by a bomb or even worse of being buried under tons of rubble horrified him. As he raced from the castle in search of a vehicle and driver to bring him to Chantilly he was thanking his lucky stars he had got away from Richter.

He had also managed, for the time being at least, to avoid having to confront his parents. He was convinced Richter did not fully understand the impossible position he had put him in. As he ran there was pandemonium everywhere, even as the sound of the bombers died away into the distance. There were still explosions as he arrived at the transport pool.

Soldiers were milling around everywhere amidst the shouts of orders and the general clamour of battle. A staff car was sitting with the engine running and the driver was standing with a group of soldiers gesticulating towards the castle. Aveleine stopped running when he saw them and changed to a fast walk.

"I'm commandeering this car for Colonel Richter," he said.

"I'm sorry Captain," the driver retorted. "You can't. It has already been commandeered by someone else."

Aveleine calmly withdrew his pistol and pointed it at the soldier's midriff. "We'll go now," he said emphatically.

The driver looked at Aveleine, and then at his colleagues, who despised but nevertheless feared the *SS*. "You'd better," Aveleine heard one of them say.

The driver shrugged and returned to his car and Aveleine got in beside him, re-holstering his pistol.

"Chantilly," he said grimly to the driver. "The Police Station, and make it fast."

The driver put the car into gear and accelerated down the road towards the front of the castle, and then hard left towards the front gates.

Half way down the road Aveleine shouted to the driver. "Watch out," as the figure of a woman suddenly appeared in front of them, but she'd already stepped out of their way.

Aveleine spun around in his seat, convinced that he'd seen Madeleine. He couldn't understand what she could be doing there, and just as he had turned to face the front again he saw a column of Kubelwagens driving towards the castle without lights. He was about to tell the driver to stop when he thought better of it and they continued towards the gate to the open road.

Suddenly Red O'Hanlon swore, as he braked and swerved to avoid the same young woman who had appeared out of the darkness and in the glare of the approaching Staff car's lights. If the Staff car had not come at that precise moment O'Hanlon would almost certainly have knocked her down and killed her. Instead she was hit a glancing blow and thrown onto the grass verge.

Paddy Mayne swore with annoyance, but despite the desperate urgency to get to the castle before they were discovered, he ordered Red to stop. He jumped down as Ruddell and Kelland swung their guns in an arch to cover them in case the Germans attacked. Holmes climbed down also as the woman struggled to get to her feet.

Then they heard rapid gunfire behind them and they crouched low but Paddy Mayne quickly dismissed the threat as only the Baker's Dozen dealing with the German Staff car.

The woman was obviously in pain but did not appear badly injured. Believing they were Germans, she nonetheless spoke in French. "I'm all right," she said, catching her breath. "Just let me be. Colonel Richter knows where I'm going."

Paddy Mayne looked at Holmes, who interpreted for him. "Tell her that we're British," Paddy Mayne said. "And ask her what she was doing in the castle, and if she knows where the prisoners are being held."

Holmes looked at Madeleine and smiled. "We'll not harm you," he said in French. "We're British. Look at our uniforms and we're here to help the French, but *you* must help us. We need to know where the Germans are holding the French Resistance they've captured, and we're looking for a General Scholtz whom the Germans have arrested. Can you help us, quickly?"

Madeleine hesitated. "You've got to hurry," Holmes insisted kindly. "If you know anything tell us, and you're free to go. I promise you, just help us, before the Germans come."

"You're really British?" Madeleine said in awe.

"Of course we are," Paddy Mayne said interrupting Holmes. "Do you know anything?"

Madeleine immediately perked up at the sound of an English voice. Then in her own faltering English she asked. "If I help you, will you help me save my husband and son from the *SS?*"

Paddy Mayne looked at Holmes. "We'll do everything we can," Holmes said. "That's a promise."

Madeleine pulled herself up gingerly and climbed in between Ruddell and Kelland. O'Hanlon accelerated as Paddy Mayne resumed his place in the front. Holmes's Kubelwagen followed close behind.

The road towards the castle still wound its way through trees on either side and then suddenly, without warning, they found themselves in the open, facing the front of the castle. Arc lights lit the approach, and as the two Kubelwagens suddenly slowed, Paddy Mayne had a quick glance around him and then he turned and stared blankly at Holmes behind him

He shouted out to Holmes above the din. "The pylon Bob. Your explosive hasn't blown it. This place should be in darkness. They'll cut us down like ninepins if we go in now."

German soldiers were milling around the front door. Vehicles of one kind and another were parked a short distance away. Most had their engines running but nobody paid any attention to the two Kubelwagens.

O'Hanlon brought his Kubelwagen to a halt a hundred yards from the front of the castle. Paddy Mayne turned round and looked at Madeleine. "You'd better keep your head down," he said.

Then he jumped onto the ground oblivious of the Germans a hundred yards from him and walked calmly back to Holmes.

"What's going on Bob? It should have blown by now," he said.

"You know the timers are unpredictable sir," Holmes said. "But have faith." And he smiled knowingly. "Let's keep our heads down and sit it out for a minute. They may still go, and if they don't we'll just have to go in anyway. The Jerries still won't know what hit them and at least we'll be able to see what we're doing."

Paddy Mayne shook his head in exaggerated despair. "That's what we've these bloody searchlights for," he said. "Anyway I'll see if this woman knows anything, but the first sign that those soldiers are looking suspiciously at us we're going in all guns blazing, so be ready."

Paddy Mayne went back to his vehicle and settled into his front position. Then he turned to Madeleine.

"No offence lady," he said. "But we know nothing about you so if you lead us astray, you're dead. Now we're going into that castle to bring out French prisoners and this German General called Scholtz. There's going to be a lot of shooting so you'd better keep your head down, but I want you to come in with us. Now do you know your way around this castle to where any of these people are?"

Madeleine nodded. "You'll still help to save my husband and son?"

"Of course," Paddy Mayne said. "Where are they? In the castle?"

"No," Madeleine said. "They're being held in the Police prison in Chantilly."

"Then we'll try and deal with that later," Paddy Mayne agreed. "In the mean time we've a more pressing engagement."

301

"But you don't realise," Madeline said. "Colonel Richter has ordered Jacque Aveleine to send them to a concentration camp. He's on his way to the prison now. I saw him leave the castle."

Paddy Mayne saw the pain and anguish in Madeleine's eyes and suddenly felt compassion for her and he had to bottle up his curiosity about Jacque Aveleine.

"All right," he did his best to reassure her. "I understand, and we really will do what we can, but first of all what can you tell me about the whereabouts of these French people and the German?"

"Bring me with you and I'll show you," Madeleine said.

Paddy Mayne turned again to look at Holmes. He had seen soldiers at the front of the castle pointing towards them and a couple of them had actually waved at them. "We can't wait much longer Bob," he shouted.

Then away in the distance he heard shooting. At first it was only a few shots in rapid succession but they all quickly recognised the unmistakable sound of the twin Vickers machine guns. And then there was more and this time it was sustained bursts of fire and Paddy Mayne and the rest of the men knew that their colleagues had finally engaged the enemy.

It was just what Paddy Mayne wanted, something to distract the attention of the Germans at the castle. "We'll have to go in Bob," he shouted to Holmes. "When we get in, the lady here will help us find our prisoners so we'll need to watch out for her."

O'Hanlon revved the engine of his Kubelwagen and accelerated towards the castle. He quickly gathered pace with Holmes close behind them. Then just as Paddy Mayne was about to order Ruddell and Kelland to open up with their guns, they heard an explosion, followed quickly by another.

"Slow down Red," Paddy Mayne shouted. "That's the pylon. Let's give it time, another minute won't hurt anybody."

He turned and signalled to Holmes who looked back at him with a huge grin on his face and he gave him the thumbs up.

Chapter forty one

The pylon where Holmes and his men had left the plastic explosive carried electricity cables to a small sub-Station, which was also within the camp. The explosions blew off two large pieces of the legs of the pylon. For a moment nothing appeared to happen as the strength of the cables held it. It was only for a moment though, because slowly the weight put too much strain on them, and the pylon lurched forward, resting for a second on the two legs shortened by the explosion.

There was a huge flash and a bang as cables snapped and fell against the steel and then the pylon, like a great prehistoric monster crashed to the ground. Sparks flew everywhere and the explosive had done its job.

Suddenly as Paddy Mayne and Holmes halted yet again the castle was thrown into darkness. "Now," Paddy Mayne shouted. "Well done Bob, let's go before a generator comes on."

He flicked on the powerful searchlight that had been fitted to the Kubelwagens, and Holmes did the same. With the sound of the other Vickers machine guns blasting away in the distance, O'Hanlon accelerated again and then Paddy Mayne, Ruddell and Kelland opened up with their twin Vickers machine guns.

By now Holmes was driving alongside Paddy Mayne's Kubelwagen, towards the unsuspecting Germans. With the searchlights blinding them the Germans didn't stand a chance and they were mown down like corn before a scythe.

The shooting was over in a matter of minutes, and the ground in front of the castle was left littered with dead and dying German soldiers, and vehicles in flames.

There was pandemonium inside the castle, which now in complete darkness. Richter had been in his office, pacing up and down in utter frustration. Then when he heard the explosions from the pylon he stopped suddenly at his desk and pulled the drapes from across the windows again. He looked out and saw the flash from the broken cable, and suddenly the place was in darkness.

He stumbled towards the door of his office and yelled out an order. "Get the generator on now."

Somewhere in the distance he heard someone reply. "Yes Colonel; right away."

Then he heard the shooting and it was coming closer. He stood outside his room and heard the yells of pain and anguish from the soldiers. "What the hell's going on?" he screamed. "What's happening out there?"

Paddy Mayne's Kubelwagen stopped right in front of the great front door of the castle, and it was wide open. Holmes had drawn up to one side of Paddy Mayne. They switched their searchlights off and the cries of the wounded and dying men sent shivers down their spines. Holmes and one other man left their vehicle, and they were fully armed as they fell in behind Paddy Mayne's Kubelwagen.

Paddy Mayne switched on the searchlight again and ordered O'Hanlon forward. O'Hanlon accelerated just as two other searchlights came towards them. It was the other two Kubelwagens, and they raced to the front of the castle and took up positions at opposite corners. With them in place the other two men left Holmes's Kubelwagen and followed the others into the castle.

Corporal Bell and Private Tim Anderson left the driving seats of their Kubelwagens and took up position behind two of the twin Vickers machine guns in Holmes's Kubelwagen. By so doing they were providing maximum firepower in the event of the Germans managing to regroup and attack.

O'Hanlon drove the Kubelwagen through the doors of the castle and right into the great marbled entrance hall. The sound of the engine reverberated around the hall and the smell from the exhaust and cordite filled the air. Paddy Mayne jumped down with a torch in one hand and a Bren gun in the other as if it was a toy.

The place was still in darkness and Kelland switched on the searchlight and shone it around. The blinding light caught soldiers unaware as Paddy Mayne handed Madeleine the torch and lifted her like a rag doll onto the ground.

"We've very little time," he shouted. "Lead the way to the General?"

Madeleine ran frantically in front of Paddy Mayne, desperate to get the job in hand finished as quickly as possible. She was nearly demented with fear at the violence all around her and at the thought of not getting to Jean and Louis in time.

As Paddy Mayne raced after Madeleine, Ruddell and Kelland fired a couple of quick bursts at the soldiers who had been caught in the glare of the searchlight, which temporarily blinded them, and left them totally bemused. They were like rabbits caught in the glare of the headlights of a car. Just as their colleagues outside didn't stand a chance, neither did they. Chunks of marble and slivers of wood flew everywhere. Windows were shattered and a huge ornate mirror came crashing to the ground.

The heavy calibre bullets tore into raw flesh. Heads were almost severed and limbs torn apart. It was wholesale slaughter and even Ruddell and Kelland winced at what they witnessed.

Richter was beside himself with rage, totally at a loss to know what was happening. The only thing he could think of was that the Allies had sprung a surprise attack, and that the aircraft he had heard had dropped off Paratroopers. He was convinced they had come for the General, or perhaps even for him. He appeared suddenly at the top of the stairway trying to see what was going on and looking for a way of escape. Soldiers behind him were trying to regroup, to mount a counter attack but they lacked the will to fight an enemy they couldn't see.

Such was the controlled ferocity from Ruddell and Kelland's firepower, they wouldn't have stood a chance and they knew it. The searchlight picked out Richter, and Ruddell fired a quick burst, but he had vanished out of sight just as quickly as he had appeared.

Holmes and Corporal Southworth stayed close behind as Paddy Mayne followed Madeleine to the room where General Scholtz was held. The guard had left, and the door was locked. Paddy Mayne fired at the lock and then kicked the door open and they went into the room.

He took the torch from Madeleine and walked over to the bed and shone it on the General's face. He was very still and his face was contorted through the agony of cyanide poisoning.

Paddy Mayne looked at him for a moment and then he turned to Madeleine. "Are you absolutely sure this is Scholtz?"

Madeleine shuddered. "Yes," she whispered, more than a hint of tears in her eyes. "It's the General. He said the Gestapo would never get him. If only he'd known you were coming."

"Damn it," Paddy Mayne said.

"All this way for a bloody corpse," Southworth muttered.

They turned and walked quickly out of the room.

"OK," Paddy Mayne said, turning to Madeleine. "Where are the other prisoners?"

"But what about my husband and son? Please, you must stop Jacque Aveleine before it's too late," Madeleine cried.

"We may already have got him," Paddy Mayne said. "I'll explain later, but for now we've got to finish this job before we leave. Lead us to where the prisoners are being held."

They quickly retraced their steps back to the central hall. The agonising screams of the dead and injured pierced their hearts. An occasional shot rang out from somewhere in the castle where an alarmed soldier fired at the slightest sound. In the mayhem more than one German died at the hands of one of his colleagues.

Richter had gathered a group of soldiers, and they made their way along the first floor to gain access to the ground floor by another route. From there he hoped to be able to mount a counter-attack, but he didn't know if the invaders outgunned him.

Meanwhile Paddy Mayne gathered his men around the Kubelwagen and was about to give orders when suddenly the whole place was lit up again. Someone had got the generator going.

In an instant Paddy Mayne was able to see the devastation they had caused in the short time the battle had raged. Instantly a few bursts from the Lewis guns extinguished the lights in the immediate vicinity. However corridors leading of the entrance were now bathed in light.

At first Paddy Mayne thought it could be a disaster for them but he quickly realised it could be to their advantage. Because of where they were, they couldn't extinguish the other lights, but they lit up the corridors so that nobody could approach them without being seen. The main problem was that at the top of the stairway it was conceivable that someone could come on them unseen!

He immediately despatched Southworth to the top of the stairway, armed with a Bren gun and grenades. Southworth was so placed that nobody could approach the top of the stairway without a serious risk to themselves.

Paddy Mayne then took Madeleine by the arm. "Quick as you can," he said. "Bring us to the other prisoners."

"This way," Madeleine said. "They're down in the dungeon."

Paddy Mayne swallowed hard and followed Madeleine, watching closely for the slightest sign of movement. Holmes, Bannon and Kelly followed.

Madeleine led them along a long corridor, and half way along it she brought them down a flight of marble steps, which quickly gave way to bare stone. The steps soon gave way again to another corridor where the only light was what filtered through from the floor above.

Paddy Mayne switched on the torch and turned to Bannon. "Chris you'd better go back up those steps and guard our exit. I don't fancy having to fight our way out of this corridor."

Bannon ran back to the top of the marble stairs and waited.

Paddy Mayne and the others hurried down the corridor. It was cold and damp. Water trickled down the stone walls and there were no doors or windows visible. They were in complete darkness apart from the torch.

Then the torch lit up first one door and then another. Each door had a small iron grill. Paddy Mayne shone the torch through the grill of the first door. At first he saw nothing except a bucket, but then as he shone the torch around the cell, huddled in the corner he saw two people, a man and a woman. The woman was moaning softly.

As the torch shone on their faces the woman raised herself up, shielding her eyes from the light. "Leave us alone for pities sake," she cried out. "Haven't you done enough? Can't you see my husband's ill? He needs treatment or he'll die."

Paddy Mayne immediately knew it was Anton and Marie Aveleine. "It's all right," Paddy Mayne shouted through the grill. "We're British. Keep well away from the door; I'm going to shoot the lock off."

He fired two shots at the lock and kicked the door hard. He swore when it remained closed so he fired two more shots and this time when he tried it the door opened.

He turned to Kelly. "Help them out," he said. "And bring them up to Bannon and wait there for us. We'll try the next door."

Kelly felt his way over to the two prisoners, reassuring them as he did. Marie grasped his arm as he came close. "You're really British?" she asked with obvious disbelief.

"Yes we are," Kelly said. "We're here to get you out, but we'll have to be quick."

Meanwhile Paddy Mayne and Holmes had reached the other door and again he shone the torch and saw Andrea huddled in a corner. She shielded her eyes from the bright light.

"Who is it?" she whispered.

"It's me," Paddy Mayne said. "Keep away from the door; I'm going to shoot the lock off."

He fired two more shots and this time when he kicked the door it opened first time. Andrea pulled herself up and fell into Paddy Mayne's outstretched arms. There was a momentary embrace and then Paddy Mayne took Andrea's hand and led her out of the prison cell and into the corridor. She clung to him as they retraced their steps back along the corridor.

"We've got your parents," Paddy Mayne said as they passed the other open door. "Kelly will have brought them back along this corridor."

Andrea stopped suddenly. "We can't go without Gary," she said. "And Simone and Charles, I'm sorry, but we can't leave them."

308

"Who's Gary?" Paddy Mayne demanded.

"He's the British pilot we were hiding."

"We're going to run out of time here," Paddy Mayne said. "Where are they?"

"They must be in cells below mine," Andrea said.

Paddy Mayne and one of the others went back and found Tucker's cell. He had heard the shooting and was standing at his door when Paddy Mayne shone the torch in. They shot the lock off and helped Tucker out and although he was weak he was able to walk unaided. Simone's cell was also close by and of them all he was in the best shape. He was able to tell them that Charles was dead, as he'd seen the guards dragging his lifeless body away.

They made their way as quickly as possible to the bottom of the steps, where Kelly waited with Andrea's parents to join up with Bannon at the top.

Paddy Mayne didn't hesitate. "Follow me," he said as he led the way.

At the top, Bannon turned around with a broad smile on his face. Paddy Mayne looked up and down the corridor. He was surprised at the silence but didn't hesitate.

"Quickly," he said. "Let's get out of this place; it's beginning to give me the creeps."

They made their way back up the corridor, which led to the entrance hall. Andrea helped to support her parents while the others watched out for Germans. Suddenly out of the blue, there was a burst of gunfire from behind them. Andrea and her mother screamed. Paddy Mayne and the other SAS instinctively spun round and fell to their knees. The bullets ricocheted off the floor and walls but nobody was hit.

Paddy Mayne swore when he found they were faced with over a dozen heavily armed German soldiers. Most of them had MP 40 submachine guns. One soldier lay prostrate on the ground. His hand was firmly round the stock of a lethal MG 34 GPMG, his finger nervously on the trigger.

One man stood out in front of the rest. He said nothing in the standoff, obviously confident that he held the upper hand. Paddy Mayne knew that even if they all fired at once, every one of them would surely die in the ensuing exchange.

"It's Richter," Andrea whispered to Paddy Mayne. "He's cruel and vicious and there's nothing you can do Paddy, because if you make a move or try to shoot them we'll all die."

"What do you suggest," Paddy Mayne asked her.

"There's only one thing you *can* do," Marie said coming to stand beside Paddy Mayne. "We'll give ourselves up, and if we stay between them it'll give you a chance to get away. He wants us alive more than anything."

"No, there's another way," Andrea said, breaking away from the group.

Before Paddy Mayne could stop her she started walking towards Richter. Marie called after her, her hand outstretched. "No Andrea, don't do it."

Anton reached out a reassuring hand to Marie and she sighed heavily.

Paddy Mayne turned to Marie. "What's she going to do," he asked.

"It's Richter," Marie said. "She knows he loves beautiful young women and she's going to offer herself to him as a hostage, but I can't let her."

She began to walk after Andrea but Anton held her arm. "Wait Marie," he said.

Paddy Mayne nearly exploded with rage but Anton turned to him. "This isn't the time," he said. "Let's see what happens. Andrea's a courageous young woman and she knows what she's doing."

Andrea walked slowly towards Richter, who was smiling at her. He stretched his hand out towards his soldiers warning them not to do anything. Andrea was pale and desperately tired but to Richter's lustful eyes she was still ravishingly beautiful. Already his carnal desires were getting the better of him.

He made a move towards her but she stopped him. "If you touch me," she said. "We'll all die. That's the deal."

"What deal," Richter quizzed her.

Andrea managed a faint smile. "It's me you really want," she said. "Let the others go and I'll do what ever you want. Otherwise there'll be a bloodbath and you're certain to be the first to die. And remember there are more of them outside waiting."

Richter's hand was still outstretched. "Anything?" he whispered.

"Yes," Andrea heard herself saying.

"And what about the names of these German traitors, these General's who've sworn allegiance to the Allies?"

"I'll tell you what I know, and my parents don't know anything that I don't know."

"How do I know I can trust you?"

"I'll give you the name of the lone assassin you've been trying to find."

Richter immediately looked up, and his face brightened. "That's good," he said. "That would be very good. But how do I know the name you give me will be genuine, and not some fictitious name you make up? Nor some poor misguided Frenchman who's already been killed by a firing squad or tortured to death by the Gestapo?"

Andrea was weary and trying desperately think clearly. She didn't want what she said to make things even worse. In the end she saw no other way of convincing him to allow her parents, as well as the others, go free.

"When I tell you who it is you'll very quickly put two and two together and realise I'm telling you the truth," she said.

Richter lowered his hand and his brow was furrowed, his eyes squinting, expecting some trick.

"Go on," he said slowly.

"You must not touch this assassin," Andrea said. "Or you won't *have* me."

"All right, all right," Richter said trying to hurry her up. "Who is this mystery man who's murdered so many of our Officers?"

Andrea smiled faintly. "You knew that my father was a cripple? And yet if you look at him now you'll see that he's standing all by himself. I'm surprised you didn't notice."

Richter hesitated and couldn't help looking surprised. "So, he was a cripple, what's that got to do with anything?" he growled.

Andrea smiled, enjoying the moment briefly. "Well it was the perfect cover," she said. "My father was crippled by gunfire from an English Spitfire and supposedly never able to walk again. He was befriended by General Scholtz whose life he helped to save. Except that although my father was badly injured he recovered well enough to terrorise you Germans. But of course you all thought of him as a cripple so he was never a suspect; it was the perfect cover."

Richter swore.

"Yes," Andrea said. "You know I'm telling you the truth. My father *was* the assassin. But you must not harm him. You've given your word."

"And on the strength of that information you expect *me* to allow these murdering bastards to go free?" Richter said with undisguised hate in his voice.

"It's your choice," Andrea said. "If they don't walk away you'll die and a lot of others besides."

"And this information you've promised?" Richter said.

"I've already said I'll tell you all I know," Andrea said wearily.

"Everything?"

Andrea smiled. "Of course." She hesitated, choosing her words carefully. "I know your methods and I'm just a woman, so I've no doubt you'll get your information."

"Very well," Richter said. Then he looked beyond Andrea to Paddy Mayne and his men, and Marie and Anton and Madeleine. And his eyes fixed on Madeleine as he thought of Jacque Aveleine sending her husband and son to die in the gas chambers, and he was satisfied.

Then Paddy Mayne stepped forward. "We'll not do it," he said, looking at Richter. "You'll let us all go or we'll all die. It's your choice."

Richter was about to speak when Marie moved over to Paddy Mayne and spoke quietly but firmly to him. "Please," she said. "If we get out of here at least there's a chance, but we must go now. Richter will have sent for reinforcements. There can't be much time left."

Anton added his approval to Marie's advice. "I don't like it," Paddy Mayne said. "I don't bloody like it."

He turned and looked at the men. "We'd better do as they say," he muttered. "Get ready to move out, but keep them covered."

Then he walked purposefully the few feet to where Andrea stood. He hesitated for a moment beside her and then walked towards Richter. He stopped and pointed his finger at him, ignoring the looks of the others Germans.

"You'll pay for this you swine," he said and then turned around and walked slowly back past Andrea hesitating briefly as he came level with her, his back to the Germans. Without looking sideways he whispered. "We'll be back."

Reluctantly he ordered everyone to back out of the hall, keeping their eyes on the Germans. They made their way quickly to the Kubelwagen in the great hall. Paddy Mayne ordered Marie, Madeleine and Anton to cram themselves into the front passenger seat of the Kubelwagen. He and Ruddell took up positions in the rear with guns at the ready, and Kelland ran before them, with Tucker and Simone following as quickly as they could to the front doors. O'Hanlon reversed out, and Paddy Mayne breathed a sigh of relief as he felt the cold night air brushing his cheek.

O'Hanlon swung the Kubelwagen round and on Paddy Mayne's instructions he accelerated towards the front gates. Tucker and Simone were bundled unceremoniously into one of the other vehicles, both of which still had their full complement of SAS and they followed in hot pursuit.

Paddy Mayne's mind was now in turmoil. He thought of only one thing, and that was how he was going to rescue Andrea. He didn't care about the dead General or the names of his associates. He didn't stop to think that all their efforts had been to no avail. He just couldn't get the thought of Andrea out of his mind.

They raced at full speed towards the front gate, stopping briefly where the Baker's Dozen had been guarding the intersection. Paddy Mayne saw the German Staff car, which Jacque Aveleine had commandeered. It had crashed into a tree when a hail of bullets from the Bakers Dozen struck it.   He briefly noticed one figure in the passenger seat slumped forward and still.   The driver had been propelled through the windscreen and his lifeless body lay half in and half out of the car.   He didn't stop to ask questions about what had happened and told them to follow as quickly as possible.

O'Hanlon accelerated again, as the Baker's Dozen and the ambulance crew gathered themselves together and followed Paddy Mayne out of the castle grounds.

At the front entrance the others who'd guarded it jumped into their vehicle and followed the convoy.   Half a mile up the road Paddy Mayne ordered O'Hanlon to stop.   He jumped onto the road as the other vehicles pulled up.

"Everybody," he shouted.   "Gather round."

The men gathered in the darkness at the side of the road and waited. "We've been amazingly lucky," Paddy Mayne stated.   "I haven't heard of a single casualty and you all did a fantastic job."

He looked directly in the dim light at the motley collection that made up the Bakers Dozen.   "If any of you men want to join the SAS, come and see me afterwards."

They cheered.

"We've done all that was asked of us," Paddy Mayne continued. "Not our fault that the General was dead.   But there's one bit of unfinished business and that's to go back in there to get Andrea.   That bastard of an *SS* Officer is not going to have his way with her.   If any of my boys want to help I'll not turn them away, but with or without you I'm going back now.   They'll not expect us."

As one man all his colleagues said, "Not on your own you're not sir."

Paddy Mayne allowed himself a brief smile.   "Just as I thought," he said.

Then he paused.   "We'll play it differently this time.   As many of us as possible will pile into the ambulance.   We'll race up that road to the castle with the lights on and the siren blaring.   The Kubelwagens will follow but they'll not come too close to the castle and hopefully the Germans will believe they're there to support the ambulance.   The

314

men in the Kubelwagens will only fire if necessary. We're looking for the element of surprise again so we want to be into that castle and out again before they know what's happening."

He paused. "We'll back up close to the door and try and slip in without being seen."

He looked for Phil Graham. "Phil, how many white coats have you in that ambulance of yours?"

Graham hesitated. "Three I think," he said.

"Right," Paddy Mayne said. "Get the coats and whoever fits into them put them on."

The coats were quickly collected and O'Hanlon, McIntyre and Weir just about fitted into them after they removed some of their gear.

"You three will lead the way," Paddy Mayne said. "And we'll try and let you be seen. The rest of us will be right behind you. If you're spotted, then if at all possible use your knives. Shoot only if there's no other option, at least until we've located Andrea."

He looked again at the men around him. "Our aim is to get into the castle as quickly as possible and get Andrea out. We must try and avoid any distractions."

He turned to the Baker's Dozen. "You men have done a great job," he said. "Now I want you to go straight to Chantilly Police Station, and release Madeleine's husband Jean and her boy as I promised, and bring them back to the forest. We'll rendezvous back there again as soon as possible."

Finally he looked at Madeleine. "Is it possible to ask one more thing of you?"

She shook her head. "You can't ask me to go back in there. You can't."

"Nobody else knows their way around as you do," Paddy Mayne said. "We'll be in and out before you know it. And Jean and your boy will be waiting for you back in the camp."

He pointed to the Baker's Dozen. "Look," he said. "It's just as I promised. They're going now."

Just then Anton Aveleine stepped forward slowly. "Leave the girl," he said. "I know the castle better than she does. I probably even know

315

it better than the Germans. I played in it as a boy, and you've forgotten my friendship with General Scholtz. He invited me here many times, all be it in a wheel chair!"

"I don't know," Paddy Mayne said. "With all due respects sir you're hardly fit to go with us in there."

Anton smiled. "But look," he said. "No wheel chair and all you need me to do is to show you around."

Paddy Mayne shook his head. "We're losing valuable time." He hesitated. "OK, but for goodness sake keep your head down."

He turned again to the Baker's Dozen. "Take Madeleine with you," he said. "And bring Marie as well. We'll see you back at the camp."

Beaufort ordered his men and Madeleine into the two half-tracks and they started up their engines. Marie Aveleine was standing beside her husband Anton, clutching his arm. Beaufort called to her impatiently. "Marie we've got to get moving."

With that Anton kissed her and told her to go. "I'm going with Anton," she said, looking at him fiercely.

Paddy Mayne was about to protest but he saw immediately it would be hopeless. "On your way Beaufort," he ordered instead. "And no secondary targets on the way. You've one job to do now. Get it done and get out of Chantilly as quickly as you can."

Beaufort nodded and the half-tracks turned slowly on the road and accelerated towards Chantilly. The convoy of Kubelwagens then turned around and headed back towards the entrance to the castle grounds behind the ambulance.

Chapter forty two

Back in the castle grounds the evidence of a massacre was everywhere. It had taken some time for the Germans to realise that the raid was over. Only those who were in the castle itself were aware of what had happened inside it. For everyone it had either been a daring commando raid or the start of the expected invasion. The bombers overhead had given weight to the argument that it was the beginning of the invasion. Only Richter now realised that the raid was set up to free the prisoners.

Dead and dying soldiers lay wherever the SAS had been. So rapid and unsuspected was their attack that nobody had a chance to put up a credible defence. Now those who had survived sought to attend to the wounded and dying. They believed the danger was over. Weapons were cast aside as first-aid kits were brought out and medics did their best to help the most critically wounded, and stretchers were called for.

Richter had resented the fact that he wasn't able to take control as soon as the raid started, and when Paddy Mayne and the others left the castle, he determined to take his revenge on Andrea, but only when he'd extracted every last bit of information from her.

The fact that Scholtz had taken a cyanide capsule galled him, and he was furious that had been allowed to happen. He was still convinced that Andrea knew some of the names of the treacherous Generals, whose identity Scholtz had brought with him to the grave. He knew, that armed with those names, nobody could stand in his way. He left the Whermacht to clear up the mess the raiders had left behind.

As the last of the raiders left the castle, Richter dismissed the men he'd commandeered and told them to return to their posts. He stood in the corridor looking at Andrea. He was pale with stubble on his face and his eyes were red. His uniform was untidy and he had lost his headgear but he remembered what Andrea had said a few minutes previously, and he was determined to get that information. Andrea stood motionless, defiant with her chin tilted slightly upwards and the faintest hint of a smile on her lips. Paddy Mayne's last words were ringing in her ears, 'We'll be back again.'

The ambulance led the way back into the castle grounds. As they came closer, O'Hanlon, who was driving, turned the lights and the siren on and accelerated. The men in the Kublewagens were tense and alert, with their fingers on the triggers of the twin Lewis guns. As they reached the intersection again Paddy Mayne noticed that the crashed Staff car was still there, but he only saw one figure, the driver. He didn't stop to think about it.

They drove flat out to the front of the castle. The front door was still wide open and it was obvious that some power had been restored because lights were showing. The Germans who were stumbling around barely paid any attention to the ambulance and none at all to the Kubelwagens some distance behind it. In the darkness it was not possible to make out who the men were in them.

O'Hanlon swung the ambulance around and reversed towards the front door of the castle. He climbed out and went around the ambulance and opened the rear door and McIntyre and Weir stepped out. Their weapons were hidden by the white coats, which showed clearly in the night. They were in full view of a small number of Germans who looked but did not come over.

The Kubelwagens remained at a distance from the castle to try and avoid arousing suspicion.

Once inside O'Hanlon looked around and then beckoned to Paddy Mayne and the others to follow. Paddy Mayne led the way with Anton Aveleine close beside him. Inside the hallway of the castle the evidence of the carnage was everywhere.

Paddy Mayne grasped Aveleine by the arm as Marie looked on. "Come on," he said. "There's not much time. Where would Richter have taken Andrea?"

Marie looked at Anton. "He'll have taken over Scholtz's suite," Anton said. "That's up that flight of stairs. General Scholtz had an office with a lounge and bedroom attached to it."

Paddy Mayne turned to O'Hanlon. "Red," he said. "The three of you lead the way up those stairs. The doc here will go with you. If anybody spots you, the white coats will put them off and give you the edge."

He turned to Anton. "Stay well behind them," he ordered. "There could be shooting. Your job is simply to point the way." Then he turned to Marie. "You stay here – please."

Marie nodded and when Paddy Mayne realised she had no weapon he handed her his pistol. She smiled and nodded. Two men stayed at the bottom of the stairway whilst the others moved up it. Paddy Mayne and Anton kept well back until they were sure the coast was clear.

At the top of the stairs O'Hanlon walked forward just as two Germans appeared as if from nowhere. They stopped when they saw the men in white coats, but undaunted O'Hanlon and Weir walked towards them as if ask them something. Then like lightening they drew their knives and killed the men instantly. They pulled them across the floor to another door. They opened it cautiously, and seeing the room was empty, pulled the two men in and closed the door behind them.

Anton then stepped forward and pointed out Scholtz's office where he believed Richter would be with Andrea.

O'Hanlon tore off his white coat and threw it to the ground as did the other two. Paddy Mayne came forward and stopped outside the door of Scholtz's office. He motioned to O'Hanlon and Weir and they stood on either side. Paddy Mayne put his hand on the door handle and turned it and burst into the room with Weir and McIntyre right behind him.

The room was empty, but there was the smell of stale smoke and a half finished glass of whiskey on the desk. Paddy Mayne put his finger to his lips as he walked silently across the office to another door. Again he motioned to McIntyre and Weir to follow. Anton Aveleine had by now come into the office and he nodded as Paddy Mayne pointed to the other door.

Paddy Mayne listened intently and then instead of turning the handle he lifted his right foot and with incredible force smashed the door to the other room open. Paddy Mayne, McIntyre and Weir were in the room instantly, guns sweeping the room.

It was a bedroom, with a large double four-poster bed. There was a dressing table at the window and a large wardrobe against the wall. There was also a writing desk and an ornate chair in one corner. Heavy ornate curtains were pulled across the window.

The three men took it all in at a glance and then Paddy Mayne's eyes fastened on a woman's blouse thrown carelessly on the bed, and they saw a skirt hanging over the side of it. There was a bra and a pair of shoes on the floor.   He recognised the shoes as belonging to Andrea.

They looked at one another and around the room again and then their eyes fastened on a half open door leading into another room. There was a dim light coming through into the bedroom. Paddy Mayne motioned to O'Hanlon to stay at the door of the bedroom, but Anton Aveleine walked past him and followed the others.   Paddy Mayne pointed to Weir and McIntyre to move across the room, so that they were out of the line of fire when he opened the last door, and Anton Aveleine followed their lead.

He pushed the door open very slowly with his Sten Gun, until he could see into the room. It was another bedroom, smaller than the first, but again with a double bed. There was a large window but the curtains were open. Paddy Mayne noticed how dark it seemed outside and then he froze for a moment as at a glance he took in the sight before him. Richter was standing at the head of the bed. He was sweating and his tunic was unbuttoned.

He held a Luger pistol in one hand, pressed into Andrea's neck. His other hand was clasped across Andrea's mouth so that she couldn't speak. He was using Andrea as a shield, her naked body covering his so that Paddy Mayne didn't dare fire a shot. He felt his blood chill as his temper flared and finally he swore in a way that in all the time he'd known him, McIntyre had never heard him swear like it before.

For a moment Richter was visibly shaken, but he managed to keep calm and smiled faintly so that it was all Paddy Mayne could do to keep from throwing himself at Richter, whatever the consequences.

"I didn't think you'd have the nerve to come back," Richter said. "But then with all that this little lady knows, I should have known that you would. Just a pity you're going to have to leave again, without her."

"I'm damned if I will," Paddy Mayne fumed.

"You're damned if you don't," Richter said. "You see reinforcements are already on their way here so you're trapped like rats in a trap. You and your rabble of troops won't get out of here alive, and that's a promise."

He shuffled forward slightly, forcing Andrea to move with him. Her eyes were wide and staring, her hair was a mess and she was obviously terrified.

"We can make a deal," Paddy Mayne growled. "We'll throw down our guns, and you let the girl go. Then you can do what you like with us."

Richter laughed. It was a sickening laugh. "That's rich," he said. "That's exactly what I'd suggest. I let the girl go and you know perfectly well one of you would get me before I could shoot all of you. Give me some credit."

Paddy Mayne lifted his gun menacingly and pointed it towards Richter. McIntyre and Weir moved across the room. Anton Aveleine stood grim faced and pale just behind Paddy Mayne.

Chapter forty three

Pilot Officer Wilson Goddard was the last one to leave the stricken Lancaster. It had been a strange mission from the very beginning. At their briefing they were told it would be the easiest mission of the War. Three Lancasters were to fly to France and quite simply 'buzz' a castle near Chantilly for fifteen minutes and then fly home. 'A piece of cake' their CO had said.

As he saw the last of his crew who were left alive bale out, he couldn't help thinking to himself, 'some cake'. Then he knew every mission; however straightforward it may seem carried an element of risk.

There was a fairly stiff wind so that Goddard drifted quite a bit as he descended. He didn't try and correct the drift because in the darkness he couldn't see where he was heading anyway. So he let the wind take him where it would.

It was too late when he realised he was heading right for the very castle they were instructed to fly over for fifteen minutes. It looked so different as he descended rapidly. The castle was almost in complete darkness and as he descended even lower he heard the shooting and explosions but he had no idea where they came from.

Then he made out the canopy of trees and open spaces surrounding the castle and he tried to head for one of those, but he had little control over his final descent. He was just drifting down one side of the castle, missing a large wooden flagpole by a few feet, when the wind caught the parachute, and he was blown sideways.

The parachute caught on the tip of the flagpole, which ripped a hole in it, and it finally snagged at the base of the flagpole. Goddard was jerked to a sudden halt that took the breath from him. He found himself swinging backwards and forwards, as he brushed against the rough wall of the castle. The shooting was still going on as he hung there limply with nothing to catch a hold of. He heard the parachute rip again as he felt himself sinking lower and lower.

In desperation he looked down and some feet below him he could just make out a narrow ledge edged by a low concrete parapet. He hung there, thankful to be alive and desperate to get free. He tried to judge the distance, which was difficult in the darkness. Then the cloud cover broke and the moon shone briefly and he gasped as he realised how far he was from the ground.

He knew that if he released the parachute and allowed himself to go that he would fall to his death if he missed the ledge. He hung on and waited, but every now and then he felt the parachute slip a bit more. Then suddenly it gave way completely and he felt himself fall. He tried desperately to land on the ledge but he missed it by a couple of feet as he plummeted to the ground.

By sheer luck the parachute cords became entangled in the concrete parapet. Breathless, he hung without moving, fearful that the slightest movement would send him to his death. Then gradually, and ever so slowly he reached up and grasped the parachute cords and began painstakingly to pull himself upwards.

The cords held as he slowly drew himself up until he was finally able to grasp a hold of the parapet and pull himself onto the ledge. He released the parachute and gathered it together as best he could before stuffing it into a recess out of the way.

The ledge he was on ran around the castle wall, and in the darkness he began to feel his way around slowly. The moon had only shone for a brief moment and it was dark again. The shooting and explosions had long since died away and he presumed that whatever had happened, things were near normal again.

As he made his way around he was pressed in close to the wall of the castle, fearful that he might stumble in the dark and still fall to his death. Then he came on the outline of a window. He could feel the glass and he thought he could just about make out the backing of curtains, but there was no evidence of light.

Further round, he came on another window, and again he saw the unmistakeable outline of curtains, and where they were not completely drawn across, he saw a chink of light. He moved forward slowly and peered in and saw what looked like a bedroom, but he saw nobody.

Then he thought he heard the faint sound of voices and he slipped past the second window and came to another.

This time it was evident that the curtains had not been drawn because light was coming from the room. As he crept closer the voices became louder and he could have sworn he heard somebody speak English. He eased himself around, conscious that if he was careful he might be able to see into the room without himself being seen.

He came to the edge of the window and glanced into the room. He heard himself gasp at what he saw. He blinked and looked again and then he remembered the last words of his CO as he led his crew out to the Lancaster. "Just for you Bill, not to be shared," the CO said as Bill pulled himself into the cockpit. "This may seem a trifling matter to you but what you're doing tonight may help affect the rescue of some highly prized people. Top secret mind."

He was staring at British soldiers, possibly commandoes. He couldn't believe his luck, and he was about to rap the window with the butt of his pistol when he stopped himself. The soldiers were obviously engaged in a conversation, or at least one of them was. He was a very tall individual, and he was very angry.

Goddard lowered himself below the level of the windowsill and pulled himself forward a couple of feet, and then slowly looked in again. He couldn't believe what he saw. A German Officer was standing with a pistol at the head of a ravishingly beautiful naked woman, and he was using her to shield himself from British commandoes.

Inside the room there was stalemate. Then Richter sneered. "You had better back off, because you're not getting away with this. If you want her to live," and he pressed the pistol harder into Andrea's temple. "You'll leave right now."

Outside Goddard couldn't quite make out what was being said. He lent on the stone windowsill to get closer, not realising part of it was lose. It gave way and fell to the path. Goddard swore softly as he lost his balance, and although Richter had heard nothing, the sudden movement caught his eye. He saw a shadowy figure through the window. He immediately assumed it was more British soldiers, and he fired wildly at the fleeting shadow, shattering the windowpane.

It was a dreadful mistake for Richter. Andrea, frightened though she was, had never lost her cool head. She had been waiting, feigning terror, for such a moment as this. In the instance Richter pulled the gun from her head and fired, she tore herself from his grasp. He was completely taken by surprise, but he reacted swiftly and swung the gun round to cover Andrea as she tried to flee.

Paddy Mayne's reaction was even swifter, and like a panther he flung himself at Richter as he tried to bring the gun to bear on Andrea. Paddy Mayne's great bulk and the ferocity of his attack flung Richter to the ground. He fired his pistol wildly, and one shot hit the ceiling, sending chips of plaster flying. Paddy Mayne heard Andrea cry out.

For a heart stopping moment he thought she had been hit but then she screamed, "No father, no."

Paddy Mayne was on his feet instantly, whilst the others in the room still stood bemused by what had happened. Anton Aveleine had fallen to the ground with a bullet to his head. He died instantly.

Andrea picked herself up and ran to her father and threw herself on his lifeless body, crying bitterly.

Paddy Mayne stood towering over Richter with one foot firmly on the hand that held the pistol. His weight crushed his fingers like matchsticks. Richter cried out in agony, as Paddy Mayne bent down and grasped Richter's other arm by the wrist and pulled it back until he dislocated his shoulder.

Richter cried out in agony as Paddy Mayne then turned and in an amazingly quiet voice said. "OK boys; take her out with her father. We'll bring him back with us. I'll be with you in just a moment."

McIntyre and Weir looked at their leader with the utmost respect, nodded, and Weir pulled a blanket off the bed, and wrapped it round the broken hearted Andrea and they led her outside. They returned in a moment and gently lifted Anton Aveleine's body and brought it outside also.

Meanwhile O'Hanlon slipped into the room and stood just inside the doorway. He watched almost dumb struck, unable to say anything as he stared at Paddy Mayne.

All the while Richter was crying in agony as Paddy Mayne kept one foot on his pistol hand and kept the unbearable pressure on his other arm. Then he bent down and took the pistol and threw it to the side of the room. Richter was by now moaning and crying and talking incoherently.

Paddy Mayne was in a cold calculated fury. He took a step backwards, and allowed Richter's now useless left arm to drop.

There was a British Lee-Enfield rifle with a bayonet, resting on two wooden brackets on the wall. It was a relic of the First World War and had belonged to General Scholtz. Paddy Mayne reached over and pulled the rifle down and held it in the middle with his right hand.

Richter tried to turn as he sensed something of what was coming and he tried to beg for mercy, but all he saw was ice-cold hate in the eyes of the man who was about to kill him. Had he known what Paddy Mayne had in mind he might have passed out in sheer terror.

Paddy Mayne bent down and grasped Richter by the top of his tunic with his left hand. Using his incredible brute strength for which he was famed, he lifted Richter so that his feet were barely touching the ground. With a roar he slammed him against a large wooden wardrobe. Richter screamed in agony as Paddy Mayne drew back his right hand, and with the rifle held in a deadly grip and with another fierce roar, he impaled Richter through the midriff to the wardrobe.

At that point Richter mercifully passed out as blood from his severed aorta poured into his abdominal cavity.

Paddy Mayne turned without another glance, and seeing O'Hanlon growled. "What do you think this is Red, a bloody Punch and Judy show?"

O'Hanlon, who had seen more than his fair share of gruesome acts and killing, paled as he stood to one side, whilst Paddy Mayne walked out of the room.

Goddard was by now trying to clamber through the shattered window. O'Hanlon turned, amazed at the sight of the British airman. "What the blazes," he said, stopping mid sentence.

"Guess I'm the cause of all that," Goddard said. "Very sorry, but is there any chance of a lift home?"

O'Hanlon smiled then as he felt the tension ease. "What the hell were you doing out there?" he asked.

"It's a long story," Goddard said, trying not to be sick at the sight of Richter hanging lifeless. "Can I tell you on the way out?"

Andrea was kneeling at the top of the stairs beside her father. She was rubbing his forehead with her hand and sobbing quietly. Paddy Mayne walked over and he desperately wanted to take her in his arms but instead he touched her gently on the shoulder and nodded and smiled. She stood up and Paddy Mayne bent down and lifted her father in his arms as if he were a child.

Andrea wrapped the blanket around her tightly, as O'Hanlon led the way warily down the stairs with Weir and McIntyre taking up the rear. Marie was distraught when she saw Anton, but overjoyed to see Andrea. She couldn't speak. "I can't tell you how sorry I am," Paddy Mayne said. "Andrea will tell you what happened, but for now we must get out of this place, before our luck runs out."

They walked quickly to the hallway of the castle and out through the front door to the waiting ambulance. Paddy Mayne laid Anton down gently and Phil Graham looked at him briefly and shook his head. Marie and Andrea sat close together, holding hands.

"Right let's get out of here," Paddy Mayne ordered, and they closed the ambulance doors and Phil Graham turned on the lights and siren and drove off.

The engines of the Kubelwagens were already running. They drove to the front of the castle and turned and accelerated away after the ambulance as German soldiers stood and watched.

Paddy Mayne sat in the back of the ambulance, grim faced but inwardly pleased that he had accomplished his mission without the loss of one of his men. The convoy turned at the gateway leading from the castle and headed back to the camp where they arrived without incident.

At the camp there was no sign of the Baker's Dozen. Paddy Mayne and his men set about winding down after their Operation. A campfire was lit and food prepared as they waited in hope for their comrades in arms. It was suggested to Paddy Mayne that a detail be sent into Chantilly in case the Baker's Dozen required assistance but he declined.

Instead he asked the Padre to make arrangements for Anton Aveleine's burial. McLuskey took Andrea and her mother to one side and went over the details of the burial with them. Together they sought out a suitable spot for the grave, insisting that after the War he would be given a proper burial befitting his contribution to France's War effort.

The grave was dug by some of the SAS and then in the quiet of the early hours of the morning they prepared to lay Dr Anton Aveleine to rest. Just then there was a commotion at the far end of the camp.

The Baker's Dozen had just arrived back and they were jubilant. They had managed to release Jean Boussiene and his son Louis, together with some other prisoners who had made their own way, once they were released. Madeleine was obviously out of her mind with joy and as soon as she saw Paddy Mayne walking from the newly dug grave she ran to him and threw her arms around him. Inspector Marius Regnier, and the priest Father Michael de Bourbon had also been contacted. Regnier decided that it was time for them to go into hiding, but the Priest still refused to leave.

Father Michael and Frazer McLuskey shared in the burial service and the Inspector paid a moving tribute to his friend Anton and a bugler from the SAS played the Last Post. Marie and Andrea lingered for a while at the graveside. Then Regnier walked over to talk to them. They were all so used to losing friends and loved ones, but Regnier knew that Anton's death would be a particularly hard blow for Marie. He did his best to console her

Andrea was standing with her head bowed, praying for the soul of her dear father. She was still wrapped in the blanket that Weir had

328

pulled from the bed and she shivered slightly. She looked up and saw Paddy Mayne watching her. She smiled slightly, and then walked over towards him, leaving her mother and Regnier to talk. They strolled slowly over to the fire that had been started, and someone offered them coffee and Army rations.

They sipped the coffee slowly. "I'm afraid it's the best we can do in the circumstances," Paddy Mayne said.

Andrea smiled. "Paddy, I can never thank you enough for what you have done for us and for France."

"I'm glad we got there just in time," Paddy Mayne said. "But I'm just sorry the whole mission has been such a waste. I mean we came all this way to save a German General and to stop the Gestapo from getting vital names from him, or else to get those names ourselves, but we were too late. Scholtz took his own life, and who can blame him, except he's brought possibly the most vital information of this War with him to the grave."

Andrea looked up at Paddy Mayne and smiled. "Well that's not strictly true," she said with a twinkle in her eye."

Paddy Mayne raised his eyebrows. "What do you mean exactly? What do you know that I don't?"

"I've only just found out myself." She took Paddy Mayne's hand in hers and squeezed it. "Gary was helping me out of the ambulance and he asked me about General Scholtz. I told him he had died in the castle, and naturally he hadn't heard. He said he was sorry, that he seemed not to be the typical Nazi and of course I agreed."

Andrea paused. "Go on," Paddy Mayne said impatiently.

"He reminded me of a night at the Château. My parents had invited General Scholtz for tea, when at the same time they were hiding Gary Tucker until he was well enough to travel. Unfortunately, or perhaps now fortunately, Gary unexpectedly walked in when they were having the meal. My parents were horrified. There was nothing they could do or say, but the General told them not to worry, that their secret was safe with him. They couldn't believe it, but the General said one day he might call for their help. Anyway, none of us knew that the

General had a secret conversation with Gary that night. He entrusted Gary with the names of his co-conspirators."

Paddy Mayne squeezed her hand. "But why?" And he looked across to where Tucker was sitting on a log beside the fire in conversation with Weir and O'Hanlon. Tucker looked up and realised they had been talking about him and he got up and came over.

Paddy Mayne looked at him for a moment. "We came all this way on a highly secret mission, and I thought we had failed. Now Andrea tells me you have the information we came to get."

"Well so it seems," Tucker said.

"And where exactly are these names?" Paddy Mayne asked. "I'm assuming you didn't carry them around with you."

Tucker winced a bit as one of his many injuries played up for a moment. "I did what the General said," he replied. "I hid them that night in a safe place near the Château."

"Phew," Paddy Mayne gasped. "That's a relief. But why on earth did the General confide in you?"

"Well sir, it seems he was concerned that the Gestapo were closing in on him. He told me they would never get the information out of him, but he was determined that it should get to the Prime Minister, Mr Churchill himself. He believed I was simply a British pilot who'd been shot down and that the Germans would never think to quiz me about the names if I were arrested, or indeed even interrogate me. Obviously he hoped I would escape back to England and that a trusted agent could then be sent to retrieve the names."

"Well I'll be damned," Paddy Mayne said. "Thank you Tucker."

Then he turned to Andrea. "How are we going to get those names to Churchill? There's every chance any one of us might yet be captured."

"That won't happen," Andrea said. "Anyway it's not your concern anymore."

Paddy Mayne looked at her. "Joe will get the names and bring them back. That's what she's good at. We've only to pass on the information to her."

Andrea returned Paddy Mayne's gaze for a brief moment. "When are you going to leave us Paddy?" she asked quietly.

"We'll rest up here tonight of course, and tomorrow," Paddy said. "Then I'm afraid it's back to the War again. We'll have to move out under cover of darkness and liaise with more of our boys who've been dropped in behind enemy lines. It's no secret that the invasions coming soon and we need to be here to harass the Germans at every turn."

"I wish you didn't have to go," Andrea said.

"Not 'till tomorrow," Paddy Mayne said quietly.

Andrea looked around the camp. The fire was burning brightly and the men were talking together in groups as they drank coffee and told stories and remembered friends who were no more. Her mother was still talking to Regnier, and she was glad he was their friend. The Padre was talking in an animated way to Father Michael.

"Can you get me a coat Paddy?" Andrea asked. "I'm beginning to feel a chill."

Paddy Mayne smiled and found her an Army issue sleeping bag. "It was a coat I wanted," Andrea said. "I'm not sleeping tonight if you're taking yourself off tomorrow."

Paddy Mayne shrugged and was about to discard it when Andrea reached out and shaking her head at Paddy Mayne, tucked it under her arm. They slipped away quietly from the campfire without anyone noticing. Anyone, that is except Frazer McLuskey.

Chapter forty four

Paddy Mayne's funeral had been a grand affair and many of his comrades in arms were glad they had the opportunity to say their farewells. Frazer McLuskey had been very moved by the tributes so many paid to him. He had been particularly pleased to meet Andrea and Marie Aveleine again, and Andrea's son Patrick.

He woke from a night's fitful sleep, with all his memories of Paddy Mayne spinning in his head and for the rest of that day he could think of nothing but the reunion. Part of him believed it would be wonderful to see as many as possible of those involved in the attempt to rescue General Scholtz and the others. Another part urged caution, knowing that it could rake up all sorts of feelings and memories that had long since been buried.

A telephone call from Andrea the next day convinced him to go ahead.

It was not a difficult task ten years after the War to bring together all of the members of Paddy Maynes's Task Force that had set out on the mission and who were still alive. Josephine Butler – formerly Jay Bee - was hale and hearty and delighted at the opportunity of being reunited with old friends. Pilot Officer Gary Tucker, though still suffering from the effects of his plane crash said he wouldn't miss it for anything. Former colleagues like O'Hanlon, McIntyre and Weir had survived the War as had Major Bob Holmes and others.

No one turned down the invitation to travel by coach to the Aveleine's Château near Chantilly to meet up again one more time, just for old time's sake. McLuskey made all the arrangements on his side of the channel, but he left the French side to Andrea. This meant that McLuskey had no idea who, from the French side would be there. He could have easily found out, but decided just to wait and see.

It turned out to be a lavish affair with the people of Chantilly coming out in force to greet the English heroes. McLuskey and the others had been given no idea of the kind of welcome that was awaiting them. The people of Chantilly, who at one time had shunned the Aveleine's because they believed they were collaborators, now recognised the great risks and sacrifices they had made during the War.

They saw this as their opportunity to make up for their attitude to them at that time. As the coach approached the Château the road was lined with well-wishers. Colourful bunting was strewn across the road and a beautiful arch had been erected at the entrance to the Château.

The mayor was there to greet them and a great marquee had been erected in the grounds where everyone was free to mingle around and meet old friends. The local brass band played and added greatly to the carnival atmosphere.

The Baker's Dozen was well represented, and they were given pride of place on the French side. Some of them had noticeably aged, partly because of the years and partly because of what the War had done to them. Father Michael circulated amongst everybody, as did Andrea and her mother and of course Paddy's son Patrick.

One person in particular, Francois Desjardine kept apart from the others. The War had affected him badly. He had been so young when he saw his family butchered and he witnessed other atrocities that nobody his age should have seen.

He had played a Major part in the Resistance after Paddy Mayne and his men left Chantilly to prepare for the invasion. He was nearly always a loner, but very dependable, and Beaufort had tried after the War to see him settled in a job. Then Beaufort returned to England and his own people and he lost touch. In the intervening years Desjardine moved from one job to another but never really settled.

Marie Aveleine had quite a job tracking him down for the reunion and an even bigger job persuading him to come.

Late in the evening, Wartime music was being played and everybody was socialising and enjoying a wonderful meal. Desjardine unable to feel at home, slipped out unnoticed from the Marquee, except that Father Michael noticed him go. He got up to go after him, and followed him for a short distance, but then as he watched him, a solitary figure, walking towards Chantilly, he changed his mind and went back and rejoined the others.

Chapter forty five

Desjardine admired the Aveleines and knew they had suffered as he had done. However he could never rid his mind of the fact that it was their son who had massacred his family before his very eyes. Because of that he just could not feel comfortable with them. He did not blame them because he knew it was not their fault.

It was the War, but memories were memories and he could not erase them.

Although Jacque Aveleine was dead, he felt he had never properly paid for his crimes.

The reunion continued unabated as Desjardine walked slowly back to Chantilly. He kept his head down and barely noticed the lone figure walking towards him. They passed and looked briefly at one another and both walked on.

On that awful night of the War, over ten years ago, Jacque Aveleine was driven by fear. Fear of what Richter might do to him if he did not succeed in the task he had set him. He had told the driver to make good time and they nearly hit a woman on the road in the dark. He knew in his heart it was Madeleine, but he could do nothing about it. And then there were the Kubelwagens and he was going to tell the driver to stop to see what was going on, and then suddenly everything went blank.

When he came too, it took him a long time to realise where he was, and to remember what had happened. He did not remember the gunfire or the crash, but eventually when he saw the driver dead beside him he knew what had happened. Vague recollections returned to him. He struggled out of the car and even in the darkness he could see the bullet holes. He knew it was a miracle he had not been shot to pieces. His head hurt, and his hand still pained abominably.

He struggled up the road, back to the castle and eventually he made it in through the doors. He could not believe the sight that met his eyes. Soldiers were everywhere trying to get some order into the situation. Most ignored his plight until he stopped a Corporal.

"What's going on?" he asked. "What's happened here?"

"British commandoes," the corporal said. "We thought it was the start of the invasion, there's been a massacre, and they've got clean away." He paused and looked at Aveleine. "Where have you been sir?"

Aveleine ignored the question and numbed by the news, he walked towards the stairs and up to the landing. He went over to the office Richter had commandeered from Scholtz, and went in. Puzzled, he walked into the first bedroom, and then into the adjoining one.

He stood there for a moment and blinked and rubbed his eyes. He could not believe what he saw. Richter's body was still hanging there lifeless, impaled on the bayonet. He looked around him in desperation and then ran from the room.

Things then began to slip into place and he walked quickly, ignoring everyone, till he came to the prison cells. One after another he saw the cell doors lying open and they were empty.

Almost in a panic, he walked and then ran back to Richter's office and lifted the telephone. Eventually he got through to an operator and asked to be put through to Abwehr headquarters. He asked to be put through to General Oster and was told that would be impossible. He tried explaining that it was an emergency, but it made no difference. Then he tried someone else he knew and again he got the same response.

Finally in desperation he asked for a corporal he'd known and worked with. This time he got a different response, but was reminded of the very inappropriate time he had chosen to telephone. At this point he lost his temper and demanded to be put through immediately. The telephone rang for almost a minute before a sleepy voice answered it.

"Hans," he said in exasperation. "It's Jacque Aveleine. I need your help."

"Jacque, it's 4 o'clock in the morning. What's so important? Hans replied sleepily.

"I must speak to General Oster immediately," Aveleine said. "It's vital that I speak to him and nobody will listen to me."

There was silence for a moment and then Hans spoke very quietly and deliberately. "Jacque," he said. "I'd advise you to get off this line. Didn't you know? General Oster's been shot for Treason!"

Aveleine gasped. "That can't be true," he said, but he knew the line had gone dead, and he knew why nobody would put him through.

He stood for a moment, panic stricken, as the reality of what had happened sunk in. Gradually it dawned on him that he was now a fugitive in his own country. If his parents were alive, he knew he could not go to them, and there was nowhere in Germany he would feel safe, now that Oster was dead.

He was relieved that none of the soldiers, not even Officers were paying any heed to him. He left the office and went down the great stairway and outside and into the darkness.

Away in the distance, corpses were being lifted and put into trucks and brought to a temporary mortuary until they could be identified and buried. Aveleine mingled with the soldiers until he found himself in a large corrugated iron hut, helping to identify the bodies.

One by one he looked over the corpses, judging their size and age and general appearance. Eventually he found what he was looking for and then slipped away into the darkness. When the last body had been brought in and laid out on the ground, the soldiers detailed to the gruesome task were only too glad to close over the doors of the hut and leave them there in the stillness and darkness of night.

When the coast was clear Aveleine went back into the hut and grabbed one of the corpses by the heels and pulled him out of the hut and into the surrounding trees. He quickly undressed him and put on his uniform, having checked that he had all his relevant papers. Then he dressed the corpse in his own uniform with all of his own papers.

Finally he found a large piece of wood and so disfigured the face of the corpse that it would have been impossible to recognise it. It was a horrible business and even Aveleine found it hard not to be sick.

When he had disposed of the piece of wood he melted into the darkness and through the trees until he came to the entrance to the castle. He stopped at the gate as a lorry full of soldiers drove in. He took a deep breath and walked away from the castle.

From then on, until the end of the War, he remained a fugitive, constantly hiding, always on the run, until finally the opportunity came to hand himself over to the British.

Jacque Aveleine was listed as one of those who had died during the commando raid on the Whermacht Headquarters in Chantilly. He was buried along with all the others with full military honours, and after the War his mother and sister were made aware of the circumstances of his death.

Epilogue

When the War was over, Jacque Aveline managed to change his identity yet again, once more becoming a Frenchman. He had heard of so many reprisals against those who had fraternised with the enemy that he did not dare reveal his true identity.

Five years after the War he met and married a War widow from Paris where he had been living. They had a son, but Aveleine didn't settle and had an affair. His wife found out and they separated and then divorced. He went to live with the other woman and her young daughter by another marriage.

It was a brief article in a Paris newspaper that drew his attention to the reunion at Chantilly, of the SAS and the Baker's Dozen. At first he dismissed the idea, but as he thought about it more and more he realised he was desperate to try and clear his name and make a new beginning with his surviving family.

He arrived in Chantilly on the afternoon of the reunion after taking cold feet, and returning to Paris the day before. It was with mild trepidation then that he finally found himself retracing his footsteps along the road out of Chantilly to the Château.

His heart was beating faster at the prospect of being reunited with his mother especially, and as he came close to the Château, he was finally feeling glad that he had at last determined to try and make a break with the past.

Aveleine was so preoccupied with the thoughts of meeting his mother, that he barely looked at Desjardine as they passed on the road. Desjardine too, was deep in his own thoughts, because not for the first time he was again contemplating suicide. The War had just been too much, and especially his failure to extract revenge for his family's death. That above everything led him into deep and black moods that he could hardly shake himself out of.

He had walked a few paces past Aveleine when he suddenly stopped and looked back. Something, he did not know what, clicked in his mind. He knew he recognised the face from somewhere, and it annoyed him to the point that he turned around and followed Aveleine, without making a sound. He felt the blood coursing in his veins as it did during the worst days of the War.

His breathing quickened as he drew closer and all thoughts of ending his life had suddenly and inexplicitly left him. He didn't understand what was happening, but he knew he had to confront the man he had just passed on the road.

Then he slipped quietly over a wall that he remembered so well, and walked in the field until he was ahead of Aveleine. Then he jumped as light footed as ever over a gate and was suddenly in front of a very startled Aveleine, only a few yards from the entrance to the Château.

"What the blazes," Aveleine cried. "You scared the life out of me. Are you going to the reunion?"

"I've been," Desjardine said quietly and menacingly.

Suddenly Aveleine felt cold all over. There was something very familiar about Desjardine's face, and for a moment he couldn't place it. But it was a face he would never forget. In a blind panic he turned to run, but Desjardine was on him like lightening, with his strong hands around his neck.

Aveleine's lifestyle in the past ten years had done nothing for his physique and his attempts to break Desjardine's hold were futile.

Desjardine was remarkably calm, as he slowly strangled the life out of Jacque Aveleine.

He took his lifeless body and dropped it over the gate he had just climbed. Then looking carefully around him he made his way back to the reunion. Father Michael met him half way up the drive.

"Father," Desjardine said. "I just stepped out for a breath of air and I'm feeling so much better now, so I'm going back in to join the festivities. I didn't really feel like chatting earlier, but I'm a lot better now."

Father Michael frowned and followed him back to the marquee.

Aveleine's body was found the next day, and when Inspector Marius Regnier saw the body in the mortuary; he called Father Michael de Bourbon. They both agreed that despite the documents he had carried with him, he was in fact Jacque Aveleine, but they never revealed the truth to anyone.